Mirage

Book One of The Elements

Heather Munro Hilliard

R. Roan Enterprises, LLC
New Orleans ~ Pittsburgh

R. Roan Enterprises, LLC
New Orleans ~ Pittsburgh

This is a work of fiction. Any references to historical events, real people or real places are used fictitiously. Other names, characters, places, incidents and events are products of the author's imagination, and any resemblance to actual events or businesses or places or persons, living or dead, is entirely coincidental.

Originally published in hardcover by R. Roan Enterprises, LLC - May 2016
First R. Roan Enterprises, LLC ebook editions - May 2016

Published by R. Roan Enterprises, LLC
3945 Forbes Avenue, #225
Pittsburgh, Pennsylvania 15213
www.rre-llc.com

Mirage/ Heather Munro Hilliard. - 1st ed.

Library of Congress Control Number: 2016939609

ISBN: 978-0-9975414-0-3 (hardback)
ISBN: 978-0-9975414-1-0 (eBook)
ISBN: 978-0-9975414-2-7 (paperback)

Mirage

The word comes to English via the French words *mirage* (from *se mirer* (to be reflected) and *mirus* (wonderful) as well as from the Latin *mirari,* meaning "to wonder at." There are also clues in etymology that indicate the Arabic *mi'raj* was of influence; however, the meaning there connotes ascending or climbing. Misleading images are frequently mistaken for reflections in extreme heat. Most often, a mirage is the mistaken identification of an oasis (of water) in the middle of a desert.

It also may be defined as something that appears real or possible, but is not in fact so.

For KJS - thank you for encouraging me

Helpful Acronyms

AI: Artificial Intelligence
ATF: Bureau of Alcohol, Tobacco, Firearms and Explosives
BCG: Boston Consulting Group
BDS: Biohazard Detection System
BDU: Battle Dress Uniforms
CI: Confidential Informant
CO: Commanding Officer
CST: Civil Support Team (62nd, Louisiana National Guard)
CFATS: Chemical Facility Anti-Terrorism Standards
DEA: Drug Enforcement Agency
DEQ: Louisiana Department of Environmental Quality
DOD: Department of Defense
EMS: Emergency Medical Services
EOC: Emergency Operations Center
EPA: Environmental Protection Agency
ETA: Estimated Time of Arrival
FBI: Federal Bureau of Investigation
FDA: Food and Drug Administration
GIS: Geographic Information Systems
HSEEP: Homeland Security Exercise & Evaluation Program
HUMINT: Human Intelligence
HVAC: Heating, Ventilation and Air Conditioning
IAP: Incident Action Plan
LAN: Local Area Network
LiDAR: Light Detection and Ranging
LZ: Landing Zone
MEU: Marine Expeditionary Unit
MSB: Management Support Bureau
MTSA: Maritime Transportation Security Act of 2002
NIMS: National Incident Management System
NOAA: National Oceanic and Atmospheric Administration

NSSE: National Special Security Event
OCS: Officer Candidacy School
RICO: Racketeer Influenced and Corrupt Organizations Act
RFP: Request for Proposals
SAIC: Special Agent In Charge
SAT: Satellite
SBA: Small Business Administration
Seabees: U.S. Navy Construction Battalion
SIM Chip: Subscriber Identification Module Chip
SNS: Strategic National Stockpile
SWAT: Special Weapons And Tactics
TSA: Transportation Safety Administration
TWA: TransWorld Airlines
USCG: United States Coast Guard
VOC: Volatile Organic Compounds
XO: Executive Officer

Mirage

Chapter 1

Though she didn't work for the company, the front desk girls knew her. When they saw her striding purposefully to the entrance via the camera by the elevators, the security lock released so she barely had to slow her pace as she opened the door when arriving to the meeting.

It was an awkward space. She had been in there years ago, when it needed "rehab" from a huge teardown. Back then, it was cement floor, raw pillars, exposed ductwork, piles of dust, loose wires - even little plug boxes popping up out of the ground making everyone watch their step to avoid tripping or getting shocked. Glue still held strands of the awful blue and grey industrial carpet, where ghosts of the past occupants tried to hide the criminal acts of the feet that trod there.

Now, the space was refinished with blues (again) and browns - it wasn't much better, and neither was the layout. It was uninviting and unattractive, even awkward. The man who designed it possessed the primary motive of utility. His office was literally in the middle of the once open space, with his frosted windows making it easy for him to see forms approaching his space yet impossible, with the placement of his dark faux-wood furniture, to determine if he was within his office. The massive space oriented his ranks around the perimeter. On the left were low-topped beige cubes for the minions, and two offices - one positioned for the watcher, the other for the finance woman - were also relegated to the worker-bee area. Cubes in six rows, only two or three to a row, breaking up any camaraderie by division of labor, trying to stave off an opportunity for mutiny.

Sweeping forward, looking for someone, she noted the kitchen was in the back again, still in block form and still not functional. Cube-dwellers had to exit the workspace and pass the boss' office even to get a glass of water or use the copy machine placed in the eating area. (What the heck?) Bathrooms in the way back, the same as before, presumably still equipped with showers for the unending days sometimes required. A creature comfort if it was actually designed with the user in mind, but it was just another serviceable space so small that you barely could turn around (and practically had to go outside in order to change your mind).

The right side she was now approaching remained undivided, but strewn with many tables. Copied from a 1940s era newsroom spread, as if varying layout here would counter the regimented environment where they had to sit everyday doing busywork. Supposedly, this "system" represented the man's idea of functionality. Right. No production, efficiency or accuracy would necessarily be generated anywhere.

Her eyes swept over the two guys on the far side of the tables. The first one had his back toward her while slightly slumped over his computer. He was shorter with only a little hair up top and dressed almost sloppily, wearing baggy unpressed light-olive khakis that held three-quarters of his red-checkered oxford, well-worn mountain hiking boots and was even wearing a gray and maroon sweater vest. Good grief. The other, also sitting but with better posture, had a watchful presence. Back to the row of windows, dark eyes forward, definitely more hair in a high-and-tight cut that seemed to shimmer with silver on the slightly longer top, crisp white shirtsleeves and a dark tie; he barely glanced up before he blinked and returned to working on his laptop.

Coming the remaining way around the center office's island to complete the u-shape layout, the conference area wasn't quite finished from its redo, but apparently that is where they were to meet. Still wide open with hints of walls to come, the light-and-dark blue-flaked carpet was installed here just as it was everywhere now. Several of the men with whom she needed to discuss business were talking over their paper cups of office coffee. Taking a deep breath to help repress an eye-roll as she had to take these boys step-by-step through the next phase of the weapons project, she moved closer.

Not many people outside of their small group (handpicked by the politicians but vetted for clearance) were allowed to come so freely into the office. This came from a hard lesson learned. The former mayor was elected as a change to his predecessor, the mayor of two elections prior, bringing reported business acumen to a region coming back after the oil bust of the eighties. Voters wanted someone to handle the city budget like a business rather than a cookie jar. Coming from a well-respected century-old corporation that had been named as a Top 50 Company in Diversity nationwide, the assumption was that fair-play would be given by their new mayor in a region known for favoritism first and discrimination second.

The first few partners brought to the table were great. They started making some modifications to line items, reviewed former audits for areas of 'slush' and even cut administrative costs, though new players were somewhat hypocritical as they were still compensated at the same rates as their former highly paid commercial positions. In working with civil service, departments were able to have some streamlining as the workforce was aging and several managers were hanging on to finish the final term of the previous mayor, since they had worked for his daddy when he was mayor, too. There were quite a few pairs of father-son mayors in this city's history.

A hallmark of this newly elected public official was that a focus was given to homeland security. Unfortunately, this was as a result of a terrorist attack that occurred just months before election. The increased funds were directed to port security, equipment for first responders and even some infrastructure protection. City Hall was getting old, so barriers were erected (on the unwelcome advice of the Feds), but an evaluation was beginning on a new location - building new or green with rehabilitation of some Class A office space. And that's precisely when the old ways started to resurface.

It began with one or two new appointments for technology and an engineering evaluation. Proposals were starting to be awarded in strange ways. Personal gains and connections surfaced. Side business deals became "not so side" work. It continued through a huge incident that brought tremendous strife for the city along with a city council member or two being indicted then jailed and the same for a U.S. Congressman with connections to the mayor, too. Nationally televised swearing and mental break downs, the Feds got him good through his own actions and he was found guilty of nearly two dozen federal felony charges. (Then again, so was the politician next door, who was a trained attorney that became a politician - with almost identical charges and nearly identical results, just assigned to a different federal penitentiary.)

The peripheral people involved also were taken down. One by one, family members of the Congressman, acquaintances of the lawyers, people who gave payoffs to the politicians or their relations all were receiving target letters from the Department of Justice. It resulted in true bill indictments from the grand jury or bills of information giving way to plea deals. Even school board officials ended up swirling down the temptation bowl and serving jail time. So when outsiders had been allowed in the past, it turned into a federal indictment nightmare spanning years and family dynasties - executives, appointees, and even elected officials. Some of those criminal deals likely took place on this very floor.

The woman striding through the space didn't give the air of sales or splurge, and had passed rigorous screening. It could be guessed that the secretaries that guarded the door and access to the sanctum helped ease her way as "one of their own." But they weren't really sure who she was, either. The guy by the windows would never directly ask, but if they knew her, they would have talked about her around the copy machine or while eating lunch. That had not happened.

He was fairly certain she had noticed that he was seated facing her entrance. She didn't seem to be the type to miss much. He always sat with his back to those windows as they were high enough in the tower to be clear of ground-level action - anywhere else, a solid wall was a better backdrop. He was glad he could see her sweep into the room. At his vantage point, the corner around which she appeared was the only access into the space and he purposefully positioned himself to see who would come and go - ingrained from his intel training. He had no idea who she was or why she was here, but he was pretty sure that she had not been here before while he was working.

Typical attendees of any of these meetings were men. Only men. And only military men, typically Marines at that. All kinds of dress, but that was the wrapping and helped judge the branches. Even when informally clothed, the grunts were crisp - though not so far as ironing jeans (that was a different group of men). Army could be a little slouchy and frequently left their shirt layers untucked (whereas grunts untucked to shroud weapons, ground pounders just didn't waste time on those things). Rare were the flyboys or swabbies here, but if they held special intel, they passed through on a temporary pass.

So, when he heard the soft sound of a determined stride coming around that corner and saw long legs and fierce blue eyes in a skirt suit, he blinked. Totally outside of training, but better than a deep breath - or a whistle, as if he were at a bar, but his silence wasn't for a lack of appreciation. Legs and those eyes. Blink. Natural blonde. Eyes down on computer. Use scope skills under eyelashes for anything else.

But he didn't see anything on that computer screen when she continued around that corner. He only saw saw that under that blue Brooks Brothers suit that she had a nice chest and a great ass to match.

Chapter 2

She approached the men, who each gave her an arm around her shoulder in turn and a kiss on the cheek. Condescending, except that was the "way of the south" - and they had no idea how to handle her. She was there because she was smart, but keeping her an arm's length away was necessary. She was not part of the club, but they needed her brains and intel. They had to treat her as any southern gentleman would - with a kiss to the cheek no matter how much she unnerved them.

Ha. Like she didn't know they were all uncomfortable. Yet time and again, she gave intel none of them could gather. She helped solve problems they didn't even recognize and kept them off the radar before they had to explain to bosses how things "went sour." She smiled, as her grandmother taught her - smile and then they won't know what you are thinking. Her smile this time was from the allusion that the 'way of the south' was to be nice to the little ladies even though the ladies ended up saving their butts at home and at work, and when it goes bad, the saying is that things went south. Irony. She loved it.

She didn't prep for these meetings. She knew she was ahead of wherever they were. The same format for every meeting, traditional military men were so easy to predict. Use the MilCom system - tell them what you were going to say (or said last time), say your update, then repeat the update to make sure everyone was on the same page. No wonder the greatest nation was struggling in the war on terrorism.

The first twenty minutes of the hour-long meeting would be spent yapping about what they thought was discussed the last time they met. About seventy percent of that would be accurate but when it gets off track, she would inject a "didn't we say" phrase to which they would all agree. She kept them moving forward by providing updates as if they had gotten past the point in question. These men were not dull (as in intellectually challenged), but they had the commonality of a few things: they didn't care, were there for the check, really didn't remember from one day to the next as they were used to receiving orders rather than giving them, and tried very hard to lead. *Bless their hearts,* she often thought - they just could never measure up to their tasks.

Conversely, she had never been labeled dull or slow in her life. While her own talents masked some of her flaws, and she used common sense to always play to her strengths. She was strong in logistics. She found it easy to complete jobs that used her near-eidetic memory, nearly perfect recall; her keen attention to detail allowed her to recall nearly everything she heard, though she had found on a few occasions that this could get her into trouble. At a young age, her teachers discovered that she had wicked spatial manipulation skills that also somehow linked her to patterns, remembering how to get in and out of places with ease (proving valuable in later field work and sometimes was just plan fun when messing with people). Her professional toolkit was powerful enough to get her to where she was today, along side of the ultimate boys club.

In this meeting, they were to discuss staging and storing activities of their Strategic National Stockpile supplies. De facto, these men slotted her into a secretary role since they were used to women keeping the notes. Using their bias to her advantage, she had three locations identified and knew which they should choose. She just had to convince them it was their own idea while withholding her frustration that they hadn't agreed upon an LZ first for receiving the items they wanted to plan on storing then dispersing. Typical. In truth, it was called "Receiving, Staging and Storage" because it was better to know chronologically how it was getting to you prior to where you would to store it since the components of the shipment could be broken into small transportable containers. The guys chose to look at storage first, however, as if options for landing an A380 or 747 were plentiful in the state or could be created from swampland easily; likely, they only considered the tractor-trailer methods. Reversing the order of confirming the two steps could cause headaches that she would need to fix later.

Sarah finally spoke into the coffee cacophony. "If we want to discuss logistics and staging areas from which ops can take over, then I have some ideas. I've been doing other fieldwork, keeping my eyes open for this project, too. Three options rose to the top of the list."

It wasn't in her nature to be patient, but with this group, all of their chest candy from various missions, it was best to try to play demure. They knew it was far from Sarah's character, but respected her effort to allow them to save face. When the full bird colonel who served as the unofficial chairman of the group nodded to proceed, she presented the three options in the order that would "help" them pick the right answer.

"There is the old base building along the river. Great interior space, ingress and egress clear, easy to secure. However, no room for expansion and access is only on one, maybe two sides, because of the river. No helo access. There is a trap factor." She looked at each face, watching the various speeds at which they comprehended what she said, with the man to her right remembering the last time he was trapped.

Luke switched to the past when he heard the phrase "trap factor" at the end of Sarah's description. Not one to try to grandstand, members of his small team in the military gave him "Pierce" for his nickname, because he would get straight to the heart of an issue. It suited him outside of those tactical situations, but no one in this room knew the nickname his buddies had given him. He had been clearing a building with his squad in an area known for rebel activity. Someone had called clear, so they relaxed a little and slowly congregated at the side stairwell.

There was an ancient stained glass window in the pinnacle of the stairwell that acted as a skylight. Mosaic tiles forming patterns and old symbols on the pillars reached up to that window. He was staring at it, noting the star in the center was a deep lapis not used anywhere else in the design, and the background glass moved from a robin's egg to a faded spearmint color. The amber and ochre geometric design on the very outside of the circle had an inner ring of diamonds that appeared to have shapes inside, but they weren't close enough for him to determine what was being shown.

He was obviously staring, and thought he saw a small shadow intrude on the rim of the circle's far side then vanish. There hadn't seemingly been a way to access the roof, but satellite intel relayed to them said it was clear from above. Maybe it was a bird or one of their planes high overhead. He turned back to the team, to see the eight coming together. But, there were only seven.

Luke held up his fist and no one moved. "Trail" wasn't with them. He was supposed to be "trailing" the team and covering the rear of the clearing ascent: hence his name. Team members each took a real name rather than a Hollywood-esque "call sign" because in public, when they traveled together, they needed to be able to call out without calling attention. Trail sounded like a real last name. Pierce sounded like a solid first name.

Right now, there were no sounds. Total silence. What happened to Trail? With his hand still raised, he lifted his head to look at that stained glass skylight just as three dark shapes shattered through it.

Taking cover was nearly impossible on the landing of the rotunda's stairs. The team split, up five steps versus partially down two steps to the next doorways. Luke had just cleared this area so took his three guys into the room to the right, then around left. A defensible position, with a window as escape, he considered the next move by the assailants.

It's always better to know who is attacking, so certain measures can be anticipated. Luke didn't like being at a disadvantage by not knowing who these guys were, or how many there were. Using the new technology distributed for this mission, he glanced at the small touchscreen embedded in the sleeve of his jacket to see where the team members had previously swept and where Trail was now - and if he was alive.

The integrated intel solution used on this mission had been deployed piecemeal ten years ago from a U.S.-based manufacturing company. Starting small more than 140 years ago, the first inventor began a revolution of ideas that crossed from consumerism to weaponry. Over time, they developed wireless technologies from biometric monitoring to encrypted comms and could actually build a new building from the ground up without outside contractors. Very helpful to the Department of Defense, who wanted security for sanctioned - or covert - missions. Though he was by nature skeptical of "gifts" offered from private corporations, this one worked quite well in spite of the nonvolunteer nature of soldiers being used as lab rats in real-world test cases.

Adapting some of the in-house smaller scale devices for the battlefield had become a niche market for the company - one not publicized for stockholders, yet the dividends kept on coming. Smaller, lighter, faster - each was an apt description of the teams themselves as well as the assistive devices they used. The one Luke deployed showed the results from integrating organic material (cotton undershirts, in this case) woven with biologic receptors for all standard vital signs as well as hydration, blood sugar, end-tidal CO2 (which helped predict efficacy of oxygen to carbon dioxide exchange and metabolics), and a host of other parameters shared on the team's own encrypted LAN. Not even the Pentagon could monitor activities of teams using this equipment as an interface would be open to hacking.

Looking at the screen, Luke saw Trail had no stats populating through his "scent" - markers as tracked through pheromones and other individualized biological indicators by these tech-K9 noses - showed his last twenty minutes of locations. The other three team members were down in what appeared to be a kitchen. The remaining four were here in a large closet area. Two sides of the coin to the team's current positioning: good they were here because there were two ways out; bad if projectiles picked up strands of material before entering the body - greater chance of infection.

The great thing about this new technology was that the shirts also created a virtual web. Just like the slightest variation on a spider's thread alerted the master of the roost to an intrusion, the team's paths created a virtual web using biologic indicators that mapped detection of other people within a 50 meter three-dimensional radius of any given team member; it would display a symbol for "friendly" if they had the right military material or "unknown" if it couldn't identify them. It appeared on his arm like the two-dimensional images of a thermal camera's screen, but had the 3D capability that could be projected for other members to see and rotate for various perspectives such as sniper positioning. Changing the screen's settings, he was able to ascertain the location of four attackers: one down by Trail's aura at the front and the three who had rappelled in through the skylight. Damn, he really wanted to know what those symbols were in the diamonds. Archaeology depended significantly on colors and patterns, and likely all of that glass and those symbols would be lost.

They would be, too, if his team didn't begin the counterassault. It took a while, and losing another member of the team or having anyone seriously wounded was not a viable option. Their 'kitchen team' would be able to get out and come back through the front to begin their own assault. Luke sent them silent messages on the screens they had, causing vibrations to the sleeve when the device had received the relay. Meanwhile, Luke and his three were trapped, locked into defense so they didn't hit their own guys that were countering the assault. It was a good position to choose except when the battle pinned the opponent between two lines of the good guys.

Waiting was not one of Luke's strong suits. Rather, he was a careful planner, typically approaching analysis paralysis if it was described by anyone else. It's why the politicians liked him. He would gather and gather and gather data, sorting and cutting information in various ways to pull the most reliable intel. That all took time. That's what he did before he was pulled into teams like this; his analytic skills in his "day job" post-military career laterally transferred to these teams quite well, even when on these types of missions.

The politicos could say they were working on a problem - when they had him in the backfield working on it - but they could still make their decisions based on personal profit and buddies and positioning themselves for the next job. That's what this boss certainly did. That man thought if he said a lie often enough it would suddenly emerge as truth from his lips. Luke could usually find information to support statements, but sometimes it was tough. Really tough.

This was one of those times when a trap factor could not be spun into truth that it would be a good choice. The river front property was a no-go. He was starting to consider actual facts to turn his boss away from pushing for this option, the wrong solution as far as his opinion went, He didn't realize at that point that Sarah already agreed with him. They could each do only so much, but most of the men in this room knew their roles. It was the ones, well really the one, who didn't that caused the problems.

Chapter 3

Sarah could see Luke already heading down the path she'd opened for him. Good. One down - two, if you counted him and his pathetic boss. So predicable, so readable. That man was a travesty to human kind and these locals voted for him once, with all appearances that they would vote for him yet again. She felt some empathy for Luke in having to work for him. Luke had some great skills. So glad for term limits. Anyway, she started presenting the next option.

"Another prospect is located in a development zone. It was promised to a buddy of the mayor, however. With big equipment moving in and out, and a design of "mixed use" space already announced, it would be feasible to repurpose the inside while maintaining the outside facade. Multiple access routes by a variety of methods, too. But, the main investor poses an obstacle of sorts."

The inaudible groan was nearly deafening. Big money plus big politics equaled big headaches. No one wanted to go up against either the boss of a few of them or the man that got so mad at the mayor that he created not only television ads against him personally as well as some of the infantile policies he instituted, but also took full-page newspaper ads to drive home his point. Anticipating this response, she rapidly moved into the next choice.

"Then, there's always the lake as a third option." She let people think about the lake, the buildings out there - the crime basin at one end and the rich mountain at the other.

Sarah continued, ensuring she appeared the most enthusiastic about this option. So typical of these guys, three options so the last had to be best, right? Wrong, guys.

"There's some room to grow in the wooded area at the end of the marsh. There is a swath in the middle, offering access to "normal" services and speedy access to interstate. The west isn't as appealing because of the high-end housing established there. If we had moved six years ago, perhaps - but not that area, not at this time."

Pausing, looking at each man except the man she knew would be looking at his phone, she then open the floor for discussion about the final two areas. "What do you think?"

Beginning with the third option, the business man (the grumpy one looking at his phone and one of two lacking military experience among other things) spoke without looking at anyone. "Jason, I don't know about you," ignoring Sarah as always, "but the third option sounds best. Increased business and tax revenue, so your boss would like it. Undeveloped space, frame it around community clean up and opportunity, couch a community center or whatever in the midst of our project, cover it with newly created non-profits that provide a service and hidden benefits for us. I think that's the win."

Cringing, Drew replied, "But Wayne, do you know the PR nightmare if anything co-mingles, or when the media begin asking about the real motives of the development, or what if we have problems with the feds because that's so proximal to their babies out that way in the past few years?"

Sarah enjoyed knowing that the predictability factor was still the same as ever. These men could do great things, but the self-serving mode was so strong here it was suffocating. She continued to smile as Andrew, the consummate worry-wort, issued reason after reason for why it was horrible. The last point was the best, and she was actually slightly impressed. She hadn't considered he'd pick up on that quite so soon. Of course, it was the wrong reason, but the right opponent.

Wayne continued his earlier thoughts as though no one else had spoken, with points regarding reduced complexity as there was only one owner to the property in question, fewer residents nearby, easier wavers of building permits or zone changes. Real estate investors and little men with big ideas of grandeur sadly made it clear - no matter what came out of their mouths - what was in it for them with a project was more important rather than the whole picture. He also made his decision based upon how to go head-to-head in order to get ahead of the guy in the second option, a man he hated because he was born with a silver spoon in his mouth. Whatever. Somewhat easier to manipulate the mayor than the pretentious self-righteous side or the granola dirt-practical side. And this "manipulation" wasn't for nefarious purposes, but to get the project continuing faster than it would otherwise without her propulsion.

Though Wayne, and indirectly Drew, had addressed Jason, he had yet to speak. He's the yes man, and usually doesn't speak until told what to say. Recently, he has even been told to say something opposite on the same day and he had done it. He was cultivated into a great mouthpiece for the mayor. There was still a little bit of the old soldier, though, and in meetings such as this where the mayor's spies weren't directly involved, he would absorb information for his own protection later, but still try to say yes to the one he thought the mayor would like the best.

She wanted to make sure they stayed on track, so she turned to Sean and said, "Thoughts?"

Sean wasn't anxious to reply. *That's probably why she turned to him, damn it.* She had to be watched. She somehow always knew something the others didn't. It didn't pass his notice that she was an outsider in more than one way. Obviously, gender. Obviously, formal education, more than any of them. Obviously, outside the region, most notable with her speech and the composition of ideas. Not so obvious were the influences of her upbringing and Sean couldn't understand her.

They knew she had a single mother. Everyone knew she was an only child. She didn't pigeonhole into only-child-syndrome, however. Seemed to want to give things away rather than hoard "her toys." Ludicrous that she demoted her own status under the guise of generosity, he thought. She also had this front of not wanting to hide things, so she'd dig up skeletons of others to display for all to see. *How could anyone not want to hide things?* Sean was certain that she was hiding some huge career-crippling secret, and he was itching to discover it.

His time at law school highlighted his struggle with research, however, especially when it came to supporting his ideas. He preferred to just say things and have people take them as true. He didn't like to be questioned. The oldest of all his siblings, he felt (and had been repeatedly told by his mother) he was born to lead. People should just follow him. This woman just grated on his nerves and he could barely contain his irritation. At every turn, he believed she made moves purposefully to box him into a corner, pressure him into mistakes, and he was constantly afraid he'd make a non-recoverable error that would cost his career, unable to control ramifications from her antics or other people's sabotage.

He had all brothers, and he had all sons with his now ex-wife - he never had a healthy relationship with a woman, let alone a good bond. Though he couldn't see it, his boys were following the same path as he and his brothers and living a dysfunctional dream. He went against his father by choosing a different high school than where the family always sent their boys; his oldest son did the same thing, though effectively returning to family tradition. His father divorced his mother; he left his wife. His father operated in back rooms to support the political machine; he wanted glory so employed grandstanding, glad-handing and politicking in the open. He used women as props and as a mechanism to increase his votes, as that was what they did best - look pretty and should be always ready to serve. It's what made him so inflamed about this *girl*. He was attracted to her, gave her signs that he was available, and she not only ignored him, but refused to even acknowledge that he existed.

Sean didn't understand her. He only saw great legs and beautiful hair and a nice body. That's what women were for, though you couldn't say that anymore. She would be a great one to use and had all sorts of ideas for exactly how he'd like to use her, but she'd never do that. It was a great turn-on to have a strong woman on his arm in public, but behind closed doors she needed to know her place. This bitch didn't know her place and somehow, she kept getting one-up on him. That had to stop, but he hadn't figured out how to stop her.

Boy, that inflamed him when a woman placed her loyalty in the wrong place. He had been fueled by his mother's lip service and empty promises; his oldest had the the undying devotion of a devout mother. Family dynamics really screwed him up and that, too, carried over from one generation to the next, leaking into the public eye in a few ways. Anger wasn't even close to pinpointing his emotion when the family's private angst was splashed throughout the media. Things happened smack center in campaign season, and the news targeted all the blame to him - none to the woman who was really responsible. He wasn't at fault. It was an embarrassment that he would never forget and he would get revenge any time he could in order to defray embarrassment. Retaliation had been taught early and used often between his parents and betwixt siblings, and now the next batch of boys was doing the same thing. He would get what he wanted - and right now he wanted to put his hands around this woman's throat for asking him a question he wasn't prepared to answer.

Sarah knew Sean's weakness went beyond ego, including but not limited to a stunted intelligence that he tried to hide with smooth moves and circular motion. It never dawned on him that people wouldn't want to follow him, or that people would tell him no. Blame that on his parents; well, his dad. 'Bring 'em up southern and they have to be gentlemen.' Wrong and far from the truth. She could use it against all of them, which she did but they could never figure out how she did it. She made sure that the outcomes looked good with the decisions they made - and though less than a stellar group of men, they at least were smart enough to realize she added something that made them look good - except for Sean, that is, so she asked him again.

"Anything?" She got a little kick out of provoking him, and tried very hard to hold back the smirk that went along with the word she didn't utter: idiot. Sean wasn't just socially rejected from the group; he was geographically outside as well. To anyone that had an Introductory Psychology course, it was obvious that he desperately wanted to be an accepted insider rather than a mere participant in this circle. That he had no control over the assignment of his classification drove him to the brink of insanity. He never seemed to digest the overt knowledge that his little suburban town had distinct links to the mafia. No one seemed to deny that down here - it was actually worn as a badge of honor.

Sarah realized Sean somehow was a was member of that group - through his father or through his own practice. The ties to various prosecutors being just a bit too convenient; the way that *no one* spoke of his father, and when they did, it was with more fear than reverence or respect. Something had to be connected there, something that Sean tried to bury. Sean belonged to that environment and tried to hide it, whereas he didn't belong as part of this collection and was desperate to be accepted. The more he tried to belong, the greater the crack in the door leading to his exposure so she kept her eyes open.

As for herself, Sarah recognized that she was merely a participant in these meetings. That was fine. It was actually the best option - always an exit of exception, of never fully-included culpability. But Sean, he salivated to have a pat on the head and have these men to open their arms to welcome him as one of their equals. In his delusional grand plan (that he believed he hid well from the others), he would become one of them and lead them all in due time. She shifted her stance from centered to her right hip and raised and eyebrow when he still had a blank stare as his reply. He spoke through a touch of a malicious smile.

"We haven't heard from Jason, and really since these are all in his space, I'd like to hear his comments first." He always wanted to try to throw Jason under the bus, as a way to get closer to their boss. That's the power source, so Sean thought, with Jason's and Luke's boss. The only two to answer to the same guy, but for very different reasons and not too problematic for Sarah.

Chapter 4

Jason knew that snake would try to push him before he was ready. That's his schtick, because all he has is his weary game. Very short on substance. Jason didn't get to be a full bird colonel without knowing how to do homework without his dog-robber. A trusted aide-de-camp that was efficient as well as creative was quite useful, but they had to ask for information all over the place in order to get filtered replies when they assisted their bosses. He knew how to do it himself when it was necessary, when unfiltered information was the most important to have in his pocket.

For instance, he was able to ascertain rather easily that post workouts, Sean used foul language with the assumption that the intimacy of the locker room was sacred. Wrong. That's how Jason also found out that although Sean was fond of degrading people on race - talking trash and using absolutely unacceptable language in the old prestigious athletic club - that he dabbled every now and then with ladies of a darker tone (even if he had to pay for it from exclusive lists).

And a big chuckle was revealed when Sean's best friend and ex-politico was outed by a madam for having certain proclivities that bent toward a pedophile role-play nature, that those same obsessions distracted him to the point of missing huge votes, and eventually caused him to miss the win in the biggest election of his life. Sean had patterned himself for years after that man because he came from the "right neighborhood" with the "right sized checkbook."

That friend, the now ex-politician, recently finalized his divorce from the ex-wife that was even from the same church, held the same kind of job, and shopped in the same stores as Sean's ex-wife. Only difference is that Sean's choice was shorter and though his buddy was a short guy, his wife was taller. Sean didn't have an original bone in his body. While Jason's boss openly took other people's ideas and pushed them as his own (at least he took them from other cities so not everyone knew of the blatant theft), Sean took them from people down the street, deluding himself into thinking that he would be liked when he became big-time, that imitation was the highest compliment.

No, it was just stealing. *How he and my boss got out of law school is simply amazing,* Jason thought. Well, it was the same law school. And how it hasn't leaked that Sean was investigated back then for cheating on exams, or that he couldn't go to the best private school not because, as he publicly bragged, "he wanted to be different from his dad and others in his family" - it was truthfully because he just wasn't smart enough.

And on more than one level, he wasn't smart. He had locked himself out of that locals' avenue, the golden ticket that boys from that school (that he rejected) received upon graduation when he refused to attend that school. His ignorant refusal nixed one of the ways the boys would have overlooked him growing up in that ratty little suburb instead of within the heart of the city. That "get out of the dregs free" card was tossed with intention, regardless (or ignorant) of the implications - no matter what he did now, because he snubbed his nose at them thirty years ago. More recently, he reminded folks publicly of his choices, which made the circle close ranks against him.

At least Jason wasn't totally from here. Funny, he was from just enough away and just enough rural that he could skip both the "wanna be" and the "outsider" labels. It's one reason his boss hired him. He could fit in, be accepted without being a threat. When he was hired, he was very physically fit and put forth a good image. His economy of words, his need of a local job to support his ailing parents monetarily as well as proximally, and his military background loaned some legitimacy to his boss' decision.

When first hired, Jason stood his ground and would give honest opinions. It morphed into being that yes-man, a position he hated but took (elections were approaching so he could keep the role and not relocate again). Others with whom he had worked at this level went away to work internationally, and there were many moments where he wondered if he could get away, too, but it came back to family. Not precisely a decision because of family. But obligation. Duty. Obedience. From day one and he planned to the very last day. God. Country. Corps.

This was one of those times when he wished that he were back active duty and could deal with Sean in grunt fashion. Though faint, there were still moments deep within that wanted to roar as if he was back with the infantry. Shooting - or directing the shooting - of the Howitzer or as a provisional rifle company commander was always preferable to the other assignments. His missions later in leadership were more to coordinate civilian-military operations. His current role was a far cry from what he was born to do, so he suffered in silence with the temperature rising; he just waited to see what made him break, as not even the mayor had forced that to happen yet.

The main difference between then and now was simple: his leathernecks were trained to assess and react. He was on the orderly side, civilians were the "messy" side, and the civilian politicians who always tried to exploit federal funding - like the bridge to nowhere - were the despicable side. What happened to the first stage of preparedness being at the individual level? Where did the accountability and self-sufficiency go in the past twenty years? Who were the people that were supposed to step up and fill the shoes of those who sacrificed so much for freedom?

Right. It's guys like this prick. Slick hair, fake silk suits made of polished polyester and pieces of paper were more important than ability or desire. Honesty. Resolve.

Character. Nope. Connections. Exploitation. Deception. Check. The realization that this man would have never made it out of boot camp put a smile on his face as he finally replied to him.

"Well, Sean, it is all in my yard as you say, so the best approach would be having everyone else's input, including junior participants such as yourself, and then us hearing my thoughts and coming to agreement. I don't want to influence your feelings with the facts I have. Who knows what you might be able to contribute."

Oh good grief, the boys' pissing contest has started, thought Sarah; *here we go. Reroute, get back on track, people.* "So it seems we agree the first location is out. We've heard a few negatives about the third and some reluctance to endorse that. Anyone have comments on the second proposal?" She tried to maintain a two-second hold of the gaze of each man, starting with Sean, who dipped his head and looked sideways to Jason. Sarah looked at each in clockwise order and none of them seemed to be able to hold her gaze. The man next to her finally spoke up as she noticed the shirt-and-tie-guy by the windows glancing in her direction.

Marcus couldn't help himself and found himself staring at her. Damn, who was the woman that was running that meeting? Or, rather, running those men like it was effortless to tell some of the most powerful 'behind the scenes' guys what to do - and actually have them do it? He was starting to let his mask dissolve, drifting away from his work at the table and becoming very interested in what was happening in the construction zone.

That's what they called the half-finished area. Not certain if they wanted a big room or several small ones, there was a hiccup in the build-out process; then, it just didn't matter for a while. So while it was semi-private and had a door along the right wall to the boss' office, those having 'meetings' easily forgot that it was a huge space that wasn't segregated from "the minions." As if workers in this office were described appropriately or accurately were "minions," thought Marcus. They all have background checks, held security clearances, were certified on a myriad of weapons. Hell of a group of minions.

If he shifted just right in his seat, he could hear nearly perfectly from the reflections off two non-windowed walls. He couldn't blatantly move his seat, but he had a good enough location for catching more than a phrase or two. The added benefit is that he could watch the woman without being noticed by her, and the view was priceless. Her back side and the long bare legs coming out from under the blue pinstripe skirt, legs set off by the black patent leather high heels.

Marcus was drawn in by her classic looks - not only with her suit, but her natural hair and that she wore very little makeup. Unlike some southern women, he neither smelled her perfume before he saw her nor saw brash lipstick overtake her fair features. Very pale skin, her heritage was likely nothing like his own.

He thought about it every now and again, as it was hard to say with any precision or confidence on his background. There was a little French and Spanish, some Native American, some Haitian, and who knows what else. Sometimes it helped not knowing. Yet, knowing how some people could trace back their lines by centuries and could grasp a piece of their ancestry was something that he wished he could do. They could relate to whole different eras and know literally where their family started, what they did, who was married or had how many kids.

But with the instability in the world, who wanted to bring kids into it right now? They would be nice and they would be good looking with that woman - his darker features and her lighter ones. They'd be tall, driven; she looked like she was an athlete as her calves were muscular and well-defined not only from her heels, but presumably from a good deal of exercise. Their children would be intelligent as she had to be smart to get to where she was. He'd teach things from the land that he knew were his own, explore things that weren't, and watch them learn things from their fair mother, too. He could only imagine the things she knew and what she would teach their daughters and son.

What the hell? He didn't even know her name and he was thinking about what their kids would look like? He had a "date" with Anita late that night after a quick dinner with his parents, but suddenly that seemed uninteresting. She wasn't usually boring but compared to this fascinating light,

Anita now seemed dull and dim. Not fair to her, he texted that something came up at work - which happened from time to time and (this time) it was true. This woman came to the next to top floor for business and he was thinking about a lifetime together after seeing her for twenty-seven minutes. He bet that she had been to the top floor, accessible to only a few with an individually assigned key-code that was recorded for every entry and exit.

That area was totally self-contained, even with its own generator and HVAC system. A few sleeping rooms with maple-post twin beds, no more than six to a room, and dressers inserted between each bed. A full service kitchen, a laundry area beside that, bathing areas that were much nicer than those on this floor - these three spaces encapsulated the two living areas. All along the long wall opposite of the sleeping quarters were windows to watch one of the main streets, once an old canal filled in and paved for "progress."

The bathrooms around the corner from where he sat for this area's staff were functional, but really distractions for the politicians from the main support area. Not everyone here was allowed upstairs - very few were given permission for that space. There was a need to keep that area off-limits and if it looked like full support could be "managed" in this space, no one without the need-to-know actually needed to know about upstairs.

After all, telling Anita that he wasn't able to see her tonight meant he had time to maybe see this woman later. Step one was getting a name. If nothing else, now that he was free tonight, he would take the boat out and do a little night fishing after dinner. Peaceful and quiet - and he could let his mind wander. He'd always done that since he was a kid. His dad would take him out, leaving his sister back on shore. The two of them could go hours on the water and not say a word. Whatever they had to drink, hot or cold, would be placed in a thermos so there would be no noise upon opening it when thirst overcame stillness, so as to not scare away the fish.

He knew all of the inlets where the redfish ran heavy, or the speckled trout swam shallow and fine. Sure, you could go crabbing past his house or catch a small gator or two - but that didn't leave your mind time to wander. Fishing let your mind clear out. Men of the area swore they knew how the fish ran, as their blood would flow with the tides. Each area of the waterways was totally different. Growing up, his father taught him that, too - go fishing by your cousins and learn their waters. You may know a lot here, but just a few miles downstream nothing is the same. Same river, different waters.

He was a night owl, but loved waking up early to fish or hunt. Fish or fowl, deer or frogs - it all brought a sense of pride and accomplishment that you were feeding your family and friends, taking only what you needed by your own skill, being nearly self-sufficient. That's one reason he stayed outside of the fancy city areas. There, still city but far out, you could know and trust the neighbors, do a little trading, like shrimp for venison. You kept an eye on certain things as strangers will be noticed. It was another reason if he met up with a girl, he didn't take them back to his place. Everyone would notice, though they might not say something directly, someone there was always keeping notes of some sort.

Chapter 5

Drew picked up on this second proposal question and tossed it back to Sean. "What about the second one, Sean?"

Cursing that he again felt pressure for which he was ill-prepared to handle, Sean didn't want to commit to anything. He was still contemplating how he could bring about Sarah's demise, and here was little old Andy-boy, pushing him for answers, too. He knew he hated to be called Andy, so he always made sure to use it when they spoke around others. Sean needed his people to give him the background on these new options. He was preparing a separate proposal himself, as his vision was going to be a long-term lucrative arrangement that he wanted to give to a potential supporter, garnishing unwavering dedication for the things he could produce.

He could think of a few things to say, but they were all derogatory about her and nothing positive about anything. So he tried to turn on some charm and yielded the floor again. "Well, imbedded in the heart of the city sounds both good and bad. I'm not familiar with how things have changed around there in the past five years, Andy. Wayne, that would be your neck of the woods, at least until the mayor gave the dog a bone instead of to you."

Oh, sweet pain from above, this would go on for hours. Sarah had already managed to narrow down the hour's first-third habit, the pointless habitual review, with her injection of locations. But now that discussion was bleeding over into the second twenty minutes, which was ideally the time to be doling out little duties to the little men to keep their little minds busy. She had to turn to the side to calm her frustration.

She purposefully turned to the windows over her left shoulder, just for a change of scenery from these indecisive men. She had been looking at the white plastered wall that ran perpendicular to the windows, that canvas waiting for artistry. When on the roof of this building, the best view was directly over the edge where these same windows defended against the heat rising from the asphalt, that being down a main boulevard that by some happenstance still had the greenery down both sides. The buildings weren't well maintained, but the sight of lush trees and the trimmed lawn space was relaxing.

It helped her think of the quiet during her last venture to the roof. She was working an event here. Stressful; buildings were going down one at a time. One of the guys was giving wrong information in the command center, and when she tried to inject updated information to keep the conversation going in the correct direction, he snapped at her. She merely stood, walked into an office where the commander was getting ready for a meeting, told him that she was "taking a five minute break before she punched a guy in the nose," and went topside. She literally said that, and a gentle smile began wisping its way to her lips as she recalled the blank look on the CO's face when she exited.

No winds up there on that night, but the air was cool enough at that height. It carried a fresh smell, unpolluted as everyone had been evacuated for days. The view without the restraint of windows, without having a guarding edge, was stunning even in destruction. Well, it wasn't as bad as the world media had hoped, but crap was down and blowing around.

Power losses, water instability - typical, but far less than tragedy from several years prior.

Sarah had walked around the large roof, just to be in open space without chatter. Up and down the steel stairwells that climbed over the HVAC and generators, under pipelines and cabling. A slow moving lap, that's what she needed then, far above manufactured pressures to outdo and overshout for attention. She couldn't walk out of this meeting to do another lap - though one of the men here was part of that incident - so merely taking two seconds to absorb the same view would have to suffice.

The lap in heels right now would have been amusing. But she'd done other things in heels, always to men's amazement. Going on deck for an inspection - were those brown heels or those blue floral print toeless ones? Hoping on the pontoon for an intercept? Black. Running to a victim during a sporting event? Cream. It was irony at its finest that she mentally reverted to frilly female topics like fashion when she needed a break from the men - after all, when anyone asked if her mind was drifting, she could honestly reply that she was thinking about shoes instead of blurting that the boredom had her thinking about asphyxiation for diversion. She prized honesty far more than people around here. Funny, that sentiment went both ways as she prized honesty more than she prized the men around here and she prized honesty more than these men prized it. What did they call that? Structural ambiguity? Syntactic? Her smile grew to its true form as she let the men do the "who's dick is bigger" dance.

Her smile precipitated a final deep breath before turning back to the task at hand - managing these men - and she noticed that man at the laptop again. He was watching her. It could have been innocent enough as her movement during a very still discussion on the opposite end of the room would have caught his eye. She let her smile rest upon him, then shut her eyes as she turned around so her 'eyeballs to the sky' would go unnoticed by them all as she returned to the conversation. As she closed her eyes, she didn't see the hint of a grin returned to her.

His thoughts were pleasant thoughts, too, though totally focused in the present. She was definitely hot... and absolutely controlling that meeting. Marcus wondered what made her smile so softly when it was obvious she was involved in a discussion that did not warrant messing around. He knew that she was catching every flippant phrase while ignoring the speakers at the same time. Was she playing a role or playing them?

He decided he needed to get up and move, now that he had seen her turn around again. Her eyes were stunning - and sharp, bright, as well as direct. His instincts were right - all indications pointed to her having her shit together. However, he actually felt like he was not in her league, and he had never felt that way previously. He knew he was good looking and appealed to women, that he could draw attention whenever he wanted. He didn't take advantage of that all of the time, but it was amusing during a slow work night or at the bar with friends.

But now, it seemed as though he shouldn't distract her from her task at hand. That meant he had to distract himself (by getting up for coffee across the room). He was supposed to be coordinating intel for the investigation on the local gangs shifting shape. They had been running one predicable way prior to five years ago, just about manageable or at least not expanding. Upheaval then caused a rift and total realignment, shapeshifting of those crews, floating of the enforcers from one side to the other and back again. There seemed to be a new pattern rather than haphazard reengineering, but his team couldn't put their finger on it. With the recent influx of the Mexican cartel halcones and sicarios, their low level street runners and hitmen, they needed to figure out the local guys quickly as violence was escalating. Historical networks could be managed; the new developments could be actually frightening.

When the two gangs named after the city's founding brothers decided to merge into one downtown gang in order to take on the uptown gang, things got complicated. Some of the selling districts no longer had buyers - they were gone, migrated away from the area. Now that both downtowns and an uptown had a Texas connection, and there were links with Mexico (in these two cases *against* Mexico as well as the new Mexican cartel components), things were heating up quickly.

Same guys, same cousins, same weapons, but this time the stomping grounds were asymmetric. A hundred years ago, the lines were drawn (in some cases literally with the neutral grounds) and hadn't been changed until five years ago. With that shift in geography as well as economics, there was an inevitable modification in the opportunity patterns - that led to a shift in transportation routes they used for delivery. Urban redevelopment as envisioned by the mayor's office wasn't the gangs' boots-on-the-ground story playing out on the streets and in city crime statistics.

The demographics shifted for the buyers, but not the suppliers. These suppliers, though, had additional competition for the resources available. The Ivy League economic theories of "Guns versus Butter" held true - and the gangs knew this. If you limit the availability of supply distribution channels, the price could then be raised because the volume of buyers was the same, or prices could be increased even further given the purity of the wares.

This purity increase came via the Mexican cartel connection. True, non-gang Latinos were infiltrating and building in the uptown area, but contrary to rampant ignorance, Latinos are not all the same. They don't all like one another. The only generalizations that were applicable were the group that came here was hard working and fairly close-knit among their countrymen. Marcus knew this posed a problem when trying to gain intel as their street contacts were not as adept in recognizing the differentiating factors between these newer groups. The only thing they could recognize was the increased tensions, the increased shootings (though less accurate), the shifting of personnel monitoring - for both them and us.

Beyond nationality bonds, the women were just as ruthless when protecting their own. Even when seemingly protecting the millennial injection to the business along with their shameful work ethic, the women didn't cower to them and didn't let them run the show. Funny, but even in more "legit" gig work, the men worked out of the house doing odd jobs but the women controlled the money. The women were the brains behind the family and the men were the front. There's got to be something to this gender segregation, but like the "staff" reengineering, he wasn't quite there yet. And as he started to think of the gender differences and how the networks could be impacted by this, it brought him right back to where he was mentally trying to leave - her - at least for the time being.

Chapter 6

The clock was ticking. She felt that they were closer to picking option two, and gently proverbially nudged Wayne into seeing how it would be a direct win for him to wrestle the property away from his nemesis by waving "no right to know" cards at the mayor, thus helping the politician get control of that loose playboy cannon again and regaining leverage. Stripping the opposition away from the opportunity nailed that punk's wallet, too, so that appealed to Wayne directly and greatly. Drew was still muttering things against option three, which was good. And he was right on some of his rationale, wrong on other parts, but hadn't hit the dangerous spot yet. She would keep that to herself, only sharing if that option reared its head again.

Tasking Luke and Jason to obliterate option one and Drew to enumerate the perils of option three - of course in a gentle feminine way that made her want to gag - she nominated Wayne to "skillfully lead the option two plan" and resurrection of this lagging project that just wouldn't get moving. In no way, shape or form did she - or any of them - want Sean to get his hands on some of the details. But, he was there as he had been nominated for "helping" by another politician who believed he was the lesser of available evils and could be controlled. So far, that had proven correct. She had a dossier on some of his dirty deeds that would help shut him up, and she was pretty sure at least one or two others had pieces of the puzzle for when it came down to that.

Thus freeing up the last fifteen minutes of the meeting and having a path forward, she let the boys do their small talk golf score bullshit and went to cube-ville. She wanted to talk to her girl - who "they" all discounted in the scheme of things, but if it wasn't for the two of them in the last incident, none of the 5,000 troops would have eaten. For real. *Imbeciles,* she thought. *For as much as people yammer that men think with their stomachs first and then their second head, knowing what crap happened last time they forgot about food, you would think they could remember just a few years later to handle the basics of Maslow's hierarchy. Hell, no.* Dummies. She should have let the troops revolt.

Simply cruel to have them not eat. No matter if they were told to self-supply for a week; when you have to take care of kids and spouses and pets and send them out to prepare for battle, your own needs came last. Sustenance for oneself came after protection in a reversal of the first two stags of the scientist's algorithm - so extra time to saddle up the weapons came before food, too. The main guys had contracted for themselves to be fed. Twenty-four meals without consideration for thousands. She had hers, but it didn't sit well.

It had taken her just two phone calls. She was able to make sure meals were distributed four times a day (for the night-watch lunch, too) at three locations in the city and the only thing they had to do was be in uniform and/or with their vehicle. Support crews, like the truck drivers that moved things between sleeping zones, staging areas, and forward base, also were included in her counts. A confirmation call from her or Lorrie (and only her or Lorrie) made an hour prior to meals ensured the feeding team had the last minute maneuvers and safe zones for travel.

Plus as an unintended side result, it got the troops indebted to her when she made sure they were fed. She also provided them the phone numbers they needed for assistance before anyone else and she made sure there was a *private* assistance area open exclusively for first responders available around the clock, away from the public. This time, they were told before the public or even politicians. The time before, they were all but forgotten, except when something went wrong. What assholes. *You have to cover the ones who have your back - or they will stab you as soon as its turned.*

The private gratification came when some of the troops found their way to her, that woman in the tower who sent the emails out about where to get help, to get questions answered at command, to send someone to them with grub when they couldn't get off post - and usually within 15 minutes of them sending the email to her phone, be it day or night, she handled all sorts of things. Moving hot food pickup when platoons shifted locations, more cots needed, remind me what SBA does again, can a tarp be put aside for my wife to grab, could you send extra ice to the slab that was a fire station but the neighbors are using as a distribution point? She walked around with that damn laptop everywhere, making sure she could carry the ball. No one realized until later how key she was to that event's success. And it opened a lot of doors because she knew she belonged and they now knew it, too.

It also helped to know where some bodies were buried with first-hand experience. People use that phrase figuratively, but Sarah also used it literally. When you could drop a line that may seem a little out of place to ninety percent of the people in a room, but ten percent knew you were going to hand them their own shit on a platter if they got out of line any further as their toes were already too close to "that line," people shaped up. Some quit their jobs just to be free of those facts. So be it - they weren't any good at what they did. And when a guy lied about sleeping with her, those that were there and knew how full of bullshit that disgraced jarhead was, well they put an end to that man's fantasy and big mouth very fast and "downgraded" his career future just to make sure the message got home.

Funny that she was never the belle of the ball, but guys would stand up for her. Even if she didn't consider herself the "fairest in the land," she knew she topped almost everyone with her brains and various skills. One gunny once said it's because her boots have been on the ground and she takes care of the troops as she goes up the ladder, knowing she only ascends with the help of the people behind her. She stands up for her people, even if she ends up taking fire for it (usually getting a few good shots in herself if the heat intensifies). Even when exhausted, that all held true.

And when she has that rare moment of down time, she goes home to unwind with no distractions. Oil painting, working her body, or stretching her voice as a coloratura. Even calling a friend from the past to speak French and keep her fluency - yes, these little private things were her own and none of these slovenly blokes could do any one of them. But she goes home alone, left to handle the frustration of incomplete projects, slow-moving counterparts, or to do the work of others as they lay on the legs of those around them.

Sometimes she pushed people away that wanted to get to know her, but that was because their intentions weren't always about her; instead, it was about using her network or her body. It was really difficult to trust people after seeing the ways manipulation was used as a weapon, and men frequently chose to use sex as a substitute for all sorts of things. Other times, folks were just scared to approach her because she seemed to operate only on full-throttle and that put her out of reach (bringing up their insecurities of rejection because she didn't settle for anything). If they only knew how she would have liked just a normal conversation with someone without speculating on their end game. She tended to keep people at arm's length - well, men. It was easier to know if a woman was friend or foe as women were more transparent to one another.

Finding and hugging her girl in cube-ville after some laughter about those idiots (always, together, trying to reaffirm that they were just giggling girls and just "increasing the aesthetic value of the environment"), they passed some information in whispers, as usual. Leaving that desk with some interesting news, she poked around to see if anyone else was around the office. Finance woman was gone already (at least the men put the woman in charge of the most important department), so she left a little note for her, to make her smile in the morning.

She saw the clock beside the blotter on Joann's desk and realized she wanted to scoot. She could cut out today a little early - she was still available by email and cell, anyway. She knew none of the men from the meeting would say a word about her schedule. If she was lucky, she could go home and change to walk by the lake before the sun set. She turned to leave, heading back toward the kitchen before that u-turn to exit stage right.

Because he was in the kitchen thinking about the cartel again, Marcus was pouring coffee as he saw her enter the cubes through the reflection in the window. She was tall enough that he could watch her navigate to various destinations. There was one corner where he lost sight of her - behind the watcher's office. There was a nook that afforded a small luxury of semi-privacy, though the assignees in that space were rarely around. She was out of sight for maybe two minutes, so someone was in there or she was leaving a note. Interesting.

As she appeared around that corner, she directly looked at him. Straight into his eyes, unblinking and unfazed that he was waiting for her. She knew he'd be watching. Damn.

She kept that contact as she navigated the paths, coming right around the watcher's office and exited the only rabbit hole leading from the maze. That's when she broke their gaze as she completed the u-turn around the watcher's office and left in the direction of the door. He heard her cheerfully wishing the two ladies up front to have a nice evening, and the tell-tale click of the latch securing. That's when he blinked.

He had to know. He didn't want to directly ask; that wasn't being a good detective. The five men were obviously off-limits, the girls up front didn't use her name, but she had been giggling with Lorrie before he poured his coffee. He doesn't interact routinely with anyone in cube-ville, though, so it would be like a big neon sign asking her about that woman.

He could, however, walk over to the secluded cubes to see if she left a note on the assumption that she'd sign it. He went back to his laptop, looked at some emails that were in his box and picked up some paperwork, trying to further mask his intention. Entering cube-ville, he walked directly to the area in the back as if he had a question about the paperwork in his hand - and found it empty.

No one was around. He could look at every desk for a note, starting with the cube next to Lorrie. As he expected in that cube, nothing like a recently placed note, though he wasn't discouraged and continued to work his way around that area. Other notes collecting dust, those partially buried under other paperwork - nothing presented itself as a 30-minute past drive-by.

He went back to his work area and packed his things for the evening. He wasn't giving up, but needed to get out to the house and grill up some venison steaks from his last buck.

Hunting season was coming, so he appreciated the grilling now more than ever, knowing he would have some fresh stock very shortly. His parents were coming over since he had an early shift today and he didn't want to get home late, which would have his mom complaining that she could have made dinner easily so he wouldn't have to work so hard. Since he cancelled that previously planned drink that was set for after dinner, he started to think about things like heading out on the boat this evening.

His mind quickly had left the woman, moving to a mundane checklist of errands as was his standard routine on the way home. Living outside of the city center was fantastic, made easy with good planning. The path deviated each day on the way home, but he made sure to get done what he needed to do so he could relax. Today, he would stop at the ATM first… and realized that he hadn't checked the finance director's office. He hadn't seen the woman enter there, but it wasn't outside the realm of possibilities.

He entered cube-ville one more time and wove his way to the back corner, opposite of the watcher's office. The finance office is typically untidy, but oddly organized, so much so that a note would be conspicuous.

Well, damn - especially when it was orange. Finance color-codes everything and apparently sticky notes are orange to catch the eye. Three notes were around, but he quickly identified the authors of two of them. The third read,

We should catch up on IJs. Wine at Montagne; Thursday, same time?

He wasn't sure of the signature, however. Much freer and almost artistic in design. *Well, baby, what do you know?* The straight laced professional had a touch of flamboyance in her smooth curves and swirls, taking a bit off that cool controlled edge. Nice. Even if she wanted to meet with finance on a Saturday, he would have figured out how to cover that place for sixteen hours or more to discover her name. Baby, he was looking forward to Thursday.

Chapter 7

Luke began accumulating and then pouring over data about the wharf option, the first in Sarah's presentation. The classified portions were supposedly a deterrent to gaining access to information, but he didn't even need to pause to pull up those reports. Boring, as usual. So many intelligence reports were scrubbed and reported only what the politicians wanted to hear. Inquiries into recent DOD intel reporting regarding skirmishes in the Middle East had begun; technicalities didn't allow the term "war" to be used.

Rumors were that orders from very high levels were given to bury anything not portraying the U.S. as a powerhouse succeeding at its latest missions abroad. There were some politics as usual - the side of the incumbent president tried to link the discrepancies to top level generals appointed to their posts by his predecessor (of the opposite party). Members of Congress were looking at the president's frequent phraseology that sometimes literally said, "I don't want to hear things like that." When the Commander in Chief says he doesn't want to hear it - even when it's his responsibility to hear the good and bad - tendencies are no one tells the whole truth, just the pretty parts. Those misinformation documents cost many lives, and Luke was glad someone was at least scratching the surface. He was not optimistic that changes would ensue, but at least things were being uncovered.

Like those that covered the truth, Luke was accustomed to reading between the lines, even when there were lines "left out" though his efforts were in order to uncover facts. When on official duty, his lines were clear electronic transmissions. When he was on his own time digging in the dirt (literally), the lines in the sand were extremely faint. The message was all contextual. Signs and symbols in the colors, surrounding glyphs, medium of carving, small marks from the tools used to create the message itself - all of these were sometimes more important than what others thought was the actual content of the message.

His latest dig involved not an actual dig, but interpreting data from two Egyptian tombs. He liked combining the two - modern interpretations being validated by ancient facts. There had been chatter some fifty years ago, when the pillaging of the pyramids was at its worst and any available technology was cumbersome, that there may be more to several tombs than met the eye. Several of the most infamous pharaohs were "missing" as their burial sites had not been identified.

Though large pyramids were not located, there were nuances in several of the smaller Upper Egypt structures that didn't add up. Though the world was now well beyond the abacus in machinations, still the calculations didn't appear to meet in the middle. As in *literally* the middle. He didn't do the math side, but was responsible for physical inspections in recent years, to decipher other areas of the rooms that might hint at the elongation or truncation of certain equations.

At first appearance to anyone, even untrained personnel, it would make sense there would be some imperfections. After all, these were designed and built more than two thousand years ago and men had to manufacture ways to move each heavy stone into place. Perhaps (understandably) the slaves whipped into action made slight errors in acts of defiance, knowing the empires would fall eventually and they could help the temples to also topple. It was logical to conclude that a small act of defiance such as displaced stones helped them get through every day and night. Just because something stood for thousands of years didn't mean there weren't internal flaws in stone placement.

But as he wandered in the silent tombs with little or no air moving, he could tell there were indications in some places that the whole story wasn't presented. Deep under the sands of time that helped keep hidden the secrets of deceased royalty, he trod in booties covering his bare feet through halls where the most esteemed artisans worked and most vile slaves moved. These passageways were built long before formal national security acts and mechanized weapons of mass destruction, and it was quite possible that there were fantastic secrets buried in the temples.

Founded on mystic claims with exploitation of the people's fears, pharaohs used science to their advantage. Creating colors for makeup such as the kohl eyeliner infamous on death masks by using their understanding of chemical reactions, even varying composition of clothing dyes dependent on the tension for the cotton's weave, Egyptians had engineering feats that launched them beyond their enemies in lifestyle as well as warfare techniques - and though there was all of that, their art is what withstood the test of time. It was fascinating to behold as well as analyze. It's why he did it in bare feet, hoping perhaps there were clues under the sand that had blown inside the rooms. It also adjusted his height closer to that of the ancient Egyptians, and perspective was everything - even back then.

Recently, transportable imaging technology was making it possible to inspect what was behind the pink limestone stela, the carvings, on one particular wall. The process was similar to the x-ray vision in super hero comic books of the 1950s and 60s. Choosing the technology to capture data for determining if seeming errors with stone placement or smaller-than-expected room design was a mere slave revolt or a well-planned hidden cavern was something he didn't do. He assembled what was captured by radiology and LiDAR to determine the story. If they were able to produce images or facts, he could then present the likelihood of contents behind the wall.

He recently also used near-infrared technology from satellite images that reflected electromagnetic data. While this wasn't the type of precision that was used for something "not meeting in the middle," it had helped identify some deviations in surface density, anomalies in a color-pattern that called out "look at me." Why some of the great archeologists liked to call on him was the military allowed him to use their data with his clearance to pull only certain data to complete a report - no one without permission ever saw all the information those space birds accumulated that wasn't part of the inner circle project. He was in the middle of it and could use the secret data to produce results that could be publicly shared.

Luke could dissect and isolate various components of the captured images, pulling off layers through a variety of GIS programs, revealing previously hidden designs in the sand. Building materials (stone and mud) were more dense, and could be seen to a depth of about a mile depending on the bird used. It was like Superman's x-ray vision with routine internet mapping capability, giving subtle underground variances. Sometimes, he even incorporated ethnobotanical results, where heavier metals once digested were excreted into soils in greater density in population centers as well as on heavily traveled migration routes.

While the military used similar techniques he derived in certain terrorist-infested regions, they had no problems with him expanding the application to things like his excavation projects as long as he protected the top secret data sources. His curiosity produced stellar results that were directly applicable to their needs as well as archeological interests for world heritage sites. His results produced virtual 3D maps that could be rotated, zoomed, and more - including printing in miniature or producing diagrams for life-size assembly in warehouse space for training purposes. Elite teams could virtually explore outposts of rebels or monitor training programs without having intrusive drones or inconsistent HUMINT feeds. Some of his applications were used in the bio-units now deployed with elite teams, like those he used during that stained glass debacle.

It wasn't augmented reality, but provided reproductions with precise coordinates. With inclusion of reflective radar imaging, the designs Luke's program produced were impeccable. However, that was impractical in an enemy's lair, though they had been able to make that happen on two occasions. He did it once with a portable watch-mounted lens; once engaged with the side button sequence, it took a multi-directional laser imprint of the room in which it was placed - even compensating for the person standing with it during the twenty seconds it took to complete the impulse. After that twenty seconds, anytime thereafter a piggy-back signal rode a normal cell call of anyone nearby, the file disguised in the transmission if any scanning equipment looked for unusual signals. The second scenario had good information outcomes, but they lost their operative. Data would win any battle, and the government let him explore new ways to win wars regardless of a punch-clock.

Luke found high demand for the geospatial assimilation of the various components from ground-penetrating radar, infrared, x-ray florescence, magnetic resistivity, magnetometry and radiocarbon dating among other technology data he used were in a variety of fields, and not only in his applications for antiterrorism and archeology; he could be selective with prospective customers. He had also devised a way to incorporate some recent features that were on par with space exploration expectations. Being able to produce a hologram that would turn and spin based on the movement of fingers and zoom based on eye movements made long-distance ground travel supremely easy and yielded staggering results. Building it for mapping sites was his original theory, but having sold licensure for use of the technology to the military, he was kept on with his full access to any data he wanted so long as he provided upgrades and feedbacks from his new commercial applications to the defense department versions as well.

There was an aspect of the project he especially enjoyed. Typically, standard corporate projects looked ten meters below the earth's surface. It's what the immigration guys formerly used to detect cartel tunnels along the border of Mexico. But since they only scraped the surface, those criminal transnational organizations began buying oil drilling equipment, purchasing all the fracking equipment they could under the guise of water excavation for long-term irrigation, a nice humanitarian contribution. Instead, they used it to build tunnels to a depth of twenty or thirty meters complete with HVAC units to circulate air with lighting units all powered with solar panels in order to remain off "the grid."

Knowing some of what would be submerged for longer-distance subterranean life support made it much easier for Luke to add features to his program that searched for structural patterning of modern shapes (rather than ancient sarcophagi), and that allowed deeper penetration of the earth's crust. The geophysics models actually identified pieces of known objects and with those properties assimilated likely areas of extensive work. Whereas humans on the surface could only go so far or just very shallow, the SAT data coupled with his AI puzzle program enabled the identification and tracking of several hundred rudimentary tunnels along the boarder. The cartels thought they were slick when in fact the feds were tracking their progress, slowly scooping them up and flipping them on one another.

While archeology was much more interesting, he needed to refocus on the local near-term mission. Perspective on option one, literally and data-wise, confirmed this building was not a good selection for the storage and distribution site. Facts were easy to accumulate, but crafting the story for Jason to present to their boss was a different adventure. He was relieved that he was working on this one and not the second option, which even if it was the best choice had a lot of political baggage and demanded interpersonal interpretations. That was emotional nuance rather than fact, an area where he readily admitted to himself (not to others) he didn't excel. He'd leave it to the mogul to work that hot mess of "opportunity."

Chapter 8

Wayne, the narcissistic businessman, was constantly looking at facts, sorting them into groupings: items for profit, stronger yet cruel pieces saved for attention on another day, and then negligible details that should be facts but could be turned into different pictures more suitable for his exploitation. On one level, he refused to acknowledge his behavior thrived on his own deficiencies, where he always started an "intellectual battle" intending to overcompensate for his faults. Kids belittled him throughout adolescence and he was still trying to prove himself. On another level, he believed it was his right to take whatever he could wrestle away from people not up to his standards. In reality, it was just that he was mean.

Growing up in the city, he was a scrappy skinny kid in an area divided between groups of brothers, cousins and other relations. Most adult males were gone when he was young - either off fighting for their lives in the war or having lost the battle and never coming home. Those few that made it back often weren't right. There was no traumatic screening, no social workers to assimilate them back into society's fold. Instead, there were houses - built on Napoleon's idea of Les Invalides - places where attempts were made to see if they could be released to the community after being torn apart in the wilds of war.

His father came back, but never came home. They tried to have him at the house, but he couldn't be with his mother, sister or him. He would pace, hyper-alert to any shifts of the shadows or rattles in the pipes, bark out statements instead of having a conversation. It was better after just two weeks in the house that he went upriver to a new veterans development (under the guise of "hospital"). It was known that there was no cure for what ailed the men that came home, and also understood that they would never be discharged from the facility. The veterans could be kept comfortable, and the lifestyle was kept in a regimental manner, thus making it less of an adjustment for them.

Excluding growing boys from the guidance of fathers was an outcome of the war that the nation's leaders never foresaw. Cruelty of children intensified when authority wasn't looking. When he was very young, it only took a look from any adult to stop a kid cold in his tracks. A neighbor would call your mom, who would tell your dad (if he was around) - then there was big trouble. But with a mother working two jobs to keep them in their home and him getting an education, there was no authority figure in his life. The old uncle made no difference. The cousin that was always mysteriously appearing with handy cash didn't want to be involved.

Wayne didn't care back then. Various groups of brothers and cousins ran about and considered different corners their area. He'd do what he wanted and when the kids picked a fight, he would handle business - then hide from his mother until the bruising subsided. He knew he had to focus on his lessons and pick a job to get out of that place. But he had no where else to go, so he was forced as the first major decision of his life was taken from him, to stay around and see what happened.

He didn't like waiting around, so he tried to create his own opportunities. Sometimes they worked out, sometimes they didn't. But he always made sure he always came out ahead in cash flow. Even back when he first started earning a little money, he made sure to keep some tucked away where no one knew. He didn't feel badly about taking a little extra from his mother when he'd claim that he didn't have any left for bus fare or getting lunch. The shop keepers felt sorry for him, this young man without a father who was rumored to be trying to care for his mother, so they gave him a little extra or charged him a little less. He came to expect that he should get more, and if he didn't get it, he'd take it.

Even his short time in the military during the Vietnam conflict, he saw bullets meeting flesh, mines explode underneath his platoon brothers, and he came out with a traumatic growth of sorts rather than stress disorder. It made him hone his ability to evaluate risk factors, build his personal resilience ability, and made damn sure he'd do more than just survive even if his choices appeared morally questionable to people on the outside making judgments about his decisions.

Over time, he had found others like himself. They'd go marry trophy wives and get rid of them after a few years. They'd find fissures in the antiquated legislature and use it to their personal advantage - or find a friendly legislator to handle the perceived problem. When other people did things like this, this group screamed about the atrocity. As their friends succeeded with the same tactics, they applauded.

He had been too busy researching something on his phone about his latest project when Sarah had tried to get him to make a hasty decision about the positioning of the supplies, namely the location of the building that would bring him huge profits if he managed it just right. He had been trying to keep his name out of that endeavor, with success to this point. He haughtily imagined he was weaving a fantastic web that would ensure his legacy for generations to come.

After all, this area of the country was three hundred years old by written western history accounts, and blazed an alternative path from the country of its forefathers. It had a way of attracting eclectic and eccentric people, which emboldened the established families to consider its progeny better than everyone else. Unfortunately, it was consistently at the expense of one group to elevate their part of society, and the message never got through that it was unacceptable to push down in order to raise up. Without meaningful opposition, it stayed like that for centuries.

Along the way, a few people tried to make things better, if not right. One wealthy landholder only had daughters, no sons, and had moved to the area for health reasons in the late 1800s. Law of this area (unlike the landholder's original state) was "land is only for sons;" daughters need to marry a man with land, and could not own property. Since this gentleman didn't want to lose his property - over a million acres - while also not wanting to make enemies with local politicians, he gave the appearance that he wanted to provide for his female children in some fashion to gain support (and marshal allies with the ear of the last mouths that would speak to these same politicians each night before bedtime).

And then taking up with lawmakers, expensed with a little bit of gratitude, a statewide law was easily passed that required profits from a trust based upon the collateral of land could be designated for ninety-nine years to any blood family member, regardless of gender. Contrary to the upheaval this law wrought in smoking rooms, it manifested resolve in the tea rooms. Slowly, ever slowly, these ladies realized they could take pieces of freedom that were promised in the "new world."

Over time, the plantation mentality coupled with the flattening of higher society through wars and appropriate destruction of slavery had these same women regroup "behind their men" in order to preserve the remaining land and profits for their sons. This then meant they could marry their daughters into other remaining wealthy families, keeping their fortunes all tied up as it had been. The justice movement died for many years.

But it did not die for people like Wayne's family. On the cusp of success and bettering-by-marriages, that had all been erased with war and famine and economic changes. Clawing and fighting to get it back, families like Wayne's would exploit small opportunities, and saw the need to revert to the ways of suppressing "lessor" people so they could get ahead. The truly old-school well-heeled saw no need for that. But this group, Wayne's group, tried to befriend the monied families, to be public-facing figurative servants to the monied's needs, and scratch slowly up the social ladder while simultaneously giving lip-service to how bad repression was while serving as the iron fist that kept it in place.

One family in particular believed the wealthy landholder from over one hundred years prior began the downfall of their family's rising to rule everything and everyone. Though of slightly different means, this put that man's and Wayne's families on the same side. Generations would bide their time separately waiting for the ninety-nine year trust to come near its expiration, yet also not realize how significant it would be when the time came.

Thus, Wayne (and Jason's politician boss both) fought for that near-century old trust to dissolve - Wayne by taking it piecemeal through legal loopholes and the politician by just ignoring the law. It allowed Wayne to freehandedly start developing projects within those areas; but actually, he had started that more than a decade prior. It allowed the politician to have unfettered unrestricted access to nearly three million dollars annually (in addition to natural resources for personal use) and elevate his family to higher status - to the point where people called him benevolent dictator without his knowledge, the public recognizing the fact he was still raising himself up while pushing others down - the same "others" that had voted for him before and likely would again.

Prior to the trust's dissolution, Wayne convinced some politicians of contiguous neighborhoods to help erode what would eventually come under their competing thorn's control. They resented the city for its name and fame, and desperately wanted it to fall. Chipping away at the trust property under the law meant "eminent domain" and "right of way" and "protecting the environment" all would be rezoned for his project. After all these years, he could claim successful revenge in the way that mattered to those higher-class people the most - through their bank accounts.

And so with the wheels moving and a natural disaster to help the Feds turn a blind eye to many things, he began to have state and local government personnel take pieces of land, under a myriad of reasons, for his big pet project. Five years ago, he even was able to have the state pay the majority of the infrastructure funding under the guise of economic development post-storm. The completion of that project saw a dirty money maker when the gates opened, with people fascinated how he pulled it off. Positioned as a huge entertainment attraction, he created a fantastic way for running smaller side businesses within the new property, on which he had been working when Sarah had spoken.

Yes, he would push people down to stand on their backs, even if it included the ringleader politician who had his beady little eyes set on grandeur. He just had to play along for this last project, and then he would be elevated to the ranks of the fabulously wealthy, being able to leave more than ample supply of riches and projects for his sons and daughter. The mean streak had served him well. Though lonely (a series of wives became ex-wives, all having left him long ago), he funneled that loneliness into projects like these that took him further into the depths of antiquated aristocracy. He would get to the bottom of how the second option would make him a bunch of money.

Chapter 9

Andrew was inherently a worrisome man, which actually helped determine his career path when he joined the military. Described as a rather compact guy, he wasn't overweight or disproportionate by any means. He was just... short, though he felt himself fortunate that he still had the same full head of light brown hair that he'd had since childhood (since taller people had to look down when speaking to him, he was extremely grateful for the natural blessing of no baldness). When he entered the military after going to the "right" high school, he knew from his academic performance that he would be heading to Officer Candidate School at some stage.

He chose to enter the Army *after* the global turmoil of the 70s had quieted, leaving it to the rank to figure out the direction he would take. He could do any mental task to which he set his mind; the problem was that he wasn't invested in anything he tried. It wasn't necessarily that he didn't care about the issues, but rather the overwhelming concerns that manifested when he was considering the "what ifs" - such as when given the post-high school graduation choices he was drawn into a quagmire of what if he chose the wrong college, what if he chose the wrong subjects, what if he chose the wrong wife... A lot of time spent thinking and not as much physical activity contributed to Drew's nature.

It wasn't that he wasn't athletic. On the contrary, his stature made him ideal for some sports. He just didn't care for group activities really. Going back to his middle school days in parochial school, the boys had their favorites for each sport. He would invariably get picked close to the end of selections for any physical match up - predominantly because of appearance. It was in middle school that the weakness of appearance began weighing on him, knowing that it was something he couldn't change.

In his mind, and that of his father's, he had to compensate for his lacking physical stature with something else, and he wasn't a child given to bouts of pettiness to take up bullying or a bounding ego that would have led him to pontificate while becoming a tragic bore. Instead, he took up a variety of studies that produced interesting facts for the evenings families of his ilk would spend at the club, intriguing both adults and other boys as well.

Learning how to identify things that may interest others (or turn them away from a discussion) had proven especially useful in high school and then in his early military career. By engaging his instructors (teachers and then Sergeants) in topics they found interesting, it elevated him to a point where they would see beyond his physical size and endow him with additional intellectual stature in conversations, especially useful when assignments were being distributed in the barracks.

The fact that he could discuss topics that interested his direct supervisor in the armed forces meant that he had extra time informally devoted to him. The Army was infamous for just throwing people into spots to see if they would sink or swim; his supervisors usually gave him tasks that required more thought or required detail work. They knew Drew's proclivity for thinking things through meant that a project that had "rolled down hill" to their unit and would be inspected (or highly visible) by senior officers would be handled in the best fashion possible with him assigned to the team.

When the time came for promotions and direction-setting for members of their unit, the engineering corps came to call on him. Understanding from other officers that he was responsible for the analysis of certain tasks and designing the best method to reach completion, they thought he'd be a perfect fit for civil engineering. While starting some of the evaluations that determined if he was prone to a specific style of engineering, it rapidly became evident that he had talent for structural engineering. He could see the integrity of an entire system, then decompose problem segments in order to attack swiftly and resolve issues.

The Army put him through engineering school, all expenses paid. His father had expected nothing less, but his mother affectionately told him at their annual winter visit that he made her very proud. She always said the same thing, whether dad was angry or belittling, trying to defuse the situation. Before returning to an engineering assignment, Drew completed the officer training before his last year of college.

The intersection of his enlisted years, then graduating from a civilian college as well as completing OCS furthered his reputation for being congenial and approachable: enlisted guys respected him for putting in his time; academy graduates respected his hard-earned degree from a private university; other officers appreciated his completion of OCS without "skipping form" as many war college post-graduate guys were pushed to the top of the ranks by virtue of the ring on their finger rather than aptitude.

Drew was pleased with the Army's selection of engineering. It always fascinated him that in medieval times, the master builder of some of the great gothic buildings had to be architect, structural engineer for static load-bearing components, fluids engineer in churches for sound patterns, part physicist for fireplace design and chimney drafting, and more. He admitted that he enjoyed many components of being the master puppeteer behind the scenes - and all of those brawny big guys got to carry the load literally while he commanded all the movements.

What he didn't enjoy rang back to his memories of those days in the 80s, of the Middle Eastern conflicts - in particular Libyan aggressions - and the rushed logistics of hurry up and wait to be blown to bits. He had friends assigned to the Gulf of Sidra in the Mediterranean, a lovely assignment during the winter months so it seemed. His buddies were on an aircraft carrier that was operating in international waters, but close to Muammar Gaddafi's random-ass "Line of Death."

The year prior to the water's line being drawn, a TWA flight had been highjacked and Libya was responsible. Since that June, the United States military, itchy from a decade away from aggressive combat fighting, only needed an excuse to engage in battle. Being the defenders of democracy in the Ronald Reagan presidency, the branches of the military ensured their bases in Europe were fully staffed and operational.

Just as Drew had done a bit earlier, many young men were enlisting at that time - they felt left out of the Vietnam and Korean conflicts, so were searching for their own personal identities and wanted to exhibit the strength of their patriotism. Idealistic as they were, the media back then did not shield the public from graphic war pictures that came over the wires. Nothing was real time at that stage, but the eloquent words used to describe the bloody battles and occasional images were enough to get any American ready to fight.

The leaders in the military were no different. Ready to show military prowess as had their predecessors in the twenty years prior, they began operations under the broadcast "Freedom of Navigation." Three of his boot camp friends, one being his bunkmate, were assigned to the USS Saratoga. Along with the USS America, Coral Sea, Detroit and Savannah, the American public thought it insane for Gaddafi to tempt fate and instigate a battle when these ships crossed the his made-up Line of Death - clearly established in international waters - in order to keep sea lanes open and free.

Rationale was not a strong attribute of the Libyan leader, and he attacked that March, literally moments after the first two destroyers went over the line (albeit with a sledgehammer for a tack). The United States calculated that they would be attacked, which is why they put members of Army regiment on the ships - prepared is better than surprised. As planes positioned and swarmed in the air, destroyers cut forward into the disputed navigable waterway, firing a Harpoon missile at a patrol boat targeting the aircraft carriers. The damaged Libyan ship was towed back to Benghazi, as were many others that day.

Geez, thought Drew, *that place has been a thorn in the side for American politicians for decades, before drifting back to that tour.* The airstrikes began, additional targets were successfully struck by the U.S. military and no damage or injury to any of the nation's assets - troops or equipment. Drew took pride in that. He wasn't there with them, but he had designed the new weapons launching system for the AMG-84 Harpoons, which was a new weapon at the time and not previously used in combat. It was his first project after he graduated from OCS.

He took no qualms with the destruction of people or property. It wasn't because they weren't Americans, but it was his job to look at the potential of a solution and make it better. His evaluation of complications was highly valued by the upper ranks, as they were the risk management guys, the ones that always didn't understand but knew they had to make a call. With men like Drew training and naturally excelling at analysis and evaluation of the options, they felt they had an ace in their pocket every day of the week.

The greater his exposure to the flag officers on the ships as well as in the infantry and other places, the more he began understanding some aspects of the interpersonal relationships that had eluded him for years. Hearing them in a room yell and hash things out, it gave him a direct perspective into how those kinds of people think. They invited him into those insecure spaces because of how he used what he heard, and never repeated what he witnessed.

After he served sixteen more years in the Army, the events that catapulted him back home and into the private sector used every drop of what he learned to make himself a richer man. These past four or five years were different than his previous thirty after high school, and he knew how to make them count with every politician and every man who wanted to get ahead in risk business. If only his father could see him now.

Chapter 10

On top of trying to locate the federal asset storage location and playing footsie with at least one joker in the room earlier that day, Jason had received the official memorandum that the upcoming championship game was facing a credible threat. This was a nightmare, not because of the threat - the city handled more tourists for special events year-round than any other city and did so on a regular basis. In fact, the only reason the last championship game was actually played a few short months after the attacks on the World Trade Center and Pentagon was because it was in *this* city. Ops were set for this type of event.

Back then, the game so close to the attacks, response ideology was "prepare for it all." No idea what could be thrown their way, but prepare to use the ready-fire-aim method was the way they went. All parking within three city blocks was cleared prior to three days before the event - and they towed anything left in that radius with the option to cite owners with a felony for impedance to homeland security operations. (Some bureaucrat always thought more paperwork was helpful; death by one million paper-cuts, but for the wrong side.)

It was a full land-sea-air operation for that game. They had erected cement barricade perimeters with a distance of placement calculated for a typical sedan-sized car bomb. Razor wired steel fencing was placed to keep sidewalks and open spaces pedestrian-free, with the exception of ticket-holders. The train and bus uni-station had bomb dogs and special teams continually on premise. Proximal office buildings were locked down, swept by bomb-teams and had snipers placed on the rooftops.

Some grunt with an artillery specialty arranged with the DOD to bring in some tanks and the Guard to assist in any take-downs and secure the lock-down area. Any hotels within the lock-down area had security checkpoints for incoming guests, complete with x-rays of luggage and VOC detection sweeps. Canine teams from all over the nation assisted, and the impressive Mounted Patrol had a lot more activity than the normal tourist areas and parade routes.

It was fascinating as the Seabees constructed an on-river docking station exclusively for the Coasties doing their navigable waterway patrol - both on and under the water. Port-catchers (virtual netting crossing above the river like a big invisible spiderweb out of a comic book designed for explosive component detection) as well as field radiation detectors were deployed for weeks before the port was closed. Even behavioral detection officers were undercover around the clock along the river's edge as well as in the crowds.

A no-fly zone was set over the region - flyboys picked the radius. The FAA even rerouted flights from South America and transcontinental flights that normally passed near the region. There were additional U.S. Marshals working the airports across the coast along with intermodal transportation security experts, aviation security inspectors ("TSA" didn't quite exist yet), as well as an additional new joint terrorism task force in its infancy stages to use facial recognition software for people on federal agency watch lists well before any young kids developed it for social apps.

The scene for that event was pretty impressive even given the circumstances, and had all the public-facing bells and whistles that could be expected for the first football game to be classified as "National Special Security Event." The game was early February that year - the first game ever to be played in February - so the weather was mild but atypically gray. Cloudy skies reflected the feeling of the nation. The president was coming to do the coin toss, so there were additional security measures with the Secret Service. That much domestic fire power on the streets had not been seen before by the average American citizen, and certainly not in such concentration. With the additional behind-the-scenes activities, including the inter-agency command center, the city prepared for countering an act of war and was ready to "press the button."

Some evidence of "ignorance is bliss" went into that short-term planning situation. Back then, they didn't really plan for secondary attacks, where first responders were targets of helping the injured from an incident - it could have been an open season on emergency personnel soft targets. The sophistication of secondary incendiary devices to hit first responders in a second attack hadn't gained momentum in the terrorist play-book until about three years later - it just wasn't on the domestic radar for preparedness and modifications in response until well into the Iraq conflicts. But it certainly was now.

Incorporated into the standard planning was always a bit of hope that the attractions (drinking, gambling, entertainment) outside of that first post-attack game would provide competing "interest and diversion" for any malcontents (and it usually worked). While the world watched the greatest nation riled like an angry hornet's nest, it was obvious that it would not be the time to attack while American emotion was so high. That was then, this was different. Same game, different era.

The current headache came because of political players' aspirations. They were all over the map. Incumbents wanted a smooth operation though there was a wistful hint of wishing for catastrophe with superstardom response to propel them to Washington (or an eight-figure national consulting contract). The ones who wanted those jobs, the biggest elected jobs in the land, actually silently hoped for horrors to come true (but certainly not hurt any of their friends) - they could nearly taste victory on the failure of others, to the point of hiding information to try to cause failure. And this was the beginning of high-season for campaigning.

The president's seat was open as he reached term limits. The candidate from his party who ran against him before (and lost eight years ago) was trying again, pulling all sorts of punches. The difference this time around was the advent of cell phones that included recording technology. No longer could candidates say Statement A to Group 1 with Statement B to Group 2 with directly opposing promises - they would be ripped to shreds on the internet via blogs, video services and the dwindling power of the mainstream media.

All kinds of conflict from the past of the incumbent party's candidate were coming to light. No sort of spin was changing facts, though the campaign was desperately searching for distractions with manufacturing opportunities not out of the question. No longer was age a typical motivator for supporters. No longer were family values, abortion rights, gender equality or the typical strongholds of their organization. Violent crime was out of control, but curbing access to guns (the good ole' standby for one side) was actually a crippling point. Many people reverted to the Second Amendment's declaration of the right to bear arms as a fundamental right of being American. And the president's party was this mayor's party, too, so even the standard blame game wasn't working this time around.

Other constitutionalist ideology was succeeding in elevating the other large party in their quest to gain younger voters. Race issues were of tremendous importance, with events at least weekly being cast or portrayed as motivated by color rather than action. After several incidents where the sensationalist media got it wrong, the millennial generation reverted to social media and other outlets for reports. Traditionally younger voters are anti-establishment/anti-incumbent; but in this case, they were aligned with the party holding the highest office. Sort of. Seeing the impact on their safety and constraint on movements, the backlash was not against the politics of their parents but those of any politicians that wanted to limit their freedoms and the methods to recover a more-equal society and oddly, a third very vocal party was emerging stronger than ever seen in the country.

Jason had a few on his staff of the younger ilk because the mayor told him to hire them, but they didn't have the drive to complete tasks or dedication to freedom as did earlier generations. Holding out their hands (an entitlement mentality, be it for salaries or grades in college or even entertainment offerings), they held these dichotomous beliefs that they were entitled not only to unearned benefits but also stuck to the traditionally more rigorous conservative platforms. It made for strange ideological bedfellows - hard to predict, difficult to plan, seemingly impossible to forecast actions or reactions.

And all of that made politicians very nervous. Removing predictability from their toolkits increased irritability and irrationality. It was absurd to create contingency plans for everything and for everyone, yet that was the constant request - and without financial resources. Magician extraordinaire. Maybe Jason could be a ventriloquist in his third career. Not just rabbits out of hats, but the release of saying what you think without repercussions of verbalizing them because it is a puppet with an integrated "it wasn't me" factor. Politicians at all levels made it much more difficult, and he tried not to roll his eyes when they inevitably asked, "how likely is this to happen?"

There are many factors that go into preparations of large scale events, but when there is evidence of a credible threat, it all intensifies. To be credible, there is a difference between a legal definition versus an operational definition. A legal definition considers merely that it is "real and immediate." Subjective legal terms are a nightmare when preparing an operation. There is always a degree of uncertainty, but case law based on semantics was a nightmare for security officials, at any level. It means, too, that someone is scared harm will come to them. Hell, in this city, that could be every day and anywhere.

An operational, more functional review of a threat to determine "credibility" must be grounded in intelligence from a reliable source (preferably corroborated by two or more sources) that has a method or mechanism affiliated with realistic ability to achieve or deliver by an organization delivery and - the key component - within a specific timeframe. As it had been more than ten years since the domestic terrorism event, the list of detection, tracking, and intervening methodologies had grown significantly as had the price tag. Yet that did not directly translate into easier ability to track and intercept criminals. Nor did it make things easier to explain to politicians.

The elected folks want a "yes/no, happen/won't happen" kind of assessment. They don't pay fortune tellers, but maybe the meteorologists could give it a whirl. Nothing happens to them every time they are wrong or grossly off-mark. That's what happened in Washington with reports from the Middle East - only deliver good news, spin that we're doing an excellent job, give us the positive numbers. If it is going to be bad news, they want three good-news stories prepped for delivery to the media, so the bad news will be pushed down the page.

He needed some one-on-one time with Sarah to sort through the details, determine an intermediate location of the SNS and antidote assets, and figure out how he was going to tell the mayor "good news" with the chaos starting to swirl.

Chapter 11

Sarah made sure to swing by her office so she was seen by a few folks that would attest she was there. With the biometric locks on the doors, the previous administration thought they were being slick to monitor movements of staff. Yeah. Except that all of these departments reported to her now and she knew the information systems group was really quite sweet and had areas of expertise - but this was absolutely not one of them. Nor were filtering and pulling emails from the system for investigative reports. Bless their hearts.

It was very easy, really. But not many people understood it. One guy in particular was a true bastard about things. He tried to hold what he thought he knew over people that didn't have as much power as him. One day, she had enough. Always up for challenge, in a group meeting about some minuscule business issue, the egomaniac threatened her after she provided information that showed he was wrong and she was right.

Repeatedly that day, he tried to put her down and embarrass her. His skill was bullying and he didn't have enough intellect to know when he should shut up. At one particular meeting, it came to the point when she told him in front of the others that he had no clue what the systems could do and he should stop talking while he thought he was ahead. He threatened to pull a report on her movements to show her skipping work and not doing her job, so she smiled while saying, "Go right ahead."

The following week, in the same standing meeting when the subject came up again, the boss was asked for details on Sarah's movements. He was forced to report that she had not entered the building - according to the system - in eight months. Yet here she sat, with a smile on her face while looking directly at her nemesis. The time and effort wasted on little people's actions and to keep them in line wasted energy that could be directed to solving real problems.

Anyway, enough of that runt-routing. After grabbing some things from her desk and exchanging documents with her assistant, she went to the cave. This was the best room in the building. No windows, buried in an area with an additional outer level of restricted access as well as the control panel on this door, the Feds (as in the Federal Bureau of Investigation in this instance) put specific restrictions on this room. She was one of *three* in the whole company allowed in this room. Unescorted, unmonitored. And it meant that man couldn't barge in while was working with sensitive documents on the table.

The cave was so private and so silent that the one assistant would give her time updates every now and then, under the guise of gently knocking and handing her a water when the assistant went to get her lunch, or asking if she had anything to go upstairs when she would deliver the afternoon update to the top floor. She could get so much done in the cave - and not worry if she walked out of the room that someone could access her documents. The other two persons with access knew what she was doing and supported it one hundred percent. Wanting to help in any way they could, they remained silent about her preferred work space.

Right now, Sarah wasn't wasting time in there on anything but the latest intel reports. There were alarming feeds on various lines of chatter about the upcoming event. A particular domestic splinter cell had been busy using some repetitive code words for planning something. So far, the pieces that were deciphered showed intent with the stockpiling of "something" as well as organization via apparent tests of abilities. Thus, capabilities and intent were established.

Yet there were still parts that were not clear - where specifically were they planning the incident and exactly how did they want to launch the attack? When planning a response for any type of incident, the objectives always considered are specific, measurable, action-oriented, realistic and time-sensitive. As chatter is filtered down from data into information and then produces intel, it's important that the person or people doing the sorting don't make assumptions.

The problems with this situation had been reverse-reviewed and it had been identified that the origin was with certain visa categories being rushed through the process to meet "a certain federal elected official's" campaign promise. Statistics were demanded that would reflect swift change and transparency as well as indicate a clear reversal in direction from the predecessor's policies. Without much thought into the havoc it could bring and simultaneously rushing to continue the "yes, boss" mentality to the then-new guy, fields left blank by applicants just didn't get flagged for denial and they didn't get held for research if the majority of other components checked out.

With fewer staff in critical divisions as many jumped-ship in the year following a party-change in leadership, those remaining had to increase daily passthrough with fewer eyes looking at the various documents or completing validations. Visas had the constraints that certain countries had priority access, applications of limits on certain work visa were rapidly met, some types were practically rubber-stamped as approved because of the short time frame or intention-of-request as declared by the hopeful applicant.

These small holes in the system could easily be exploited. Blatant offenders weren't allowed into the country, but perhaps their relatives were granted visas or some of their other known associates. Slightly sloppy writing harkened back to the days of Ellis Island in the late nineteenth century, with intake specialists misspelling the names immigrants said it was all in the name of the "you're-here-now-get-the-hell-on-down-the-hall" attitude. More recently, when taking an archaic and similarly handwritten form and Federal staff typing it into the systems for research, a sloppy N could appear as an M, and it's suddenly a totally different person with a clear background. (People in this line of work didn't like to consider the intentional mistakes; the accidents were about all they could absorb on a daily basis.)

Admittedly, more than one or two on the watch-list have entered the country in this accidental manner - straightforward and just not caught. One or two of these activists now resided in urban areas with marginalized populations, people who were looking for an answer to their problems and a short cut to getting out from "under the thumb of the man." These people weren't outcasts per se, but did not participate in community niceties or obligations. In some ways, it made them standout more - but only if you were adept at noticing something different.

Changes in people being radicalized didn't happen overnight, but really over the course of weeks and months. This, in the eyes of many lower level boots on the ground, was where higher-placed government officials needed to have a better understanding of this flipping of a switch and provide funding so the ops people could devise methods to intervene and prevent. Observant residents were not the standard anymore, as people just wanted to do their own thing with self-gratification, taking what they wanted for themselves while leaving others behind, and the fabric of the society essentially had started to erode from lack of interest.

Much of the work reviewing the anomalies (meaning situations or people that just didn't seem to fit into the community) relied more heavily on local resources and luck than anyone cared to admit. A neighbor noticing increased traffic with multiple-state license plates and alerting someone about it made all the difference, from situations of criminal arrests on narcoterrorism as well as national security threats. Another example was changes in a garage being converted to living quarters, allowing fugitives to hide from authorities by remaining "off the grid." The "see something, say something" slogan was really infantile and made you question if those in charge had a clue - right until you knew of a concrete example where it worked (while trying to ignore all of the crazy things people shared). It still sounded juvenile, but whatever; it's how this one particular group's strangeness was noticed.

The group they were monitoring now appeared on their radar from a citizen-reported anomaly. Knowing they don't fit into a small town, these kinds of people pick suburbs of larger metropolitan areas that have a somewhat migratory or transient populations to form their groups and activate plans. People coming and going usually isn't noticed if they pick their location well. As emigration from urban centers pushes outward, it's natural that new people move into neighborhoods.

The current people associated with the latest credible threat were just smart enough to pick an area of new development, near interstates so they could travel on the road with cash and leave a minuscule trail. Their footprint was small, but in each of the locations where the three possible cells with high volume data was originating, they had done things to make neighbors and the local police just a bit suspicious.

With teamwork and the good old phone-tree method, one area reached out to some people who knew some people and happened to have similar occurrences in their jurisdiction. This wasn't the sort of thing, at this stage, where they issued bulletins or documented things in emails. Though incident management "rules" of the feds wanted a paper trail on everything and a very tight protocol that left little room for maneuvering, no one locally thought that a wise approach, and they didn't want to present anything until some facts were known.

They figured out by cell phone tracking that the members involved did indeed have a connection to one of those visas that came in through a hole. At the early stages of each of the relationships, electronic communications had been captured. Not long after it started, those lines had been severed and it could have gone unnoticed. However, since the visa-holder was placed on a watch list *after* entering the country, the termination of relationships by the individual was noticed as well as the cascading self-imposed isolation of the people with whom he once regularly communicated.

Cooperation with Federal officers to try to get details on the group's ideology was paramount. But the right questions had to be asked because sometimes territorial posturing happened. Incredulous, because they were all on the same side, but personal gain over community safety is frequently a driver of "sharing" intelligence. Carefully crafted questions to get pieces of the puzzle without giving too much of their own, exhausting but hopefully fruitful.

The feeling she was getting made her very concerned. It seemed that some components of this organization, of the three cells, pointed to activities here in the next two weeks, right in time for the championship game. She knew the area had skated through some events ripe for man-made catastrophe - and with some of the "leaders" in place playing shell games with the funding that was intended for security, knowing they were basing their planned mea culpas on the hope the federal budget would bail them out when security forces were necessary, their play was all geared to cover themselves and everyone else be damned.

Right now, she needed a drink.

Sarah finished her paperwork for the afternoon and secured it in the safe people didn't realize she had hidden in her office. She almost couldn't get out of there fast enough because she suddenly needed a break from the mounting stress and it was likely the last break she would have before the event. All work and no play… blah blah blah. It dulled the senses and took away the edge, just like if you were building model rockets too long (like she had done as a child) and didn't get into the fresh air every once in a while, you would miss what was in front of your nose.

It would take about twenty-five minutes from this office to get to the Montaigne. But she had well over an hour, actually an hour and a half, before she was meeting Joann. Sarah didn't want to wait and cause herself to gear-up about 'wasting time' instead of being in-motion. It was getting dark early, so she thought she'd change at home and then go to the wine bar. She'd check her snail mail, maybe order that new pair of shoes online and then head down the street.

To relax, she consciously made the choice a while ago that she shouldn't wear her "work" to play. She tried to have her work clothes portray business with an overt hint of femininity. After all, the majority of the men down south were intimidated by her - the speed at which she spoke, the pace that her mind worked, her empathy for things they just didn't understand. It isolated her, but she outwardly ignored their insecurities and even preyed upon them. Of course, she wore high heels at work - these men were much shorter than those up north or out west, so it frequently put her at eye level or even taller than them. That didn't sit too well, contributed to their nervousness since they couldn't just loom over her to intimidate, but she wasn't hired to just sit pretty.

Heels, skirts, delicate silk scarves, frilly blouses under suit jackets. Work appropriate, nice business clothes but not designer typically. Not that the men would notice, at least most of them. There were a few, though, like the chief of staff. He knew. And he would give her compliments, noticing the shoes or a new top - it was nice to be appreciated for her attention to detail without any overtones, with no expectations, and still he knew the good work she did.

In fact, that gentleman (and down here, she used the term rarely) had been in his position for more than three decades. He had elite training that he used outside of that particular role, so he appreciated her background. When it surfaced that in her new position she wasn't pandering to anyone and was here to do a job, the level of respect increased across the aisle. He approached her one day to go to lunch, and she really enjoyed it. The surprise aspect was that she got a lot of unsolicited background, a personalized tour, and introductions to the guys who answered only to him (directly or indirectly).

Being introduced as "she's one of us" to his crew was a priceless gateway that he opened for her. He knew it, and it was a way to express appreciation for the job she did so well. So, when it was getting crazy, she'd think at least there was one rock in the storm that wouldn't be be hurled in her direction. Rocks made good friends and were conduits to building good things.

And rocks were optional in her bourbon whiskey that she would soon pour. She enjoyed a strong drink. There were echoes of an odd tribute to the Whiskey Rebellion in its history. Bourbon was a special American whiskey, and the mash had to be at least 51% corn from one particular county in Kentucky - a toast to the nation's bread basket and making it entirely from domestic products. Then it was aged in new, charred oak barrels (harvested from American forests, of course).

The aging process actually reduces the proof of the bourbon - it can't be over 125 when it goes into the cask and doesn't come out until it drops below 80; gets to be called straight bourbon if it ages over four years and the oak can do its thing for twelve. In the 1800s, it used to be bitter and fairly awful, but good things over time get better. So did the recipes for bourbon, and it got a bit sweeter and heavier. Funny that the name was derived from the French - again, a tribute to the countrymen that help liberate the colonies from The Empire Where the Sun Never Sets. The final touching tribute to La Liberte is the mimicry of naming rights - akin to champagne, unless it's made in the USA, it's not bourbon.

This city itself also was a tribute to the rebels and men of France. Perhaps that's why she liked it here to some extent, why she liked bourbon and Champagne, too. Her heritage ran through Alsace, so maybe it still accounted of some of her preferences more than two hundred years later. A reassuring atmosphere that didn't change over time, but that was one of the annoying drawbacks, too.

During the drive to her house to change, she decided to have a glass of Appalachian gold before leaving for the Montaigne - sans rocks. Once inside and picking her outfit out of the closet with her left and and with her right holding the tumbler bought and carried home from Waterford's factory, she selected something a bit playful. Definitely something she couldn't wear to work, and would not remind her of work. She felt herself unwinding already.

Living fairly close to the wine bar, there was no need to rush. Things operated on their own time here anyway. Inevitably, something always happened to create delays, and many locals started to explain their tardy arrivals with "what had happened was..." Her friends were typically not cut from that lateness cloth (some of her colleagues were), and they enjoyed selecting places for atmosphere sometimes and other times, for food or drink. She had to admit that the food at the Montaigne was the antithesis of bar food, and that's a lot of the reason why she liked going there. The other was for the wine selection; even the environment was pleasant. She loved a good trifecta.

They had a large variety of spirits for being such a small location. Rather than crushed, it was intimate. Whereas other places had failed in this very location, this team succeeded. They just did things right, relaxed, and with a bit of finesse. The twinkle lights year-round were a bit odd, but in this setting, it just blended with the local flair. So many parties and events all year long, no need to redecorate this way.

She arrived and because she was totally away from work as well as dressed so differently, she sat in the bay window bench seat table. Enjoying the view partly up the streetcar tracks as well as the few other tables in the place and seats down along the bar, she started with a glass of champagne. Knowing Joann would be there shortly, she also ordered some tapas. Oh, the gluttony - pommes frites fried in goose fat with a drizzle of a warmed brie, petit garlic steamed shrimp with a sweet fig and ginger sauce, and last but not least, slices of zucchini fried in a pummeled nut paprika breading topped with a sweet lemon-parsley dollop.

As the waiter set her flute on the linen cocktail square, Sarah leaned back on the pillows of the window seat with her legs crossed in ladylike fashion and sipped her champagne. Since she was looking out the window in the same direction as the door, she didn't notice that the waiter stopped at the bar to place a call before continuing about his duties. Marcus was on his way.

Chapter 12

He figured that Sarah would pay in cash. That's what most of the folks in their field usually did. Many reasons for it, but among the top were 'leave no trace' and 'plausible deniability' when needed. Well, at least that was the case in the era before all of the security cameras in restaurants, around grocery stores, and even on private homes in a network sort of project, those schemas held true. Now with facial recognition capabilities, movements were easier to piece together - especially with law enforcement's controversial license plate recognition software, which sped the tracking process immensely.

It wasn't necessary for his contact to hover or be extra attentive this evening - just so that he was there for the heads up. He had let the waiter know ahead of time, and the guy arranged to work a double just to make sure he saw the woman Marcus described. She was vaguely familiar per the description provided, but the guy agreed to ask for the card under the guise it was busy or new manager or something with their register system. Marcus didn't care about those details, only her name.

The waiter notified Marcus that she opened a tab with her card, an indication that she was planning to relax and stay a while - he guessed then would likely pay with cash at the end. When holding a tab, some nicer places didn't run it, only held it until the customer was ready to close the bill and leave. And if she went there often, as some of the haunts with loyal local patrons were known to do around town, they sometimes didn't require the card to hold the tab. When the phone rang from the bar, he answered it and waited for him to speak her name. Sarah Steinbrunn.

Damn, it was like soft butter. That family name had overtones of Germanic origins, which made sense given her complexion and stature, not to mention her posture. While he couldn't envision her in lederhosen, her European ancestry was as visually clean as his ethnicity was murky even in its appearance. His mind started to drift again to her fair skin that was such an appealing contrast to his olive tone. He had to really pay attention as he arrived near the bar, driving on the bad roads - dangerous from sink holes as well as crime that drifted on the wind hitting every area without discriminating.

This area of the city had gone through all sorts of changes over the centuries, over the past two centuries. Originally, it was the outer reaches of the earliest settlement, designated on maps of large plantations streaming out from the river with lines fading after so many arpents were noted as they were bequeathed by the King of France to "deserving" supporters. The land then was so new, so alien and exotic that they didn't even know what was at the back of the properties. It was just noted by cartographers that each family owned to the ends of their vision.

Each plantation was a small faubourg, a little self-sufficient community that was the foundation of ever increasing farther-reaching suburbs well-beyond the city center. Named for the owners as a reflection back to the bourgeoisie European roots, all of these "Faubourgs such-and-such-insert-family-name-here" were still just middle class families trying to self-promote in the new world and portray themselves as more prestigious than defined by reality. While in Paris the faubourg ran out from the city's center, here they ran from the heart of the region - the mighty river.

When designated and as they started to evolve, the faubourgs carried the connotation of middle classes striving to retinue heights. It wasn't the very wealthy or noble families that were pushed to marginalization in the swamps outside the urban center. The city was founded by those well-recognized courtiers who named streets after themselves and had large homes in posh locations. Those families weren't relegated to far-flung mosquito infested castoff lands, where frog-led chamber music could not be silenced and the glow of swamp fires could penetrate even the darkest nights. These were the areas where they parceled some of their holdings to poorer relations or to those whom they owed gambling debts - and some of the shadows of such "inheritance" followed these new owners up river, "uptown."

These areas now, just as with the plantation owners back then, were focused on materialistic gains, perpetuated conservative values, and envisioned creating economic engines that would outlast any single monarch so their name would live beyond one generation. And though they tried to escape their own past to create a petit-royale future, the dichotomous undercurrents of hedonistic behaviors continued to run strong along side of the large river in small rivers of extreme pleasure-seeking acts perpetuated and expanded. It was ensconced in the design of the expansive homes with the garçonnière for the single young men of the family that had separate entrances for the late-night returns, shielding from female relations' view the biconjugate reality the mixing of races that was so chastised in public as white owners privately cavorted with black slaves.

Patches of conservatism ended up surrounded by liberal neighbors and some "original" families decided to continue their move in search of fortune and increased grandeur. When expansion continued further upriver, a train system was built to take people from the heart of the city four miles out to the new outer reaches, which was two miles beyond the fringe of commerce. The rails were now for streetcars, and Marcus was crossing over that set of tracks now as he reached his destination.

Parking just down the street, he checked himself one more time before he got out of the car. Not sure what he was going to say or do, he determined he would go to the bar to pick up an order to go, get a drink and figure out how to say hello casually. He called that order in quickly. Dressed in a pale blue oxford with his deep blue tie hanging slightly loosened, he had matched them with dark blue slacks but soft black calfskin shoes. He wore no watch. It was two days since he had seen her; he worked half the day from home and changed three times before he went to headquarters for the afternoon so he would be closer for tonight's call.

Stepping out of his SUV, Marcus took a deep breath and walked down the street. This area was one of the worst when it came to the annual spring celebrations because of the popular restaurant that was about a block and a half from the wine bar. Typically on certain days of the year, the area would be crowded with underage kids, reeking of marijuana smoke, and the pungent smell of decaying food made it to the top of nearly every cop's list to avoid. The only ones who couldn't avoid it were the mounted patrols, and even they were fighting a losing battle anymore with the disrespectful masses. Right now, the throngs of kids and revelers weren't lined up waiting for parades to roll but the memory lingered in the mind of anyone who has tried to navigate the area during an event.

He was reeling a bit from the fact he was nervous. He really wanted to know more about her; he wanted to remain calm without appearing slick. Since that day in the construction zone, he hadn't seen her again or heard anyone talking about her - not even on projects where he suspected she could be operating currently. He felt like he was going in blind, and intel staff don't like to do that. Yet nothing about this was "normal." This was not a normal pickup under any circumstances. Sarah was inside.

Just inside when he opened the door, actually. The door opened inward with the handle on the right side, so he naturally scanned length of the actual bar and seating on that side first, just by mechanics. After turning to make sure it was closed and before he started walking to the bar to get a drink and enable that to-go cover order, he saw her in the window seat.

Perfectly framed and looking right at him. Again. Damn. She could be so unnerving, but that was so alluring, too. The stutter steps he took were totally natural, so no excuse was needed to head over to her. Walking her direction, he smiled and opened the conversation as he arrived at the table, no corny line as that would likely get a smart reply.

"Hello. I'm Marcus. Saw you the other day up at the operations center. Nice to get to say hello now as you were quite involved with Jason and the guys that day."

Sarah had seen him walking up the street, and was amused that he was here. She never saw him here in the years since it became the wine bar, so she decided to wait for his eye contact and see how he proceeded. When he came directly over, she was pleasantly surprised. Clean cut slacks, thoughtfully assembled attire, relaxed stride - confident but approachable at the moment, and thank goodness his hands weren't in his pockets trying to be suave. Nice body, too. And tall, like they may just about meet eye-to-eye with him having a slight edge.

"I saw you by the windows, with your watchful eye on the hallway. Nice to meet you." Let's see how he plays this, she thought, as she didn't give her name.

Luckily for him, the waiter came over seeing Marcus arrive. "Miss Sarah, would you care for another cocktail while you wait on your food?" *God bless this waiter,* thought Marcus.

Curse this waiter, thought Sarah, but he was a mighty fine one and she'd rather have...

"I'd be happy to get this round, if you don't mind? While you wait for someone?" Marcus gave a general wave of his hand to the second cocktail napkin on the table and the two plates stacked in the center by the candle, along with two artistically folded cloth napkins.

Perfect. "Perfect, thank you." And she was sincere. Nothing trite or displeasing in her tone, or as she looked directly at him, again, with eyes sparkling and even smiling. He was in so much trouble.

He ordered his scotch neat and she indicated another champagne with a tilt of the flute in her hand, letting the waiter nod and depart. She turned in her seat and indicated he should join her on the pillows. He struggled to keep his mind here rather than her on pillows somewhere else. They made some small talk, of course. He discovered she did indeed like the sporting aspect of the coming event and it wasn't necessarily all work.

Sarah learned Marcus was more articulate than she imagined a well-built man skilled in the art of combat would be under usual circumstances. Neither directly said what they did - after all, this was a pretense for relaxing on a warm Thursday night towards the end of January. This time of year literally ran hot or cold, and he was in luck that it was on the warmer side, because she looked stunning and so feminine.

With a bit of coolness still in the air, she had let that amazing blonde hair out of its tight coif in which he saw her last time. It just billowed over her bare shoulders, down the front of her flowing sundress. Her outfit was a very loose-fitting brightly colored purple-based paisley on a cream background, slightly low cut but not drastic - it was perfect for her. And she knew it.

Its length was not too long but absolutely not too short, and Sarah loved this dress. She felt good in the sleeveless shift, and that altered her confidence to a gentle aura that was almost a seduction. Purple looked good on her. Shortly after the storm, she had to travel to San Francisco and she found the perfect pair of purple heels that strapped around her ankle. The salesman was an evacuee and that's what sealed the deal. It was a sign. She knew that someday, she would find the right outfit, and indeed she had.

She had a light wrap with her that was essentially black but with some purple that matched the dress, and it had fabulous fringe. She kept it around her, but low on her back and only over her forearm of the non-flute side at this point. She needed only a gold chain bracelet and hoop earrings to complete the outfit, and that contributed to why she liked it - low fuss factor. Classy. Cute.

And Marcus absorbed everything. Even though he knew that Joann would arrive at any moment, sitting here where they could talk not about work, he could watch her gestures openly, and he could smell her light perfume that just enhanced the whole feeling he had before and really had now - he wanted more.

"Well, hello, Marcus. Thanks for keeping my spot for me. It's starting to get crowded in here." And just like that, the spell was broken, for now. As he rose, he didn't take his eyes off of Sarah after he greeted Joann. He merely said, "Nice to formally meet you, and I'm sure we'll be seeing each other again soon." With that, he went to the bar, picked up the food he had ordered after he had parked, paid his tab, and walked out.

He did steal a look at her as he exited. Watching her so animated and laughing, he was hooked. He had to have more.

He looked forward to the door and when he began opening it, she looked up, smiled and slowly blinked, then returned her focus to Joann's story.

Chapter 13

Luke went up to the construction zone to see if anyone was there. He had assembled the intel about option one, and was ready to give it to Jason for their boss. There was another report, too, about the current credible threat to the upcoming event. He felt like he was missing a piece or two, but needed to share what he had gathered.

As he was buzzed into the offices, he noticed that the atmosphere of cube-ville had a relaxed nature, as though there was nothing pressing. Three of the guys talked in one aisle and two others were in a separate area. It amazed Luke every time he witnessed these guys hanging about, waiting for someone else to do their work. Jason protected them, however, and someone would pick up the slack eventually.

Not that any of them would be the actual workers. They would take credit for the output, of course. He remembered one guy would claim to be the Operations Chief but was drunk eighty percent of the time during one particular incident - one meeting, he was told to stay upstairs and sleep off the alcohol because his whole body just reeked of rum. He had taken it from some of the others as they worked, gone through their bags. Who knows where he disposed of those bottles, but the other people weren't happy about the invasion of privacy or his immaturity.

Sarah actually ran that particular meeting for him, extremely well in fact. Sending him to a room to sleep it off (in the middle of the day), and in spite of not having attended any Ops meetings prior to that due to her attendance at the commander's meeting and press prep that occurred at the same time. She apparently had told the CO she needed ten minutes, sailed into the Ops space to set the plan for the operational period, and launched the team to go get the job done.

Luke was in that operational meeting every day - prior to that and subsequently thereafter. It was obvious that they loved her for the economy of words, not to mention the efficiency of tactics was such a divergent course than what they had with their slow-speaking discombobulated inebriated chief; they were glad to be acting right on the money and faster than usual. And to think the woman didn't drink coffee! She was so professional and really nice, too, even when having to be blunt due to time constraints or stupidity of others.

Yeah, Mike must have been powerfully drunk when he thought claiming he had sex with Sarah during that same event was going to go over well or that people would actually believe him. She worked 22 hour days well into nights during the height of the situation, and the nap she took at hour twenty-two on day one was only considered when someone she trusted literally sat at the door with her laptop, watching for anything she would need to handle. With the guard outside of her door, that guy wasn't with her then, that's for sure.

The second night of the incident, a few of the old-timers (of which Sarah was part) were able to get hotel rooms in a very nice section of town in a very classy hotel. The owner was friends with one of her friends, and he gave them ten rooms on one of the floors as long as they wouldn't tell anyone - the building was empty except for them since the city's tourists, businesses, and residents had all been evacuated. They had all looked forward to a hot shower and fluffy beds... but got lured by the quiet of the night and some good drinks to explore the soul of their city without noise pollution and people congestion. They did get their showers and to sleep in fluffy beds, though they had also stayed up talking like it was a big sleepover, too.

Nor was that damned alcoholic with her the third night when he forced - yes, forced - a group of people to sleep in the stadium because *he* arranged for it. He thought it would be cool and fun. He planned to take the claim to fame when the event was over, about resource allocation, public-private partnership, blah blah blah. Walking them over as if it was a parade, Mike couldn't understand why Sarah's steps slowed as she approached the building. He did not understand the depth of her commitment to NOT reenter that building after the storm just a few years prior, but this trigger made it seem like yesterday for her.

Friends literally had to prepare to die in that building, considering various methods of how they would drop bodies as barriers if they were charged by the overwhelmed masses. Seven days of a living hell and this jerk wanted her and the others to sleep there, be locked in there, for seven hours. Her discomfort was more than Mike could fathom because *he wasn't there for it,* wasn't even in the state. She was.

She nearly knocked him cold when he tried to put his hands on her and push her inside; Luke thought she should have done it. He had seriously thought about it, even though he had already entered the foyer. So did the Guardsman that was standing watch at the building, seeing Mike go back to where she stopped, and then as he began to shove her. That soldier, a stranger, gripped his weapon tighter, frustrated that he couldn't leave that door. She would have packed a mean punch, loaded with sadness and fear and anger from several years prior not to even mention her revulsion at his unwelcome touch that he tried to make intimate.

The fourth night into that same incident, Sarah was able to borrow another hotel room through a connection who was going to run home to check on things out of town and be back in the morning. The quiet and solitude was so welcomed - both as people were not yet allowed to repatriate nor were there any guests or others on the entire floor where the room was located. She gave it to Sarah to get away from the guys and again have hot water. She was very happy to have it. Unfortunately, because she was sometimes too nice, she saw Mike on the street a bit tipsy and told him to come inside and sober up in the hotel restaurant… where he met another military guy. And hell, a reporter, who luckily for Sarah was lovely and discrete, shutting her ears when Mike blurted out classified information.

The local reporter shared with Sarah that the guy with her, a colleague, did the same thing when he drank, and said any time she wanted to share a lead on the record to call her, even sharing her real name not just her journalistic handle, so the connection of that night would be recalled while she was on the desk. Sarah was so mad at Mike that evening that she literally yanked him out of the establishment so the bartender could leave, and those witnesses (including the one who became nearly as drunk as Mike) recognized there was no physical connection and he was in no condition to force one.

In fact, the witnesses to each of these episodes knew that absolutely there was no way she allowed him to sleep with her. They - and others - made sure everyone else knew it, and someone helped spread the word that he had a little problem involving burning and dripping when he urinated, too, so it would have been tough for him to perform, even with a great woman like Sarah. He soon thereafter lost his job under the premise of going to work in oil and gas - kind of a parallel to how he exited the Marines after eleven and a half years. Who the hell is honorably discharged after that odd-ball timeframe? Gone from their world after two and a half years, and good riddance.

At least the guys left in the office were not that offensive. Asshole.

"Who?"

Luke didn't realize he spoke it out loud as he set his bag on the kitchen table. Marcus was coming toward him as he continued, "You know you have to be more specific around here."

"Yeah, I was just remembering that guy who tried to say he had sex with Sarah during the last big event. Total ass. Disgrace to the uniform, and just guys in general actually. Do you remember Mike? Drunken sleaze ball."

"I don't remember Sarah during that, but I remember him bragging about bagging some girl during that time. He was canned from his part-time job shortly after he 'resigned' here. Tried to do some side work and no one would hire him. Bad attitude and didn't really know what he was talking about. I saw her that day of your last meeting, and happened to run into her as I picked up takeout last night, but I don't remember ever having worked with her."

"Dude, remember how the last event was so organized, with our own chow lines, our own federal assistance areas, how we knew crap before the politicians did? You should thank Sarah for that. You should have seen her up here - when it was a real construction zone. How Mike ever thought he could reach that high - or that any of us would have allowed something to mess up her hard-on groove getting everything done… alcohol can mess a brother up." Luke shook his head and again wished he had punched him that night when he tried to force her in the building with the group. He gripped the side of the table while taking a deep breath in order to get rid of the tension.

"Wait," Marcus said. "I remember that woman. Well, emails from a woman. She answered at least two questions for me about the SBA and sending ice out to our neighborhood that actually arrived with supplies of crap I never even asked for but we really needed. That was her? I sent her a thank you email back during the incident but never met her." He remembered the vast differences between the back to back deployments, recalling, "It was so different than the last event - we were all less stressed, actually ate and had cots, whatever we needed. And the media were kept away from us. I didn't realize that was her." Marcus couldn't believe it, but he could see her doing all of that even just from the meeting he witnessed, how she handled the men and the conversation.

"That's our Sarah. So where are the real workers? I see the A-Team over there is just yapping as usual." Luke knew Marcus, though laid back, couldn't stand lazy people either.

"Jason should be back any minute. Whatcha got?"

They started to review the intel about the credible threat. Marcus wasn't really involved in the countermeasures at this stage, though he would be in the near future. Luke would be told when to bring him into the loop. But he was absolutely part of the counterterrorism unit that needed to know about the current situation, and likely supplied some of the information they were reviewing.

As they were talking, Jason walked up to them. "Looks like trouble over here." They brought him into the discussion and Luke highlighted the weaknesses in the current intel.

"Oh, yeah, there's a meeting about that this afternoon," Jason revealed. "Sarah and I just spoke, and she has some intel, too, has some gaps she wanted to discuss. You should both come. My office, 1400 hours."

"Yes, sir," they both replied immediately, with Luke straightening as he said it and Marcus nodding, both in deference to Jason.

Chapter 14

Wayne was again looking at potential blueprints, though not for the western land-grab development, but instead for the things submitted by his competitor to the permits office for buildings on the greenway that Sarah suggested were ripe for "modification" to the storing of counter-terrorism materials. He really didn't care what they wanted to store - it could be bodies, for all he cared - so long as he could make a profit.

The "nouveau design of the integrated sustainable environment" included (apparently) "a local 'farm to fork' concept restaurant that overlooked a well-manicured garden facing the greenway (away from the nightmare road), a small independent book nook, several shop areas roughed out for a 'haberdashery' as well as a fine stationary store, a wine bar, and of course the obligatory trendy condos." As one of the largest undeveloped spaces in town, there was so much potential and of course his competitor would try to gentrify the area with his island-themed upscale design. It wouldn't flip to locals, but he was already advertising to customers out of state - domestic and international, to sister cities and locations with direct flight access.

Wayne had proposed to build time-share property with his bid to the city, and the politicians wanted ownership over transient. They were so fickle, the city council members, especially as this ownership would be practically the same as his proposal (and then the whole 'rental' issue would rear its ugly head yet again). The mayor could always be sold (or bought) on an idea if it incorporated good press for himself, as long as he also got to time the actual announcement using a good story to bury any sort of unsavory story. It was so strange that Wayne and the mayor were on the same side of projects, yet Wayne gladly gave the mayor his own PR time and let the man claim ideas as his own (since he never came up with any via independent generation).

In reviewing these plans, Wayne was trying to literally see where the space could be carved out of living areas. That was the only flexible space at this point, since face time had been given to the stores already with modifications for their designs and leases. Huge press coverage of the "rebuilding of the fabric of our uniqueness" had been overplayed for months. He didn't see a viable way to save the mayor if he eroded those public areas.

But the living spaces were just hollowed out, estimates of development. In fact, he was under the impression that these items for anti-terrorism could be moved in during build-out, so no one would be the wiser - just boxes and crates. The interior components needn't ever be completed for the "residential" space. He figured if he could secure ownership - for free, of course with a wave of the mayor's wand - of the middle units, even interior spaces that would have sold cheaper by his competitor - that he would have income generation for the mayor coming as under-cover federal payments, perhaps with a personal guarantee for both of them. His payment would be considered eligible for the construction to specs as his guys knew how to shut up, and for the mayor, who would sing the tune of any bird in paradise as long as it made him look good.

Yes, the mayor had actually been known to literally sing in public if he thought it could boost his image. As a child, he wanted to be on Broadway. The first problem, according to his parents, was Broadway was in Yankee-land and a second problem was that endeavor was unbecoming to the family, strutting around on a stage like that. His career was planned for him from birth, so every now and then - likely just to make his dad cringe - he would sing, or dance, in front of the cameras.

Shifting from dancing to floor space, the other nice feature about the interior space condos is that they were just about complete with the footing. From the time of starting footing to finish would be less than three months (not sure he would ever want to live in that type of shoddy construction), so they were probably two and a half months away from completed homes. However, he didn't want a home - he wanted a shell that allowed him to manipulate the inside visually without structural integrity alterations. That could be accomplished in three weeks of a normal schedule, perhaps a week on rush.

If these packages weren't marked obviously as anti-terrorism components (as they shouldn't be to move around in public), then putting them inside "housing development space" by his guys as they were taking in things for drywalling, outlets, and other roughing materials would be simple. He wasn't sure of the volume, but he knew an office was required in addition to the storage buildout. They would need one kitchen, one bath, one office out of the three whole units - the project was reducing in cost by the minute. And if this was indeed a rush with two weeks to the expected event, it would be staffed 24/7 and no extra security needed as his guys would build around the boxes.

Inside was fine. Knowing the exterior had to match his competitors "high end tourist play ground" (a joke in this neighborhood but tourists don't appreciate the difference until arrival), he planned on interior blinds that looked more like full length wooden shutters that could have open slats for monitoring exterior movements, but would not open accordion style. This rendered extra security for the windows, as these wouldn't be wooden but steel; the windows would be lacking opening mechanisms, so provided another layer of security. Drapes had to be hung over the shutters, but whatever. Cost still minimal. He didn't even think they would paint inside these rooms, but did need good insulation and HVAC for the pharmaceutical components; he at least remembered that from the conversations. Maybe some lamps on timers, placed on boxes so outside it seemed like people were home and moving around at normal hours.

Open floor plans made for an easy project. The second floor of each of the units could also be open - no need to do plumbing at this point for upstairs work. But that would probably look shady to a future buyer so he'd make them lay lines but leave the pipe ends at the wall. Cheaper and cheaper, meaning more went to his pocket. And the need for cash flow from this real estate operation was nearing critical stage to help fuel the gambling operation across the river in the "non-profit" development that the legislators helped him build.

His efforts here were to support the other, supposedly this last, investment. With four units and the profit from this dumped over there, he should quadruple his money and secure trusts for his children. He had to be careful, though. In spite of a new U.S. Attorney, they were still breathing down the necks of some white collar guys they thought needed to be put away. The last U.S. Attorney railroaded the longest serving governor - anyone around knew that hotshot manipulated the whole system to put that notch on his belt. And didn't that backfire when his goons embarrassed him to the point that he had to leave office. Yeah, karma.

Yes, Wayne had learned a thing or two about racketeering from one of the finest in the business. Still only got that man on seventeen counts for ten years. He'd be out soon and looking for new things to try. Wayne wanted to be ahead of the game and show his mentor, who had showed him how gentlemen got business handled, that he had learned his lessons well and would be the one to stay out of the federal penitentiary. But my, he did get himself another fine young wife while in there!

Shaking his head to bring him back to the prints on the table, he figured he'd call his architect and get him to do the new layout right away, also incorporating open archways between all of these units, a view-blocking wall beside the front door. The offices in the two outer units would be staffed with someone; Sarah, he supposed, was handling that. He was leaving any monitoring to her, too. She had said temperature controlled but not that anything like a refer unit was required. He supposed the old kitchen space should be wired for commercial refers, too, in case that came up later. Costly to incorporate after the build out, even if it was only a rough stage. Ripping out and redoing was never beneficial to a bottom line.

With the general intentions outlined, Wayne went to work on how to tip off the mayor and get the downpayment started for his work as well as an annuity, of sorts, channeling the syphoned rent to an offshore account that would reroute back into his gambling project. This was going to be the crowning glory in his professional career - and then he could find trophy wife four and begin the fun part of life, leaving the kids with some cash and not having to interact with them again.

Chapter 15

Such a cliche, but Marcus couldn't believe his luck. He had gotten to see Sarah last night and now would see her again today, this time without pretense. He would get to hear how her mind worked during this meeting and be able to watch her unabashedly while the meeting progressed. She should be coming to Jason's office in about two hours.

And only an hour later, the mayor had called Jason to an off-site meeting. He ended up calling Luke and telling him to bring the intel to him (and they wouldn't be showing anyone just yet). Since he didn't know if the two of them were still together, Jason next called Marcus and gave instructions to wait for Sarah as he couldn't reach her on the cell. Relaying her number so Marcus could intercept her and bring her along, he hung up abruptly.

Well, now Marcus had her phone number. Hot damn. He gathered up his belongings and pulled his car to the front of the building, watching for her to come around. And he had to try to remain calm even though he was quite aroused when he saw her - what hot blooded American male wouldn't at the picture she made.

She was in a chocolate leather skirt suit, with a silk maroon top and chocolate high heels perfectly matched to her outfit. Sarah's long hair was blowing in the wind, several strands crossing over in front of her sunglasses as she headed toward the door. With her long strides to the front of the building, he nearly didn't move fast enough to intercept her because he was frozen, staring.

"Sarah."

Though he didn't speak loudly, she heard him. She stopped in her tracks, and in almost slow motion, turned to him. The wind shifted and her hair was blowing over her shoulders. She started moving toward him. She pushed her sunglasses onto the top of her head and then used the same hand to continue in motion, sweeping her hair back over her right shoulder, straightening her gold hoop earring at the same time with the other hand.

He opened the car door for her and gestured for her to enter as he simultaneously said, "Jason was rerouted by the mayor; we're going to him now - without the mayor joining us, is my understanding." Closing the door gently, he exhaled and trailed his hand along the roofline as he walked around the back of the car, to drive them across the lake.

When he got in his seat, he expected her to be on her mobile handling email or something. No. She was posed with her seatbelt already fastened - *oh, mercy* - and was turned in the seat to look at him. With both front windows slightly lowered, as he started to drive, the breeze coming into the car made the air swirl and lifted her fair hair in slow motion as they began to talk.

"And where, pray tell, is our new destination? Not that I'm surprised that the mayor caused upheaval in everyone's day. Typical." Sarah had an irritated smirk on her face as she withheld what he was sure was many derogatory comments. He could nearly read the script across her face. Some kind of willpower to bite her tongue that way.

"We have to text Jason when we get close. To the bridge is a bit of a hike, but I'm going to swing past my house quickly.

Actually, it's shorter with less traffic across the old bridge anyway."

"Beautiful day for a drive, and I'm so rarely driven. Thanks for the lift. So, what is it you do with Jason? We didn't get into that over scotch and champagne." She could gather that they could talk a bit more freely, as it was just them in his car, but maybe she could learn a little more. "And by the way, where's the SUV?"

"My personal car is at my house, which is why we are going that way. I need to grab something out of it. I live out by the lake's edge - away from the crime and chaos. I can actually hear birds in the evening, fish jumping out of the lake sometimes. It's great when the rushes blow at night, rustling like a deer coming toward you through the underbrush. An occasional bullfrog sounding, breaking the calmness of night. They don't just sound once; usually runs for twenty minutes, so it becomes quite loud, but then when it stops, it's the strongest quiet you've ever experienced."

He was simply fascinating to her. It wasn't even irritating she ignored his first question but yet dove right into more intimate details of his personal routines than describe what he did. Normally, that was a non-starter when someone said what they wanted and disregarded her like that. He was sharing who he was, intentionally or not. This man was too much, describing nature as if he actually sat in it and listened to its sounds.

"Well," she said unpoetically, finding herself unsure what to say. Lost of words wasn't familiar ground for her, as she didn't know many people that she'd actually care to hear them continue to talk - or ones that actually had something substantial to say directly, with interesting snippets of information coming through indirectly.

Fortunately, he wanted to keep her interested in what he was saying, have her keep looking at him even if he was driving and couldn't watch her directly. He didn't want to talk about work or what they were doing that day, where they were headed or what brought them together. He decided to stick with what he knew, the stories of his home and the stories his family would tell when they'd go camping or have crawfish boils. Safe enough subjects.

"You know, I haven't traveled around much, like you've probably been to a lot of different places. I've stayed pretty close to family and the job, but I know about the spirits that keep the fifolet burning in the marshes. Those lights are actually gorgeous and you can look at them for hours. Some people that hunt in the bayou and those woods were said to have never returned because they are chasing the treasure where the fifolet lead. I guess it's like the northern lights, with stories that have been handed down over generations to explain fascinating things."

He paused while he took the exit that would take them toward his home. Sarah stayed in utter silence, somewhat entranced by the spell he was weaving of the area and very glad to hear his story, to listen to his voice pull the cloak around her. Dodging some traffic, he quickly made it out to the older and somewhat abandoned stretch of highway. He continued after they were on the two lane road, with no markings and driving deeper into the trees, with the city far behind them.

"My last name, Rougaroux, is actually a French derivative... well, the Canadian French as in the Acadians that came hundreds of years ago when the British exiled them from Canada, from an area just to the east of the Laurentian mountains that was populated by Indian tribes and settled by the French, the actual ones from France, so my background includes Montagnais as well as true French. There are even traces of Irish in that tribe.

Anyway, my name means werewolf. It's the predominantly Cajun variation of loup-garou, the pure wolf-of-the-darkness, and I don't mean just of the night."

"Do your typical criminal prey realize they are being tracked by a dark wolf that is prepared to hunt to success and demand fear as well as obedience?"

"Surprisingly, some do. When they glance at my name tag if I'm in full gear, their eyes go large and they stop fighting, dropping their heads and take a step back, kind of in the way of old time class deference, maybe to hope I don't make them into one, too. They have no loss of pride being taken down by a werewolf." He smiled at a memory of a particular arrest, but quickly returned his focus to Sarah.

"So anyway, what about your story, background, things. I've said enough - what about you? Where do you stay? How is it you get to attend secretive meetings and waltz into anywhere you please?"

"Ah, and here is the inquisition I actually expected from a detective such as yourself, rather than the description of tranquil nature at dusk," she said with an amused chuckle as she shifted in her seat to be nearly facing him with her whole body. "In a poolside cottage, because I'm very good, and I actually prefer the tango with the turns that make you catch your breath. How's that?"

When she cocked her head to one side, the airflow in the car changed a little with her shifting, and he caught the scent of her - citrus and light flowers, slight cypress and spice in there, too. All femininity and blissfully not the boring scent of vanilla. Her choice in perfume left him more interested than ever.

"I think you are trying to distract me by providing pretty answers but not to questions I asked. The first reply was the only one that nearly answered what I asked, assuming I was asking the type of home rather than its location. The last one is quite distracting. So I will go with your change of direction and ask when the hell you have the time to literally tango."

"Well, with my beau at the time and four friends about fifteen years ago, we enrolled in a ballroom dance course. My boyfriend managed to switch his schedule - I mean, quote - had his rotation moved through no suggestion of his own - endquote and insert the eye roll here since you are driving and cannot - well, should not - watch my storytelling. So, I was frequently partnerless in class." She relaxed a bit, with shifting her shoulder back over the corner of the passenger seat.

"One evening at the start of class, a dark haired woman, who I later learned was first generation American and her parents were from Italy, confided in me that she didn't like to dance and was here for her husband's sake. He was actually the dancer of the couple. Noticing I was alone after the first evening and often was partnered in haphazard form with the instructor (who never completed steps with me as he wandered off to correct other people), she felt sorry for me because she thought it appeared that I liked to dance. She asked if I would take her place in the lesson that night. That was the evening we learned to tango," and she turned her head as if she could see the scene out of her window.

"He was Italian, too, just like his wife, so you can imagine how he looked at class, no matter what was the designated style of the evening. That old instructor chided us that even if you found nothing else in the closet to wear other than jeans, the ladies were required to wear heels. I was taller than him even without the heels. The height difference didn't matter. Because he was so skilled and a great leader, I learned to tango the right way, and with skill. I loved moving around the room and being quickly turned in a different direction. I made mistakes and he covered them with ease. One of the few times I probably totally gave in to the moments. Simply marvelous. I was so glad the guy I dated didn't come after that - and he didn't feel as sheepish, either."

They continued talking a bit about nature, the lake, briefly figuring out topics of mutual interest similar to last night's conversation. There wasn't much time to say more as it was only a few miles more to arrive at his house. As he stepped out to go over to his personal car, she stepped out onto the oyster shell drive in order to have a better look around. It wasn't quite as she expected.

From the outside, it was raised - that much was expected. Damn, he lived on the lake so nature herself determined where the first floor could actually begin, which in this case was maybe sixteen feet up, possibly twenty, so that you could see straight to the water behind the yard. It had a large stairwell to a grand porch that wrapped the whole way around. Gorgeous sunsets could be watched over the lake from that porch. She found herself drawn to the edge of the water that came up to the left side of the house and nearly to the road, looking through the reeds he had described that were indeed sounding as though a softly babbling brook were passing at her feet.

"Do you like the view?" He was closer to her than she realized, his voice low and whispering just behind her right shoulder, as he stood between her and his home.

"Mmm, very much, and also what I hear." Closing her eyes, she continued, "It's as you described, with the breeze coming off the lake. You hadn't described that part of you that comes from here - that salt scent that comes on the wind also comes with you." She turned around with her eyes still closed, the sun now on her back. "I like what I smell, too, and feeling the warmth here in the middle of the day is just heavenly. Imagine waking up to that every day - you must feel as though you are the luckiest man on earth. Sunrise," she said while facing him and then turning back around to the west while opening her eyes, "to sunset, with barely anyone around to change your plans you have each day."

He took a step closer. "I would love to show you the view from the porch, all the way around. Inside, too." He came around to her right side, just beside her and slightly in front. While looking past his shoulder to her, he reached with the hand closest to her, tucking some loose strands behind her ear. "But we have a meeting that calls us both." His arm slide naturally around her shoulder and it took all his might to pivot them both to the car.

They each took one look over their shoulders at the house, and continued back to the car. Slowly, with his arm still draped around her shoulder, he walked her to the passenger side and opened the door for her with his right hand. As she lowered herself to her seat, he took the small luxury of letting his hand be caressed by her hair, and then gently closed the door again. He paused to look at the front door, down at her and then made his way to the driver's side to set off across the lake.

Chapter 16

They arrived at the meeting, with him a bit on edge and wanting a cigarette (though he was trying to quit) and her looking a bit tousled with the perfect wind-blown look (except it was a business and not personal setting). It was an odd building, seemingly a repurposed old motel. There were outside stairwells at either end of the two-story building and a newer secured glass door at the end of the interior corridor upstairs. Once keyed through that south upper door, it was a shotgun approach toward the north entrance. Horrible for security, but if you didn't advertise the activity on the converted second floor, perhaps the cost-savings could be applied to the bells and whistles on the other side.

To the left, there were three doors evenly spaced down the two hundred feet. The central corridor was about the width of a single bowling lane, gutters included. To the right, there was a door thirty feet from the entrance where they stood, and a mirror along the side setup at the other end of the hall. Not a single image or item decorated the space, but it still had the aura of motel, likely from the grey carpet and dingy darker beige walls as well as florescent ceiling lights.

Marcus stepped around her and opened the door to the right, motioning her to proceed him into the meeting. She walked into yet another room full of men and one female, who was relegated to a corner on a triple-screen set up sync'ed to a laptop.

As there were never many females in the room, she always noted these potential allies first.

Though not always friendlies, gender in this field brought more women together than most other industries. Quicker to collaborate with intelligence and situational reports, women in domestic security (not mere "law enforcement;" that field was a coin toss where typically women were considered too manly or only as prospects for bedding) rapidly assessed and understood that if they had gotten this far that it was on skills not on sheets. That allowed a bit of traditional tension to be erased along with a quagmire of other assessments being rendered unnecessary.

The respect that was given by the female gender regarding achievements in the old boys club still allowed for evaluation of expertise. In a rather ironic twist, if you made it to this level of the playing field by thwarting the club's advances and subsequent pigeonholing as a result of doing your job exceedingly well rather than by favors or blackballing, you knew that the other females had to know their stuff; they would never be included as a "token" or political favor. Women in these spots *earned* them, just as she had earned hers. A single nod between Sarah and the other woman, then they were ready to work.

The look toward her by the men, conversely, was always priceless. Rather predictably, they knew team members were coming from the city to participate in the ops meeting, but no one had said who would attend. Typically when she showed up, there were three "faces" in the room - first and easiest to recognize as well as most prevalent, the incredulous "it never crossed my mind a woman would be here" face, and the owner may or may not have the stamina to keep up with the intellectual activity of the fore-coming meeting (always a factor to be determined… this look could have outcomes of smart or clueless). This was usually lower level guy, commonly boots on the ground or street guys allowed to present as they were being considered for leadership positions - these situations were part of the evaluation process. It was a good filtering system, as their bosses could see reactions just as this meeting showed, where reaction and subsequent action could not be staged.

Then there were some of the boss' reactions. This second group of men tried not to let it show that they first recognized her femininity, but it was painstakingly clear. They were just under the "need to know" level, but in fact knew these kinds of meetings were not transparent. The screening process required a certain level of achievement and verified contributions, unless it was an outright political plug. These meetings intentionally did not typically have plugs, so politicians could claim a certain level of deniability. Typically, if the "duh" faces were 60 or maybe 70 percent, this second stoic face was about 30 percent - the old fashioned "I-can-take-a-yelling-without-blinking" guys.

The remaining ten percent or so didn't even consider women as participants that they could make contributions, and would either dodge her or treat her like candy. These stupid guys had risen to the level of their incompetence and it was only a matter of time before their ineptitude would be revealed. Though of the same cloth as the guy Sean from the previous meeting in the construction zone, these guys in the third category didn't try to hide the lack of interest. Instead, it was overt avoidance or bar-room magnet for them - but both were the same category because they would never recognize a woman's professional contributions (and quite often were sneaky enough to try to abscond them as their own achievements).

A rare fourth category sometimes appeared, and this was actually more intriguing than the nuances of the American financial "one percent" club. This particular one percent evaluated simultaneously on a contributor's intellect, future value to ops, and weighed past achievement with grains of salt. Only then was gender factored into members of this percent's equation, and if the object of evaluation was female, it actually got extra points for dodging political bullets and making it to this elite "playing field."

Luke was one of her first encounters locally that met this description. His analytical prowess and dealings with ancient Egyptian female leadership likely colored his present-time evaluations, too. Those women who rose to Pharaoh in Egypt were cunning, brilliant, and even sometimes downright ruthless. Luke gathered information and wasn't biased by appearance (though she caught his glances of appreciation in certain outfits). She had a feeling Marcus was a member of this rare breed as well - an ops "one percenter" that liked and respected a few pretty things.

Smiling, but not chuckling as the Ops Chief walked over to greet her, she realized the four groups of men fell into the BCG business organizational plot that still proved accurate today though designed in the 1970s. It was really a growth and revenue mapping matrix, but it applied all the same here: Question Marks versus Cows (as in cash cows, not fat men), Dogs versus Stars. Same experience curve applied, too. If only more people could put aside their personal agendas and evaluate facts instead of biased images, but that was asking a lot.

Introductions were made to Sarah of three people by the captain running the meeting. She had heard all of their names previously, on other large ops. Typically, these meetings were attended by high level people, with the intel folks feeding them, and then the outcomes of what the high level folks wanted handed down to worker bees. Extremely inefficient, and with time working against them, they cut out the middle step - the high level men. There was a saying by the Civil Support Team to just get the job done first and work on the paperwork after you save the day. Applicable in this instance, for certain.

In total, there were twenty-five people present when the meeting began, and a few drifters came late. In recognition that many of these players from a wide array of agencies had never met face to face, but likely used each other's work on a regular basis, the captain encouraged the suggestion of a round-robin introduction. Great for the men, but seemingly a bit obvious of a ploy aimed by a few to understand her role. She could care less if they understood.

At the appropriate point in the round-robin, she provided, "Sarah Steinbrunn, and what I do is a long story," knowing that that should keep the dogs and some of the question marks out of the way while the others worked.

Marcus was standing behind her, slightly right, just as he had along the water's edge at his house. He introduced himself next and the wheel kept turning. She knew it was no coincidence that he placed himself at her six, and she appreciated the connection in a room of unknowns. She leaned back into him a little and without averting her eyes from the robin, she whispered back to him, "I thought Jason was going to be here with us?"

He was able to lean toward her ear, also keeping his eyes on the reaction of others to their exchange. It was obvious now that they had arrived together, though upon her entry it was likely no one noticed Marcus enter the room, or thought they were all separate as another guy entered the room behind the two of them.

"Jason is with the mayor at another meeting near the train station. When he's clear, we leave here and meet him - maybe even at the side of the road. I'll get the text when it's time. But this is the meeting that was hastily assembled to talk about the game and share what we know. Too rapid of an assembly to have someone scope and bug this thing."

Chapter 17

She knew he was right on that last aspect. As the building was an old motel and had some recent work done, because of the era of the structure, it was all cinder block and steel. Made for enduring wind safety rather than creature comfort, even the rehab completed in the last two years didn't provide any luxury. What it provided on this half of the second floor was a room half the length of the building, with the high and small rectangular portals that seemed large enough only to determine if it was raining or the sun was shining. Breaching this back wall would be tough, as would any extrication if necessary.

Suspended from the ceiling approximately four feet in front of the left wall were six flexiglass panels - clear glass that had microscopic pixelation enabling them to show images similar to computer screens or the old overhead projection screens, but that were visible from both sides. At six feet a side, you could see a lot of detail if you wanted to zoom in tight. They also could roll up to be deployed at an area command, which is why they were called flexiglass - and they had stands that power them for field deployment, but those weren't necessary here. The room was about 50 feet by 100 feet, thus giving them plenty of distance from the panels.

They were programmed redundantly at the moment, so the set on the left was a mirror of the set on the right. Currently in each set, these were showing ground level view on the left and an overhead schematic of the arena's interior on the right; the center display was a satellite picture of the area for a square mile. They could actually load several public venues, but everyone knew they were there for review of intel on the championship game being held in just days.

Additionally, Sarah knew that they could have a locked internet feed to a lone panel that was hung practically invisibly along the front wall, ten feet back from the front of these panels; it was isolated and controlled independently from a separate lone laptop. This was to prevent any interface for potential hackers to the system used for drills or during actual events. The laptop for the drone feed or satellite - even if one of their snipers wanted to integrate his post view back to the command center - it was all done through the single laptop on the one screen. Thus far, they hadn't needed a second live feed but that took about ten minutes to run a new one next to the one already installed.

This new geomapping system the kids produced was unique in that it was an actual production of radar sensors sending millions of signals from the transportable boxes they took into the stadium. And these, too, were not internet capable - so the data couldn't be exported to a system with internet and extrapolated by a worm. With full access to the stadium granted by the owners for as many days as they needed it, all under the guise of "structural engineering inspection" (which wasn't entirely false), they now had a complete replica of the actual building - significant from all of the work completed over the years and after the storm. There wasn't an accurate complete set of blueprints anywhere.

That happened frequently in older cities and with multipurpose or government buildings. With changes in personnel and elected leaders, some things just got shifted. Hard to believe that there were buildings with no plans, but in reality, it happened more often than not. It worked to their advantage when bad guys tried to plan just based on the original or a recent blueprint, but these were never complete (sometimes on purpose, usually not). Like with maps, a way to tell if someone copied efforts, purposeful errors or omissions were included in schematics to ensure authenticity.

With the development of more portable and higher powered optics in the last decade, there was the ability to translate portable medicine endeavors as well as minute transportation devices capabilities to portable security efforts. These lasers, sonar, radar and other gamma-knife accuracy components made planning more complicated but alleviated many time constraints. The result of all the various components being assembled - all in a non-internet environment - made a lifelike image that could be zoomed in to the smallest of rivets in a supporting beam's structure. The only downfall was they were stagnant from the moment of capture, so on-site inspection wasn't rendered irrelevant, just reduced to last-minute walk-through.

Once virtually "assembled," actors (the bad guys), players (the caught-in-the-middle-guys) and responders (the good guys) were also programmed into the system - using actual data, if available, for all of them. There were interactive maps that could respond to voice commands, or compute timed movements of a crew. For instance, if they had a fully equipped SWAT team roll through the club level outside hallway, the computer could time the accurate coverage of real estate made by the team. Likewise, if parameters were entered for an event (like a bomb near an exit), the effects and timing could be played out through the software.

Tabletop exercises for these good guys in homeland security were no longer paper-pushing machinations of guesses and speculation. It was more reminiscent of a full-scale drill, where each virtual responder represented an actual person's height/weight/training level/etc, each unit based upon real teams comprised of those real responders. Overtime budgets weren't problematic. Running scenarios ad nauseum wasn't fatiguing a crew. A known actor or his gang of terrorists could be programmed as virtual actors for known habits or to have artificial intelligence randomly direct them - and the virtual responders wouldn't be conditioned at the beginning of every scenario to anticipate the actors' moves; they would react to the presented simulation as they would in the field.

Each individual in the stadium (and even surrounding it) was programmed - the sports teams on the field, the spectators, the media personalities in the press box, the grounds crew, pedestrians and traffic on the streets surrounding the building. Considering there were 80,000 players attending and working the events without considering first responders, it was a phenomenal bit of programming. It was an amazing achievement that few people did realized they had accomplished. It was nice to have enthusiastic students and a private sponsor for things like this.

And it was nice to have a motel-looking building in which to do it all. The front of the building still looked like a shabby longer-term motel. An office still existed to give the appearance of a functional motel, and handled typical office items such as phone answering, mailing services, provided a copy machine for "guests," and minimally assisted the office upstairs. The first floor in fact housed the kids who designed the program they were about to put in play - in luxurious suites and private spa baths on the "front" side and their work room was directly beneath the meeting. The front side of the second floor still looked like the old motel but on the inside had been remodeled with a great kitchen using all the high end appliances, plush living room with a theater system for them - and a secured entrance within the first floor to the second, so they didn't have to exit their bedroom suite area and go outside in order to head upstairs.

They got free housing, great security (though an internet disrupter was employed and they were warned to not to try and hack), and paid to do what they thought was cool - a virtual reality video game. The private funder actually owned a video gaming company, so they got paid legitimately for their work with guaranteed employment afterwards; they just had restrictions that they couldn't spend the money now - it was all escrowed for them. That was no problem as currently their utilities, food, non-attention grabbing vehicles, some toys were all covered and paid for at this location under their contracts. They had another restriction that they couldn't bring home guests - but the amount of money in their accounts and what they were doing, they didn't care. These three guys and two girls were geek coders, and the project was way cooler than human interaction.

The location was great not only for building design and housing these brilliant kids, but it was located on an old indian trail - so it wasn't in a new snazzy industrial park that screamed for attention and had loads of people passing through every day. This trail, now roadway, had been used for well over 250 years. Just like up north, where the pioneer trail ran from east from New York to west at Chicago along the bottom of the snow belt (which became Interstate 80 once cars were developed and the federal roadway system was formed), this trail became a road, too.

Originally used by Indians when hunting, it ran as close to the lake as the changing of tides and storm surge would typically allow. Frequently using it for hunting, and then when it was used as a trade route to the New Americans settling in the region, it became a busier thoroughfare. When cars were introduced, it became a wider roadway, but not heavily trafficked. Other areas across the lake within the city were like that, too, like the ridge with the bayou road that led from the river to the lake.

Some of the people in the room knew they were embarking on historic ground, but didn't know the full extent of what they were about to witness. They just knew mentioning it to anyone outside of the room would cost them their freedom. It was a Kantian ethics battle, is the good of one man worth the price for the good of many? Everyone in here knew they have a ticket toward ultimate sacrifice and didn't hesitate in the service for the good of others.

Chapter 18

Drew had been considering option three and how to not drown in the myriad of negatives of the proposal, attempting to create a succinct no-go summary. Community memories were still strong from a few years ago, as well as from a century past and even longer. The eastern area based for this proposal was young in that respect; it was never developed prior to the early 1900s, as there was no need for the space. Urban life was content and compact; there was actually no easy way - or good reason - to commute toward the city from that direction. You either worked in town and lived there or moved everything beyond its boundaries.

Little by little, and with increased water traffic and new waterway completion, expansion began to happen. Sure, there was always an area of camps. It was a Cajun version of camp, mostly often out onto and over water as those were originally built, in order to go shrimping or crabbing by the house piers, fishing off the porch, even doing cannonballs into the water for those who knew how to swim; these were opposed to the traditional Yankee camp in the mountains or woods for hunting - both camps intended for the same purpose, just not parallel prey. This area of camps was along the lakefront from the times of the voodoo queen (which was historically spelled voudou, said va-doo, in this Creole area as a blend from Haitian and African religious beliefs). But now, there were easier ways to drive a boat and soon, automobiles puttering out to the rich fishing areas at the edge of the marsh permeated nature, where the largest animals were deadly silent, producing ripples of water barely moving as the alligator approached blue herons and white egrets that launched into flight with the advance of the predator.

As the city grew and industry grew, this suburb grew. To make an even more idyllic pastoral environment, utilities had to be buried in all new developments after 1960; and so the scenery remained lush, undivided by poles and wires. However, when the oil went from king to crow in the 1980s, people fled again from the entire city - including the east.

As with crime of any sort, opportunistic voids were filled by the shadows. The apartment owners needed rent for the complexes abandoned; they began allowing subsidized housing vouchers, though preferred cash payment tenants, with a little lagniappe to turn an eye and keep away. The landlords didn't mind as the cash flow made it easier to cook the books; they actually could charge a little more to give their new tenants the "freedom" these new clients sought.

Crime began to increase in outlying areas, which came as no surprise to anyone as policing changed then as it had today within the entire city, yielding reduced protection nearly everywhere as resources were directed toward the city center and where the tourists kept the money flowing. Legislators had moved too slowly take more and more of the city's tax revenues for other state projects - an oddity that the state constitution allowed, and the city couldn't figure out how to fight. Thus state troopers augmented the local officers in the areas the state deemed "important" in order to protect their own interests, while other sections languished.

Long abandoned were the plans to continue the outgrowth of the city to the edges of the marsh. Healthy forests of the east remained thick, natural hiding spots for bodies, drug deals or other illicit activity best conducted when camouflaged. Granted, the storm of several years prior had washed away much of the evidence of past crimes, but there were ties to this land, a hard variety in varying degrees that made the web dangerous to navigate.

Thus began Drew's argument as to why option three was the absolute wrong avenue for development. This was an area that was considered "bequeathed by abandonment" to the members of the majority of the city. Federal, state and local government personnel had dedicated time and television speeches to restoring other areas; a significant deployment right now so distant from the heart of town - and contrary to the pomposity of pundit logic for environmental conservation and resource concentration - would draw too much attention.

If this group that met on the top floor to identify a location for covert anti-terrorism activity was to prematurely establish a brand new facility, even boldly incorporating multi-use functions and extend invitations to house community groups in the building, there were many issues. Some were obvious - why develop at the farthest region of the city prior to rehabilitation and development of the residential areas. That was an explanation he wasn't sure the best verbal tap dancer would be able to handle.

In addition, everyone in the area was extremely skeptical of anything associated with the government. Even though engineers proclaimed their building efforts complete, no one believed them. They were told the same story by the same group about the last round of protective structures built, that those would protect them and look what happened. The perception held by many was that government guys failed the very areas that the majority of the residents lived in order to create a resort atmosphere that lined their pockets and helped their buddies. To hell with the families that worked in the area and tried to stay in the area - building familial empires was more important to these southern politicians via eminent domain, legal loopholes, by whatever means necessary it seemed.

As painful as it was to live in the situation, it was more confusing to try to explain especially when progress was made in other parts of the nation. Thus, while locals had aversion to develop what they didn't generate and seek themselves, the federal "partners" didn't want to do anything that would seem like repeated forcefulness like Reconstruction, didn't want to do more than specifically instructed; at times, they actually sought to stop other endeavors from changing their new grand engineering experiments. And that was exactly the word locals felt they were living - an experiment that had no beneficial outcome for them.

This was all part of the argument against option three. For three hundred years, provincial governance maintained a distinct manner of law found nowhere else in the country. It was hard to figure out how to fit into the system in order to change the system while safeguarding against it changing you. For outsiders not in tune with the tides of the community members, it made no sense so they wanted to alight to fix a superficial issue and leave. Very few came to touch the differences that needed to be made. Lipstick on a pig, patting themselves on the back and away they went.

Drew knew he was one of the insiders and 'landed gentry' with a twist; his father's grandfather had inherited land from *his* grandfather (et cetera for more than two hundred and fifty years), and they still held some of these old plantation lands. The original house was long gone, but the family held onto the grounds by the river for inheritance sake, and to validate the fact they were insiders. This group didn't want changes, and somehow didn't consider there was any problems sending the folks away without incorporating or adopting improvements.

It didn't surprise him, however, knowing how his father and people that surrounded him handled things. He wouldn't say his father had friends; he had no pattern for how to make or keep "friends" growing up, something that he should have learned from his father. What he did know of his father he kept to himself, because it would hurt his mother. Just like the typical stories of poor maids getting pregnant by the rich man of the house, his father slipped one day and gave Drew fuel to use in the future.

At some point in middle school, he remembered a warm rainy afternoon when after school sports were cancelled. It had rained for days on end, and though the days prior the teachers had orchestrated activities in the gym. It was Friday and the teachers had enough. The kids were told to go ahead and walk home. School administrators had been kind, but it was the week's end and they were drained of ideas as the mud filled the school's yard.

So he headed home, and went into the house through the kitchen door, laying his backpack on the smooth wooden bench. Removing the muddy boots and putting his wet umbrella in the stand as he had been trained to do (if he didn't want scolded), he grabbed some cheese out of the fridge and munched a bit. Washing it down with some juice, he left the empty glass on the counter beside the sink and headed into the hallway, down to the library.

As he approached the doorway, he heard his father talking to someone, or rather two people. He knew the tone of his father's voice, but he couldn't place the other two voices. He knew for sure one was a female, but only heard a quiet higher-toned whisper in reply to his father's short clipped sounds.

Having no reason not to enter a room in his own home, Drew came around the corner standing straight and tall so as to not be admonished by his father for slouching or having a stature unbecoming to a man of "good breeding." How he hated this connotation of his father's ideal child, appropriate conformation, intentional goading into doing what he preferred. Nonetheless, it was easier to just do it to please his dad and keep the peace in the house rather than explain why he wasn't keeping to instructions.

Turning the corner around the open pocket doors and entering the lush library, appointed with much finery in a masculine decor, he saw his the back of his father's head in the deep green armchair. A woman was standing on the opposite side of the matching ottoman, on which sat a young boy. He seemed perfectly formed to his father's idea of what a child should be - he sat up straight, looked directly at his father as he spoke, hands folded on lap, legs perfectly bent at the knee. Resembling a little Michelangelo angel with light sandy hair that matched his father's, within one blink Drew knew it was another son.

The woman looked at Drew, and only raising her eyebrows with suspicion, his father turned around. Without missing a beat, his dad complimented the woman on what a fine young man she had brought to see him. As he stood up, he gently and fondly placed his finger under the boy's chin, tilting his eyes upward as his father smiled down lovingly, patting the boys head and thanking the woman for stopping at the house.

He didn't even acknowledge Drew as he exited the room, making the left turn toward the front door with the woman and her child following him. Drew went with them to the door, and stood at his father's right hand as the door was opened for this woman. When she passed to exit, Drew stated, "Thank you for stopping by and visiting our home."

With that perfectly phrased sentence, he showed the politeness required of his family with a quite obvious reference to the fact that she did not live there. Drew nodded goodbye to the boy, who appeared perhaps two or three years younger, and as they stepped onto the porch, he walked back into the library allowing his father some privacy again for his goodbye.

When Drew returned to the library, he sought out the book he wanted to continue reading, sitting in the window seat that was not facing the front of the house. Instead, having his back to the front of the house he was looking into the side yard, with it's immaculate boxwood border planted in a paisley-like pattern, each tear-drop filled to the brim with pink petunias, pure yellow daffodils, and whips of lavender filling the dollops of design and the crushed oyster shells creating the path in-between. He turned his gaze back to the room when his father cleared his throat, indicating that he waited for an explanation as to his early return from school.

Nothing was ever mentioned about the woman and the boy. He never said anything to his mother, knowing it would deeply wound her. He thought about any stories he heard or discomfort, trying to place what could have been the impetus for his father to stray while also knowing his father didn't part with money easily so there had to be some significant reason for the non-typical behavior.

But Drew knew that even if his father would belittle him or chastise him, with one raised eyebrow he could remind his father with the same tone of voice as his departure sentiments of that day. Indeed, his father went too far one day nearly ten years later, and only that once did he implicitly yet indirectly remind the man of the secret he maintained. Shortly after that, his father announced he would be traveling to Europe for an extended stay, with his mother traveling with him. That was more than fifteen years ago and he hadn't seen his father since. His mother came to visit once a year and they always had a pleasant time. She never asked why he tore out the library, converting it to a music room.

Chapter 19

The captain called the meeting to order after the introductions were completed. One of the petty officers was called to present the known facts to date. Beginning with a streamlined history of the event, those present tried not to look disinterested. Important in the analysis, but these were the pieces everyone already knew if they were in this room. Bless his heart, he just had to do his speech and then the significant components would be discussed.

Sarah leaned back into Marcus again, nearly pleading, "More of this and I will need a drink." He apparently agreed, as they were still connected so she felt him chuckle once, though he remained silent for a moment before adding, "I came to find out what I don't know, but you know their process. They have to tell us the outline of what they are going to tell us, then tell us, then repeat what they told us - meaning, we can leave after we hear what they tell us."

She turned and smiled in appreciation, then tried to direct her attention back to the guy across the room, still relaying what anyone could find on the internet - and they all memorized this information already. But what she had seen over Marcus' shoulder was more interesting, so she kept her body facing the front while she continued rotating to the right, focusing her vision past his left ear. The right screen was playing out a scenario of the interior of a programmed event, as the kids downstairs must be making some final adjustments, obviously uninformed about this meeting.

Apparently not realizing she was leaning more into Marcus with the right side of her body, he was doing all he could to pay attention to what the next speaker started to say. This guy was talking about the precautions and ops orders already in place. Since he had composed one of the police ops orders being presented, he wasn't necessarily listening for comprehension, but filtering content for accuracy, to correct anything if they had decided to adjust things without rationale. Sarah was unknowingly making it difficult not only because he wanted to see what she was watching, but her body had warmed the leather that was now leaning into him and it was very distracting.

What attracted Sarah's attention behind them was a scene on the flexiglass of all the avatar players, trying to rush toward exits as well as those they thought would be accessible by leaping onto the field. The colors of figures on the screen showed they accurately coded the rent-a-security-guard folks in bright yellow. Some yellow folks were over-zealous in trying to contain or fight people from getting onto the field; others were trying to run toward the locker room archway or crawl into the stands by the gates that they knew were in the wall from presumably their prior work details to balls and concerts at the location.

The point of incident was in red haze. Coming from the fifty yard line's box seats, where the most expensive tickets were sold and the highest profile spectators would be located, the screen accurately represented smoke as well as collateral damage to the building, blocking routes of escape. The concentration of explosives used for the scenario they were running before the official demonstration illustrated rubble blocking three aisles from the floor, decimation of the box level, structural integrity compromise, and the level of hysteria seemed appropriately dichotomous - the drunk unmoving fans versus the hysterical panicked ones.

Interestingly, there was an additional area of impact opposite from the main detonation point, but not directly across. Explosives positioning produced a reflection point that was not a geometrist's predicted trajectory. Rather, it was off by perhaps five or six degrees lateral and fifteen degrees distal, causing additional mayhem on that side of the field, but not identical in nature as there were more people injured or dead, thus slowing evacuations. The kids downstairs probably didn't realize explosives were their last concern, but it was good for testing programming as they could most easily relate to that sort of event from movies and adjust algorithms accordingly.

She was listening to what the third guy was now saying and decided to return her gaze to the speakers. When she relaxed her shoulders a bit as she rotated back to the discussion, Marcus shifted his weight behind her and she realized she had been maintaining contact. In recognition of the adjustment, she pushed her hair behind her left ear in a similar move to the one hours earlier at city hall, and shifted in the opposite direction of him, though oddly (yet not uncomfortably) their legs - her right and his left - were still touching.

Marcus made note that the ops orders presented were all what had been submitted, and the staffing was still reflecting accurate levels. In the past, the department forgot how to do math. Seriously, in one ops order after the storm, they triple-counted available officers. When an independent editor reviewed it, the first notation was a simple math sheet that showed they needed three-times as many officers for the "wish-list" plan and they needed to create a realistic framework based on available resources - not one based on "if we ask our friends and neighbors, this is the party we could do" nor one based on no one just adding up the officer count from every component. Terribly embarrassing for the brass, but he didn't work on that one. He was placed in the MSB shortly after that debacle nearly went public.

Other errors in that document were pretty obvious, too. Multiple divisions didn't cover their respective area but instead covered what they thought was a district's responsibility. Two divisions would cover the same locations. Shift changes were all different - some with erroneous hours for the tour of duty as though no one knew what times to use during an emergency deployment - another embarrassment for senior staff. Some platoons were used three times (what a magic number). Specific officer names were used rather than rank and title (and invariably, promotions and transfer lists would occur before the plan was enacted, so were the people assigned or the position the person held tagged for the role they held when the plan was written), causing more undue tension.

The submitted list of obvious deficiencies was fourteen pages long; that editor wasn't a trained officer though no one knew who completed the review. Invariably internal people found additional problems and tried to discredit the list. But that editor was skilled in English, and the general editing "red marks" were all over the place in addition to the critical thinking notes. In spite of this, the department just waived the requirements for sixty hours of college credit to work on the job - because no one, of course, needs to write anything down in a report or anything. Good grief.

The voice changed to a fourth person. Both Sarah and Marcus stood straighter as the recent intel was being presented. A lieutenant commander began speaking. "Chatter has shown that there are several distinct people involved in four countries in planning an attack that we believe is local. No direct indication that our event is a target has been identified, but timing of planned movements, phrasing, and keywords strongly yield evidence that we could be in for a ride." Glancing at his notes briefly, he continued.

"While we cannot confirm specific locations, we are creating a web of activity and known actors within the regions. We have the Colorado/Four Points region, New York, Germany and the Middle East, with that specific region hard to negotiate at this time. Additionally, the participants are using multiple routers or public locations, and some other governments are reluctant to provide any surveillance material as they suspect the U.S. of our own use against their elected officials or general public. So we only can continue to process what we access directly ourselves." Handouts started circling through the room, giving all of the details accurately to the attendees. There was a short pause until the papers stopped rustling.

"In addition, we can eliminate the typical explosives or shootings as the intended mechanism. While we know we like our weapons in the south and blowing things up, there is no indication that bombing is the method of disruption and as far as active shooter scenarios, the supply on ammo in the recent months has a tracking on all purchases. There is no evidence that there will be enough actors to engage in infiltration to accomplish significant disruption in that type of mass action at our event location due to its configuration with either of these options." He checked his notes for the last time.

"Further, there have been no unauthorized movements of radio-nucleotides, no thefts of significant amounts of particulate to craft dirty bombs, no strategic or tactical missile engagement possibilities within the response radius, including the Gulf - mobile or stationary in several locations are being monitored

24/7. This leaves biological or chemical concerns at this time. Colonel."

Picking right up where the prior gentleman stopped, "There are groups with the expertise to coordinate such an action proximal to our event, and I'm not being disrespectful, but our Al Sha-bubba neighbors are not one of these groups. Earlier indications were that they now had access to a credible scientific party contributing to their cause, but that has since been disproven. For your own awareness, the gentleman in question there calls himself "Doc" as do his compatriots but it's more because he knows how to set a bear trap and disembowel quicker than his buddies rather than his knowing how to use a test tube or beaker. He hunts illegally and likes to sound more sophisticated than he is; this was confirmed yesterday."

He continued, "We have not been able to rule out any cells from the Colorado region that have been under watch or any of those more proximal to the event. The rapid identification of the threat has made it nearly insurmountable to monitor them all, but we are doing what we can and simultaneously diverting resources for this NSSE. There is a greater presence of untraceable funding for domestic groups than in the past; we all admit that has been an issue for several decades and even though Silk Road is shuttered, there's always another waiting to take its place." While none of this was new information, both Marcus and Sarah hoped it was somehow relevant to their situation.

"There has been a specific threat on a large gathering for the timeframe in question. It is unlikely, though not impossible, that the pre-game activities are targets, but we know that actions like this type have predators that prefer media coverage and no one watches how far some nine-year old can kick a ball in the family events before game day. Sorry to all you parents out there in the room, just not scalable for results as important to divert additional assets.

"This leaves us with biologics and chemicals; a list of agents from the Type II lists within a five hundred mile radius will be displayed on this screen, and we will go through them phase-wise with notes about how we eliminated certain possibilities. It should be noted the observation mechanisms for routine disturbances remain in place, such as the airspace monitoring and other anti-fanatical techniques. Our next portion is presented by," as he gestured to the corner, "a chem-e from Case Western, as you learned when she introduced herself, but she also has a PhD in mathematical modeling of dynamic systems." Everyone turned to the regular screen located at the opposite end of the room from the flexiglass panels. The female Sarah noted earlier began the next part of the presentation.

"The 12,271 locations that are covered under the CFATS and MTSA regulations in this region are mapped for you. Removing the MTSA locations, as those come under the USCG and have been routinely inspected and documented in the years since the storm, show no significant vulnerabilities at this time. That leaves 469 CFATS locations remaining in the area in question." She was more organized than the other presenters and used no notes as she presented slides and maps with overlays that went along with her speech.

"As these chemical facilities are the ones identified without a navigable waterway and thus are outside the parameters of MTSA, they have greater susceptibility to penetration, both theft and accident, for two reasons: they were identified by federal entities as being more susceptible and published accordingly in the public domain in addition to not having the federal funding behind the regulation for inspection. Thus, they stand as a beacon for those looking to steal with intentions of using the items to create a chemical incident elsewhere or using the location itself as the incident for chemical release." She shifted the map again, focusing it tighter to the region.

"Taking the Type II list as well as the MTSA regulatory specs and recipes for destructive agents, the Type II would expand the vulnerable locations by 621." As the woman spoke, the scenes shifted on the map using color coordinated beacons on the screen. Dots representing MTSA and CFATS, fading for MTSA and adding of others for Type II, varying intensities for theft versus incident origin - all contributed to an ebb and flow as the information was visual presented with her verbal depiction of the damage that could be inflicted.

The female chemical engineer continued. "Splitting the screen into two maps, one for locational incident and one for theft, right versus left respectively, we see that theft is significantly narrowed as the components accessible in significant quantity are available to be formulated into a useable weapon. This map takes each substance at the identified storage facilities and considers what is needed for weapon mechanization, cross that national map with this one, and significantly reduces the suspected targets because of the length of time that the recipe, if you will, needs to be completed as well as the placement and transport time for deployment at our event. The resulting eighty-six locations have Federal personnel staged on site for the next nine days, overstaffing by two days for certainty to cover the potential for actors going for effect rather than impact, meaning less product would need crafted and released.

"The chemical incident/accident display is on the right, and shows a geo-sensitive map that incorporates comprehensive weather patterns for the area, as shifting as they may be. We can inspect and have people on site in the days ahead, but incident management will be intense on the specific day of the game. And in these locations, it's not just interior security but outside as well. For instance, the facility down in 'da parish' wouldn't normally be considered but for the sulfuric acid and ammonia that, in gaseous form, is fatal to people within ninety miles in mere minutes if the hydrocracker is targeted by a rocket launcher along the main road. Another facility upriver seven miles from the event location uses hydrofluoric acid, just as dangerous depending on wide direction, or perhaps more as it has no scent to indicate release and exposure. Considering the different variables for location, this is reduced to fourteen CFATS and twelve MTSA locations. USCG can be deployed to MTSA, relieving personnel burden but the other CFATS sties must be covered by ground personnel."

Chapter 20

The chemical engineer continued, "If you would turn around to the panels behind you, we will look at the modeling developed by our gamers downstairs that incorporates the chemical mapping. You have all been made aware of how the programming for the teams worked; your own profiles have been loaded, too, though generically and not with an avatar at this stage."

Silence filled the room as the screens Sarah watched previously were reset. Weather patterns for the day were inserted and appeared on the upper left corner of the first screen. Avatars of outside people and vehicles adjusted accordingly, in volume as well as concentration of available "pieces." Time of day was entered, day of the week, and other minor details.

And then all three (well, six) screens shifted with the play initiated. The details of game day started rolling, with emergency personnel appearing, staging, pre-game outside beginning, on-field preparation beginning, vendors inside staging food and souvenirs, gates opening, and people flowing everywhere. It was in rapid pace, so even kickoff seemed to come more rapidly as the first ten hours completed.

When the center screens' images started getting hazy, someone in the back of the room inhaled loudly. It was a vivid reminder that not all good guys even with high-tech (or standard low-tech human intelligence) were always able to win. The cliche of *the terrorists only have to be lucky once* was on display for all to see. The unknown chemical had been released in the stadium. At this point, timing during the game was irrelevant.

Apparent to everyone in the meeting was the rapid decline of each and every person based on proximity to the release point. Chemical weapons took people down based on dose of exposure, reliant on the concentration of the agent given to the person, and length of that exposure. In this space, there was no simple way to inject fresh air - and no one wanted a scenario of several years ago with a damn hole in the roof. People near the release point went down fast, likely 'ceased to breathe' within just a few heartbeats as the medical responders say, and it was like a horrid reverse stadium wave, where people went down and stayed down rather than standing at their seats while waiving their hands and then sitting back down.

It didn't matter the color of avatars - chemistry is non-discriminatory. Blue police, red fire fighters as well as EMS staff, green sports team members, purple drunk spectators, pink generic spectators, yellow security staff, orange vendors, and more - every single one falling like a domino or stumbling as the effects impaired movements or permanently inhibited them.

Outside the stadium, it was surreal. The effects were contained inside, though the first responder colors could obviously been seen jumping into action in various ways - and thankfully none were running into the scenario. At early stages in situations like this, nothing can be done without full respiratory protection, but they could seal the scene until proper personal protective equipment was delivered.

For some of them in the room, such as Sarah and Marcus, this was the cue to leave. No more could be gleaned as there was no more intel on the responsible party, and until the predictable mechanism of choice was narrowed in scope even response couldn't be enhanced. It was all about pre-emptive capture of the suspect or suspects and derailment of the intended impact. This center was staffed at all hours and they could come back later, reviewing other chemical scenarios or a few biologic ones - though that would not have the immediate media impact of a chemical event. That was one reason that they were focusing on chemical: biological took longer to manifest symptoms whereas chemical incidents took mere breaths to begin and end. Biologics were typically better at high-volume but low media events whereas chemical or dirty bombs (previously discounted from this scenario) loved the lime-light.

But really why they had to leave was deeper than just this scenario running on the plexiglass and the background commentary by the gathered experts. Only a few years prior, in the worst natural disaster in the nation's history, a very similar event was playing out in the mind of twenty-two of their close friends. Back then, there wasn't a math model, there weren't facts and outside impartial evidence to reveal what would happen - it was their imaginations creating the end of their world. The police in there were planning for their own demise, with the assailant being not chemicals, but the other people in the building that were expected to turn against them at any moment during those seven excruciating long days and nights isolated from any other realm but the Lord of the Flies outplay. Some of their friends and coworkers should never see this modeling example; Sarah and Marcus were both in sync with their thoughts, knowing when they simultaneously turned to each other, they needed to get out to Jason and begin modifying resources, responders, and pray for a break in the responsible party aspect of the threat analysis.

Though they were in the front of the room at this point, the men parted when Sarah turned and headed toward the door. It also signaled that the meeting was over - no need for anyone to review what was said again or to see a replay. The screens and math and research showed exactly what the enemy was likely planning, regardless of the mechanism used to poison nearly 100,000 people on national television with a billion people watching live, one hundred twenty five million at least in the continental United States. Silence continued through the room as Marcus slowly inhaled and followed her, with several others filing out behind them.

Neither spoke as he opened the car door for her again. Nothing was said as Marcus texted Jason while walking to the driver's seat in order to determine where they would meet. Sarah looked out the window as he started the car and some seeing her in the passenger seat may think she was overcome with emotion. While she was impacted with heartache at the scenario, she was actually calculating the next moves against this unknown assailant. She was more angry than sad, and when she was angry she was very, very quiet.

Marcus pulled onto the trail and made a right. He, too, was thinking about the unknown now that the "where" and "when" were fairly established. Let those experts in that room determine the "how;" he was focused, as he had been, on the "who" - the "why" was just as revealing, yet it was usually secondary to the other question and could be revealed during potential identification filtering stages.

They moved down a lesser used state road, coming to a spot where they could pull off and stand by the lake to wait. A few trucks with empty trailers were parked here, across the road from the boat ramp. In the middle of the bridge just a little further down and heading across the lake was an old drawbridge - she had been on a boat out in this area. That was a nice day, similar to today's weather, but a totally different atmosphere and a quick trip around the edge of the lake to get out of going back to the office.

Right now, they were both thinking of getting back to desks. After a few minutes of the continued silence, Sarah spoke first. "When this is over, I wouldn't mind going out on the water here again. I haven't been fishing since I was a kid, but it would be nice to just be out on the water, quiet and still, where cell phones don't reach and you can imagine nice things instead of planning counter-measures for something sick like this."

Marcus agreed, quietly saying, "We'll do that." They remained in each other's company, looking out over the new dock being built for one of the houses being rebuilt. When Jason arrived and after giving him the short story, they also outlined the next steps. Marcus began by stating what he was going to do with some of the detectives and IT guys from the joint task force, even though some of them weren't included in this preparation. They frequently helped one another without a complete need-to-know.

Sarah suggested it was best to keep the other folks with the stockpile project in the dark. She directly stated, however, none of them needed to babysit anyone at the moment, and she could contact the state physician that had command and control over chemical weapons antidotes to start moving them. There was also another system that had never been deployed for indoor use, but seeing as their stadium practically and literally had it's own meteorological system being so close to (and under) sea level as well as the way it was built that she wanted to investigate deployment inside and underneath the roof.

Jason concurred, knowing that letting these two just get to work would be best. Marcus and Sarah got back into the unmarked car and Jason watched as Marcus drove headed into the city. As for Jason, he wanted to do a bit of investigating on his own, as when they shared the four locations of the loose web for the potential suspects, the first thing that came to mind was military deployment locations. It could be a coincidence, but a few other strange things lately got his mind working in an uncomfortable direction.

Chapter 21

Over the next few hours and into the next day, Marcus gathered a select few specialists to create a mini-task force, consciously choosing them from the various branches of federal, state and local agencies to work on identification of the mastermind behind the suspected attack. They had to build a framework without the four-point web constraining their processes. Nearly as important was the attitude of the personnel chosen in addition to their prowess. Considering their experiences, the seven members including himself brought various talent from the field to this table.

He chose a Fed for the data-mining guy, whose endeavors could have linked him as a founding member of any geek club. Strangely, the outward appearance of this bureau agent looked like he could have been a model with the body sculpting he had perfected, his dark thick hair styled with mousse, the pale blue eyes clear as the sky. His clothes fit perfectly without any special tailoring, causing women to be drawn to him while men were repelled by his effortless appeal to women marking him as instant competition.

While the guy could excel in the gym or any fitness test required, that wasn't his calling. His best performance came when he sat alone in front of a bank of computers. Having created his own supercomputer of sorts, he constructed an independent network with his own redundant servers and an elaborate client group to maintain parallel processing of far-reaching information as he was able to retrieve it from a variety of locations. With one computer, he programmed an algorithm to assemble the pieces of disparate information to create a more cohesive story based on probabilities, reliability of data source, weighted redundancy of similar components to refine the final story. His badge carried federal weight, but his toys were privately funded through a few modeling jobs he completed in college. If you've got it, use it; the guys on the larger joint terrorism task force didn't pick on him too much.

The second team member was also a Fed, assigned to the Public Health Service. Regardless of professional designation in that hierarchy, he was an infectious disease epidemiologist. Prior to the terrorist attacks in New York and Washington, D.C., police and public health personnel didn't interact much - unless someone was shot, it seemed, and even then it was a stretch for communication let alone cooperation. Immediately following 9/11, everyone assumed the only need for collaboration would be for an anthrax attack. But once some tag team trainings occurred, both sides realized the need was much greater.

There were some scenarios that public health staff could solve - or nearly resolve - in the matter of a few hours. The critical thinking skills were very different from the traditional criminal analysis training of law enforcement. Cop mentality was predisposed to creating an image of perpetrator and associating behavior patterns with the classification of crime. Health staff, however, looked for signs and symptoms, clues and evidence of activity, before pulling information together to make data sets then seeing where the facts direct them to search.

One exercise Marcus distinctly remembered had all of the alphabet soup groups of multi-jurisdictional teams in a room with an "illness" and explosion incident at a festival. The questions the public health team members asked were so very foreign. The law enforcement folks branched their own way after hearing what they considered to be odd questions, preferring to solve this their way. However, thirty minutes later the public health teams knew the illness-agent used, had a profile of mechanism of deployment, a scope of exposure, and already were down the path of reviewing key schematics as well as video from the entry points, significantly narrowing the possible guilty persons. The way they described how they arrived at all of the correct information confirmed for him on that day that even if something wasn't medically related, the next "big thing" needed critical thinking. He tagged this guy from D.C., who would arrive six hours later on a charter flight.

He decided to pick someone from the newest industry to invade the city for the third slot: movie folks. He had worked some details for a variety of shows and seen how they viewed situations very differently. Be it a still shot, video, or live on sets, the videographer made the magic happen even when the director was behind the staged area. They were trained to make the pretty picture, but in order to achieve that, experts had to see the big picture as well as how the details mattered all in seconds, with the pressure of time is money.

Staging was a big deal, and the people behind the lens looked at so many things - and also knew about gels and screens or other things that would alter how an image was received. He had seen one camera woman make changes on the scene of a television series and actually stop a director because the roll of a particular sleeve wasn't coming through in the best way. Talented people behind the lens noticed variations in lighting, texture variables even down to stucco pattern variations`, coloration, angles, height - you name it, they caught it.

For this big picture-small detail position, he chose as the third member of the team that same woman who worked on the animal show, able to override the director on a call for production the day he was on set. Working with the animals, too, she had to have talent to read and anticipate movements, recognize emotional detail as well as non-verbal cues. She would be assigned to review the networked crime camera system (well, the footage from ones that actually worked... ones that helped the indictment and felony conviction of a former mayor's pal) and she could do some profiling not of the racial sort, but the behavioral sort.

As he was also acting as team leader, he needed a second detective, an experienced person with contacts in the city. Undercover experience and a set of confidential informants would prove extremely valuable, especially as he had been working his own leads with the drug case lately. His CIs were focused on narcotics and he needed a different kind of lead. He picked one of his own department's longtime officers, one who had been in Vice for seventeen years.

This twenty-eight year veteran detective had a shoebox full of complete identities to use with his various contacts. It was a pretty impressive collection that was destroyed by torrents of swamp water in the storm. Swept out of its hiding place, the box was on the top of the pieces of his family's life smashed and piled against the front window of his home as the surge entered, overtook, and exited the home. This guy never wanted to move up the ranks, so he kept his ear to the ground for decades. Able to blend into a variety of places, he could work the street quickly as the fourth addition.

Only two more types of specialities were needed in this ad hoc team's tool kit. One was a forensic evidence specialist. As it turned out, a cop (a detective at that) came to mind who might be the solution. She went to nursing school when the new administration's bureaucracy exacerbated her frustration with the police department. Doubling up on her classes, passing with high scores, she now worked for the coroner. While she seemed less than friendly, quiet yet bitingly direct and usually accurate when she spoke, she was obsessive, too. Having an axe to grind and make sure the politicians didn't get any glory moments out of this event, Marcus thought this project would be right up her alley.

She wasn't exactly a conversationalist or a collaborative team player. Her style was do her part and hand over for the next piece of the process, so she definitely contributed in that regard. From that aspect, she was a good team member, looking at facts and pieces of information that were brought to the table, but she never gave a warm impression to people - even when out drinking with friends. Marcus remembered a time when out at a favorite bar with a group of friends and a different blonde girl was with them - the one nearby store owner drinking with them mistook the new woman for the cop and actually made a funny comment about the (new) blonde was so much friendlier, she must have had a lot of stress lifted from her shoulders. Mistaken identity in a dark smoky locals bar, but the guys got a kick out of it and the cop-now-nurse was never told; it just stuck in the minds of the guys that were there and heard the third party revelation.

The last piece was someone who would identify physical weaknesses, like a surveyor, architect, structural engineer. By his thinking, there were major gaps not only where they were looking but where they should be watching. No criminal investigation skills needed for this role, it was more necessary that the person had an ability to study composition of space, light, structure weakness, traffic flow (people and vehicles), and again apply the 30,000 foot elevation start and zoom into blade-of-grass minutia quickly.

He didn't know many people that qualified. It wasn't his world. The guys that helped elevate and rebuild his house as well as his parent's house weren't technically trained to do what they do. They were great, but not right for this position. Similar to the cajun fisherman that knew their waters and the tides of the bays and bayous near them, this was a bit different. He needed someone with impeccable professional training and community credibility.

Starting with the local prestigious architecture school, he looked at the full-time faculty. What concerned him with this obvious solution (other than it being a lazy one) as he browsed the faculty directory was the academia bureaucracy ingrained in a tenured professor's mentality. There was no sense of urgency in their consideration of scenarios, no structure of penalty for missing a deadline - or for being wrong. They were accustomed to setting priorities and guiding discussion that frequently had no correct outcomes. Here, with days to go, urgency and accuracy were paramount.

Adjusting his target, he looked at the architectural school's board of advisors at the same leading university. Unfortunately, names started leaping out immediately. One very wealthy gentleman had a seat on the board, and was connected to the mayor as well as most other local politicians. He had other dubious backchannels and was implicated in some voter manipulation schemes in the largest parish, the one with the highest percentage of registered voters. In addition, he hadn't actually *done* any work in drafting or design for perhaps twenty years. Next.

He glanced down the list to look at the whole thing. Twenty-five members weren't even in the state, most not even in this time zone. Of the remaining local people, only ten were actually architects. What the hell? A renowned musician was an advisor of an architecture school? That begged other questions as that particular entertainer was under investigation for fraud in another city investigation. Marcus was only on the periphery of that case, but he would pass the information along to the white collar crime division.

Back to the list. Two of the remaining ten were well known owners of local firms, and likely were more focused on business management. At least one of those same men had a well-publicized problem with some politicians, and that was a distraction that would not help. Pass on all three, and down to seven remaining options. Shoot, he thought this was a smart way to proceed. He kept scrolling down the list of the remaining seven anyway though less-hopeful than ten minutes ago.

The fourth name of the ten in-state names just by going down the list posted on the website graduated sixty years prior. Number five going down the list… and Marcus began to wonder again if this was the right way to go. He could try to look for an engineer, but right now they were all questioned by locals and sometimes didn't do well when put into the light of day, meaning when put on the line they had no definite answers. They didn't have to know regulations, didn't ever answer questions on the news with direct answers about anything - be it the marine industry building ships here, or aquatic engineering, aeronautic engineers at the space shuttle program, the damn guys working on the bridge expansion upriver… never mind, back to architects.

The sixth one actually went to school with the fourth, so skip that, too. The seventh graduated when Marcus was born. But the eighth held promise. She actually graduated within the past decade. He knew AIA was the abbreviation for the American Institute of Architects, but she had TSA behind her name. Of course, he thought of Transportation Security Authority, but that wasn't right. He looked it up online to see if this would be his lucky number.

Interesting, but it was an abbreviation for Texas Society of Architects. They seemed to be recognized members of the AIA according to the website, regional component whatever that meant. If she was elite enough for the school to consider her as an appointee to the board, he could start with her. Very little exertion gave him the home address, some stats, family overview - and that an armed robber chased by SWAT a few weeks prior had been caught hiding in their kids' treehouse behind the pool.

A quick call to the captain that was on that scene gave additional information that indicated she may be the right choice. He took care of some additional things for this new team and then went by her house when her children would be home, too, getting ready for dinner. He was not in uniform, but had his badge on his belt and headed to ask her to help them. When he arrived, they were heading to soccer, but she and her husband agreed to assist any way they could.

Actually, the husband was in real estate management and had floor plans for some of the buildings in the potential hot zone, according to the earlier avatar drill. Her husband would get the kids to soccer and she would gather a few things and head to the nondescript office away from city hall where the bureau guy had his network already drilling through information.

It was very difficult to create a crime scene team without having an actual crime scene, but he hoped her blueprint skills would help. In so many industries, particularly since the 1980 oil bust, people and even students still in school were instructed to think reactively instead of proactively. The decline of the American imagination accelerated, though its repercussions weren't felt until recent years, particularly when foreign markets were increasingly diversified and had a greater growth trajectory.

People in the United States didn't work on identifying new problems to solve. Instead, citizens - and companies - moved to a "firefighter" approach, tackling the urgent and emergent issues without planning for the moderate issues to progress to important and then evolve to critical mass. There was no forecasting, even in business or politics - kicking the can down the road in federal budgets all the way down to mortgages and car loans.

There would be no kicking problems down the road this week. In the morning, they would be four days away from the game, this team needed to figure out who could be masterminding this attack and find him. Or her. At this point, all bets were off and they were rolling up their sleeves to catch this slippery pig.

Chapter 22

Marcus certainly had good people working with him, and trusted them to keep at the task at hand while he had to go to other meetings. His mini-intel unit was making good progress on the two-pronged assignment: defensive netting and getting closer to tagging the suspect.

Playing for offense (as that's really how that portion of the team saw it) were the model-looking computer-loving geek, the former detective-gone-forensic medical specialist and the long-time detective. It was natural for the former detective to pair with the current one, but that's not how it worked. Vice unit members were very much alone in the world, without anyone to share their burdens. They frequently had to have their toes on the line that distinguished legal from criminal, and it would weigh heavily on a person - sometimes breaking them, turning them straddle the line instead of enforcing it. Having different identities and personas for each character they had to play was tough, too - but not as tough as letting in someone who wasn't a vice detective. Even if she had been a good detective, Sibyl was investigating after an event. None of the vice group thought they were elite, they just had different skills to be part of the action going down and be in the thick of it when a decision was made.

So Alex, of vice, tended to work on his own to pull information from all of his various street contacts as to what they had heard about things going on with the game. He didn't care about the "lemonade stands" - the shifted locations of drug sales to attract tourists to play. Nor was he particularly interested in the influx of "day cares" that served as human trafficking zones specializing in young boys and girls available for spectator pleasure. He certainly passed along information inside the department and to the bureau, but he was trying to flush out anomalies of deviants not typically associated with their city's underground.

Within 48 hours if he worked around the clock, he could hit most of his reliable sources as long as he kept changing clothes. He wouldn't be able to change cars, but for most of them, he parked farther away from the contact point and would just circle through a couple of folks in each area. Sometimes, this meant going to three bars in one hour and having a drink at each as the contact would walk up to share information and then he would leave first - on these rounds, he would have to go expel every drink or he'd never make it through the full two days. He was closing out all of his contacts on the third night before the game, and would head back to give the computer dude, Herman, what he knew from all these street dudes - a new player was in town, a ginger (the one CI that always made him laugh gave him the best intel of the two days when he swigged from his can in a bag and animatedly offered, "you know, man, like a white cat with reddish hair and that skin that's always looking sunburned"), walking around like he was some body in areas they weren't sure he should be. But when a white dude comes walking around like that and the times he was passing through, it was bad news for them because he was a stupid new cop or he had some dirty business to handle - and the street guys had talked on the side and figured he was up to no good.

Even though he literally knew how many days he had before he could retire, Alex was exhausted. His body was breaking down from the years of stress. It hurt his soul to have to put himself in some of these positions, and tried to convince the people around him that when the Big Guy upstairs decided it was his time to go, he just hoped he'd have a smile on his face. His pressure had been going up for years. Now, he had diabetes, too, and his diet eliminated both salt and sugar as well as all alcohol. When this was all over, he wasn't sure he'd even be able to remember who he was from thirty years ago, to pick up his personal life from thirty years prior and be the person he wanted to be instead of the person he had to be. Knowing he wasn't like the guys who enjoyed vice kept was one thing that kept him sane, but he couldn't wait until it was all over - this assignment included.

The other detective-gone-nurse preferred to work alone, too. It's why her switch to dead bodies matched her personality so well. She didn't have people talking back or misdirecting her. The evidence present on the corpse didn't lie. The environment of a killing was distinct, with traces of reasons, rage and rationale. The facts gave pieces to a puzzle that should always be able to be solved. Looking at her, anyone would have thought she could have had the world. She wasn't superstar pretty, but she certainly wasn't coyote ugly. But she never smiled. Ever. Even when she was able to pull the residual evidence together and give a good lead to a murderer or closure to a family on their loved ones' demise, the corners of her lips just pulled wider though not upwards.

She worked alone, just like her detective training encouraged. This time, she was focusing on the dead bodies left in the emails from the discussions pinpointed as likely contributing to planning this event. She didn't look at buried metadata or the routing; that was Herman's job. Sibyl's job was to look at the word evidence, the times, the strength in syntax - those sorts of things to try to ferret out information that would give more details on the suspect's motive, any angle on the planned incident or even if there was a weakness that could be exploited to stop it. It wasn't easy, but it was kind of fun. She had determined the trigger moment of moving from concept to engagement and she was referencing other information to see if she could identify the trigger mechanism that got him over the point of no return. This was way more fun than being called on the carpet for a screwup of a detective on another shift doing batshit crazy and trying to bring you down in the process.

Sibyl left the department reluctantly. She made great friends and formed some really tight relationships, mostly with other detectives. She never took a supervisor test because she wanted to actually work and not just tell other people to work. Her pride got the better of her on a few occasions when supervisors whom she did not respect told her to change something in a report or rerouted her efforts when she felt it unwarranted. There was only one supervisor she liked, and he encouraged her to go before it was too late. So she set her plan in motion, finished school, and transferred to another city department (that was also linked to the state for funding purposes). She was free to do her investigations her way, and no one would undermine her. The only "under" happening here was when her evidence would be buried in the ground.

Conversely, Herman was trying to elevate pieces of the virtual underground to light. Just as with the other two, working alone was his strength like the other three offensive line members. He created his exotic interface of servers and software to analyze the smallest of electronic trails and do prospective forecasting - where the suspect may emerge next. He had determined to a level of confidence within two hours when the suspect had gross relocations (meaning outside of a telephonic area code) and was creating a map of sorts in escalated time lapse, so he could compare with the targets on the watch list for symbiosis in movements. He felt he was getting close to accurately determining what the suspect was likely to do on game day.

He and Marcus had worked together once before on a similar project, though it was on a "normal" drug dealing task force (and there, too, the feds called their sweep "game day" for different reasons). Every so often, the federal agencies tended to show their prowess to locals - both law enforcement types and the communities - and pick a timeframe to do a big sweep of narcotics operations. The last one was before the storm, and they had gotten a few players in each of the project areas. But Marcus had been fascinated by the 'behind the scenes' aspects of the computer modeling, and said he would keep him in mind when he needed to have a solid team for a high-profile case. In this line of work, you always knew it was a matter of time when projects surfaced, and Herman was always ready to help his friend.

He found it interesting that the energetic cinematographer, Rae, was assisting both "sides" of the operation. She asked very good questions about his modeling, and was reviewing camera images, sometimes returning with two or three follow up questions. With the answers Herman gave, she was able to refine some of the search techniques once he modified the filter he designed the first day they were in this house all together. She pulled up some graphics that were interesting and he planned on updating his algorithms on the feeds as soon as he was done with this last segment of coding. She noted it wasn't only about facial recognition, but slope of shoulders, spacing of strides and arm swing - these were all features they should be monitoring in the existing camera details for this particular event.

She also was playing defense, however, and noted where new cameras needed to be installed. With the commercial cameras available online, they didn't need to do RFPs for government strength interface units, all of which would add too much time. They just needed more eyes in the right places and could just purchase under the emergency declaration given by the president for this NSSE, which allowed a whole new set of law enforcement powers (and finance exemptions, too). After she looked at the placement map - and the layer of which cameras worked and what didn't - she made a priority list of what cameras needed new units installed (they could fix them later, she didn't care; she just wanted more eyes right now and one particular brand of baby-cam could provide what they needed).

Rae then went to each of the locations and determined what lenses needed swapped of the existing functional devices. Some of the images were really grainy. She knew all about the past indictments for the technology scam pulled by the previous mayor - it was sick when she realized the volume of money extorted and wasted on these crime cameras. With her knowledge of filming and the less expensive ways to capture quality images, her shopping list had been turned over to Marcus to give to a construction team to mount the new devices on poles, walls or whatever was necessary to give them additional images around the city.

But on several key areas, she also requested the installation of flexible gels - designed as tiny overlapping lenses that would have optic adjustments when bent. They also had an uncanny clarity in humidity and didn't degrade as rapidly with air or water exposure as the regular lenses the city was using. They were a newer design available to the film industry for higher-end productions. Instead of the traditional mix of lower grade plastics, these were composed of a special silicon oxynitrate and newly patented hydrocarbon compound called parylene. The tiny lenses that fused images together through software were strung together by polymer light emitting diodes (which also acted as light enhancers) and organic photodetectors - both of which contributed to the sharpness of the 4k technology imaging that was clearer than even the human eye could detect. She considered it an investment in their future, because the way the crime was in general all over the city, she was sure these would come in handy sooner or later. and reliably be active when they were needed for high-quality evidence in a courtroom.

These defensive tactics were enhanced with a second part of the list with the architect-developer team. They knew the buildings in the presumed hot zone, and the architect (Betty) was able to take the external lines of the walls in order to determine best angles for near-100 percent coverage of all foot traffic in the radius. Betty's husband, Peter, was working the outlying buildings for ownership and potential access listings to mount internal cameras at choke points or escape short-cuts. Together with Rae, they were able to design a new-install grid with a different camera design using those flexible lenses, where the images could be enhanced through a simple editing program Rae used at the film company's office, which was not too far from the secondary (now main) EOC. She should have the clear images routed back to the house with a little handiwork by Herman.

The couple's children were in school and while they couldn't devote all 48 hours of these next two days to the team at the house, they would still discuss and work from home and send messages back or have quick calls with additional information. The infectious disease epidemiologist, Tam, interacted with the couple a lot, as he took the list of priority chemicals suspected for use and tried to create ways with the married team members to redirect pedestrian traffic, where they could locate the sniffer devices that would have the greatest "capture" rate of suspicious air for every single person approaching the game, and where they could mount the newer device that looked like a misting box though it actually "inhaled" air to identify toxins.

Once these three offensive team members had a list of locations and an idea of the height at which they needed mounted, they had contacted Marcus. This was about two hours before the meeting at the EOC with just a few days left to the game. The offense called Marcus, who conferenced in Sarah, and they heard an update of logistics needs as they were driving in opposite directions to accomplish the same thing: eat, change and get back to the EOC before the next meeting that started in about two hours.

When Sarah realized what was needed, she immediately considered the archways used at the city's annual food festival. They were the right height and made for the various crews to mount things to the open beams. There were, of course, about three different sizes used on the fairgrounds, so they had few options they could employ around the game. Banners could be created to shield from wind and vision to some extent, and would give a sense of direction, too - the cattle channels (the pedestrian walkways) would be able to be expanded easily around these arches as the same considerations for mass exiting at any festival were things needed for sports events... when chemical weapons events weren't the typical consideration. These arches were aluminum, too, so wouldn't react with most of the agents being considered as possible by the suspect - easy to decon and wouldn't create another event because of unplanned reactions.

When the offensive team hung up the phone, Marcus was still connected to Sarah as they sped through the city. He asked how she was going to abscond the property from the for-profit group that ran the food festival, even with the situation they faced. She reminded him of a time about thirty years earlier. Knowing he wasn't on the department at the time, he may not have remembered. But with the upcoming indictment of yet another public figure - this time, the former deputy superintendent of the police department - it was going to be "refreshed" in the media soon anyway so she was pretty sure she could get them "donated."

The director of the festival was quietly known to look for action between the sheets wherever he could find it. Literally. He would bring women and men from various "homes of ill repute" back to his place, which at the time was nice but not as fantastic as the one he had now. It was known in the industry that he liked to mix drugs with his rock and roll, and he would share them with his bed-mate of the night. Usually, they all did drugs anyway, but one young female had never tried anything before that time, but was willing to try it because she knew this famous foodie wanted it. And it was the last time she ever tried it, because she died in his bed.

Panicked, the man called a buddy for a favor - and this buddy happened to be the deputy chief (though at the time, he was just the captain of the district where the man lived). The two of them hid the crime - both of underage prostitution and the murder. This deputy chief was now, thirty years later, coming under fire for a wide range of unsavory things, just like so many other public officials in the region. People actually placed bets on which public official would get a bill of information or indictment next, how many counts they would face, and if the prosecutors would get them on everything the public knew should be coming.

Sarah called the food man, and while pleasant enough, reminded him that it was possible that ghosts of his past would be calling when the ghost of the future came to pay a call on his buddy. She could help silence that portion of the present ghost if he was willing to "help defend the nation in the time of national security" with some of their resources. Gladly and immediately, he donated the use of whatever they kept in the warehouse, and said he and his logistics director would go over to storage right now to meet the federal team members that would take whatever they wanted "for the good of the cause."

Chapter 23

Sarah did not go straight to house or swing by her office. She went to the old parking garage, to talk with her former colleagues in the pharmacy unit for the state. One of the craziest things was the office being at the top of the parking garage - but it was very practical for no one could make a crawlspace or dig through a parking garage deck to try to get into the pharmaceutical stockpile.

No one even really knew that's where the office was. On half of the top floor, it appeared from the ground that it was blocked in for the garage manager, perhaps to protect the elevator and generator from storm and wind damage. But once a pass was used to get out of the elevator on the fourteenth floor and exit into the stark hallway and pass through the reinforced door, it was a different world.

Wrapping around the end of the building's elevator shaft, the nearly-black tinted windows kept the ultraviolet rays from heating the offices. The storage areas were kept at cooler temperatures, but the offices were generally comfortable. After entering the main door (which had no windows and looked like an access port to a generator room), a choice was needed for right or left.

To the left were storage rooms and work rooms for pharmacists - both dispensing areas and research areas. The compounding of certain medications could be done here at cost well below market rate. Since this state was one of the few remaining in the entire country that handled all indigent care as a direct provider, they staffed physicians and pharmacists, nurses and other clinicians in health units all over the state. These staffers were typically paid below market rate as well, but the benefits were great and the pension used to be wonderful.

The lethal injection drugs were kept in this area for the state penitentiary, as were the antidotes for a myriad of weaponized agents. One of the main drugs housed in this location was for response to an incident at the large nuclear plant 23 miles upriver. Just as not all power plants used the same radioactive fuel to produce power, it was true that not all antidotes worked on every radioactive source. For instance, she recalled that when the Japanese earthquake and tsunami devastated the ill-positioned plant on that country's coast, when salt water eroded fuel rods and nuclear waste was dumping into the ocean and air, there would be problems on America's west coast carried by tide and jetstream.

What the hippies and ill-informed film industry folks out there didn't realize is that people can't take just any pill to chelate and bind to just any radioactive particle. Akin to a puzzle, only the right agent would fit into and "stick" to the right particle. Yet millions of dollars in prescriptions (not covered by any health insurer) were wasted on a high demand for potassium iodide. Helpful for this nearby plant, just an expensive placebo there as it didn't match the fuel type from the Far East. The stockpile at the "garage" was enough for the federally required radius of dispensing to be filled along with first responders in the hot zone and all the plant employees. None of the chelating agent was stored out there because of fear of contamination (if there was a leak, it would all be inside the hot zone) and as it did expire, the controlled substance needed to be restocked, and the feds helped fund that - as long as it was maintained under certain security conditions and an approved pharmacist.

And that particular pharmacist was to the right of the main doorway. A very warm and gentle man, soft-spoken, he was willing to help anyone yet did not allow himself to get roped into anything that wasn't above the line. Sarah saw him stand up to some bullies in the state capitol once, and it was all done in a gentile manner and even-toned statement: "Well, how about you just put what you said in writing and we will get started right away." Everyone knew that appointee would never put it in writing, so no resources were wasted by trying to meet unconscionable demands that were in all likelihood illegal, too.

The two assistants outside of his office were watchdogs for this nice man. The doctor was always welcoming and had spent over forty years doing this particular job. They tried to help keep his pressure down and demons away by keeping on top of inventory, meetings scheduled in locations convenient for him (as in not at the state capitol), and ensuring local protocol always was signed off by him rather than the politicians in other places. It was very cute, too, as the ladies has the same first name, so he would just raise his voice a little when sounding the first letter of the last name when he needed them in his office.

Neither of them were there at the moment; the one on the right was a leader in a local club that had a prominent role the week after the game, so she had flex hours this time of year when that community work had the craziest schedule you could imagine. The one on the left was likely in the back adjudicating inventory for the weekly order and transfers of supplies. Sarah walked up to the larger office door, knocking lightly while her head peaked around the door jam.

He was obviously expecting her. Dr. McPherson came around his desk and hugged her and motioned for her to have a seat beside his desk, and waited until she was seated to resume his own seat. She knew he would never say where he got his information and though he was partial to old-school methods, he stayed very well informed.

After their greetings and catching up, Sarah began, "Don, you know why I came. I need your help on two things and possibly a favor. The first item is the stockpile antidote. I know you can get it moved and between us that could happen tomorrow, but where are we going to put it?"

Touching his finger to the side of his mouth, he paused, never speaking before he was ready. In a slightly shaky voice of an older gentleman, he began to answer as he lowered his hand to the desk. "I was thinking that maybe my wife's sister's boss would have room. He has that large warehouse along the river but not in wind-shot of the game. It's temperature controlled because of all of the computers. The gaming equipment is all rented out for these tourists - you should see it in hotel lobby bars and set up everywhere you could imagine. So the space is empty. It's far enough away that the owner couldn't entice anyone to use it for the game." He waived his hand around as though he was indicating they were all over the place.

"He's also an aspiring politician - and wealthy. Always seems to be on the wrong side of the coin, but that's more because he's against the establishment. I heard rumors that he's going to buy a paper, too, just to have the other side of the story told. Won't let those guys buy him for a headline, he just has too much money for that. That also means we might be able to use it for two days, no questions asked and no invoice. What do you think about that location, you know between the hospital and the bridge?"

Sarah agreed it was a good plan. Don spent a lot of quiet time in this corner office thinking, looking out the window at nothing in particular. When that happened, he could be remembering the hostage situation and fire at the hotel across the street that happened about when he started his job. He could look in another direction and remember when the two theaters held competing presidential candidates on the same evening, and then those two men went to a fine old restaurant together afterwards with no one else in attendance. He could lean to the side of his desk to look down the street where one presidential assassin was holed up while the feds were looking for the suspect - all from the top of a simple parking garage.

"That's great. Here's the next item. You know the arena practically has it's own atmospheric system inside that dome, and it was restored when the repairs to the gaping hole were complete. What do you think of BioWatch?" Sarah knew there were many conflicting opinions at the highest levels - politically, academically and practically - about this monitoring system. And there was always a catch as the EPA mounted the sensors on their monitoring stations, to effectively control yet another non-related program. The DEQ also liked to poke there nose around the state and try to cash in on some action, throw their regulatory weight around with citations or good publicity.

Don began to speak, stopped, and then turned to face Sarah. Leaning forward, he began again. "BioWatch is a great public relations piece for the United States federal government to illustrate an "action item" in response to Ameri-thrax. However, it faces some intrinsic problems."

"First, it's bio. The only thing that the EPA will review is biologic agents. It's almost like their beach monitoring program we do nationwide - you are required to test for the bacteria, but there's no funding to monitor, no mechanism of response or rehabilitation if detected. It is, for all intents and purposes, a facade. Unfortunately, the head of the EPA is from the city, so there isn't anyone locally that will try to convince her to reduce her power sphere." He unwrapped a cough drop and continued.

"Second on the list is the method of detection. Think of it like fly paper that you hang in a barn or on the back porch. You have to have a fly actually touch the paper to get stuck. This system is the same in that the wind has to blow a certain concentration, a certain number of particles over a given time that actually make contact with the paper and adhere for the sensors to detect the substance and then only certain ones mind you, in order for the alert to signal a possible event. In the barn, you know you have a fly problem and that's why you place it along the rafters. They deployed this fly paper to cities designated in the first UASI round of funding, and we were in the first security initiative designation with twenty-one other cities so we have it."

"Lucky us," injected Sarah. He nodded.

"Another reason it's not practical, and not the last but it isn't insignificant, is that the number of Federal agents and work crews and permits and the almighty paperwork to be processed couldn't necessarily happen in time. But there are answers that could be employed, deployed," and he leaned back in his chair as he listed some positive answers.

"The CST will do this somewhat off the books. The state has tasked them with the monitoring mission for volatile organic compounds, so bio and chem may be detected. Their equipment is pretty good and their technicians are top notch. So that works in our favor. However, there is better technology out there and we should really get our hands on it.

"Several years ago, the feds put out an RFP for sniffers. I know it's crazy, especially since the gold standard for hydrocarbon detection is still the human nose and a damn taste test, but don't get me started on that right now. The government wanted artificial intelligence sniffers that could be programmed better than a bloodhound's nose for scent. They hadn't gone public, though there was talk about using them with TSA. The main sniffer company didn't get that contract; their main competitor persuaded the feds to choose just a higher sensitivity x-ray machine.

"But this sniffer still exists. There are machines that went through an FDA type of testing process, because of the human exposures. They can look like x-ray machines at the airport, the ones that detect metal and explosives, well sometimes they detect them. Anyway, the mechanisms can be established in various other forms - like an event's archway, a new signpost giving pedestrian traffic flow, you see where I'm going?"

Sarah nodded and picked up the line of thinking, "So if we can get the inventors - the manufacturing company - to "donate" as a live test run these components, install them between now and the days before the event, we could have in essence an invisible web to detect... whatever items the coders have created in the interest of national security. Bio, chemical, explosive - even radioactive. We tried to do something like that over the port a few years ago, to screen all cargo coming in, but the project was stopped."

"The same guys who stopped that project were awarded the national contract for the 'enhanced' x-ray machines. And you can see why - a simple x-ray could never compete with one successful capture using that sort of technology, regardless of the cost. The DOD and others will spend exorbitant amounts for the oddest things, like a $43 million dollar gas station overseas, but it also used dark money to protect troops and develop capabilities exactly like this."

"Then why isn't this already being set up around the perimeter and other target zones, even the interstate coming from the airport and the lake on the multi-lane signs? If they can install truck weigh station scanners on interstates, this should be no different. We'll need to do BioWatch if, for no other reason, it will keep certain fed folks out of the way and they can do all the PR dog and pony they want, but BioWatch is really just like the big box in the post office distribution centers that only detects anthrax - and when a white powder mail item reaches an office, they still do a full response because no one really trusts the BDS in the post office basements anyway."

"Correct, Sarah, and starting with your last point - and it's the same exact technology in both programs, the BDS and BioWatch. As for the first point, that is a question for another day, but we have a solution and just need to work our contacts for possible acquisition or a demo unit test of significant proportion. Don't you still talk to that legal guy at your old company? Yeah, they are the ones who make them. Make the call to Wisconsin and I bet we can find some answers quickly. The appeal of post-success accolades is worth a lot of goodwill dollars, especially this early in their fiscal year. Jot yourself a note and then we can get to the favor you need."

Chapter 24

Jason had been thinking about those four locations that Marcus and Sarah relayed from the early afternoon meeting. He went back to his office after seeing them by the lake after the media event with the mayor; the next day he tried to focus, but went across the river to his house, where he maintained a home office. More importantly his personal military effects were there, in the second floor office that was elevated much higher than the 500 year flood maps ever projected, almost directly across the two story open foyer from the front door, accessed by the large curved dark hardwood stairwell coming up the right side of the entrance. He needed to dig through some of his old files and maps for something; he just had to get his hands on it.

His deployments had taken him from Cuba to Fallujah. The other three locations mentioned by Sarah and Marcus from the briefing weren't part of his dossier of assignments. And Fallujah wasn't much of a link given the tech team couldn't narrow down the "Middle East" pingbacks. There were so many forward area locations that had fairly reliable internet access that one of the grunts commented while on deployment with an offhanded joke (but not untrue), saying they had better connectivity in Iraq than Cuba.

It wasn't a large group of military personnel that could move through those locations or make local contacts that wouldn't be relocated over the years. To him, it meant that these locations had ties to Marines, probably lower level officers that could get off-base everywhere but Iraq - and there, when support personnel rotated in and out on regular intervals, the same group could have three tours. It wouldn't be hard to buddy up with an intermediate repairer for computers or a data network technician - particularly if you were in the logistics element.

Opening the long shallow oak drawers of the antique map cabinet, he took a deep breath and ran his hand over the wood. While the remainder of the pieces in his study were darker toned, he was partial to this piece as it also had a top that would fold open to make a display area for the map once removed from a drawer beneath. He also appreciated that this antique piece stood nearly four feet tall, so he didn't have to bend over to review a map like as would normally happen on a regular table-top or the pool table in the next room.

He was a bit nostalgic away from the office. So much had changed, even in the past few years. Now that politicians were organized again and short-term memory loss created a selective amnesia of sorts for who helped them rebound from the devastation of a few years ago, even specialists were rendered back to the pawn positions. He hated chess, not for the strategic thinking involved but for the lack of repercussions some participants needed to feel. Without deterrents, stakes were diminished. Without reminders, memories of the important things would be replaced with superficial self-absorbed agendas.

So he kept this cabinet, with maps from his missions and deployments, as a metaphorical lock-box of ideas as well as battleground acquired and lost. He removed maps sometimes to remind himself of what mattered. In recent years, he was going to the drawers more often. While he liked to use the special display board integrated into the piece, at the moment he preferred the pool table's felt as he could align some Middle East maps in the hopes of sounding the bell loudly that was now only a faint ringing, to create a more profound reminder of what bothered him about the suspected network.

He lingered, calculating that it was time well spent. It was approaching sundown. Still not having a specific answer as to why this was really resonating with him, he departed to make his way back across the river to the emergency operations center. Things were in full swing, with complete (though skeletal) staffing around the clock at this stage, with only a couple of days before the big event. Over that time span, they would have redundant staffing established and because of concerns about the threat (with the proximity of the traditional office to the game site), they were actually established in the backup location, so that's where he headed.

Of course it would appear chaotic to anyone not integral to the operation. Certainly it would look like that to a reporter, trying to take pictures of "behind the scenes" for exclusive footage, and that feeling unfortunately would be portrayed to the public. Since the events on September 11th, smart public safety officials declined all media requests for interviews in EOCs.

There would always be, however, elected officials that thought they could never be targeted and doubted what any terrorist could learn from a little television interview. He half jokingly told the mayor to stage photos in another location and just claim it was the game's emergency command center. At this point, they couldn't risk the integrity of operations or images taken of their intel modeling with the flexiglass program for a smile-n-shake shot.

Oddly, the mayor listened. That made Jason concerned, as he then would be expected to appear in two places at once - the press conferences fully covered by international media as well as the working center. If anything should happen, it would not be possible to hint even in a whisper that showmanship overrode safety; his job would be finished. And while that may not be a bad thing, as his son was deploying for a second tour and his daughter's wedding was about six months away, it's not the way he wanted to end his second career.

Being a politician was the mayor's idea of a second career. Though he had the generations of politicians and strategically placed in various levels of government jobs, through high school this man thought he'd go perform on Broadway. He wanted to be a showman; well, so did his dad in a manner of speaking, but in politics rather than on the boards. He was forced to follow the algorithm for the family, but was known to burst into song for cameras. It took Jason a long time to create his political battle face of a blank stare when that happened, as he only ever had a fighting battle face for motivation and unbridled emotion directed at opposition with live fire involved.

So two grown men in their second careers, neither where they expected or quite chose to be. One with the battle tested experience that wasn't sure if real bullets were better than proverbial knives in the back; the other wanting to be paid to put on a show with memorized lines from others and yet he managed to do that exact same thing using other people's ideas to put on his own show. Jason couldn't help but roll his eyes thinking about recent antics as he got off the elevator in the old paper warehouse away from the business district, the backup location for emergency operations.

And as the elevator opened directly onto the secondary EOC location, he saw it was relatively controlled and quiet inside, with the late evening light fading so that the overhead halogens were in full use. That illuminated the teams in their various areas, hard at work. The whole floor was key encrypted rather like a loft, like refurbished luxury living that was becoming so trendy and very hot real estate at the moment. They had an additional floor one level up that was all infrastructure and could only be accessed through the spiral stairwell they installed between this third floor and the fourth floor - the top two of the building. They welded shut the shaft's door to the upper floor after installation and erected a bulletproof wall in front of its freight door during ops use.

As he looked around, he always loved the windows. They were the old large warehouse style, the kind throughout the south that ran floor to ceiling - industrial height ceiling - and that would slat open once upon a time for ventilation. It actually worked pretty well, though these windows had been sealed after the storm and the new HVAC system installed. For visual protection, they stuck the cheap frosting contact paper over them that they bought at the hardware store so there was no line of sight to the interior before they started the build-out. Pillars still ran throughout the open plan but there were no other walls save restrooms on one side of the elevator and kitchen on the other. No other obstruction for view on the whole floor. He actually preferred this space to his own office and the construction zone; they didn't have multiple voices directing the build-out traffic in this location.

Old red brick on the outside, and the beige stone arches surrounding the windows were original. The stone was exposed inside and when they did the build out and insulation, they ran the studs and drywall to the edge of the stone but didn't wrap it. Thus, when they "decorated" the room, using the term loosely, they pulled the natural element in from the outside, and they used similar tones throughout the interior. The beige stone complemented the pale reddish-brown wall color that whispered of the exterior brick, but used a white on the ceiling (behind the drop air vents) and left the huge glass panes unblocked (though frosted)in order to keep the interior bright. The baseboard matched the beige stone as did the carpet - yet furniture was modern in stark contrast to the building's design but in alignment with the exposed utilities. It made for an interesting space, conducive to actual work.

He saw Sarah on the far side of the room, to the right of one of the rows of pillars. Sharp as a tack, it also caused her unintentional problems with some of the members of the group that met last week. She had a few people that were unfamiliar to him at the table with her, so he approached to see what they may have discovered.

"...yet the BioWatch only detects very specific biologics and is meant to be deployed outdoors to catch particulate as it blows in the breeze," spoke the older gentleman in a kindly, instructional tone. "It won't be effective, though we are putting this system inside the stadium. It's been talked about a lot as the way to save people from a public anthrax attack, for instance, but it has only ever had false positives and never detected an actual event. So don't rely on this for your own safety, just consider it a tool to keep the media busy. Ok?"

The older man looked at the team members around the table, some of which were familiar - from SWAT unit leaders, FBI team members, a sheriff's elite team colonel, fire department hazmat experts, et cetera. Jason's gaze stopped at Sarah, who was to the left of the man and both of whom had their backs to him. She must have known he was approaching, noted by the shift of eyes behind the man to him and over to her. Taking the cue as the man began to speak again, she backed up to get Jason up to speed.

"This is the director of the state pharmacy, an expert on all the bells and whistles in the state, really beyond, and the actual effective items that aren't made public. He's briefing the guys on BioWatch, the great PR tool-slash-not-so-great ops tool. He and I figured it would be easier to digest coming from him." She had no need to relay the alternative was her, as it was her 'intellectual space,' but he knew that's what she meant. She was a good leader in that way, knew when to back up in order to make the mission move forward because of other people's frame of mind. Sometimes they would talk about the struggles of leadership together, as each had their challenges. By far, however, he felt more sorrow at her situation at his own as there were things she couldn't change that slowed her down from the place she should really be in her career.

"The guy two to his right on the opposite side by the corner window is in charge of the state and federal chemical countermeasures. I'm not sure if you've ever met Elijah, but by the look on your face likely not. Great guy. Has a personal interest in snakes and anti-venom. Amazing. Fascinating international adventures. Anyway, he's then going to go right into the need-to-know portion of the countermeasures. Obviously, we can't put them in the new location as it's not finished yet and there are strict climate control needs, not to mention asset management requirements." She paused as the older gentleman was wrapping up his comments.

"I'll explain the part about the sniffers in more detail to you later."

Jason turned sharply, looking directly at her now. "The what?"

She smiled and repeated, "The sniffers. I didn't tell you about them, but you'll hear the update. The politicians buried the technology but it's very precise. Went back to another buddy from a former life, so to speak, to ask for the units - and since I worked there, I could tell them how to demo it off the books so it wasn't traced and there's no cost linked to the event... so no RFP requirements because there's no payment, rental, nothing. Anyway, my turn."

She stepped up to the table again next to Don, and began to describe what she told Jason were "the sniffers." Apparently already programmed for a homeland security test, but then put away up in Mequon after the politicians rigged the national bid. Brushing that aside literally with a sweep of her right hand, she continued to describe the compounds that were able to be detected, the sensitivity, the collaboration of the sensors as well as the direct scanner routes that were currently being flown in that evening to be erected tomorrow for Sunday, noting the pedestrian entrance points to the environment around the stadium.

Hazmat peppered her with a few direct questions about particulate drift in the open environment rather than a controlled interior design for which it may have been made. She adeptly countered with the mass spectrometer detection capabilities and the way the devices would be mounted would ensure draft exposures directed into the areas for analysis. Then she described a bit of the terahertz radiation options that would give insights to the fingerprints of their composition. Continuing about ion mobility spectrometry, when the members' eyes started glazing, he knew she had them and they were ready to move forward.

He learned that they would be detecting for the common explosives even though that had been discounted through intel they kept it included in the scanning as it was a "freebee" for the installation. They did disarm the controlled substance detection as that could be a nightmare with the spectators, possibly the team members, and almost definitely (and sadly) with the city's own employees. Enhancements had been incorporated for previous tests for several "common" chemical weapons, and that was the key for the approaching weekend. They even incorporated organic compound detection via millimeter wave capabilities, too, as the weapons would have to be stored in something. Hazmat seemed impressed, especially Chad, the lead of the team who was tagged to be the next deputy superintendent.

Chad wasn't easily impressed, either. At six feet six inches tall, he couldn't be physically intimidated. They couldn't do it during his football days when he played on the line, and no one had seen anyone that could successfully do it now. One of the few to have a degree of any sort in the fire department, he held a masters degree as well. Done all on his own time after college, his masters was with honors and very few people knew he completed it. No need to broadcast it and put another target on his back.

After all, even in today's city, not many civil servants had degrees, and fewer Creoles had any degree let alone two. It would set him apart even more than his stature. Jason noticed that at the moment Chad was slumping, trying to conceal his height. Amazing that he had perfected that over the years, but he used it to pick up a lot by listening and watching without intruding, and sometimes passed along interesting intel to Jason.

His attention was drawn back to Sarah as she rolled out old-school butcher paper upon which someone had mapped the anticipated hot zone area. It was larger than the GIS printers in the corner, and she appeared to have six copies to hand around for the teams. Directing everyone's attention at the top sheet, she used a laser pointer to illuminate the choke points intentionally redesigned for the sniffer deployments. In pure redundancy, she also had decorative archways that would provide directions for the crowd and serve as mounting devices for the sniffers in the same channels fifty feet apart. The dichotomy of the technology topic on paper was ironic, yet showed that just because a method was old didn't mean it didn't work.

Jason turned his attention to the other clusters and stopped to get a five minute brief. He heard updates on the navigable waterway changes from the Coasties, utilities task forces formed as they were being forced to play well together for the sake of the ancient infrastructure, the airport adjustments from the two airport teams co-located for practical purposes - the warehouse space was big but not indefinite. It was certainly bigger than the regular office, but with the installation of the second set of flexiglass devices like they had out on the old trail building, it reduced space significantly. Essentially, they laid this out by geography of support functions, which was the best way to have the multi-jurisdictional teams interface.

But he noticed that the one empty space was Marcus' special team that was working on the "who," the suspect causing this upheaval. He knew why they were off-site, but thought by now they would be here with updates ready. Walking over to the table, there was little left on it; just like a good detective, not leaving a trace of where he was or where he thought this was going. Jason texted Marcus asking for a ETA; of course, he was getting on the freight elevator now.

Chapter 25

"Here's what I know about our guy," said Marcus as he opened his laptop and synced to the plexiglass in the command center to show the beige silhouette of a man on a black background with a dim grey web surrounding him. It was hauntingly reminiscent of Leonardo da Vinci's *Vitruvian Man,* though not a double exposure. Luke followed him in, and took up a spot to his right. Sarah came standing by on the left and some members of her group drifted around the table while others filled in behind, more for curiosity than need to act on this intel. Marcus used the Prezi format to show the first area of interacting results, beginning at the man's torso, which illuminated with a low intensity red orb.

"While we are still processing lots of data and the team is at the secure house working around the clock, analytics of the syntax of the messages reveal that the author, our target, is likely a middle-aged male, possibly midwest formative years, rather regimented. Tries to maintain formal comms but slips sometimes - particularly mid-afternoon our time. Anomalies appear that the team determined are attempts at command-and-control verbosity that doesn't always achieve the target's goals. Sometimes, the reply or following chatter makes fun of things previously said.

"There are indications that there is military training, though not of a respected officer level - or if so, was just promoted when reaching the plateau level of promote or decom. He wants to try to give the impression of control and it seems very important he do so. Target gets energized when others in the comms threads seem to be supportive or relay information that pleases him." Marcus floated to the part of the silhouette's web that illuminated the head of the shadow.

"Further, there are no triggers that he has any qualms about ethical or moral dilemmas. There is no wavering from the path the target has established. Indications are also that he suffers from narcissistic personality disorder with evidence of arrogance, self-promotion, attempts at manipulativeness and power grabs. There are frequent demands for members of the threads to recognize his authority and prowess, which also reveals insecurity. The use of this event disruption will be the defining moment for him, though we cannot figure out his motive.

"Traces of delusional grandiose disorder are also present, as more than one thread went sideways with presentations of how the his self-proclaimed high-intelligence would lead to great recognition, though never indicated that those supplying him or assisting would also rise to greatness. But he also used language to reveal some trigger recently pushed him to take action and his plan is one of revenge. That is still under review for additional parameters."

Shifting to the hands, "There are no indications that this person is a weapons expert, or even routinely familiar with a variety of arms. The team eliminated Army as the background on this as well as Air Force; his language is not as sophisticated as required to be a fighter pilot or other USAF support personnel. There hasn't been any language that narrows it to Navy or Marine at this time." He switched the suspect's highlighted point again.

"The feet are lit as we continue, but interestingly, we cannot tell what time he would normally be awake and walking, to help determine his current whereabouts or recent travel pattern.

There are episodes of mania and insomnia, where chatter is initiated for days at a time at all hours, and then there are other stretches where there has been absolute silence. We have crossed it with days of the week, and there is no correlation to weekends or gives any suggestion of a steady full-time job that would limit ability to communicate during certain hours."

The generic suspect's avatar rotated, showing the back to the group with a backpack enlarging to become the focus and opening to reveal the next pieces of information. "Although the team believes that this man was military, you see we have a few blocks coming out of the pack. There is no indication this person has special capabilities or special weapons background given some of what he's relayed in chatter. In fact, it seems as though our target was primarily an office dweller, papers and logistics rather than actual operations, though may have - again - delusions about his actual role in events."

Looking around the room for any questions and seeing none, he continued. "We strongly believe this guy is going to be a lone wolf, using something that will allow him to fulfill his need to be recognized as a leader by others, likely that he is saving the day in a megalomanic fashion. There's no indication that he's sophisticated enough to acquire a biologic (forget about manufacturing anything), and the chemical most probable is going to be something that doesn't cause mortality but morbidity. Though he wouldn't hesitate to kill necessarily, the ramifications for him are perhaps too dirty for his preferences and well above his skill level."

The plexiglass image morphed as the silhouette reduced and once it was reduced to a pinpoint, it reformed as it enlarged into a world map, with the once dim grey web that formed the background becoming brighter. Marcus began speaking again, focusing on the four areas indicated in what everyone called the "avatar meeting" (as it made it a little less doomsday and there was no doubt about which meeting was referenced when they used that nomenclature).

"With the transmission of comms bouncing around the globe, but primarily tracked in these four locations, it was difficult to determine from where the origin of our suspect's initiations was occurring. But, we were able to take some of the imbedded metadata and determine the initiating ping was always in the United States. It is possible that the subject was stationed in these areas briefly for training or staging."

"Shit." All bodies and eyes turned back to Jason, who had been leaning on the nearest pillar, the one closest to the elevator side of the building. No one spoke. "Sarah. Marcus. Luke. Come with me. All you can stay out here, generally speaking. Don't go far."

The three summoned approached the spiral staircase as he ascended. The swearing wasn't uncommon, but Jason interrupting a presentation such as this was absolutely out of character. They followed him up the spiral stairs. On the infrastructure level, they had built out sleeping quarter rooms that were in the center of the pillars, like boxes almost in the middle of the floor. At either end of that center "tube" were also small meeting rooms, one of which they had assigned to Jason and the other was a conference room. Passing the men's shower (above the third floor kitchen whereas the women's - essentially Sarah's - was above the downstairs restrooms), they went to his office - directly across from the welded freight door and bulletproof wall.

They entered, and sat around the cluttered table while Jason went around the back of the desk, lowering slowly to his seat, then leaned back in his chair. Silently they stared at him; Jason rubbed his face, starting top to bottom and then grunted as he leaned forward, placing both elbows down and hands out in front of him.

Shutting his eyes again, then opening them, he swore again before beginning a more interesting speech. "Sarah. Marcus. When you told me by the lake the four locations of the routers, it reminded me of something. I went home and pulled out some of my old maps from my thirty years in the service. There was something about the pattern that was ringing in my head.

"But that wasn't it. I kept those maps out on the pool table upstairs until it dawned on me today and I drove here. Location wasn't the key piece of information, but what was in those locations and when, actually, that mattered. And who I think was in those locations, would have been able to make friends with people in the surrounding areas or in the case of that broad category of the Middle East, a pal with someone that wouldn't be rotated out necessarily - or would rotate out but then back in again."

Sarah was growing impatient. She daren't glance at Marcus or Luke sitting to her right, as she didn't want to disrespect Jason. He was nice, and sometimes over his head in the politics, though when he was wearing his Marine hat, he morphed to a different person - quite commanding and knowledgable. She didn't stir, but Luke did lean back in his chair, showing he was prepared to wait this one out as Jason continued and also giving him a line of sight to her around Marcus.

"To me, it's a Marine. I hate to say it. The Navy needs exposure with navigable waterways for deployment. They don't travel to Four Points unless on vacation, and naval guys... well, it doesn't fit. I called a buddy to ask to use the VA system to map who was where and got a list of folks. He couldn't map who would care about the game, or people coming to the game, or anything like that.

"What I did have was a suspicion about a grudge. Not held by me," he clarified as he leaned back in his chair again, rocking a little bit. Marcus leaned forward, elbows on his knees. Sarah noticed that he frequently assumed that position when looking at his laptop screen and processed things in his head. Luke still leaned back, moving his left arm. She still didn't move.

"Let me give you the framework. Marine joining right out of high school, has to do boot camp. Comes out wet behind the ears and the absolute lowest man on the totem pole, with a chip on his shoulder because maybe," Jason nearly squealed that last word in contempt, "he just wasn't up to par with a sibling, a sister, that got an honors scholarship. So he enlists to piss off his parents as many a boy has done. But when he's out of camp thirteen weeks' later, the unit where he's assigned has just been pulled out of one of the nastiest evacuations of an embassy that had happened in a long while. Ribbons for all involved, but not him. He's missed the fun. The resentment builds over time, first because of the sister then from missing his first chance to prove himself.

"But, they ship his ass to the Middle East for the early days, the 'sitting around and doing not much of shit' days, to a friendly base in a neighboring country to Iraq because the Pentagon knows trouble will happen. It stages troops in the area. But this guy's got nothing. They assign him to paper. Even when stuff starts happening in Desert Storm, he's already out as they had set up everything that was needed and they ship him off to another place, causing him to miss another high-profile military action.

"For years, he pushes paper. He takes low level courses, pads his resume for when he can get out. Starts taking online college courses for undergrad when he can. Whatever. That automatically got him into OCS, which can auto-bump people that don't get shot or commit a crime. And yet something happens in 2001 that fucks up his trajectory and they boot him. Eleven and a half years and he's out of active duty. Obviously not honorably discharged exactly. Bounces around, two years later finishes an undergrad degree while he bides his time in reserves to get a final promotion and an awkward thirteen years of Corps that he decides to list as active duty on his resume. Keeps floating between little jobs after the degree, starts a masters that I personally always doubted he ever finished.

"Hurricane hits here, he figures someone will give him a job so he moved to the area. I needed a logs guy and brought him onboard, brother Marine and all. Semper Fi. Looking at those maps on the pool table, as I walked around them, I remembered in Fallujah we caught some errors on our maps that saved our asses when we realized it and double-checked something. Never mind that, but that's when I drove here. That error then did remind me now, however, of this particular Marine's troubles. And you'd think after all his years in paperwork, he'd know how to get it right - or cover his tracks.

"His resume. Claimed to help execute a liberation of the embassy; yet he wasn't even attached to the MEU when that occurred. He could have claimed the battalion though not the mission and maybe had it slide past, but he went too far. He screwed up what damn Iraqi War he was in. Messed up the dates with the name. Gulf War was when my son was in Junior High and I was there; Iraq War was just before that same hurricane I mentioned when my son was in college and I was fucking there again."

The three of them could tell Jason was far away in his thoughts, but this time in the pause, none of them moved an inch.

Things were clicking, far more for Marcus than Sarah or Luke at this stage, and he was biting his lip to keep things from flying out, like questions about Jason's suspect that were falling into place for him. Jason had been speaking very loudly, but the next phrases were quiet, fueled by rage.

"But this asshole," now in full-on commander mode, "gave himself a ribbon he never earned. Gave himself an assignment in a battalion that had been in one war and not the other. Even included events on his resume that were *after* he was out of the Corps." Jason looked directly at them to drill down the point, "And no good Marine will let someone defame the honor of those of us that were there, of those that fell in service to this country. He wasn't part of Sharp Edge. He sure as hell wasn't part of Dessert Fox. He was a Logistics Combat Element, not an ops expert and never part of command.

"When I got his file from my friend, I looked at dates he gave me versus the dates the military had for him. Military may be outdated in some areas, but it documents with paper like it is going out of style. The VA hospitals have troubles, but the personnel department has it on lock down. I was able to check fact to his fiction. Looked at your four locations and where he has been.

"On his resume, he's placing himself in places of the globe where he may have gone, but not when it counted. Even said he was part of the 31st MEU, that's the one that actually did Dessert Fox and Southern Watch in the early days of Kuwait. Jackass was in Okinawa for a few months with the 31st but never went to Iraq when he said - and was even discharged *before* Operation Iraqi Freedom. I was there. He was not. And you need to go find him.

"He was a drunk when he was here, almost the entire time of the 900 days I kept him around. He didn't just up and leave to start his own consulting company - I allowed him to resign because he couldn't keep his junk in his pants or leave the bottle at the bar. Before I came to the third floor tonight, I even looked at what he claimed on his resume in his online profile since he left our group - and he had the nerve to claim he was the XO. Sarah, you know him. You've seen more of him than you probably ever wanted. And I see you're surprised I know about him trying to catch you while he was drunk and naked instead of leading the Ops Section during that evacuation."

Jason leaned forward in the chair again, putting his elbows on the desk again but this time, placing his head in his left hand while rubbing his forehead, like he could erase the memory of this guy and the mistake he made in hiring him. Luke turns his head to the left to look behind Marcus to Sarah, but only his head. Marcus turns his whole body toward her, sitting back in the chair now with his left arm slung across the back of his chair. Sarah looks at them both, blinking once, and turned to look at Jason.

"Where. Is. Mike?"

Chapter 26

He had been essentially alternating between living out of his car and couch-surfing. This 46 year old man slogged between women's homes that he hooked via various sob stories that bespoke of the woes of a jilted husband, or a military man come home from deployment to find that his home had been demolished accidentally during rebuilding of neighborhoods, or even once he came up with a cockamamie story of being addicted to the traveling life of a soldier.

Relying on his superficial charisma had gotten him to a certain point, but he really had to fake the rest and he obviously kept coming up short. He had been evicted for not paying his bills shortly after his "wonderful" new consulting career never got a paying customer. It wasn't only that his ignorance of state laws made him blind to the illegality of contracting with any government entity for whom a former employee directly worked; incorporated, too, was an unhealthy dose of misplaced confidence that he was an insider with powerful connections, each of whom would ignore the law in order to work with him. His ignorance was so pervasive that he didn't even consider that his potential client list all realized he couldn't perform.

Expected favoritism never materialized (at first he had to know how to complete those RFPs, how to legitimately compose coherent competitive responses - then he may have been considered for contracts). It was tough to accomplish when the only thing used to whet your whistle all day was hard liquor. Even when someone was exposed to him in limited or moderate doses, it was apparent that he was a functioning alcoholic. He thought he was suave when he "offered" to have interns work for him, publicizing they would gain valuable experience by writing proposals and working on real-life issues. Quickly, these volunteers realized there would be no mentoring as he had no clout, no connections, no credentials. No projects. And then, he had no interns.

It was even pathetically humorous that he couldn't earn the certification he so desperately sought that would be displayed for the world to see how wonderful he was, with the papers to prove just how elite he should be considered. The application process was arduous and it was not only required to submit three letters of recommendation from field leadership personnel that would speak well of his contributions, but he also had to *make* significant contributions. The publicity around some of the events he tried to explain were really his own actually gave the appropriate credit to others, which he thought unjust. He apparently tried to take credit for certain activities anyway - even when media reports contradicted his statements. He sincerely convinced himself that he had done all of those things, and didn't understand why the evaluation committee kept rejecting his ongoing attempts for confirmation.

The repetition with selective understanding was just one of the manifestations of his sociopathic behavior. His overriding fallacy that pigeonholed him into the diagnosis was the inability to focus on multiple topics as well as his unsuccessful attempts to lead an integrated multifaceted life. He had problems to the extreme extent as he only had concentration for how to make himself look like a leader in the face of his former coworkers. (Such a shame it wasn't to actually be one.) Everything he did operated with the internalized question, *"Will this make so-and-so jealous, make them see me for the leader I truly am?"* It could be directed to the women he attempted to seduce, the area where he tried to find work, the brand of cigarettes he purchased - any number of routine daily activities that were no longer normal for him.

He had other tell-tale signs of the disease, too. He didn't really posses neurotic behavior (it was "only" classifiable as annoying). There was never a good connection with women (he understood only with his own ego, so couldn't empathize with women when they found sex with him impersonal or handled by him as a trivial event). In either professional or social situations, he lacked insight into conversation or relationships that inevitably deteriorated into closed doors (he merely tried to provide excuses - for himself - when people turned him away).

The obliviousness and strongly apparent lack of self-awareness he exhibited in the former workplace about his capabilities was also translated by his peers and supervisor (in addition to Mike's continuing to be inept) as antisocial, generally lacking commitment to a cause. He didn't learn - either from his own mistakes or from being told why he exhibited poor judgement. Disregard for both timeliness as well as the importance of honesty further isolated him, and he could not understand his shortcomings. He did not understand he even had shortcomings.

Instead in the past few years, his focus had been redirected to whomever the proverbial "they" had assigned to others when he perceived it as his expertise, his area to handle. His motivation was always about comeuppance and how to force others to recognize his superior skills. During his chain-smoking hours-long sessions at his favorite bar, he would talk at anyone he thought was close enough to hear him on the things officials were doing wrong, how he had actually created the program that clearly they were screwing up, or even if he was so-and-so how there would be proverbial "cake for everyone."

It was these final attributes that revealed some of his cunning nature in how he could manipulate facts to fiction, how his mind would start working on how he could actively cause failures of people who left him behind. However, the alcohol impaired any sort of intelligence that he ever possessed and dampened the outward ruthlessness typical of a true sociopath. What caused the troubles now brewing were the endless mental notes Mike kept on every wrong he considered ever done to him, with cascading intensity the more often an individual appeared on his cheat sheet. As the infractions escalated, he shrewdly plotted a way to upstage the people he felt slighted him and one that would ensure he would be recognized as the one who should have been given the accolades all along the way.

His mind had been trained this way since he was eight years old. His older sister was playing outside and when he joined her in their somewhat rural area, they wandered into the woods to go down to the next group of houses in order to see if any other kids were around. They did find a few playing near the creek, but those seven boys and girls didn't want anything to do with them. Said they were too poor to be allowed to play their games, too stupid to have any idea how to keep up with them. His sister didn't care and kept walking to look for some kids that might play with them, but he remained frozen, staring at the children until they left. He held his ground, though in reality there was no ground on which he could stand as their statements were pretty close to the truth. Facts never had swayed him much.

They had no money. His father worked two jobs and rarely saw the boy, didn't really care if he saw the girl. Behind on their rent, everyone around knew it. They raised themselves essentially, and kids wandering between homes to play could pick up on a few things, such as who had good toys or nice clothes or lots of food for lunch. Rural networks kept up on things like that, possibly even more so than the old close-knit inner-city communities before everyone started moving to suburbs in the late 1970s. In the country, kids drifted between homes to play as parents were out working - in fields or factories, it didn't matter - as the kids grew up pretty quick.

Unless you weren't smart, and he wasn't. He barely made average grades in school and would make up stories as to why he didn't have homework, why his report card was so mediocre. Upon listening to these stories and his father's grunts, his sister realized that she could get attention if she was good at school. Their father liked smart people, and she put her nose into the books. The distance between their grades was evident by the spring following the incident with the kids by the creek, and Judy started getting more attention from their dad whenever he was actually around.

This didn't sit well with her brother, especially when his father took to comparing them. She became the standout in books and sports, leaving nothing for Mike. He began to look to his mother for inspiration, for ways she attracted her husband's attention. Noticing she drank, tried to be casually funny and used her body to distract as well as manipulate his dad to get what she wanted, he took her pattern and used it - all of it. He began drinking at the age of twelve, started using slower speech and offering his body up to just about anyone to get a reward he calculated would put him ahead in some fashion.

Thirty-four years later, he was still employing that childish technique to try to "win friends and influence people." Not noticing it didn't work, he still was trying to get attention from a father that didn't care, not after all the embarrassments his son put on the family. Any attention given to that boy (and still to this man) came in directives of stand up straight, put that down, pick this up, you can lift more than that. There were also paternal admonishments that ranged from *can't you do anything right* to *why can't you be more like your sister*. Thus, to Mike, he had been unwittingly trained that women were just something in the way and he treated them with disrespect, distain and distrust because at any time, they could divert the attention away from you. In his world, there was no reason to have a social conscious where women were concerned, and he harbored no guilt over hurting any woman that got in the way.

It's how he met, treated and then was abandoned by his first wife. Originally attracted to him for his seemingly slow approachable nature and affability, she liked him right away. Went to bed with him on the second date. They got married only because Mike thought his dad would look at that as a sign of being a man, but his father didn't even take the time off work to go to the wedding. The new wife quickly realized that she was only a piece in a messed up man's puzzle, and when she found bottles in the garbage day after day, she quickly left and filed for divorce. He never saw what he did wrong, but didn't really care she was gone, either. He'd find another girl to warm his bed, for a few nights anyway.

His lack of moral remorse manifested as treating people poorly was sometimes misinterpreted as strength, chalked up as his focus of "mission" (people can be collateral damage when you have a big "play" coming) and nearly always there was a clique of followers that looked to him for leadership, nearly always younger men thinking they found a mentor. It was easy for him to find a few people that were looking for direction, their career to have purpose, and he could mold them into whom he wanted them to be by exploiting their insecurities. Getting a relationship, male or female, wasn't his problem. The blatant disregard for social rules seemed to enhance his status with a handful of young men who thought they were being given a chance to be "inside" a circle because of the good game being talked. They would absorb and reflect some of the acidity toward the same people Mike didn't like, even when there was no basis for the attitude other than Mike led them to that conclusion.

Leading people by the nose made him feel powerful. It was where he thought he was supposed to *be*. It didn't matter what it did to other people - if something could get him further ahead, he would take the opportunity to push himself upward on the back of others on which he stood to make himself higher. He could not tolerate being frustrated and was quick to place blame on others for problems caused around him, as he couldn't see his own behavior was the source of many work-related conflicts. Even if he was able to establish a relationship with a woman, it never lasted as they were quick to determine Mike could be callous, manipulative and applied his own definition of norms to every situation - including lying, rationalizing his irresponsibility and lacking remorse if he hurt them (or not even recognizing he had done something "wrong").

By the time his followers realized that he had nothing really to offer them, possibly some of them figured out his great 'war stories' didn't always add up, they would drift off and he would be recruiting a new crop. This revolving door didn't seem to bother him much as the new gang always fed his ego, eagerly listening to his stories, believing what he said about practically anything and replaced any sense of loss he may have felt, though it was a stretch to think he would have felt anything at all. People were commodities, replaceable and strictly generic components to satisfy a particular need he had at the time. If he exited their lives before he royally betrayed his true nature, he could call on them again when he needed something.

Thus in floating between the couches of guys he knew back from his enlisted days and the beds of women he didn't care if he knew, he ended up for a few summer months outside of Colorado Springs, at a buddy's ski condo. From there, he didn't have to worry about paying bills except to eat and he had some money to cover that or could do small little jobs here and there by bluffing his way into a few projects. There wasn't internet his friend's place, but he could go down to the mall near the military base to use free wifi in a variety of coffee houses and a book store. Every now and then, he would strike up a conversation with a younger looking non-military type, because he was at least self-aware enough that he wouldn't be able to hoodwink any of the brass based near this location or passing through for meetings; he had to keep it to someone who still was young enough to be gullible and not have connections to double-check his stories.

As he drifted between returning to the North Carolina back woods once to see his mother briefly, the friend's offseason hideaway in the mountains and along the southern coast, the anger began to build inside of him that someone needed to be held responsible for his nomadic situation. Someone who wasn't a devotee of the military doctrine had expelled him from his rightful position as a leader in his recent career. He didn't remember why he was kicked out of the Marines - actually, that was all irrelevant in his world as he remembered the story differently, in that he took an early option to leave and work on his degree. It was the more immediate past that was the center of his torture, what he believed to be the root cause of all his evils.

There was a possible combination of things (according to himself), and it usually held the theme of people not recognizing his innate ability to lead and delegate and bring people to his promised land of peace and posterity based on his infallible preparedness and planning. Some days, it was his old boss; others, it was a group of intel guys still on active duty that presented actual facts contrary to his self-invented ones. Other days, it could be that damned woman who shunned him or the entire population of the state in which he last worked.

All that mattered was that he restore himself to his rightful position, that he become the commander to lead the small-minded workers wherever he saw fit and he be recognized for the brilliant strategist he was - preferably with a healthy income in addition to a strong title that people would immediately know he was the one in charge. The longer he was without a substantial role, without a staff to whom he could delegate all work and for which he would claim credit, the more focused he became on righting his wrong. He even began to formulate that it may take an event where he could swoop in to save the day in order to rapidly retrieve that eroded elevation he thought he lost, but he never really had.

He never saw the parallels to his mental positioning and terrorists who radicalize young vulnerable people for their own devious purposes.

Chapter 27

Sean had been trying to figure out what he didn't understand in the earlier meeting of that inner circle. Whatever it was came just beyond his grasp. He directed his people to research those three locations in order to compare it to his preferred option that had high-dollar personal gains. He wanted a flamboyant partner that he could still control, one that would have the right connections and right location available but that would defer to him on all things regarding timing or publicity. He preferred an extravagant personality in an endeavor like this as a distraction for the other components buried in the agreement. The goal for him, besides lining his pocket, was to be the brains of the operation and to ensure the right people knew he was the mastermind. He'd get his media attention, even if someone else was the main spokesperson.

He just couldn't wrap his head around the idea that he wasn't wanted - or needed - in that group of people. They sure made it seem like they had their fingers in all of the important projects in town. There was no doubt in his mind that he was important, that they should be coming to him for advice and with gratitude and showing him how thankful they were for him opening doors to wonderful opportunities. Passing along cash was the best way for them to show appreciation, but he knew that some paper trails had to be created or the feds would get suspicious. He didn't need them poking around in his personal life - they were always at the office anyway, which is why he never went there anymore.

Recalling his one in-depth interaction with the Federal law enforcement guys, one which he considered quite distasteful, he didn't get a pleasant feeling. In all his time as an attorney, he did more horse trading for folks (figuratively speaking) than actually trying cases. He'd only ever prosecuted one criminal case and the only reason that happened was because "the machine" told him to sit second chair on a no-brainer slam dunk felony just to get it on the record that he was there. He asked one question in that one week to one unimportant witness - but he sure was able to make it seem like he had a much larger role in that trial as the years went past.

And it was only after the ATF guy was rotated out to another state was he able to proceed with his tall tale using any bravado or, over time, finesse about his non-consequential role. That boy had been on the job for nine years in this district, and he had been an attorney for fourteen. He knew more than him. Yet time and again as they prepped for the case, this detective kept showing him what Sean didn't know. In front of other people, he usually asked the right question as he - as the second chair prosecutor, not some lowly researcher - was looking for the pieces of information to put together. The guy got off on pulling Sean around by the short hairs, and there wasn't a damn thing he could do about it.

At least, not then. A few months after the trial, Sean found himself out at some fundraising party for some crime-fighting thing. He hated those events, but needed to get his name out there, be one of the boys, show them he knew where the "party was at" and what he needed to do in order to "fit into" their crowd. When he went to functions like that, because he didn't know the right people and had a hard time remembering names and faces, he actually had a staffer that he kept on his private dime to compile a photo album with key facts about each "player" that could be there and what he should try to get out of them. He'd review the final copy as his driver would pick him up and take him, but also the draft during the entire week before hand. During the ride to a particular event, the kid that put it all together would sit in the front and turn around on his knees to face the back seat, rapidly giving him any updates on people attending.

This included when the U.S. Attorney was going to be replaced. It was a matter of time and it would have been absolutely normal for anyone in the legal field to know what what coming, to hear the whispers in court hallways. The kid in the front seat even knew, but was certain Sean needed help because he didn't keep an ear to the ground - or if he did hear pieces of information, and this was the more likely scenario, Sean had no idea what it meant. He didn't spend time in court or even in a law office. He had some friends in the field, but they chose not to discuss those sorts of politics because they knew Sean had a big mouth and was vindictive. If he repeated something he heard and it turned out to be wrong, he would throw stones at the person for years - even if it was his fault he didn't understand the original message.

This was the first opportunity he got to throw stones, and it unnaturally landed a direct hit in his own mind. Having a bit too much of the sauce in the grand old Post Office reception hall, he paused long enough to hit the head. It just so happened that the incoming SAIC of the FBI was in there with the outgoing SAIC of the ATF. Since they try to overlap senior management rotations between large DOJ departments, this time the ATF guy was the one moving out after the new FBI man (with a specialty in white collar crime) moved into the state. Neither guy knew Sean as he walked up to the urinals, but figured since he wasn't one of them that he was either a heavy hitter on the finance side or one of the guys "moving the cheese."

After his corny attempt to converse at the urinal, both Feds figured he was a money guy as there was no way he could handle ops. When they each introduced themselves by first name and division, Sean took it upon himself to complain about the ATF's interference in his old "prosecution." As it happened, as the SAIC was leaving, he had already decided to take that particular individual with him back to headquarters as his first assistant, which also gave him a big promotion and raise (to pay off the nice engagement ring he just gave his girlfriend). When the moved happened two months later, Sean just knew he was the cause of that guy leaving - but didn't realize it was the result of a promotion rather than his complaints of incompetence.

It happened another time in his new political party, actually, with none other than rumors about the chairman of the state. Of course, he never directly asked the chairman what happened. He merely overheard something at yet another fundraiser and put two and two together to make seven. As he was throwing them back with the best of the best in the room, it started to become evident that he was not one of them. His uncouth backwater accent emerged, and he couldn't even tell people were circulating the room away from him faster than any other attendee. As he tried unsuccessfully to join one group of patrons in discuss, that's when he overheard - or ear-hustled as his momma said, but he would never repeat that term - the two couples adjacent to his about the chairman and a particular Candidate A.

Sean overheard - it wasn't even that he was told - that the chair privately backed a certain candidate for office, and it was someone Sean detested. He also felt that if Candidate A (the one the chair was said to have endorsed) were to win that particular office that his buddy, Candidate B in a different election the following fall would have a more difficult time retaining his position as incumbent. If that happened, Sean wouldn't have the creamy endorsement of the sitting guy to help him get further in the next step of his political pipe dream. Had been included in the conversation, he would have known he overheard wrong. If he would have called the chairman (assuming his call would have been taken), he would have been directly told he was wrong.

And Sean thought he was never wrong. So he didn't call and instead fueled a grudge against the new leader of his new party, the one to which he switched just the year prior in order to have a better shot at national office. He was always thinking ten years ahead, how his actions today would position him for great things tomorrow. Except he was nearly always mistaken. Nearly always needed help figuring out just what it was he should be thinking. And as he was nearly always drinking at these posh events, it was about that time that he decided he shouldn't drink any longer, too. He said it made him gain weight - he was very concerned about his looks and receding hairline. But everyone knew it was because he was starting late out of the gate and needed all the clear-headedness he could get.

Even when sober, it didn't mean he was smart. That's why he had his "people" researching and monitoring the locations the inner circle wanted for the storage place. He couldn't see a good thing about any of them. He thought pulling it away a little from all that discord and crime would be safer if they ever needed to retrieve the... whatever they said they would store there. And he knew cheaper ways of watching the goods, too. There were a lot of people here looking for work now that a lot of rebuilding was done after the storm, and they worked cheap. They worked for cash, usually off the books - so if he got a little handling fee, it would all be alright.

He figured he'd talk to one of the women of a group he was trying to court. The Latinos that went to the Catholic church out in the suburbs had a lot of connections. He never could remember what they were from or how they were related and stuff, but somehow they could work those phones and have people show up to an event like no ones business - and he needed that kind of support. He wanted people to rally and surround him, even if he didn't know what they were saying. He needed people to give him the respect he deserved and these people clamored for pictures with him, the tall self-proclaimed handsome one. He could be their American knight in shining armor and lead them to new opportunities - like having some of their younger sons stay off the street by guarding whatever this stuff was that woman said would be there.

When he went by the church for the Wednesday weekly meal, he made sure to arrive before Bible study. He always said God Bless America and stuff like that, but churches and priests made him uncomfortable. He had one he could call when he needed things, but he didn't like going to mass. He honestly couldn't remember his last confession. He thought he showed up to the baptism of all of his sons, but knew he missed the First Communion of two of the boys and at least one of the Catechism things of the three that went through it so far. Whatever. The boys would always be there for him, as he needed something from these people now.

It always struck him as odd that they held church in what, to him, was like a reception hall - a wide open space. They'd eat and have Bible study or the damn service right there. Not like in a sanctuary or anything. He guessed they prayed to the same God as did he, but wasn't totally convinced since he didn't know what they were saying. When he arrived, he noticed they were all leaving and started to yell at his driver before opening his door. Immediately changing to smiles as he exited the SUV, he greeted everyone coming over to see the "big American politico man" and took a few pictures. They always took pictures. Hell, they were almost as bad as those Asian people but he smiled away for his adoring crowd.

The woman he was to meet wasn't here, but he quickly figured out through a teenager (since he spoke no Spanish and the kids were all bilingual) that they were headed to the soccer fields. What a great photo opportunity! He told the kid to hop in with them and his driver would use lights and sirens to lead the caravan to the field. When they arrived, he couldn't figure out why everyone ran to the opposite side of the field. The teenager exited the car with him and explained that maybe it seemed like he was bringing a group of immigration agents with the cars following and the lights and sirens. The kid knew better than to pull a stunt like that, but figured the gringo could do what he wanted and it would make a great story.

The teenager started yelling something in Spanish while waving his arms and people surged back over to see Sean. He still didn't understand why it would be a big deal about the lights and sirens, figuring his web-foot driver should know better if it would have caused a ruckus when he asked for it, but took more photos plastered with a huge smile and found his little señorita. It was really señora, but he didn't know enough to care, just like everything else. Not like he would call her by her name or anything - that would mean he'd have to remember it. All he knew was she spoke English, so they could talk without a translator, who would have been an additional risk to his so-called great plan.

Moving off to the side of the field away from the team benches as people resumed the match, they discussed the options if the storage place was not where he originally wanted it outside of the city and in an area that was more inner city. He was asking if that would be a problem since it wouldn't be close to where he thought they lived and he knew she said she wanted opportunities for the young boys to keep them off the street. Sean was trying to explain there was apparent concern for the costs of transporting the juveniles and the time it would take to go back and forth.

She listened and couldn't believe her luck, that the new place he was describing was closer to their other operations. Now well established, she - along with her sisters (Cristina, Sofia, and Luciana) and two female cousins - stayed home to run the "family business" with other family members back in Guatemala that routed their wares through Mexico, under the tunnel outside of El Paso, and then through to them here. It was then split and each sibling held a "district" and the two cousins ran logistics. The oldest cousin in the states that worked in Texas for a cable company was allowed to come see family using his take-home truck, delivering the uncut products to the drop house once a week (usually Tuesdays). The young cousins were the mules, under the guise of basketball games or youth group events, to route smaller packages locally to distributors.

Meanwhile, the logistics cousins had out of state contacts go to the drop house once a week; Thursday for east coast handled by Rosa and Monday for north or western areas that were coordinated by Maria (more so because her kids were older so she had more time for the bigger region). Action was always after school dismissed, and there was a pool and trampoline around the back of the house where the driver would send their kid that they brought along to play quick while they went inside to make the deal. Kids never went inside. There were two doors and no one was allowed in the left door that went upstairs to the cutting and storage area except one guy and his newer "partner," a skinny dark-skinned young guy with shoulder-length dreads. He looked black, but he was actually a dark-complected Nicaraguan who was the only one allowed upstairs with her son and so far, this had greatly confused any police investigations.

The three places he described to her, only one made sense for whatever their government was planning on doing. She couldn't really tell what the hell was the objective of that developing operation because Sean had no clue - and she didn't want to ask too many questions. The man always seemed to put off answering questions. The second place he mentioned seemed like the best, and would allow them to branch out operations into an additional area of town, one that was particularly underserved in her opinion. Emilia smiled at the nice, stupid man - *tan bonito el* - and assured him that her sisters and cousins would make sure the boys got where they needed to go, that she was so appreciative of his generosity to help their children - and gave him another "donation" for his ambitions, to use as he chose.

Chapter 28

Wayne knew he had to work some magic with the mayor in order to show him why this second location along the greenway was a better deal for the two of them instead of the other guy; he needed to get in there as the lead partner. The hard work was done and most of the permits were already issued. It was the perfect stage in which to make the adjustment; it didn't even need a reason for the modification - the mayor could just make it happen.

That was one of the strange things about this city. The mayor could basically change anything he wanted without the council's approval. Even when the council *by law* was supposed to authorize how he used certain funding or approve project assignments, the group of seven appeared to be entranced and agreeing with whatever his honor said. With great horror to business community members in attendance, in the midst of a recent meeting, the chair actually blurted out ignorance that the council didn't know they were supposed to approve certain aspect of allocations in addition to the basic budget package. Chairs were squeaking, but miraculously no audible groans were heard. Sure, they would take turns squawking about an issue, but there were reasons that were widely known that kept putting them in their rightful place.

Take that one female district-holder. She was an attorney like the mayor, but never really practiced (also like the mayor).

When Wayne once asked a neighbor as they were sitting on her porch one evening about this woman's chances at being elected mayor as she had starting talking a lot to various women's groups about the need for the first female leader in three hundred years, the neighbor neatly replied in one breath "that will never happen because everyone knows she's crazy and a drunk and if she tried to actually run some of the old city employees that saw her stunts would just come to the meeting where she wanted to announce and she'd sit right back down when she saw 'em." The neighbor took a sip of iced tea and kept on rocking.

Then there was another woman holding a contiguous district to the crazy one. Her claim to fame was previously being the representative for a security district, an "elected" position in her neighborhood. She appeared mousy, which wasn't helped any by her short stature, her short fluffy hair, or her quiet drawn-out speech. She was elected by the middle-class group, but would align with the wealthier districts as their area was trying to reach above their status and ability. There was no reasoning with her since she couldn't make up her own mind, which meant no opportunities to *persuade* her to change it on issues. She would frequently just vote after the crazy drunk and do what she did because mousy's folks wanted to be like the drunk's folks.

Damn, he just realized that there were four women on the seven-member board, evenly split by race. When did that happen? Oh, right. When the one councilman was indicted and put into prison after the U.S. Congressman was - the local guy was stupid enough for getting caught with a bribe. His first bribe and he blew it. Dummy; he was replaced by a woman, one farthest from his appearance and beliefs as could happen. Well, none of the ladies wielded any power outside of hiring their own staff because they could never agree with each other - and it wasn't that they'd align on race issues, either. The other two women represented poor areas, where they grew up themselves and raised their children and always wanted to talk about everything, which involved lengthy and loud discussions that frequently had to be continued to the next day. They would argue with each other and anyone else, but voted together on everything when it came time to call the question.

The remaining three men had varying degrees of approachability. One was a winning basketball coach; one was a recently-disbarred attorney; one an activist who supported the indicted Congressman and continued to publicly declare his innocence even after in-prisoned. Obviously, the electorate knew that these seats didn't need rocket scientists, and two were purportedly coming up for special election; those two would have been approachable and may have actually accomplished things on a small scale, but were under high-watch status now, so forget it. The basketball coach seemed much too clean-cut to help support anything, and likely was just focused on his next job. Good thing the mayor was approachable.

Though oddly the council was now a majority female, the city's mayor had never been a woman, nor had the holder of the office ever been unmarried in the traditional sense of the ceremony. The city was extremely friendly to a variety of lifestyles, yet no one of a non-traditional status was on council, either. Wayne considered that maybe those people enjoyed the amenities more than working to preserve their predilections being voted out of fashion in other parts of the country. So strange that people didn't work and become involved in making sure their legacies were intact. Then again, those kinds of people had no legacy as they couldn't have children (naturally) and the courts still saw fit here not to allow them to adopt.

Wayne needed to complete this last project and move to some nice island, one where he wouldn't see any of these people any more and his kids would visit once a year and he'd be done. He was planning on buying a superyacht, where he could move out of harm's way while in the lap of luxury if there was a hurricane coming to the island. Plus, he figured he may get bored. And if the time came for a new girlfriend, that would be a way to attract a sexy young woman that could be distracted about his age and some details about his past business dealings. If he got tired of one woman, he'd drop her at a port and go find another one somewhere else.

But, he had to finish this project, and he needed the mayor on board to handle the change in hands as well as discuss the redirect of some of the funds. It wasn't like the mayor hadn't shifted money before and done whatever he wanted - Wayne was hoping he wouldn't need to blatantly remind the mayor of his past transgressions when it came to that slush trust he absconded (or, well, tied up in legal proceedings until it was dissolved). That would be so crass, so it meant that it was possible the mayor would need to hear things that way in order to do things Wayne's way.

It had been decided on Wednesday night that they would meet at the club the following afternoon, and the treadmills would be reserved so that the two of them could talk relatively in private. One of the bodyguards would arrive first and ensure no one else got on the machines, and would also suggest the music be turned up on an obnoxious pop station to further mask anyone listening (in the room or through devices). While the mayor used fitness as a hiding place, Wayne tried to convince everyone he used it to keep in shape. He was in fairly good condition, but per his own narcissism, tended to let everyone believe he worked out routinely and lifted more weights or doing more reps than he actually completed. He'd stop and take phone calls and the "meter" would keep running in his head congruous with the call - both in billing hours style and allowed workout time fashion.

All of the juggling would catch up with him sooner or later, which was why he needed to finish these two deals and get the hell out of there. He wasn't going to let the past catch up with him as it did other folks. They weren't as smart as him, so of course they'd get caught. But he had his little non-profit money laundering gig that was predominantly funded by the state "grant" as well as the potential for a deal as developer at the location of the first option Sarah presented to the group at the meeting. That former naval base would make great loft apartments that incorporated communal activity space, organic shopping for food and clothes, classy restaurants, a meal delivery service, perhaps a friend's latest girlfriend's interior design attempts.

His mind sidetracked as he thought of that silly tramp-turned-designer, coming here from Atlanta having been a reporter for a few years. She was shut out of the market there for being so dumb; came here and got a little degree, thinking she would strut her stuff and make a fortune. For the life of him, he could not figure out what these chits thought of themselves, going from television reporter to designer or other wacko jump (also known as non-congruous employment if he would care to be politically correct, which he didn't) — way out of her league and had no connections other than the ones she made on her back. She wasn't good at designing, just like she didn't do well at reporting. She made Henry happy for the moment (he was older, wealthy, established and she was younger so looked good in high-end clothes with the ability to follow basic instructions from him). But before incorporating space for her on Henry's dime, he better make certain she would be sticking around for a while… and ensure that no one in the building attempted to use her interior decorating or there may be another rebellion afoot.

Going back to the NavyLofts project, he quickly realized that the greenway project was familiar in concept, though not in construction. Maybe if he offered to let the mayor in on his lofts, it would sweeten the deal for him to place him as lead on the greenway development, too. He already had his towel around his neck and got his machine started at a moderate to brisk walk. After ten minutes, the mayor appeared at his left side as though it was unplanned - but everyone in the club knew that when the bodyguard reserved all of the machines, it was time to discuss business.

They looked out the window toward the facility where the game was going to be held in just a few days' time. Lots of activity. He didn't care about all of that. He avoided gambling because it was supposed to be chance and mathematics rather than tests of skill. Waiting for the mayor to start talking, he slowed his machine a little bit in order to let the mayor go faster than him without losing breath. It wasn't like he had been jogging, swimming or much of anything in the past few years - the man had been doing nothing other than running for higher office, and bringing his whole family to bear on his next endeavor.

Once the mayor gave him the opening, he started to relay information about the riverfront property first and all of its benefits. Gentrification was a huge concern to the inhabitants of the city, but he knew the mayor's plan from the time he held office previously was to make their tourist destination even more prosperous on the backs of tourist tax money. Wayne focused on the local jobs that would be created, not just the short term construction and landscaping projects that could be awarded to some of the mayor's brothers, but also the longer term project that would employ the very people pushed out of the surrounding neighborhood as younger, more affluent people came to town with the intention of setting down roots near places like the one he described. Sure, they might buy a condo from him first, but they would spread out - he was looking to make a product that could flip, not a permanent resident high-rise. Quite a bit of opportunity to make some money with promises of tax relief for incoming business, if a new economic impact zone with special permits could be achieved.

The mayor listened and asked some questions, primarily obscured but obvious to Wayne about how he could get the family construction business involved. He took that as a moment to segue to include their real estate "division" and how this project would be complementary to the one he awarded to someone else further away from the river. In fact, Wayne even pitched how he could connect the two projects to then build attractions in between the two anchor sites. Of course, leadership would have to trade hands at the greenway, and he began to explain the federal interest in the other space that was already underway.

Wayne couldn't contain himself and started explaining how he devised the interior "remodeling" would need to occur, and he planned on using a certain group of guys to handle the work. This time, he did not mention the mayor's relations as he didn't want them involved in this one - it was his get out ticket. He needed to scrape as much as possible from this gold plate. He explained the business promises could be kept, but that other guy wasn't privy to the inner workings of the federal project, didn't have the trust factor with the team, and Wayne figured it all out - blueprints and all. He began to play on the nasty blood as of late between the mayor and this other guy - what promise does the mayor need to keep if he's only getting bad press when Wayne could make sure there was something special in it for the mayor.

Boy, his dad would be so proud. He had heard how the mayor's dad (a former mayor) had talked about his son and how he was running the "family business." Wayne knew his father would never speak so highly of him. Actually, he would never speak of him it to him since he was dead. This distracted him to the point where his anger started desensitizing his filters for trouble, and when the mayor started asking questions about some of his other projects, Wayne began to pour out details, thinking the man was now his friend and ready to do some serious business with some serious cash (not to mention serious top cover for the regulatory components that lie ahead).

The mayor, however, couldn't believe how easy it was for this egomaniac to start talking about his nefarious plans that were blatantly against the law. Perhaps he forgot about him being a lawyer, since he never really practiced though he did have a nice corner office in a law firm, but that was really for political meetings. His family members were judges and lawyers and federal investigators in addition to the blue collar work that some of his siblings performed with construction and landscaping as well as a sister in cargo shipping, and it was time to remind this lower class son of an absentee father who he really was.

With a partial turn of his head over the left shoulder, the mayor's bodyguard signaled for the mayor's father to come join the two men on the treadmills. This was his regular time to workout and be seen, and his oldest son arranged the meeting at this time for that very reason. His father would be the voice, so this son would never speak from this point forward. His first words were that he invited the youngest son along, too, because they hadn't seen the baby (the 42-year-old baby) in a week. The youngest son got on the treadmill next to Wayne, leaving three remaining - one toward the locker room door and two toward the free weights.

The mayor and Wayne slowed their machines so that the other two men could warm up at an even pace. The former mayor was the first to speak.

"Wayne, I hear you have some big ideas for some upcoming plans. My son said you are quite the man about town for real estate development, but of course only on large scale opportunities."

Wayne agreed with the old mayor, now feeling as though he was in the prime deal-making environment of his life. Surely, if the daddy knew and the other brother knows, the current mayor made sure to check everything out before they came together today, so that bolstered his confidence further. He gave an outline similar to what he said earlier in the workout, and was peppered with questions by the two men on the outside treadmills.

In spite of the gears shifting to the development across the river, including details of the state funding process and allocation of the land receivership in order to claim that property, Wayne never got the signal. The man on the right would ask some questions, and then the dad on the left would follow up with how that project's processes could be replicated and apply to the new projects. The dad kept his treadmill slow, but the brothers nudged their pace faster, noticing that Wayne would think less and talk more if he went faster, the adrenaline getting the better of his sense of self-preservation. People would come and go as they could all hear the locker room doors latching softly underneath the music, but given the sunlight coming through the panes, the potential for reflection to see exactly who stood behind them was impossible.

Wayne's spirits were high. He was jogging with the power brokers of this city. He had made it to the upper echelon of society and unlike a gambler who only thought about the next bet, he was ready to cash in on this last deal and get out. He'd make the NavyLofts deal even better for the mayor, kicking some of the federal redevelopment money to his brother and daddy, too, just to help get this done and get him out of the country. He was slow to notice that the other three men had slowed their paces to walking and were about to step off the devices.

When he did notice they had moved out of his peripheral vision, he hit the stop button and grabbed his towel from the top of the machine to wipe the sweat off of his face as he turned around to face them. When he looked up from his towel, the person two paces from him was a U.S. Marshal. Not "a" marshal, but The Marshal for this district. He looked to his left at the brother and his right at the two mayors in bewilderment. They had grabbed their towels; the oldest brother was hugging his dad and they proceeded toward the locker room without looking back at Wayne, but the mayor did raise a hand to his youngest brother as he and his daddy walked out together with the bodyguard holding the door open for them (and another one right inside it).

The U.S. Marshal stepped forward, with two uniformed men following right behind him at five and seven o'clock. Wayne began to hear his right to remain silent, which confused him even more. He noticed the workout room was empty. No longer aware of how long they were alone, he blankly went through the motions, trying to control his anger and his mouth, realizing it was far too late as he realized the federal investigator (younger) brother heard every word of his deceit, racketeering and money laundering process. He hadn't been talking to the brother as an equal or the mayors as partners; he was writing his lifetime imprisonment confession.

The brother smiled as he saw the recognition of defeat on Wayne's face, and he thought how the little people will never win as he walked out before the new felon lowered his head and followed under arrest.

Chapter 29

Ironic that his mother had gotten him the cell phone so that she could use the GPS app to track where he was and when he moved, just like she watched his siblings and cousins. It wasn't about where they were, but all about the merchandise they were moving around the city for her. Because the phone was for her business purposes and not what her son was doing, she didn't care what he did on the phone. There was no blocking of the internet or tracing calls, things of that nature. It gave him the freedom to try to figure some things out for himself and make friends that weren't members of the family.

He was just six years old when they came to America from Guatemala. They spent a few years in southern California, moving around doing migrant farm work and his baby brother was born. About eight years ago, they moved to Houston for his dad to work in construction with all of the new housing being built and his uncle did landscape work for another guy they knew from back home. A sister was born; they all bounced from school to school, and finally spent two years at the International School in Monterose before The Storm where he was able to catch up and start to get ahead in his lessons.

It wasn't seven weeks after those twin storms before they packed up and came to this city. He had been about to start his third year at that same school. By then, he had his driver's license and drove an old beat up truck his dad had packed with construction things behind the mini-van that his dad drove with his mother, younger brother and sister. It took forever to get there, he felt, and they kind of staked out a home that appeared abandoned on one side and had another Guatemalan family living on the other. Well, two families were in that half of the house. They were only there for a few weeks, and then moved into a bigger house that they fixed up with his aunt's family. His younger siblings thought it was like camping, but to him, it disrupted the first recollection of stability he could remember and it ate away at his sense of progress.

Surprisingly, the area where they moved had a lot of Latinos. It wasn't a nice area of town, but that's because they were willing to work and knew about construction so could fix up whatever they got. As long as a group of guys had one that spoke English - and a car helped, too - they could all get cash work every day, seven days a week. Some people needed serious help rebuilding their homes; others just were doing touch ups or felt like it was time to make big changes though they suffered no damage like other people did. The group of guys got paid at the end of every day and soon realized that they had to have one guy in the group as a lookout - to watch for anyone that wanted to jump them for their money. It happened a lot and they couldn't tell anyone - most Latinos at that point didn't have green cards. They had to protect each other until they could wire most of it home or buy their groceries for the family and liquor for themselves.

But, they could all find work and that was good, his dad said. Work wasn't steady in Houston and it wasn't available year-round. That was just great; however, it just wasn't the kind of work that he wanted to do. He had enough English classes (even in a dozen different schools) that he spoke very clearly and with very little accent. Nothing could change the color of his skin, but he knew enough that it was still better here than in Guatemala. There, he could have been kidnapped and forced into any number of horrible jobs or to fight with the guerrillas. The problem was for him, while his parents saw opportunities and making way more money than they ever could over a whole lifetime back home, he only saw how little they had here compared to people just blocks away. He was raised in America, and though his little brother and sister were American as they were born here, they were still too young to understand.

He was raised with some American values. He still had the work ethic of his parents and was willing to work hard to get ahead. It's just he didn't want to do manual labor. Working in construction like his dad or digging in the dirt like his uncle was unappealing. He wanted to work in an office, with steady hours and chances at promotions - and no chances of falling off a roof. From all that he learned through high school, he knew that he needed to take some college classes and slowly start to work his way into an office job.

So he worked at night as a busboy for a local restaurant as soon as he finished that last year of high school. That was crazy enough - he just showed up one day and because it was in such chaos, they gave him a diploma at the end of that year without ever teaching a thing. Two years later, he lived at home but by day, he would take one class each semester at the community college - all business courses so that he could start to see what he needed to do to manage money, supervise people, control inventory. Any chance he could get, he would ask questions about things at the restaurant of managers and patrons alike - and he finally got a lead with one of the customers to work a few hours each morning as an accounting intern at their local office, which meant he could still take an afternoon class and work his night shifts.

But that was only if his mother didn't start making him take more routes or give him more deliveries or get him involved in the oversight of her distribution machine. That was the best way to describe it. Her own little enterprise was cold and calculating, well-oiled and followed her instructions with precision. Shortly after they moved here, while his dad was out working twelve hours a day tearing out wet insulation, cutting new tile, installing dry wall, painting - any projects he could get, and his mother was back at the house with her kids and other neighborhood Latino kids. She watched what happened in the area like a hawk keeps and eye open for the smallest mouse on the forest floor.

What those beady eyes saw was a rip in the action. She saw shifts in movement, like there was a river that had forgotten which way to turn. With the storm disrupting normal activity, the suppliers of the higher-end drugs had been forcefully evacuated by Mother Nature and hadn't returned. None of the distribution folks were back; they weren't staying and working on their own home, let alone someone else's. That was hard and dirty work. They wanted clean, easy, and to be paid for doing nothing.

The people who had returned were mostly the ones needing to buy their drugs, and were floating around like a river without direction. They didn't want just any drugs and they didn't want to go in the really devastated areas to get what they wanted - and they'd pay a higher price for not having to go too far to get it. Supply and demand - and convenience. His mother realized there was a chance to work smarter while his dad worked harder. They were in an area between the nicer areas and the really rough ones, so it wasn't totally off limits for these people looking for their routine to re-establish itself.

It was easy to fill the space currently vacant. She could get her sisters involved as they were also now in the city; they lived all within two blocks of one another, just like in their village. What was different now was that they picked schools for their kids to attend based on where the sales were. They went grocery shopping so they could stop by the fancy houses - neighbors always thought they were the cleaning ladies anyway. They coordinated a distribution point in an area near the lake where less than fifteen percent of the homes remained standing and even then, not all were rebuilt and inhabited. Any routine was stretched beyond the norm for them, to take the service right to the homes (or areas) that were looking for help.

She ran the business with a tight grip. Not only did she control the money his father had left after buying the groceries she wanted and the alcohol he needed, she controlled everything for the distribution locally. Because of the missing links, what she thought would be small grew tremendously - to the point of networking with other Guatemalans in four areas of the United States. This was the town where others came to pick it up at a house not associated directly with them - so they thought. This is where her sisters orchestrated days and times and which regions got supplied. His mother ran local stuff and international imports; the aunts did the coordination of vast shipments to other areas.

And that left the kids and the cousins to run point. After all, don't kids wander all over the place, seeing cousins and friends, playing basketball on different city courts, carrying their backpacks everywhere they go? She strictly enforced a dress code and the phone system, so small deliveries and handoffs of the exact same school uniform backpacks could be swapped at a pickup game that wasn't really "pickup" except in the sense of picking up a different backpack to take to the next distribution point. She made sure none of the kids attracted attention to themselves. Requiring good grades and participation in sports as well as youth group activities was all part of the machine.

Now that he was older, it was harder for him to integrate into that system. So she was trying to step him up. He more frequently was to go to the drop house, where he'd go in the left door to make surprise inspections, make sure they weren't cutting too thin or taking any for themselves. While there was machismo involved, the men were afraid of what the women would do if they were to step out of line. It would be worse than withholding sex - they would spread stories about them and they would lose face. It was easier to have some of them work normal jobs and seem like they were the money-makers to those not inside the machine, but knowing they could never escape the routine because of how far his mother's network spread was depressing.

Leo quickly realized that this was not the business he wanted to enter. He constantly tried to think of ways to get out of it. After a "pickup" game one afternoon, he walked eight blocks to just think, and stopped at the local market for a cold drink. Inside, an officer was doing his detail and making sure no one stole anything or robbed them at the end of the day. The guy kind of looked Hispanic, tall and darker skin that wasn't white, but not dark enough to be black. So he approached him and tried to strike up a conversation.

Marcus knew kids - hell, a guy in his late teens most likely - don't just walk up to the police in this town to start chatting for no reason. He made him feel comfortable, actually bought his drink for him as he was getting one, too, and then the kid wouldn't have to wait in line and break the contact. The backpack slung on one shoulder appeared empty, so he was also keeping his eyes on him so that he didn't try to lift anything. The kid actually asked about a job, when he worked there - but not like he was casing the place. Almost like a lonely kid looking for someone to listen.

When Leo went to walk out, Marcus knew not to head out the door with him, in case anyone was watching the boy. But he did step into the office to look on the cameras and see which way he went. He told the kid when he worked, and sure enough two days later, he had reappeared. Over time, Marcus started shaping him to believe he could help him out if he ever saw anything suspicious or got accused of anything - guys his age were called out all the time for things. He tried to treat him like an older brother would and it worked.

Not a year after that first encounter, Leo started feeding small bits of information about drug deals. It was just enough to peak Marcus' interest, and to know there was something more. He just had to wait until Leo was ready to give him the keys to the deal and he had a feeling it was a big one. He knew his background, that he wanted to get an office job someday, that he was interning for a mid-level manager in the business district so was taking college courses. It would come together for both Marcus and Leo if they were patient - and indeed, it had.

Marcus' "regular" CI, Leo, had information to share about the international drug trafficking scheme, while that same night Jason was revealing to Sarah, Marcus and Luke the identity of whom he suspected to be the terrorist - just three nights before the day of the big game. Leo didn't know the detective's phone was off while in the EOC meeting. He just knew now was the time and one of the biggest opportunities to get himself free.

Leo began to text, and not just the trigger phrase about setting up a discrete meeting. When Marcus would check his phone an hour later, fourteen messages would give key information, all sent very quickly once he had made up his mind and hadn't quite planned what he would say.

> Huge heroin shipment in three days. Very big fish present. Lots of cars and from different states. Bouncing thing in the yard blocking the "pickup" door on the right. Above ground pool now in backyard, along with a trampoline. Little kids screaming all day, planned distraction. Deals that evening, made in the house. All about same time as kickoff, just after. Going down near that corner store where we met. My regular night for bussing, not near it. Main lady short, will appear friendly or confused, first to talk. Her sisters are just as big for you. Local men not really part, except teens and 20s mules. They think they are smarter than you.

Ironic that his mother had gotten him the cell phone that was now going to set him free.

Chapter 30

"I don't know where he is. It has been months since I have seen him. He finally stopped coming to the office when he got the message that it was against state law to contract with him for work. I never saw him outside of work; in fact, I planned the holiday party at my house around when I knew he would be visiting his family out of state. And before you say he may have moved back to his mountain hometown, I should share a few more things." Jason looked away and paused, still not comfortable with the fact that all indications were that Mike was the suspect. He forced himself to continue because if indeed this Marine was capable of these horrific delusions, then he needed to be stopped.

"He and his ex-wife are estranged. No contact, no children. Who knows where she may be - she likely remarried and changed her name. It would make sense with his alcohol issues. His father is still alive as is his sister, not sure about his mother, but with the whole macho 'company commander' thing, his dad likely wasn't even told that he isn't employed by the city any longer. Mike always overstated his roles, overstated his abilities - even tried to get interns to do his work and submit it as his own. I caught that on more than one occasion."

The exasperation combined with the embarrassment of a military member - one of his own branch - was capable of such horrific plots was exhausting. The smallest hope they had that the plot wouldn't work was that Mike didn't know how to do hard work. He always had grand ideas that fell apart - but this time, they weren't sure who could be assisting, and considered that he may not be the mastermind of the threat. The uncertainty of his partner, or any partners, made the four of them concerned for very different reasons.

Jason shared some other facts he hadn't relayed earlier in the conversation and the other three each shared what they knew about him, beyond than the obvious predilection for alcohol. Sarah knew that he liked sand volleyball - of course, he claimed he dominated the court, but she only saw him once actually involved in a game while he was umpire when the other guy got sick. He called that game with a drink in his hand. Marcus knew that there was one dive bar out in the suburbs that he liked to frequent, though he never joined him there when asked time and again. Luke knew very little except his demeanor that he experienced that night when Mike put his hands on Sarah, so he couldn't really contribute much - except that he would wager there were people who had an axe to grind with Mike if they could find him. That could produce some valuable clues to his whereabouts.

The foursome agreed that they wouldn't share this intel with the group gathered downstairs as they were oriented being ops-ready for the game, and not concerned with the hunt. Marcus would, however, pass along everything in person to his gang at the house that were dividing and conquering identifying and derailing the plan and likely perpetrator. As they left the room to descend the spiral stairs, they discussed if any of the plans should be altered, coming to the conclusion that the plan of the day would stay intact until Marcus could get updates from the seven folks in the intel house.

Returning to the third floor, it was obvious that the various divisions were busy with their clusters and interacting with the two new people Sarah brought to the meeting - the docs that knew so much about the potential weapons. Some of the guys were gathered around Elijah, having very animated discussions. It was likely a story of snakebites or bad first responder calls. The members in this room were always looking to learn more, and were probably picking the brains of the experts about other topics than the potential catastrophe at hand. It didn't worry her because everyone was on their game in this gathering.

Other guys were around Dr. McPherson, including Chad, the hazmat lead. While Marcus went over to Elijah's gathering in the left corner of the room, Sarah went over to Dr. McPherson. The group surrounding him was larger than Elijah's, but much less animated. Everyone was standing quietly in front of him, almost in perfectly nested semi-circles like seats in a university lecture hall, being very respectful and just listening to what the doc thought he needed to say. He was faced away from Sarah and toward the back wall of windows. She stood behind him to his left side while he finished the mini-lecture about the stockpile and he answered a few additional questions. She was impressed at the advanced planning they were considering in just a short time of being exposed to the new components. They also seemed to like the idea of the festival archways being used for the same reasons she thought previously - lack of reactivity potential and easy decon.

When it was clear that those listening were beginning to take the information in smaller discussions to the next step, Dr. McPherson turned to Sarah and smiled gently. He always was a calming force, even when he was most agitated. The only time he had ever been very upset, she watched him breathe more deeply and his voice got louder, but it did not talk faster or use coarse language. He placed his left hand on her right forearm and patted gently, in a reassuring manner.

"Well, Sarah, I think that these young men and women are ready to go out there and deploy the additional assets to stop whatever's going to happen. Showing them the examples of the DuoDote injector and Mark 1 unit helped a lot. Elijah and I will get those distributed to hazmat and EMS tomorrow starting at 9am from the warehouse by that bridge upriver, and they already have a pretty good idea how to hand them out to the various crews as well as have pre-staging of replacement supplies with the sprint cars. No one has really nailed down how many assets they are putting in the potential hot zone versus response areas, but I know they're working on it. Now, you had a third favor for me back at my office earlier. What was it?"

Sarah could only grin, knowing that even though he potentially - likely - was the oldest person in the room, he was the most organized and contentious person there, no matter how the state of his actual office appeared. "You've already done it. You came here and explained things to the team, calmed them down with your voice and knowledge, and are here on site to back me up. I could ask for nothing more."

He returned her smile and noted he needed to get home to his wife. He had called her to tell her he had a late meeting and it was ok, it wasn't with the people in the capitol so he didn't mind, but he would need to eat dinner a little later. He didn't typically drive after dark anymore, as his cataracts bothered him and produced a glow around every street light, head light, and red light. He also made a joke about if he didn't get to bed soon he would never be able to handle all the hustle and bustle of the next day. So with a hug and kiss on the cheek, he shuffled to the elevator and exited, with Luke going along under the guise of questions but the intention of being a lookout for any neighborhood roughnecks.

Sarah returned her attention to the group that was fracturing to handle their business, and she focused on the blueprints and various schematics on the table. The copies intended for the teams had already been scooped up by the various leaders. She noticed a few adjustment made to sniffer positioning and arch deployment, appreciating that someone was thoughtful enough to update her copy while they made the adjustments. She'd need to give it to Marcus' team, so they could review this, too, and make adjustments given the operational guys' considerations.

As she was rolling her copy of the footprint with sniffers and arches new patterns for foot traffic, Chad walked over to her. They had met on occasion in cube-ville by Jason's office, but rarely had the time to talk as of late. She smiled up at him; she was tall in heels but still not *that* tall that she could look directly at his face. She opened her arms to give him a hug - she truly didn't mind the hug and kiss on the cheek from him.

"Chad, it's so good to see you."

Chad chuckled a deep chuckle. Sarah was one of the few people he didn't have to bend to - either physically or mentally. They had some pretty interesting discussions on a variety of operational tactics, and it was never a guarantee who would have more better ideas than the other. He figured she didn't "give in" to many people, and why would she when she was really quite fast on her feet. He opened his arms and gladly pulled her close.

"You are honestly one of the few people I like to hug. You're taller, so I fit in the right space and it never seems like a forced 'oh brother, let me hug this crazy one' like some guys. They literally have a look on their face that screams a five letter word starting with B instead of crazy one. Sometimes, you just need contact, you know, and contact that fits not contact that's forced." Sarah stayed close as her face was turned to the side, laying on his chest and still kind of looking down at the schematic.

"Do you have any idea how uncomfortable it is to slouch all day, bend over to hear someone not talking well (not that you really want to hear their prattle anyway), or give that fluffy hug to someone who is really two feet shorter? All of the Cajun blood has folks teeny tiny compared to me. It's nice to hold you, to know that you don't have a knife in that hand at my back."

He shifted the conversation, but not his hold. "So, who do you think can really be behind all of this and is it worth all the last minute shifts we are hoping the teams can bring to reality these last forty-eight hours?" When they had some of their best conversations, it was to bring out the direct questions instead of soft-shoeing and never getting to the point, like many of the politicians (and wanna-be politicians) in the city.

She continued to just relax into him, and while she couldn't share everything from upstairs, she thought it served cross purposes to not give him some information. Providing him with potential identification was being finalized and some of the things that brought them to that point, she didn't want to pigeonhole him into the same identification as the four just made upstairs. His quiet laid-back way of hearing everything and coming to interesting conclusions made for a prime opportunity to get his insight on the rationale for the threat and asked him directly - as they typically did with each other - what he thought kicked off this plan on the part of the suspect. She listened to him reply with both ears, hearing his voice resonate in his chest and from he left ear.

"I think this nut feels he has some justified provocation into launching what, to him, is the next great catastrophe for the region. He has some connection to this area, and that was taken from him. Not saying he was born or raised here, but there's some hook that makes him feel possessive of events, yet he lacks any power or authority. It's all in his mind about something being taken from him that could have ever been his, but likely there were signs to him all along and he just didn't fit the mold or couldn't read the writing on the wall. Something that was clearly not his to start, but he internalized it and is either masterminding this to get attention back to himself or as a punishment to those he saw as defeating him."

Sarah pulled back to look up at Chad. He absolutely had analyzed the little data he heard floating around and precisely articulated the MO. She still had her hands loosely around his back, and his hands had slid, too, so that they were more on either side of her waist, though partially under her leather suit jacket at this point. She stared intently at him and wanted to see what else they could determine - without him knowing the actual person they identified.

"Let me play devil's advocate. What's the difference in your two options for the motive. What would be factors in this particular case of a suspect going attention versus retribution route?"

Chad was quiet, though remained focused on her. She knew that he did this when he was thinking sometimes. He was very particular about his word choice - sometimes intentionally being ambiguous (and funny), but that wouldn't be the case now. He was actually processing the various components of his theory and weighing her question seriously. The intensity with which he stared at her likely was only a projection of what he was doing in his own mind as he searched for the answer.

In truth, however, Chad was trying to regain his focus on what the hell she had just said. The olive suit and her perfume with hints of citrus gave a spicy richness to her that was easily distracting, especially since he was part of the VOC teams and had a trained nose - literally - for scent discernment. The heat of her body that close, too, didn't help. He knew she was all business, but when he hugged her and she stayed in contact when they talked, it was still disarming. Finally gathering his thoughts without any of the distraction being read on his face, he provided her with two possible reasons for the first option and three for the second. It was off the cuff, so he made sure she understood that he had only done that analysis just now, but he was pretty sure those were things that would impact the suspect's choices.

Marcus watched via the periphery this exchange with Chad and Sarah. He hadn't realized they were so close, and it got him to thinking when had they ever met before this event. Surely, they couldn't have engaged on other events - Chad and Marcus were usually near one another for such things, but that man sure had a way of moving about quietly undetected, even for being over six-and-a-half feet tall and a former football player. He was packing up his presentation items and noticed their ongoing interaction over his left shoulder. None of them needed her distractions right now, but they all needed her leadership and intelligence. He packed up quickly, and walked over to see if Sarah was heading to the team house with him. Not that he cared about the answer, he merely wanted to interrupt whatever this was.

As Marcus approached, he heard Sarah say softly, "Yes. Yes, I think you're right. They're so different, but both could easily be generated with the things in the profile Marcus presented earlier." Turning to Marcus, but still not pulling away from Chad, she continued, "I have to tell you some of the things he said about motive, and he hasn't heard all of the pieces. Maybe when the team has the profile finished, Chad could look at it and think about any gaps we've missed."

Chad was surprised, as he was hazmat and tactics whereas he knew Marcus had a prowess and respect in the law enforcement community for detective work. That Sarah would push open a door to have another head in the identification discussion was at first surprising, and then he realized not so much. She thought about the mission and the game and the end results, evaluated the best way to achieve success and headed full-throttle for it. When people understood her, they saw that it was all about the solution of a problem and not about titles and politics for her. In fact, that's why she had really strong supporters in all the sectors of operations - but was also why she occasionally (no, make that frequently) bumped heads with those above her pay grade who wanted the job to be a success, but didn't have the intelligence to understand how to get the best end result.

Since she frequently ignored up front niceties because when it came down to what could be life or death, she always picked life and the quickest way to preserve it. She would beat herself up for it later - but only a little. Because of her success rate in saving lives (and saving the butts of politicians), she was continued to be hired by some of the biggest names in the world, and frequently would never be associated with an actual name or company. The improvements she left behind were testament to her achievements.

But that didn't matter when it boiled back down to the basics that she was a woman that some smart men found attractive. Obviously, thought Chad, Marcus was one of those because the look he was getting was primal and protective. *Whatever, bring it tin soldier*, though Chad. The past fifteen seconds was like a standoff at the O. K. Corral without anyone actually drawing their weapons - and all with Sarah lost in her thoughts about strategy updates with the information from the past two hours.

When she spoke, it brought all three back into the room where they were a team and would continue to play by those rules. "Ok. Marcus, let's head back to the house and see what they've done. The guys made updates to the plans for some positioning and walkways that we need to deliver to Betty and Peter, if not also Rae." She looked to Chad and explained they were the architect, real estate and cinematographer assignees to the group working the angles of the situation.

"Marcus, I have my car so I'll meet you at the house in like fifteen minutes; I'm going to grab something to eat on the way and just woof it down in the house. I can't decide between a burger or a fully dressed salad. I'll figure that out, so better give me 25. Here, take the prints with you," as she leaned to her left to pick up the tube from the table and passed it to her right hand - avoiding bopping Chad in the head as she passed it over his continued contact.

He backed up a little so he could remove the plans from the tub and look quickly. If he had any questions about the updates made while they were upstairs, he should find who did it while he was still here, to get the quickest answer possible. He realized it was all pretty straight forward, some notes on rationale for adjustments included, which was a nice touch. A really good modification for one of the archways and small sniffer units immediately made sense to him and unconsciously, he was nodding.

Chad watched with interest as Marcus reviewed his updates. In the interest of time when he saw the affirmative agreement from him, Chad injected into Marcus' unconscious question, "If you need any information about the adjustments, just call me. I was the instigator in most of them, but we discussed them down here while y'all were upstairs. I'll fill you in if your team wants to know from the ops side why some of those were moved - it's a plume model concern we had, for the most part."

"As for you," he now addressed Sarah, as Marcus was deep into the plans and was already heading to the elevator, "back to the first part of saying hi tonight, I enjoy hugging you, too. We should go out and get a glass of wine sometime when this is over. Next week, maybe Tuesday or Wednesday. Let me know." Chad pulled Sarah in again, this time making sure his hands stayed under that jacket that completely lifted out of his grasp when she handed over the schematic tube.

She hugged him back and agreed that would be great. An extra squeeze from her to him and a smile that would likely be the last for the next 72 hours, she really was already changing the strategy in her head. And that caused her to be totally oblivious to the fact he may have been asking for more than friends to have a drink.

Chapter 31

Sarah arrived at the house about twenty minutes after Marcus, but he waited for her to get started with the team on updates from both sides. It wasn't a hard decision to make compared to all of the other ones of late - the house had ordered pizza, so everyone was making some personal calls and catching up on life outside those walls. The whole "house team" was there, all seven of them, and Luke came back, too, to make adjustments to the profile Prezi as he ate two slices. What Sarah brought for her dinner was neither burger nor salad, but Lebanese food from the restaurant between the other two options and it had smelled delicious - not what she thought she'd get and not typical regional fare, but the restaurant was consistently good. She ate her schwarma while Marcus updated the team on feedback from the presentation as well as the adjustments on the schematics.

The team also refined camera locations, lens types, other pedestrian access routes and more. They were able to integrate the changes from hazmat's suggestions as well as the modifications the Coasties thought would be useful to integrate regarding the navigable waterway ops with other federal assets. Tam, the epidemiologist, gave them some updates that the manufacturer had made for them on the sniffer software, as he already relayed that to the field teams that were laying out the wooden shipping crates tonight, to assemble things tomorrow on the routes.

The food festival guys had actually donated their crews, too, for the segregating of the right containers for the archways, and since power was involved and some cutie lighting for the tourists, the same electrical team was tagged to do all of that. The logistics team came with the industrial farm-sized equipment to carry the storage units down the street and position them in pre-build spots just like they would do at the fairgrounds. One of the team members was a welder during the year, and he jumped on the archway component; another member was a supervisor of a public works division of a Texan town, and he drove in early to help stage and sort the pieces for the electricians. These guys were accustomed to how the pieces worked, so no one had great concerns that after they staged the boxes and lifts that the staging area was empty, as was the field area where building would begin again in the morning.

As the house team members slowly departed for their own homes for the evening, knowing it would be the last time they'd probably have quality rest (and food) for the next three days, each generally felt good about how far they'd come. The defense team members were the first to clear out that night, including Rae as her camera orders were all in-hand and going to be installed or re-gelled tomorrow during the day, and she'd need to supervise those technicians. She would get the updates on the suspected character tomorrow - she didn't need to know *him;* she needed to see him and they'd need all night to pull some of those images and for Herman, the IT guru, to get software specified to his features.

Marcus knew to let him code in solitude. That was not a job that background distractions helped when time was critical. Alex and Sibyl were very interested in the notes from Jason, and were bouncing ideas off locations and checking out the various sand beaches as well as bars that would conform to his profile.

Luke was sitting with them, and incorporating their ideas into the profile avatar - both here and a file to upload out on the trail with the kids at the data center for the flexiglass software. Marcus came over to join them, and realized his phone had been on silent for the past three hours.

"Oh, shit."

"That phrase is becoming overused in our crowd. First Jason about two hours ago, and now you. What gives?" Luke was asking as he was typing and listening to Alex and Sibyl, who now stopped given the abrupt revelation of sorts.

"My phone has been on silent and while we always get messages all day and night, I now am seeing some solid intel from a CI about that interstate drug trafficking sit I've been working over by the lake. It's going down Sunday around the start of the game, though we'd been planning to hit it about three weeks from now. I'm going to have to back out of here for a while and back to the DEA on this. Don't hate me - but also know my phone isn't going to be on silent until Monday at the earliest. I have to get this stuff to the task force." Marcus continued muttering some things to himself as he grabbed a coffee for the car and left through the front door.

Being accustomed to the lifestyle and challenges of normalcy, none of the members remaining in the house (since they were all nearly of the same background) blinked an eye at either the sudden change of his plans or that he was talking to himself on the way out. Each and every one of them had that happen - both the rerouting of plans and talking to yourself without realizing it as you organized next steps. Granted, for Sarah it had been a while as she usually found herself surrounded with people who weren't cleared to be in the know, but she recalled being the master of your universe until some nitwit had moved the ball. It's why you always wanted to be prepared - it's why she kept her fatigues and boots in the car even when she normally wore skirts and heels. You just never knew.

Only a little longer did she stick around as the four of them remaining talked through some details. Right now, it was really in the hands of the detective and analyst, as well as Luke for his ability to do both on a different platform and relate that into visual art that the less abstract-capable team members would be able to understand - no one that was in this house needed it, but for others to understand how far this house had brought the battle closer to conclusion, sophisticated picture-grams needed developed. Sarah excused herself, went to her car and went home.

And she felt like she only blinked when her alarm woke her to get ready and delver updates down at Jason's office. She walked in after being buzzed into the chambers and saw Luke already there. Jokingly, she greeted him good morning as she would someone with whom she spent the night - as not even a whole normal nighttime had passed since they were together. She didn't know much about his personal life, only the things she got from his personnel file through her real headquarters. He was certainly interesting, and she appreciated the way his mind worked.

Little did she know how much of Luke was involved in this project. From the Prezis to software to who was working on the avatar software schemes. Luke mainly kept to himself and just involved himself in various projects that interested him. He had a personal stake in this one, and while no one needed to know that, it was making the project flow that much sooner. After all, game day was only two days away and kickoff a mere ten hours further afield.

Sarah asked him to follow her, and she took him back out to the elevator bay, and into an odd corner of the farther of the two sets of elevators. There was a panel there, and she entered a sequence on the keypad that slide the panel open in traditional architecture form for the region - it was like a pocket door, so there were no hinges and no other indicators than the keypad beside the elevator that there was a door. She took him up to the interior of the top half-floor and out onto the roof so they could watch the various crews continuing to set up equipment and walkways, signage and their archways. There was a second way to the roof that the building maintenance staff used, but that was on the other end of the building and they'd have to chat to people the whole way down that office space - and then answer questions why they were going to the roof.

Once up top, though Sarah was in heels she moved with great agility and determination around the ladders and catwalks in order to position them with the most direct view of the game grounds outside the stadium. Twelve floors up (since the uppermost floor wasn't accessible for people, just extra space for the extreme steel beams that supported the huge compressors and generators on top of the building), the view was impressive. It was strangely quiet, save the deep constant whirring of the compressor fans. Each fan was the as wide as four parked cars in a parking lot, and one specifically supported the positive pressure environment that protected the tenth floor living quarters through which they just passed. While Luke was amazed at the construction components, he was as equally amazed at her ability to move them to optimal recon viewpoints - and in her heels.

Sarah looked down to the street then back to the rooftop while leaning on the edge of the roof that only came to her mid-thigh. She had guided them to a spot under the shade of the cooling tower, which also hid them from view of a nearby office windows of the neighboring building that sat directly across from the stadium. The sun's angle would help disguise them from the office directly across the street, the one that had the sun pouring directly in the windows. Most of the blinds were closed by those occupants. Crossing her arms, she directly stared at Luke, and pointedly asked, "Are we ready?"

Luke couldn't maintain her gaze as he turned his thoughts inward. He slightly shook his head from side to side as he approached on her right and leaned slightly forward over the edge. He had been asking himself that since last night and Jason's revelation that jerk Mike was most likely the impetus for all of this extra work. So many assets, so much money, so little time.

"There's rarely a day when I think I'm fully ready for anything headed my way. I do things to help keep myself ready. You know, hit the range and the gym, that sort of thing. But that's only physical preparedness, nothing you can really do for the mental game. Past experience prepares you for how you react, and you can overcome deficits to some extent. But only if you know what they are. You can keep sharpening the sword, but there comes a time when you take too much of the metal off the weapon and you shorten your reach."

He continued to watch the workers below. The street had been closed for nearly a week in preparation, to restrict non-essential staff (meaning the whole damn city, in essence) to the outside and only those with the right credentials were allowed inside the barricades. Every time the buses brought media personnel, they completely swept every bag. They had relocated the teams - with some angst from owners - to the two hotels where players could walk on escorted secured pathways. He saw the trails of effort from so many people trying to work at making this weekend fun. Fun, damn it. He leaned forward so his elbows where on the roof's edge, and bent at the waist as he let out a long breath. He turned his face up to Sarah.

"For me to mentally prepare, I try to keep my mind busy. It's one of the reasons I took my hazardous duty pay from those few crazy deployments and put it into starting the gamer company. It's worked out well, as the military still lets me keep my access and I develop things that will make games more real while I lock out key pieces of information - but I program things for the government to help them get smarter, to do more with less as the legislature always asks DOD to cut back. Those kids out in the trail building - yeah, they are all part of my team. They don't know it. They think I'm their military liaison that brings them plug ins of new data. But I'm glad I can help keep ops like this moving smoothly by taking what millennial will think of next, but giving us real world useful applications that greatly enhance our chances of winning."

Sarah just looked at him stunned. This was not in his file. There's always more to people than what's on paper, but it surprised her that the dossier was glaringly mute on this topic. Then again, if he was using his old connections for the new businesses, it would make sense that certain things could be kept scrubbed. She was shaken from her amazement by a loud clang on the ground just before Luke continued.

"I dig in the dirt to keep my mind awake, too. You know that I do the archeology as my main job. But I use the technology of today and the data it gleans in order to see back into the past. We haven't been able to do a lot of that before these past ten years. But I also thought we should be able to take that to the future, too. I set game theory on it's head when I programmed those avatars. I did the skeleton, left it for the kids when I hired them through my legit regular business. The HR person has some insights to things, so knows when I ask for certain team members, we do the final interview with me listening in and texting questions to ask. There's a camera in his office so I can watch the reactions.

Anyway, if I could do it in a tomb, then why not use the information to make sure we don't create more mass graves with future looks, too?"

Sarah was finally able to speak, and didn't focus on the shock of his multi-faceted career (and bank account). "You're fortunate you've been able to find a path so clearly. I sometimes wonder how it can all come together. I know my skills; so many people don't get beyond the image they can't consider respecting what's brought to the table. It's really discouraging and in this situation, I've tried to just ignore the ones who aren't here to play for the greater good. I've been burned a few times on whom to trust, and it's tough when there are all sorts of cultural constructs and money machines changing the environment while things play out. I know I can do this and do it well, but sometimes I'm not allowed and I don't want to do a job and not execute to the best of my ability because of outside restraints. It's not fair to the people down there or to my ultimate boss."

He knew of the past few years that she rarely spoke about her real boss. The guys all seemed to know she wasn't really from here, of here. She might be here now, but the likelihood of her being shifted to a new area could happen at any time. If the team was successful on this mission, then she'd move up. If not, then she could be shoved into oblivion.

She hadn't been speaking at Luke while she'd said this; though she was speaking to him, she looked at the cooling tower. She looked away, off to her left, and then turned toward him, placing her hands down on the cement edge. She looked at him without saying a word, back in her own place of planning and strategy, trying to re-engage herself in this event, pushing away the self-doubt that sometimes clouded her mind, though never seeped into her decision-making.

They both turned to watch some more of the assembly lines below, as if a signal reached them to keep an eye on things. After some time, she gently smacked the ledge and turned to him with a nod. As the clouds rolled in so they could proceed back to the door without the sun's rays beating them down physically as they had been beating themselves mentally, she began picking her way, quickly and cleanly, over the pea gravel and walkways on the roof, with him following behind, then heading back below to their meetings where they were trying to get everyone on the same page and stop this ass from making a mess of what was supposed to be fun, damn it.

Chapter 32

They had actually spent an hour-and-a-half on the roof watching components come together on the ground below them. They saw a lot of interesting things, including areas that didn't seem to be assembled as quickly as they had liked. For instance, they noticed a group of guys and several boxes being unloaded at the equipment entrance that seemed to have quite a few issues. The police had walked over and again inspected their credentials, just as would have happened at the cargo entrance. Additional folks joining them from operations - they could tell by the vests they wore were designated for this event - also tried to get some things organized for this distracting group. They were too far away to see which people interacted, but the apparent confusion was still being sorted when they went back downstairs.

A very loud conversation was occurring in Jason's office as they passed. No one was in cube-ville. Hell, if there had been guys hanging out in there, she would have put her perfect-ten heel up their butts and told them to get out of the office - go do something outside and help the mission. She hoped wherever they were "helping" wasn't going to hinder that aspect of the operation.

She and Luke rounded the corner and found Marcus in his usual location, which surprised them both given the great break last night in his interstate narcotics trafficking case. He was furiously trying to type away on his laptop; trying was the most appropriate description as he appeared to type and then furiously deleted and then stared at the screen and then would begin all over again. Together, they approached in silence and he blurted out what was driving him crazy - an "official" ops order needed to be created for this office as well as the police department, so he was trying to create them without giving too much information to leaders that would likely blow their mission or squander any opportunities they had.

He also told them that Dr. McPherson and Elijah were dispensing the countermeasures, and most of the supplies at their location that were meant for the street units were already in the hands of supervisors, accomplished in a bit less than two hours. He had to incorporate some of those details in the plans as it was a state partnership (so all the folks up river would be looking for inclusion, though obviously not either of the two actually doing the work). As he scratched his head, he explained it was a damn mess trying to give the powers that be accurate details but not all of the details. It wasn't lying - it was just protecting the important aspects of the truth from what would surely be mutilated by politicians.

Sarah laughed, but empathized with his frustration. "Just make sure whatever you write is not as bad as that plan the department created after the storm. Holy hell, that was such a mess. When I edited it, I had pages and pages of notes on top of the traditional spelling and punctuation edits. Literally, I had to put additional note pages on top of the front cover. I don't even remember everything I saw wrong, but I sure do remember they couldn't count. Somehow, they used every officer three times - at the same time and all over the city."

"What? You have to be joking," Luke offered. "We know there are a bunch of misfits here, but surely they could count to three?"

"No." Marcus was very abrupt. "Are you telling me you did the edits for the first plan created after the storm?"

Sarah didn't like his tone of voice and immediately reverted to her cool detached personality, which was disappointing after such an interesting and productive time on the roof with Luke. "Yes, Sergeant Rougaroux, I am distinctly telling you that it was rife with problems of a basic nature of math, riddled with inconsistencies even about the time of simple things as roll call, and above all else, they had no conception or utilization of correct English."

Marcus leaned backwards and his attitude seemed to deflate as he turned his face away from Luke and Sarah, staring at the two large screen televisions that were tuned to news stations now with no volume. They also served as display boards for ops meetings, but during events they were typically tuned to coverage of whatever they were working (if it was a public event and not an unfolding terror situation). She immediately felt like she should apologize, but wasn't sure for what. In a more conversational voice, she leaned forward and sat on the table across from him, and asked, "Marcus, you weren't the one who wrote that plan, were you?"

He shifted in the chair and shook his head as he leaned forward towards her. "No," he said more gently, turning his head away from the news to talk to her. "No, I came to the division after that was actually passed through every single officer in the department. Some of the rank that were tight with their crews shared it, and of course it was shared again. No one ever knew who did those edits. We could tell that it wasn't someone in-house, and some of the comments were written way above what we could understand at that point, having been without food or shelter and in a deluge, trying to figure out which end was up. But officially or not, everyone saw those notes, the photocopies of those pages you attached on the front, written on little sticky notes so you could reorganize them in your order of importance… there were so many damn problems with that order. Once we all saw that, I can't tell you how many people that really wanted to stay, officers who started their careers here and wanted to retire here, the number of officers that left that first year alone was more than 250. It was as if that edit was a flag that our department was failing, that the administration had no common sense and our own leaders, if you want to call them that, didn't even possess basic book sense. Hell, even guys on the street knew you couldn't be in three places at the same time."

He gave a one-laugh noise and continued, looking over to Luke and then back to her, smiling. "Though I didn't go to college, I can write well. They brought me in after they were embarrassed by that outside consultant. By you. The administration had signed off on the plan not realizing it was a draft - apparently without reading it, or our mayor had some 'splaining to do with all those problems. You don't need to be a cop to see the things you saw. A good cop should have never included some of those errors when it was written. I was put in charge of this unit after that."

He smiled at her and nodded his head a bit, relaxing his shoulders and sitting straight in his chair again. "Knowing that was you takes the edge off a little bit. We didn't know if it was a mayor's goon making us look bad or what. It just makes a whole lot of sense knowing now it was you, how you can cut to the heart of matters so clearly without seeming to have to struggle with things. It's what makes you good at what you do, Sarah. Sorry I snapped or if it seemed like I doubted that was your work. You have no idea how many guessing games have occurred department wide to figure out who was able to see our flaws so clearly. Makes you scared that someone else outside can find our weaknesses and exploit them. Which then brings me back to this mess," as he gestured at his laptop, "and wanting a good report but not too good of a report that will expose gaps in the plan."

Sarah looked at Luke and said, "We all have things we do well and not everyone knows." Turning back to Marcus, she continued, "Thanks for letting me know what people thought of the changes. On my side, typically I parachute in, fix something, and don't necessarily know how implementation works. Here, in true habit of the city, it wasn't fixed and they brought you in to redo it, adding more work to bad efforts. I hope it helped you on the next version."

"Yes - and," he now proceeding in a comedic tone, "would you like to write this version for this event? I'd gladly turn over the computer to you," as he slid the laptop across the table to rest against her leg that was still parked on the tabletop.

She was saved from sharing her funny reply that would have clearly demonstrated what she thought of such an opportunity when the door to Jason's office was flung open. They could hear the latch and drag along the carpet, even though it all happened on the other side of the wall. The voices got louder, with Jason seemingly holding his own. The three of them waited for the exit door to slam, and for Jason to appear around the corner.

And when he did, he looked like a man that needed a drink. With that unvoiced sentiment, the first crack of thunder was heard, and it wasn't that far away from them - or the game preparations.

"Watch out, the lightening may strike right here next. I have never been so amazed that a week apparently doesn't mean a week. These Federal guys who know everything," Jason yelled while rolling his eyes and swinging his arms in large flailing motions in the air over his head, "simply everything there is to know at the EPA, knew the potential to move BioWatch could have been made for quite some time. It was discussed I think six months ago in an HSEEP planning meeting. Sarah confirmed it and they knew they had to do it. So what are they doing? Having meetings. Talking about having meetings. Complaining that they only have two days left to the game. What should they be doing? Moving the asset, damn it!"

Jason stomped off to the kitchen, poured a cup of coffee, added his powdered creamer and spilled sugar as he attempted to add two packets - causing more swearing.

Charging back over toward the threesome, who had not moved from the spots where he first approached them, but didn't make it very far as he stopped after three steps before continuing the rant. "Do you know they don't have a plan to move assets? That once they put an asset in place, it is supposed to stay there for all eternity. There is no plan to test the thing, to move the thing, to replace the thing, to fix a broken thing. They can't use the plan to do a new install because it's not new, he said. We called his boss in Washington," punctuating the location by pointing in the general direction of north, "and she agreed it's not a new unit so that installation process can't be used. Hear me clearly, I don't give a fuck about how it gets done but if it isn't done, the only people responsible are the Feds and I will make damn sure everyone knows it at this afternoon's press conference when I call them out on 'here's what we've done but you have to ask them about this part' bull shit. Team my ass."

He took a sip of the hot coffee and resumed talking from the entryway to the kitchen, still being heard as clear as a bell. "All of these different federal groups pushing their way to the table for months. They've been clamoring to take charge of shit since we went to the last championship game to see how they did it there, in case we thought that would be a good model here.

Hell, no. We've done this ten times - ten! That city had only done it twice and it's nothing like here. No one else can handle ops like this city except New York, but we'd be a lot different if we had 60,000 soldiers-at-arms ready to fight. They don't even have a football team in the actual city anymore, so they don't work the games like we do anyway. But sure, we played the Feds' game up there along with the committee members from our business community; all the staff hauled our asses up there and played along."

He proceeded to walk back to them, obviously calming down a bit as his steps were slower and his volume softer. "There were some interesting things about public relations and the social media aspects that were slightly different than our last go-around. But our guy already does all that for his city department, so actually showed them a few things on implementation where they could improve. No one comes close to mass casualty care - our parade drunk tents and makeshift hospitals after the storm are actually the model they use for big events around the country, and they tried to show us how to do the model when they didn't even realize they were using our plans to put up their tents. Marcus, you know how many groups come here to follow our special events law enforcement model - even the Feds come for large event practice."

He arrived at the table and took a chair over where Sarah was seated on the table. He took a deep breath, another sip of coffee, and looked at the three of them for a moment.

With a fake grin, he asked, "So what cheery news do you three have to share?"

Bringing him up to speed, Marcus shared what he told Sarah and Luke, and they both shared what they saw from the roof. Things were proceeding slowly - they always seemed to be behind schedule in this city - but would be worked around. The

BioWatch not being shifted yet was a significant concern only from a public relations standpoint. They all knew it was not going to help anything, but made the Feds sound good and for the most part, kept certain groups of that side of the fence out of their hair.

It was approaching lunchtime and Marcus gave some background on the drug issue to Jason, too. Sometimes, it was just nice to hear about progress being made, even if it was tangential to the operation at hand. Distractions were good for everyone on a limited dose. Last event when Jason and Sarah were together, Luke and Marcus weren't directly involved, so weren't in this room when a detour was made about Jason's house remodeling. They actually spent some time talking about crown moulding and chair rails, wall paper and color schemes. The old colonel was a pistol, but even he recognized breaks were important in a mission sometimes. Of course, she needed to remind him to eat at least once a day, and took to taking his chow plate to him and standing there - regardless of with whom he was meeting. It got to be a joke as he would plan meetings he didn't want around meal times so that Sarah could make the attendees uncomfortable and they would excuse themselves or she would pointedly remark that he needed fifteen minutes to eat. They knew how this all worked, and worked well together.

So they talked about some of the connections with Marcus' case to the uprising of violence in the city, the driving force of many young working families moving to other areas and choosing the long commute over shortened life-spans. It caused a problem for employers when there weren't enough talented workers living close enough that would take slightly lower wages; instead, companies were expected to pay higher wages so private school, commutes, and the "accustomed lifestyle" could be supported by an employee. That forced a lot of corporations to leave the area, too, which left marginal legitimate opportunity and a whole lot of time on some folks' hands, which led to resorting to whatever needed done to provide for a family and also provide a lifestyle of a different sort.

When he had left for his lunch meeting with DEA, the rest of the them went in different directions. Jason went to his Friday lunch meeting with the mayor, always a pleasant treat, Luke and Sarah were certain. How could you eat with a man like that breathing down your throat? Luke was off to the team house and then had to cross the lake to check on the kids and avatar updates he dropped off last night. In the meanwhile, Sarah was going to swing out to Dr. McPherson and then backtrack to the EOC to make sure the flexiglass was installed and ready for Luke to upload the completed software package late that night. It was only forty hours to daybreak of game day.

Chapter 33

Mike was taking his time at the little grocery store. It was more like a convenience store, sitting along the interstate as kind of an enhanced rest stop. He didn't cook anyway; right now, he had no where to get fancy stuff or a means to cook it. True, he had a converter for the car where he could plug in the little hot plate, use his pot to heat up a can of soup or even fry a hamburger patty. But whenever he did that, he needed to be stopped in an area where he wouldn't attract too much attention.

This whole week was exhilarating for him. He had traveled back from Colorado over the weekend, chain smoking the whole way south. He stopped in a quick motel to sleep briefly and then shower before he would arrive at the volleyball on Monday night. He knew he wouldn't miss the opening scramble of the league, and it was always that Monday evening every year. The owner always timed it to start two weeks after all the area's colleges were back in session, in the hopes picking up some new players. Mike liked that first night because that meant sometimes he'd have some new opportunities to find a girl for a couple of weeks. When they mixed up teams after a match was won, it allowed just enough time to ensnare one with charm, but not too much time to strain his web of deceit. Making sure he was clean-shaven (as clean as he could with a disposable razor), he had finished up at the motel quickly but still wanted to look fresh for the new candidates.

After the second match, he managed to find a girl to go take him home that first night back, but didn't want to stay too long with her. Just long enough, and was out before lunch Tuesday as she showered before heading to class, grabbing some snacks from her kitchen on his way out the door. He still had some errands to run, some supplies to gather. His trunk was very organized with the items he had collected already. While he preferred an SUV, there was no place to hide things - bigger things, like canisters and tubing for instance. He didn't want that in plain view, where it would be legal for law enforcement to then use probable cause and snag him.

Instead, he traded in his old SUV shortly after he left working for the city for a nondescript older model green sedan. He quickly realized his mistake, though, as it would get hot in the summer and the car was like an oven. Since then, he had traded two more times and was now in a gold sedan with cream leather interior. He wouldn't have chosen the leather as he'd stick to it when he would sweat, but the price on the car was good and it had low mileage. Even back then, he knew he would be driving a lot, so needed something reliable and a vehicle that would blend into the masses. And since he knew he would be preparing things over the next six to ten months when the sun would be its most harsh, he had installed the self-adhesive window tinting to the back and passenger compartment windows, but in a lighter shade so the police couldn't pull him over for the tint being too dark.

While the sedan's exterior was fastidiously clean and trunk contents were meticulously arranged, the interior of his car was disgusting. Crumbled fast food bags all over the floorboards, his two gym bags of clothing strewn over half of the back seat - it was as though he planned for people to stay away and not have a closer look inside the car. The other side of the back seat had a backpack of his toiletries, a blanket he could throw over himself as he slept in the car at rest stops, and a ball cap from his youth. No one had ever seen him wear it, but he would be able to blend in with no one noticing - it would change his appearance enough for the sorry crime cameras that only sometimes worked. He didn't wear it into any stores on the interstate, which is where he visited when he needed something. The cameras there were only for theft, not facial recognition before a crime.

During these last bits of preparation, he had been able to spend Tuesday night at an old campsite he used once before in the next state over back in a hunting area (though it was off season now), Wednesday night back along the interstate in an overnight rest stop in the middle of the swamp, and then paid to spend Thursday night at a state park tent area that was about two and a half hours south of the city. One other couple was there, bird watching or something for the week out of their popup camper. He made a little small talk so he wouldn't be remembered as rude or aloof, and as it was getting dark, he used that excuse to leave them and set up his tent, which was one of the things tucked into the trunk along the front edge of the compartment. He hunkered down on the sleeping bag that he used to separate the canisters - he only removed it now because he knew the car wouldn't be moving, so it was relatively safe to do so.

On Friday, he knew he could take his time waking up - it would be a long 48 hours, but the adrenaline would keep him motivated. Finally, people would understand that he was supposed to be running things. He knew where all of the holes were for the city planners and their weak first responders. So few of them had any military experience they couldn't come close to what he knew. He was smarter than them all. That's why his plan was focused on mass effect not mass destruction - they only trained for destruction not distractions, and didn't know how to triage that kind of situation. He knew how to cause a panic and funnel people out a certain way - his main device was considered a secondary event in order to target some of the first responders. He could get past whatever little wand-screening they established for the game and create a diversion alone, no problem. When he got people to rush like cattle, that's when the device was intended to take out the very people who didn't respect him, who considered him not good enough for managing all of the big projects. He knew where they would hang out during all of this, and that's what he'd make sure was in his crosshairs.

While he was certain the mayor would have ordered the homeless out of the plaza by their offices, he knew they couldn't restrict pedestrians in that area. People would still congregate as it was shaded by some old trees that weren't torn down with wind damage or storm water toxic mix killing them. He was lucky he wasn't here for that event, but if he was he would have shown everyone what they did wrong. He didn't understand how some people could be so naive when it came to crowd control and crime prevention. They just needed to keep those folks contained and monitored all of the time to help stop them from committing crimes. He figured it was like having a shock collar on a dog. That preventive tactic would eventually be ingrained into a mutt to behave before he got bad, and the same could be done with people living in certain areas of town where the crimes happened. He couldn't figure out why they hadn't done this yet, other than they were stupid and just hadn't thought of it.

During the drive back toward the city, he figured he would go straight to his storage unit and get the hot dog cart out and clean it up. It couldn't be too clean or it wouldn't fit in. But the umbrella needed to be dust free as did the top of the service area - if the flat surface was greasy or had old ketchup or mustard stains, he didn't mind that. When he was at his buddy's ski lodge, he had made a really nice identification card that matched the last event's credentialing process. He figured he would be able to come in from the back side, toward the homeless mission that had to be overflowing with displaced "campers" from the underpasses and the plaza, hang out in that neighborhood overnight with his cart draped in a blanket and a tied-down blue tarp just like the other homeless folks.

There was a spot back in the rear of a movie company stage he considered that was more private so he didn't have to spend any more time than he had to with those people. It wasn't far down from his storage unit along the river. He could take the back brick service road for most of the way from the storage unit and it would just look like another transient moving along his wayward path. One of the good things about all the crime was the fact that people now disengaged, turned a blind-eye toward seeing strange things. No one wanted involved. Clearly, they didn't want to be a witness to things that could be pulled into court. From what he heard in the news anyway, the mayor wasn't funding the court system correctly and the public defenders were only picking up small cases that could be dispensed quickly - murders and violent offenders were being released back to the street since they couldn't get a speedy trial. Pathetic the judges here were releasing criminals in exchange for votes in the next election, targeting the population that was left in the city to actually vote. Let their children and fathers and cousins and sisters out and you could be guaranteed their vote, even if you needed to give them a little jitney money to get them to the poles.

The couple of people camped back in the small wooded lot behind the converted warehouse-now-movie-lot had been there for a while. He didn't check on it recently as that may have drawn suspicion. He knew it was there, and since it was out of sight the mayor left it alone. The path in the grass to the tree line on the right side of the overgrown patch was protected a little further back by a riverfront dilapidated warehouse. Probably a banana facility at one time, since it was such a big fruit import town from Honduras. See, more people coming in to work from these other places; he would help fix that, too, when he ran the security group, making sure only the right people got the jobs here.

The bums on the lot didn't try to break into the building and instead stayed in the open air with their makeshift tents and had a little enclave where they knew one another. But sometimes people came and went, moving around as they were passing through the area. He had a story prepared about how he was pushed out from the underpass and would only be there a night or two until he could go back - if anyone talked to him at all. He wouldn't make his camp right next to them, so he wouldn't cause suspicion, but would go a little ways off and still try to hide himself in the tall weeds and crazy bushes, hoping he wasn't allergic to anything growing there.

He arrived at his storage unit, prepaid a year in advance to get a discount (and he used that saved cash to help the kid at the counter not require the usual license and things for entering his true name in the system). It still had two months left in the annual agreement, so no one would have a flag raised about a renewal just yet - a renewal with a notice sent to a fictions person at a false address. The facility he chose was just off the river near the power substation and about a mile and a half from the bum camp. It was also a few blocks from a grocery store, which is where he'd put his car that night - across the street by the bar right there, so it wouldn't attract attention out in the lot. Driving up to his ten by ten unit, he positioned the trunk right by the rollaway door so he would reduce the likelihood of anyone seeing what he was taking out of his trunk.

Rolling open and pushing up the bright orange storage door, he was able to lift the canisters easily as well as a few boxes and place them right inside the door, along the wall that was shielded by his vehicle. He had the hot dog cart in the back under an old dark-green blanket, so it wouldn't reflect light ricocheting off passing cars and be seen by anyone on the street. He had wanted a unit closer to the back side of the property that was closer to the river, but this had been the only ground floor one available - in any size. It had less camera security than the back, too, as in theory the kid at the office could look out the window and along the front of this block of units. That suited his purposes well. When he paid for the rental last March, he realized that an explosion from here could hit the nearby substation (since it was next to the end unit in the direction of it) and any passersby could be struck if he packed it forcefully enough to blow out into the street, a main artery of the city. That would cause a lot of confusion, both with traffic and power outages.

Once the trunk was unloaded from its contents, he reversed the car to block the doorway and opened the back driver's side door, like he was getting out more stuff. He would eventually clean out the car of his clothes, the trash that seemed to be accumulating, and wash it up the street, then wipe it down like he was doing a normal interior spring cleaning when in fact he would be using a chemical that would help disintegrate any prints after the guys at the car wash had done the full interior. He would do that later; for now, he needed to arrange the unit. He would sleep there tonight, in the locker, but not have a lot of his belongings left inside. Those would go back into the trunk after he had everything spotless, including the trunk.

Removing the blanket on the cart, he saw the umbrella was in good shape. Well not good, that would be conspicuous - but appropriate for this mission. The red and yellow wedges were a bit faded, one small hole near the edge of the white piping, the pole not too shiny and it actually looked a little greasy. That was fine. The cart itself was also fine; he did take a towel and gently wave it around the general area of the top panel so some light dust and dark green blanket fuzzier would blow away. The interior compartments for hot dogs were clean - he'd get a few gallons of water and condiments now before heading down river toward his deployment area, then getting the hot dogs tomorrow.

When he put the cart in here, he had also taken the time to split the hosing that connected to the propane that would cook the hotdogs and warm the buns. That left him space underneath where there was usually a second and third backup tanks so the vendor could cook all night for the drunk people coming down the street from the bars. He didn't care for the food to stay warm longer than it took him to get into position, so those spaces were for the canisters that would feed the chemicals up to the ninth floor EOC where the old gang would be working. He paid one of the janitors last month to go to the roof and drop the tubing down the side of the building along the gutter and a few days later, he went on the ninth floor and took the end into the window by the dais with the two large screen televisions, where some people would be gathered to watch the game - they always did that. No one really used them for operations and news.

He opened the doors to the undercarriage of the cart, and loaded the canisters inside, very carefully wedging them together so there was no rattling around. The road hazards from bricks and potholes and incomplete sidewalks would make him sweat the whole way to bum camp, which suited his purposes just fine. Connecting the tubing he had previously trimmed to the right lengths, he also wound the spare coil in the smaller compartment behind the push-bar, so he could unwind it quickly to connect to the tubing hanging from the EOC windows. The space in this was skinny, meant for money drops or something, so he could use the concealed latch and once it was fastened, not open it again until he was ready to deploy.

There was still space in the cart for the extra food that these vendors were supposed to have. Health permits required a separate compartment from the propane fuel. Into this area, he put his change of clothes, consisting of one of his old homeland security uniform shirts. He would wear the same shoes and pants, but did need a lightweight jacket and the ball cap to get into the game area. The timer for the dispersion of the canisters was also in this other small compartment, as if the flimsy aluminum wall between the two sides would save him if the clock sparked and set off the binary munitions, but that never occurred to him - only prepping everything he needed in one spot. It also left room for his sleeping back for the next night - which he would leave in the weeds. One of the bums could take it. Once all his supplies were positioned inside the cart, he pulled it to the front right of the space, push-bar side to the doorway, and put the blanket over it. The umbrella pole stuck out a bit past the edge of the handle, so he had to wheel the whole thing in a little deeper than he originally staged.

He took the boxes from the back wall and set them along the same wall as the cart, the one closest to the substation. Basically old mortar configurations and some military grade explosives he got from his buddies, he intended to set this timer and blow out the back walls of his unit and the neighboring one, propelling all the crap into the power substation. The wires would be snapped or melted from the blow, so he didn't need to include additional projectiles. The left side remained open, which is where he laid his sleeping back, brought the clothes out from the back of the car and restored his duffles and moved the backpack from the backseat in the unit, too. Off to clean the car at the car detail place down the road, fill it with gas in case he needed a full tank, and get some dinner someplace nearby before he'd go back and sneak a long nap in the unit before dawn.

Chapter 34

It hadn't occurred to Mike to check the weather forecast. As he drove away from the storage facility to clean his car, a crack of thunder came from behind him, down river. He did the car wash anyway, knowing it was going to sit a few days and get pollen all over it. It needed to be as clean as possible, not having been washed in five days already. He gave the guys an extra tip for doing the insides thoroughly while he crossed the street to grab a drink at the cigar bar while they worked. It was all coming together in his mind.

Moving the car down near the grocery store, he dodged some rain drops and looked for a bite to eat just a few blocks from the place he wanted to leave the car for the night. It was still too light to just wander back and hang out in the storage facility. He ate local fare for lunch at the nearby dive and had a few drinks at the bar. When families started showing up for dinner, he migrated to the next bar, relaxing and getting mentally deep into the details of his cover plan. From the early evening hours past dusk, he sat at a tall boy table, sipping beer after beer and watching the sports channel updates and all the local coverage for the game just one full day and another half away.

He was lucky he stopped at the dive joint first because two detectives assigned by Alex and Sibyl to sweep a few local establishments where the old members of his team used to visit had gone to his current location. None of the old guard were around anymore, but between all of the current members working on this event, they created a list and set teams to go check every location. The two officers literally missed him by twenty minutes at this bar, and the dive wasn't on their list so they hadn't bothered to stop there. He came so very close to being picked up without even knowing it. The cops would periodically go into bars looking for someone and then leave without asking the bartenders to keep a lookout - they wanted to keep undue attention away from the big game; this time it also coupled with sometimes they were just lazy when hitting a checklist. And with the rain, it made the job even less pleasurable. It was like a needle in a haystack, looking for an alcoholic in that city.

Happily ignorant, Mike moved his car two more blocks down the street and went in the grocery for a snack to take into the unit. He also used the bathroom, though had a hospital urinal container to use overnight if he woke up. He figured he'd get a pretty good night sleep, actually, since no one knew he was there. The place was staffed only twelve hours a day, but you could use your code to go in and out whenever you wanted. He'd go in the pedestrian gate with his access code, wait a bit and leave again (using the code to reopen the gate). He'd walk around the back and hop the fence, avoiding the camera angles and with assistance from the bad weather fogging up the camera lenses. But again, the kid told him they only have those to look at tapes if something's missing, not to monitor all day and night. He got back in his unit with the lock hanging in the closed but not latched position, slid the door down from the inside and got some sleep.

The people on the other side of this event did not get sleep, however. From the BioWatch having problem after problem getting into the arena and then up into the rafters, everything from safety harnesses for workers to delays when installing the units, you'd have thought the world revolved around those

Federal staffers. Mandatory breaks every two and a half hours, they also didn't work more than eight hours, which meant they stopped at seven to be raised in the crane, then unharnessed, then do their checklist and wait until the clock struck precisely to hand over the list to the next one to get harnessed up and down to work. It was maddening and nothing could be done to speed the process. Sarah suggested at one point she go down to the stadium herself and duct tape the stupid thing to the beam. Luke thought maybe one of the guys that changes the lightbulbs could help. No, this is a *Federal job* and *we know what we're doing,* though the local team saw no progress whatsoever. Around two am on Saturday, Sarah and Luke had enough and left, with him texting Jason there was still no update on the Fed side of the project.

The rain helped everyone sleep that night, but it also slowed the workers' progress into Saturday morning. The last few days of a normal event were already stressful; adding the threat on top of this timetable and that they knew for whom they were searching and just couldn't find the bastard did not make anyone more comfortable. The house team continued to work with Marcus on better strategies for creating that defensive netting. Rae suggested some adjustments for the cameras due to the inclimate weather, as the depth of the feeds wouldn't be as accurate if the rain didn't give way for a significant amount of time. It involved a little higher expense, but her film company defrayed some of the cost for the flexible lens that worked so well in this area - they were on location and they would just replace them through L.A. later. She also pointed out that everyone would be cast in an angelic aura, since the humidity and heat with the actual precipitation formed an ongoing mask that would distort the images somewhat. None of this could be corrected in Herman's algorithms; she would just have to pay extra attention to what was fed through the review portal and hope a blurry image of the right guy didn't get thrown into the wrong bucket.

Alex and Sibyl were actually elated that the rain continued. Well, Alex was darn near ecstatic and everyone could tell. They couldn't really figure out what Sibyl felt but she seemed more animated and less stressed now that the rain continued for nearly 20 hours straight. She was miserable in those first hours of Friday afternoon when it had begun, more so than usual. But as it continued, her countenance was engaging and they all took that as a positive sign. She was still in the mood today, and would help Rae review footage coming into the cameras starting this afternoon as they worked in six hour shifts until game time when they would both watch the monitors together. They were starting now in case their man was picked up by the system that still had new components coming online, and they'd continue to build this image net until Sunday morning. No one expected an early capture to be handed to them, but it made for good practice of the game-day scenarios and watching how the images would scroll to them from Herman's elaborate system.

Betty and Peter had contributed significantly in the earlier part of the project, both on the layout of the detection zones as well as access through quiet channels to surrounding buildings for response teams to be staged in case the attack occurred. Now that it was only one day before the game, the couple brought some food and snacks around lunchtime to the house in the spirit of camaraderie. They had bonded with this group of people that they'd never met before, and it was likely with whom they'd never work again. It was amazing to see from their private sector lives how the hard work was accomplished on the government sector side - and the dichotomies of the workers versus the political process was not lost on either of them. While Marcus had jokingly offered tickets to their family for the game, they decided to go to his mother's house, which was well away from the hot zone and they could easily have an extended stay should anything happen - and their three adorable kids were delighted with a family overnight outing at MeMaw and PapPap's house.

Tam was delighted, too, but for very different reasons. Very much like the Wicked Witch of the West, many chemical weapons agents were reduced in power with the addition of water. Not all of them, but it made most of them extremely diluted and some of them were even rendered inactive. Part of this was simple organic chemistry, with the addition of copious amounts of water (a base) to any acid (the chemical agent), it was possible to create a dilute substance so that the "parts per million" sample was so low that it would be nearly undetectable except to the most susceptible respiratory sufferers. There were two options that could increase the volatility - one by the water splitting into the hydrogen as an acid and the other as it reacted with water. There was good news here, too, and Tam was trying to convey what he meant by even this bad news was good news. The house team wasn't following what he was saying and kept telling him to slow down, explain using a "weapons for dummies" version for them.

He finally was able to convey that of the two "bad news" choices, the first one was very low on the probability list that this suspect could use. The components to create the chemical were not necessarily rare, but getting them to combine, to actually bind in a quasi-permanent fashion and create a weapon was extremely technical given all of the variables and precise measurements that needed to be performed successfully in a very controlled environment. From the description of the suspect, there was very little chance he could accomplish this sort of advanced procedure. And there was no evidence he had been in communications with anyone that could be hired to do it on his behalf - on the comms side or from the finance side.

The second piece of the bad news made no sense whatsoever to any of them, even when the house crew got the next part of the "weapons for dummies" lecture. But what they managed to understand was there was already high humidity in the air in addition to the rain drops. The humidity was a mist they couldn't see or necessarily feel, as they could only feel the rain drops. Because it had been raining for almost a day straight, the humidity in the air was very high. The air was "heavy." None of them were meteorologists but they all understood this from living in the city. Tam explained that when the chemical weapon was released - likely in the form of an aerosol for greatest dispersion in at crowd - dry days were bad as the air was light and could carry it further. However, when humidity was high, the aerosol droplets would cling to that invisible mist and smaller droplets would collect together and fall to the ground.

Sibyl, ever the devil's advocate, immediately questioned his logic by directly challenging him on the increased concentration of the weapon descending and hitting people as it fell. From nursing school, she knew that there were a variety of ways the body would "take in" agents - inhaling (which was the anticipated route when the crowd would breath it into their lungs), absorption (when the agent soaked through skin), ingestion (not as likely as they wouldn't be *eating* the raindrops in any significant number) and sometimes even by injection (though that would be a targeted attempt at a single person's life - with no application in this scenario).

Glad for the engagement and now feeling that he was finally able to make a contribution with the team able to understand why he was there, he reminded Sibyl that the invisible mist droplets were water - the primary dilution material for any solution. There was much more rain than agent. The natural mist would say double in size for purposes of the discussion (though really not even that much) and then dilute the droplets to an impractical size for inhalation. Yet they wouldn't so big as, say, thunderstorm drops to soak through attendee clothing AND sit on their skin for an extended period of time for absorption purposes. With all of the food and alcohol vendors on site, it was impractical he could contaminate any item for significant ingestion mechanism use. And injection was pretty much just for the movies - or for "targeted killings" (assassinations) completed by intelligence officers.

With this explanation, the team members were much more appreciative of Tam's presence. They previously figured they'd just need him when the substance was released into the air, for logistics of dispersion and other scientific mumbo-jumbo. But now, they all had a sense of relief and figured it mightn't even hurt to ask Marie LaVeau for intercession and continued rainfall. Who cared if the city streets flooded because the pumps couldn't evacuate more than a half-inch of water and hour through the brand new fancy insufficient pumping system the mayor installed? Cops were naturally a skeptical bunch, but even the well-seasoned Alex was grinning ear-to-ear that there was scientific proof that backed the blue line theory of "rain keeps a lot of problems away." No one yet considered what would happen when all of the chemicals were washed down the drain, into the water system and pumped into the river and lake. They were too focused on people casualties, but the environment would be okay, too, since dilution would be extreme even for the component that could react with water in the amount that could feasibly be released the next day.

It was generally a good news kind of day, and Marcus left for his last DEA meeting before tomorrow's bust with this bit of progress. He would take all that he could get. He called Sarah to relay it to her as he sped toward the federal building, and she in turn shared with Luke as they were together at the stadium again overseeing the various stages of completion for the game. It was approaching dinner time, and they went full-bore on duty starting 24 hours before the event. Even though the two of them initially weren't happy about the rain, they now were very hopeful it would continue.

The Hazmat team was not as cheerful as they had to stand out in it while doing inspections of all of the archways and clearing the various pedestrian pathways in the potential hot zone. Depending on the colors of their rain gear, the team looked like a damn fruit salad, thought Chad. Three looked like waddling bananas as they carried the large scanners under their jackets. The two fishermen and one fisherwoman of the group had on their green waders and topcoats, so they more resembled avocados. One big guy had a red suit - no idea where he got that - but appeared like an apple, and there was even an orange (from a distance, there was no indication male or female, but Chad knew the female firefighter), who was used to hunting up in Canada in her florescent well-lined weatherproof jumpsuit. As team leader, Chad had elected to stay in the command vehicle and enter the data to the laptop as the team read the numbers back on the radio, so they didn't get more equipment wet than necessary.

Other teams were running their last minute preparations, too. The Coast Guard had their units out on the river, already doing the necessary scans for various items of concern (not only other vessels and suspicious packages, but the routine for the city such as a floating body or other contraband that would make for bad press). The four different federal and state teams at the airport had been in full-event mode for three days, but still had through tomorrow morning to keep at top form; then they'd have a bit of a break through the game. If anything suspicious had occurred, they'd go to highest alert and intensify screening of passengers in case a suspect or accomplice tried to escape their way. As for law enforcement, regardless of their division, they were pretty much operating the same way as they did for every large event in the city, but with the understanding there was more visibility to top-brass than usual.

From this point forward, with 24 hours until kickoff, there was no rest for the weary.

Chapter 35

Mike got a good night's sleep and was nearly giddy to start the next to last phase of his plan, as he was finally so close to being recognized as the real leader around here. He woke up and used only a small candle to provide light inside the unit so that no unnecessary light could filter out underneath the rolling door, just as added precaution. It was just before the front desk person would arrive, so he made sure he finished changing and opened the rolling door before that staff member arrived. He knew that the gates wouldn't open from this side unless the code on the outside had been used to enter. He planned on circumventing this by exiting with his tarped-up cart after a vehicle entered. Not that the rental (or his particular gate code) was linked to his actual name, but maybe it would slow them down on the timing of events - if anyone was actually checking details like that before the game. *Probably not, since they were all more lazy than he was and it was unlikely that anyone would think of such important details since he didn't work there anymore,* he thought.

The unit now completely opened, he lifted the edge of the tarp to secure the sleeping bag in the one compartment as well as the shirt in which he would sleep again tonight. Also shoved in there was the old green blanket that had served as a cloak for the car, but tonight would serve as an awning under which he would sleep next to the cart. Obviously it was still raining, which would make the tarp seem necessary to move stuff rather than conceal whatever he was rolling down the street. So many people in these poorer areas didn't have a way to get around, and moved by car or cart or jitney. It wouldn't seem that out of the ordinary for someone in a rain suit to be pushing a tarp-covered bunch of supplies down the street.

He wasn't necessarily in a rush to get started for his next long day in the rain, but he needed to be prepared to move decisively when a car came through that gate. Alternatively, he would wave at the office staff, hoping that they'd receive the message to open the thing from inside. With the rain like it was, coming down in sheets, he hoped they would just go ahead and do that so he wouldn't have to go inside, in the clear view of cameras and his rolling destruction visible through the window. The rain made people move slower today, not anxious to leave the dry house and run errands.

But he wasn't disappointed, and not too long after he stood there with the door partially lowered to keep any rain from blowing on the explosives placed along the side wall behind the cart, there was a large box truck coming into the property. Unfortunately, as he started to roll his cart out of the spot, the truck nearly blocked him into the unit. The truck was apparently going to load all of their belongings in or out of a unit three spots down from his. Debating if he should ask them to not block his path while snarling silently that the man driving past didn't see that he had the door open to leave, he opted to wait and see what the two people climbing out of the truck had to say.

The bulky man approached to pass him and nearly didn't speak. Merely nodding as he walked by, he muttered something like "just a minute" and continued to where the other passenger had started to unlock their storage unit. Mike thought he'd just wait where he was, as the truck blocked any blowing rain and he could always say - if the man spoke on the way back - his friend hadn't called that he was on his way yet.

That minute turned into two hours. He hadn't eaten any of the snacks or had more than a half a serving of juice from the small bottles he bought yesterday, so he wasn't needing to go to the restroom yet. Always planning ahead, he knew that's what got him farther than any of his buddies. That might not be how the friends or former coworkers perceived his dubious achievements or dubious acclaims, but it never crossed Mike's mind that anyone would actually doubt him. By the time he ended the self-serving *I am wonderful* speech in his head, the guys were climbing back into the cab of the big truck and preparing to back out of the gate. He pulled out the cart as they backed past the opening, locked his unit, and began his soggy plod toward bum land.

As the rain kept falling, the truck wasn't reversing quickly since the side mirrors were splattered with raindrops. It moved slowly enough for appearances that Mike was part of their group and it was maybe something they couldn't get into the truck while in the storage area. He was able to walk at a normal pace out of the gate and walk for one block on the main road towards downtown, appearing to go to his vehicle from the viewpoint of the storage facility office. Once at the end of this short block, he turned back the seemingly dead-end road toward the river and train tracks.

But those tracks had a fence, and the fence was placed just deep enough for a small car to drive between it and the houses' sides, so that these deceptive dead end roadways had a loop around. People that lived in the few homes on either side of each of these dead end streets could use the loop so they didn't have to back out into busy lanes of traffic on one of the most heavily used commercial throughways in the city. It made sense, even if they weren't official loops. It still served his purpose fine.

And while the residents along here weren't the finest of citizens in the city, they tended to pay attention but not say anything when strange things occurred - like a man walking a tarped cart down the back street. If something happened and needed to be said, they generally communicated just to the neighbors, not inviting law enforcement into the area unless absolutely needed. No one bothered anyone else, and there was no reason to bring people snooping unless something very serious was occurring. A man and a cart wasn't an issue, but it was obviously interesting to them as he noted some sheets-into-curtain window coverings being pulled back as he passed.

He made certain to walk slowly, as if without purpose, looking neither left nor right. It was tough enough on this dirt and gravel and shell pitted road. The next twenty-four hours of rain had certainly made puddles in the potholes along the tire paths. His wheels were just wide enough to catch the inside edge of each one, so it took some strength to keep the cart upright and not sweating too much that the canisters could be shifting. A few times, he had to really wrestle with the cart, when the water hid deep sharp drops into potholes and the cart threatened to fall on its side. Slow and purposeful, he continued down river.

A few areas in the remaining residential section on this street didn't have the loops, so he went back up to the main road for a block, returning promptly back to the shadowy path. He figured with the patrols of the rail lines that there wouldn't be cameras. In his mind, Fed Transportation Officers never considered someone could jump the fence to mess with the port's storage yard for rail cars and river shipments. It was a wrong guess, but with the weather as it was, the cameras couldn't get an image of anything but the big blue cart and the hunched over figure in a loose poncho with dark colored running pants that were soaked the whole way through.

Once he reached the area where the trucks came through to get the full cargo containers, a block prior he switched his route to two blocks away from the river. Not wanting to walk a long distance on a heavily trafficked path, he chose one that though a better residential section had a road that mirrored the back paths along the tracks. Continuing just as he had earlier, he moved closer to the bum camp. He realized about ten blocks before reaching it that he didn't want to hang out there already, it being what he estimated was about midday but he couldn't really tell and didn't want to get his phone wet by looking at it in this rain that just wouldn't stop. He tried to peak into the coffee shop at a corner, but the person sitting at the table on the other side of the window pulled back and made a shoo-ing motion with her paper. He continued around the corner and sat on a bench in a run down playground for a while. It wasn't a busy area, so no one would really notice. It probably wasn't the first time someone rough-looking was resting for a spell. He just proceeded to review the plan for the next 27 hours in his mind. After an extended stay in varying degrees of light to moderate rainfall, he moved on to the bum camp.

Still in the same location as he had seen a year earlier, as he crossed the roadway after backtracking a few blocks and continuing down the back path in this area, he saw the make-shift shanties constructed for longer-term temporary housing by the homeless group. Surprisingly water tight from a distance, the "roofs" were evenly hung with correct slopes in the direction of the most forceful and frequent winds. They were all nearly the same size, too, though not of the same construction on the top layers. Some were clear, others white, an occasional blue tarp outlined the tops of each one.

They weren't very high, either - these rooms were not made for standing and having a cocktail party. He would be surprised if anyone could stand upright in any of the tents, for even the upper end of the slope wasn't quite to standing height. It was likely purposeful, so that it wouldn't draw attention to them from view of the main street. When the grasses and bushes were tall, the roof could be raised; when it wasn't growing season for weeds and everything else, they were lower.

The back walls were all aligned, too, straight along an invisible border that did have an occasional tree or two nearby. Correctly constructed again, the back wall lip was at least six inches under the roofline, just like would be built on the eave of a real house. These rear walls were made from longer pieces of plastic, so not as uniform as each roof in size, indicating it may be a communal wall. He didn't care how the insides were constructed as he didn't plan on getting that close. The only reason he noticed at all was he was evaluating how they'd perceive him and his cart, and he worried a little that they'd see him as the transient he was for the next two days.

He was pretty certain they wouldn't say anything to anyone, like cops or social workers or any of the groups that tried to feed the homeless. He doubted those groups even knew of this enclave. He looked at the rest of the block in which he walked as he approached the structures, to see if there would be anywhere else he could make camp that night, and there really didn't seem to be an area. The left had a loading dock with open parking in front, which extended to an open parking lot that looked like an old slab of a former building. That area had equipment stored there, some of which looked like it had been parked a while and others that looked like they were used during the week. As it was a party weekend for the city, he wasn't worried about any of it moving now, but there would be cameras probably. He didn't want to bring anyone out here that he'd have to handle before he completed his mission.

Along the right side of the rough road was chained off parking for the old big redbrick warehouse that was closer to the river. No way to get in there with his cart unless he cut a chain, and he didn't bring bolt cutters as that wasn't part of the plan. Realizing he needed to go with his first thought, though it left him closer to passersby on the main thoroughfare, he would pass the tents and go to the opposite end of the grassy lot, still close to this truck access road and hopefully not get the cart stuck in the mud.

As came to the end tree and large bush, he listened for activity in the tents. He heard none, but by now these bums would have learned to be quiet and stay out of sight. No one liked a bum. They all chose to live this way and not get real jobs or have real families. They probably all slept around with whatever homeless women stumbled into the bum camps. He liked a good lay but couldn't even imagine the thought of taking a homeless bum. They couldn't have self-respect, living like this on purpose. There was no honor in being a bum, and the most important thing a man could have was honor and a respectable job.

Passing the tents and coming to the end of the lot, he also noticed that the old tall grass from last fall was severely matted with the recent rains. There wasn't much brush on this side of the lot, either - not even a good small bush. Back about a block, he knew there were some from which he could break a good number of branches, growing on the side of the loading dock around the building. Knowing there wasn't much else to do, he slowly moved the cart back to that area, and left it at the corner of the road of the bum camp so he could see it, but not have it visible from the main road. He hoped people just thought he was the caretaker or something if they drove by and saw him hacking down the branches.

It took him longer than he thought - the brush was full of water and therefore not very brittle to break. He didn't have a knife on him as he didn't want stopped at the entrance tomorrow. He did what he could and then walked back to the cart, rolled back to the lot, and proceeded to use the dark green blanket as a lean-to on the cart, with the green toward the road and hiding most of his blue tarp-covered cart, laying the branches against the blanket to break up the solid square pattern. Hopefully cars were driving fast enough they wouldn't notice too much. And from the bridge, with the onramp that could see as it twisted into the sky, he didn't care if they saw blue tarp-scraps as they could be seen everywhere. The other blue tarps could be seen, anyway.

He crawled into his lean-to and opened the door on the smaller space that held his sleeping shirt (as opposed to his hot dog vendor shirt that he wore at the moment), and before pulling out the shirt and sleeping bag, he removed the poncho he wore and laid it wet side down to make a barrier against the mud. It was pretty solid ground and had no branches (or needles) to poke through. He made sure to remove his shoes and while keeping them dry in the shelter, he kept them off the inverted poncho, making sure the maximum dry area could be used for sleeping. Quickly changing and storing the hot dog shirt - it needed to be a little stinky anyway as those vendors were never really clean - he got into the fairly clean t-shirt and a pair of dry shorts. The pants were hung across the small compartment doors, though in this weather he didn't expect them to dry. He just didn't want to wear them.

Pulling his phone out of the same small space that held the clothing, he looked to the larger compartment and checked the canisters. They were secure and the hose connections were still in place for quick assembly tomorrow afternoon. There were two stores on the way to his selection spot by city hall, so he'd get the hot dogs tomorrow and not worry about storing them overnight. If one grocery didn't have them (he'd hit the cheaper store first), the second shop certainly would - it was near tailgate parties so they would be loaded up on all the traditional food. The buns and condiments were on the cart from yesterday's snack run. He wanted fresh meat, though. After all, when he ate this hotdog and all the fixings right before showtime, it would be the best meal he would have tasted in a long time.

While he still had some daylight and a moment of dryness, he also checked the detonator and remote timer mechanisms, that they didn't get jarred about too much on the walk to the bum camp. He had wrapped them in the sleeping bag, and they were fine. Replacing those but leaving the sleeping bag out, he then removed the baggie that held his extra AA batteries as well as a little charging box for his cell phone. There had been one girl at the city that came to work with them out of nowhere, and she used it and showed off to everyone. He thought she was a know-it-all. He tried to sleep with her and she wouldn't. He tried to get her drunk and she didn't. She had answers for everything, and it made him mad. Her answer for the power outage was to use this little device to keep her phone powered up - everyone loved it and she let anyone borrow it when she was finished. He just never gave it back.

He finished out his last day as a nobody by surfing the internet on this disposable phone. No SIM chip, no tracking to him, he was free to roam the universe and get ready for greatness to come to him again. And he eventually fell asleep on that note, with no one from the bum camp disturbing him. The rain kept falling and made a good barrier to the traffic that continued throughout the night and the rain was a greater force than the cars.

When he woke, it was to silence. The rain had indeed stopped for a bit. He peaked outside the lean-to and noticed a woman entering one of the other shelters across the lot. She looked at him, and then went into the "doorway" with no comment. He preferred that. After using his portable urinal, he finished getting dressed. He would just dump it out on the walk up to the main drag and throw it away two blocks down at the grocery store.

Now in his sales clothes and the jacket overtop, but with the homeland security top underneath both of those, he would be ready to go as soon as he broke camp. He unfastened the green blanket from the blue tarp once all the compartments were secure again, and lowered it to the ground over the sleeping bag. Not that he was keeping it dry, but the branches and blanket would help it blend in more to the surroundings. He did make sure to take the poncho, as looking at the sky it was only a matter of time before needing it again.

Making his way to the street, dumping the urinal waste on the side of the dead end away from any prying eyes of the bums, he slowly proceeded to head to the first of the two grocery stores on his path to city hall. In the garbage dumpsters at the back corner of the store, he threw in the urinal wrapped in his other clothes that he didn't want to leave with the cart. From there, he had to consciously make himself count to two before taking each step or he would walk too fast. He couldn't just hang out too early at city hall in his hot dog selling spot. That would be awkward. He was wearing his ball cap as the sun was coming out a little, making it an unsavory muggy morning.

He wore his old ball cap when he went in the store to buy the hot dogs (and a coffee for himself). Upon exiting the store, he unrolled the blue tarp from the cart, put the hotdogs in the two gallons of water he emptied into the cooking bin while still in the storage unit, and after replacing the tarp, turned toward city hall. He made sure it took him over an an hour to get there. He could look like he was messing with the propane or checking on them cooking, or whatever vendors do while they just stand there.

His location was a block outside of the hot zone. He couldn't believe his luck, and as he approached the area where there were more police, he took the blue tarp off the cart's side but left it on top, though now held in place with the red and yellow umbrella. Every cop knew these hot dog carts and no one would think it strange a night-time vendor was taking advantage of a bit of day-time action. He hung his old-style vendor credentials around his neck, so that they swung with every step. But no cops came close enough to check the date or style - the just looked right past him at every corner.

He managed to almost get in his position before the rain started again. Quickly putting his umbrella into place, he actually had the idea to put the blue tarp as a backdrop to keep the rain off of him as he stood close to the wall of the building, tucking his old ball cap in the back of his pants so he didn't forget it when he abandoned the cart later. It would also then be a visual barrier to the tubing that was there, just as he paid for it to be. He wouldn't connect until he was ready to go to the game, but there were only three tubes to connect, including the one to the timer/detonator device.

Turning on the propane for the water to boil and being sufficiently dry from the rain now rabidly falling again, he started to unwrap the hot dogs and set up his little business distraction. He even had the sign ready to display when he had to go to the arena that read "Gone for more supplies" to discourage people from coming over and disturbing the cart after he left. He only needed ten minutes for the timer to activate the binary mixture (which started after five minutes, enough time for him to get away if there was a leak) and the small compressor to get the gas to the top floor, where all of the key city officials should be in the EOC as they watched the kickoff.

Chapter 36

Marcus figured that he was able to be with the team members at the house for a few hours before he stopped at the EOC that was nearby and then would make his way to roll call for the take-down. He was going to avoid the game and traffic of the inner city as much as he could. Tensions had been high for the past week, and he needed to focus his remaining energies on staying alive tonight during this bust rather than traffic or loitering tourists.

Upon entering the team's home away from home, it was very quiet as the they had even turned off the background music that had been playing for the last four to five days. The selections had covered a wide range, and everyone took turns picking the satellite station. It wasn't even predictable who would pick the heavy metal versus pop or sometimes the oldies; it all had varied depending on where they were in problem-solving at the time. There were no regular television screens as there were in the EOC, because they had visual components to their projects and needed to focus on their computer screens. Anyway, all of their information would come from a direct line back at Command Desk or through what they generated themselves.

He liked this house being a work center away from distractions. And, the location of the new EOC was a good idea, away from the real-EOC-turned-stage that would be crawling with media staff and just generally was way too close should an incident go down at the game. An area command that proximal to suspected activity was one thing, but the location of main operational support coordination should not be susceptible to high-value targets. That location decision was made by the mayor, so he could call the guys down in a display of power or pop-in to show-off. The choice to go operational elsewhere was a wise one made by Jason. Marcus wasn't certain how he pulled it off with the mayor. In fact, he wasn't even certain the mayor knew.

Rae and Sibyl were both at the id screens, bonded in silent intensity to one another and their objective. Herman had set up dual control of the panels, so they weren't locked into one being the driver and the other having frustrations mount for a turn to zoom or scan through images being sent by the algorithm for further review. It was interesting that they didn't pull someone in that knew Mike to help identification here, but the team also had two facts: no one was sure who was really a friend of the guy and this was not the likely way they'd find him. Trained visual specialists would look at the details, movements, bone structure and not the pre-familiarized image of Mike from working with him on prior occasions, so it was actually a smarter plan to have Rae and Sibyl performing this critical task.

Sarah would be down at the event. Before Betty and Peter left yesterday, they helped create a two-pronged prioritization of the entrance locations and where Sarah might be most likely to see him. Luke would be stationed at the other high-value entrance. There was a third way of the eight that he could be likely to enter, but they'd just have to hope the officers at that gate could delay a suspect that matched the description and then the team would handle confirmation through a smart phone picture and run it through Herman's software back at the house for a fifteen second confirmation in addition to dispatching Sarah and Luke to that location.

Alex wasn't around, but was down at the site doing some undercover wandering. None of the team liked that he offered to go inside in case the event did get to the point where extraction was necessary but in his words, "What the hell, I've lived a long life and going down in a few breaths by suffocating is sure better than going through another storm or being shot and left to die on a scene." He, just like Sarah and Luke, had a comms earpiece and an attached small microphone that Luke produced for them to use in the field to talk back to the house. They were encrypted, discrete, and off the radar of anyone trying to poach the operation - including Feds or state personnel that forced their way into nearly every component.

The new buddy, Tam, was a Fed that they liked - even if took a little bit of time to warm up to the scientist. They really appreciated his news about the rain being helpful, and that's what sealed the deal for the team that he was a welcome member of their gang. This actually turned out to be a well-balanced group, all things considered. Marcus stopped into his room, where he had set up the receptor technology from the behemoth corporation that provided the sniffers. He also had a meteorological workstation from NOAA and another regular-looking laptop for plume modeling. Marcus found it amusing that the most boring part of the setup was the most critical (this nondescript off-the-shelf laptop) should the chemicals deploy on the exterior of the arena or inside the stadium.

Before he headed to the EOC where Sarah and Luke were getting ready to go to the event site, he popped his head into Herman's domain on the second floor. It was the entire second floor - established in similar fashion to the EOC where he was headed - tactics on one level and the artificial intelligence one story above. Herman had a few holes knocked into walls so that he could run wires more easily and safely. Marcus wasn't sure how he'd react if someone tripped while on that floor and knocked out part of the project. After hearing all things were set and that Herman was ready to go if anything hit on any of the systems, Marcus said goodbye to everyone since there was nothing more for him to do and headed to the next stop.

Sarah and Luke were part of the briefing held for leadership at the EOC, where Marcus would arrive in less than 15 minutes. It was the last operations meeting, setting the stage for the final 12 hours of the event. Though the NIMS framework had an established pattern for the order of meetings and the paperwork involved to support the IAP, today would be run old-school in the successful pattern of so many other events here. All the checkboxes had been completed as far as the federal requirements were concerned. But this team knew this city and this suspect... the actual game was just another game to them.

Luke used the flexiglass to highlight the new locations of where Sarah and he would be the eyes on the ground. Explaining the way they would get intel from any camera shots relayed through their comms devices that linked back to a remote team (the house team, but they never fully explained where those members were located or who they specifically were), the responders felt pretty confident that all angles had been considered for the offensive net. The defensive options had been drilled by Chad and the team out at the academy, and the police had enough crowd control that they didn't necessarily need to drill their aspect of the plan considering there were fewer people visiting for this event and all in a more confined area than during their "normal" annual big event. They'd had to evacuate folks and lock down areas many times in the past. That was one thing about this region - they sure did get to "practice" with real life events on a pretty regular basis.

Marcus walked up to the group as Luke was finishing the flexiglass review and the avatars were activated to start working in real-time. The comms devices each operational leader now had issued were live feeding into the avatar program as well, though not on the screen just yet as it wasn't in the radius of the hot zone and warm zone perimeters. The people in this room were all in a "parking lot" off to the side of the avatar ground view screen, with a color representing their team and a number beside it. Fascinating technology, and the capabilities after this event were already on a checklist for Luke to integrate before the next one. They could see Alex already in the stadium, however, as he ran through a few checks and went up to see if the BioWatch device ended up being installed with duct tape or some wonderful federal overpriced clamp.

The three of them - Sarah, Luke and Marcus - broke to the side, and Chad followed momentarily just to say good luck, shake the guys' hands, give Sarah a hug and leave for the scene. While a third to a half of the room emptied and headed to their respective assignment locations to brief their teams, the EOC staff went to their stations and prepped for the day, and this involved a lot of paperwork. In spite of the fantastic technology, some things were still behind the curve - and they left it that way so the "outside" didn't see how far the homeland security operations had come, how sophisticated they were and how the success of detection led to containment of potentially dangerous threats. Plus, it gave everyone a commonality about which they could complain - internally or externally.

Sarah asked Marcus if he was ready for tonight, knowing he was about to leave to prepare with the DEA for the bust. He would be in full body armor with SWAT members, other local jurisdictions and others. These longer meetings before the bust were always painful, as the DOJ reviewed the rules of engagement and the DEA reiterated the chain of command as they deputized the locals for the task force. They were tedious meetings, but helped bring down the adrenaline that could contribute to sloppiness, so no one complained too much. They talked about texting him if they caught Mike, but Luke made the valid point that it was better if Marcus could focus on his mission, only contacting them when he was clear. Agreeing on that, Marcus repeated Chad's departure hand shake and hug, wished them luck and left the EOC.

Luke offered to drive Sarah to the event. They had extremely limited parking and Sarah suspected that Luke's trunk had some helpful things in case the situation started to escalate. Glad for the time to think and not focus on driving, they put on their rain suits as it had resumed raining and they headed down to the arena. Parking on the side closest to the interstate as that's where Luke would be stationed, Sarah began her walk along the fenced lot and then the razor-wire topped train track fence. This area was restricted for public safety use and would not have pedestrians. The street parking on this side of the small arena was ideal for first responders because of the barbed wire fencing, lack of feeder roads, and gave a safe zone for field staff roll calls and to park their units. She knew it was important to always give a mental safe zone for teams, as a way they could check their personal issues there and pick them up when they debriefed before heading home.

As she passed through this area, she did the same thing with her virtual separation of personal versus professional life, and focused on the crowd ahead. She would be walking against their direction of movement along side of their path that was delineated with barricades. She could see some of these early arrivals and make way to her post by the parking garage overpass. Wisely, they had swept the garage and kept it closed to the public, but it was used for previously credentialed media. The parking attached to the stadium was for players and coaches. They shuttled the stadium staff in busses from off-site parking areas around the city (to make it easier for the folks who normally took a bus, but they were running on very different schedules today). Sarah felt good about everything except the uncertainty of where Mike would enter the fray.

For more than three hours and closer to four, everyone remained on high alert. It was tedious and exhausting, but they watched the crowd movements and waited for the house team to give an alert that they saw something; all they heard over the comms was the thirty-minute time stamp that ensured the devices were still working without too much distracting chatter. Luke was at the top part of the event "spider," as it seemed the walkways appeared as the legs looked like a spider from the flexiglass arial view. It was the closest to the trauma hospital and the on-ramp for the interstate, so he could pursue if it came to that. They had determined Sarah would have the main artery that came from Uptown and the warehouse residential district. She was positioned about two thirds of the way down the path, so a person would be trapped in the congestion if the suspect panicked. These two ways had the most people anticipated for funneling, and by all logical accounts, Mike would keep away from the tourists entry routes as he wanted recognition for whatever he had planned and needed people to see his arrival.

But they had used logic and thus, picked wrong. As Mike sold his last hot dog by city hall and put up his sign that he needed to go get more supplies, he put away the ketchup and mustard in the open small compartment. The end door was opened under the push bar handle and he removed the long tubing to attach it to his munitions canisters. He turned off the propane, removed his hot dog jacket and shirt (leaving his homeland security shirt visible), left his hot dog credentials under the cart with the uniform top and put his ball cap back on his head. Attaching the hoses and the timer/detonator device to the canisters, he activated the compressor, ready to feed the chemicals up to the ninth floor in five minutes. He briskly set off around the top corner of the building for the game; it was two minutes until kickoff.

What he didn't notice was the new camera at that end of city hall, pointed back toward the direction from which he was approaching. He had that poncho on again, but the cap kept the hood back from his face. The image that came through to the house team was clear since this camera had the new lens installed and the software sent the picture to Rae and Sibyl for secondary confirmation along with the map location of where it was taken with the corresponding time.

Simultaneously, they realized they thought they had him. The face was turned only slightly to the right away from the camera, as the suspect was looking at the looming checkpoint crowd, so it was a good take. Rae handled the confirmation process with Herman upstairs and bounce backs to the film production company's servers as well as alerting the "real" EOC as Sibyl used the comms system to relay the update to Sarah and Luke.

"Confirming hit. Suspect at city hall checkpoint in queue. Repeat. Suspect at city hall checkpoint in queue. Time lapse, 45 seconds."

Sarah and Luke both turned form their respective locations and began to run. Sarah was closer and had fewer people in between her location at the larger checkpoint, with Mike being one or two football fields away from her. She had a direct line of site to that mass of people and began to run in her soggy combat boots toward the sighting and called in her status, forgetting the EOC would see her on the avatar projections. Luke had between four and five football field lengths to travel to come from around the stadium, but was in better shape for long distance running of the two of them. He also had more people milling about as his entrance had an open area for people to file into the event through two separate gates. He, too, marked status as he ran for the checkpoint. Inside, Alex began descending from the upper areas of the stadium and heading to the closest entrance that would let him get to that checkpoint.

Of course, since they were on the private comms system, the other first responders didn't know what was happening. The decision had been made to have the smallest circle of knowledge, in case Mike still scanned and listened to the radio transmission of 911 staff. To find him before anything happened, it was best not to give any indicators he could intercept or to spook him with lots of uniforms running in that direction. It also eliminated any loose lips from tipping him off ahead of time, allowing him to change his plans. They still didn't know how deep the situation would penetrate once they were able to get the whole story.

Sarah slowed her run as she came to the open street. People beyond two or three deep in the queue couldn't see her running, but no reason to panic anyone - or if it wasn't him and he was watching this main street for any activity, it could spook him. She approached the checkpoint and nodded to the contraflow officer, who let her pass through. She saw him. Slowly raising her hand up to her throat to activate the comms microphone, Sarah let the team know it was indeed him. Keeping her head down a bit in the lightly falling rain, she indicated eyes-on confirmation of the suspect as she put her hand in her yellow rain coat. They were designed for first responders so that they could access equipment on their person, like gloves and blood pressure cuffs for medics or guns and hand cuffs for officers.

Grabbing the butt of her weapon with her right hand and releasing it from its holster, she withdrew it from the underside of the coat out to the large pocket, still concealing it so no one screamed and got in her way. She got closer to him; he was in the back of the line, if the group of people waiting could be called that. No one to her right, the side toward city hall, she had the weapon by her side and got close enough to Mike that when she stated, "Freeze; hands up and kneel on the ground," with her weapon pointed at center mass from approximately ten feet to his left, the people nearby merely pushed forward, closer to the checkpoint. Oddly calm, they were all focused on getting into the game and seemed to understand crap like this happened in this city more often than the mayor or tourism bureau cared to share.

Mike looked to his left in shock. Who the hell found him? It was that bitch from city hall, the one he hated, the one that took his job from him and made him look like a fool. She started all of this, and part of this payback was directed at killing her so nothing would stand in his way of being a leader again. He didn't move, but stared at her like he was frozen in this small roadway, so close to his goal but not knowing what would happen now. This was never part of his plan. He never thought he would be caught - let alone by her. He couldn't move, he was that stunned.

"Why aren't you upstairs in the EOC? You are supposed to be up in the EOC. You are supposed to be with them. You're all supposed to be together. Why aren't you there?" Mike uttered rapid fire statements and questions in an eerie monotone without moving any other part of his body.

"I said kneel on the ground, Mike. Do it."

She didn't look so intimidating in that banana jacket. He was pretty certain he could take her down and get her weapon.

She was only a female and men were stronger than women. *Apparently, she only was fierce in those suits and heels,* thought Mike. He could take her, easily, this fluffy banana girl. And he turned his body to face her, slowly raising his arms as though he was going to comply, but he of course had a better idea.

It appeared that he was starting to follow her instructions, with his hands now raised to be level with his head in a surrender position and beginning to kneel. He was left handed, and dropped his right leg forward a bit as though that was the first leg to go to the ground. But with the poncho, she couldn't see that he was assuming an attack position with his legs, ready to leap at her from the posture of a sprinter. In his mind, it was still perfectly clear even with the twist of events - he'd rush her back to the fence and knock the wind out of her and simply take the weapon. Maybe he's smack her once good and hard across her face for all the demeaning things she had done to him. She personally should pay now that she was there and calling him out, spoiling his plan.

And just before Mike could leap, he was knocked flat on the ground. Luke announced his arrival with a tackle and a simultaneous punch to the right side of Mike's head as they fell to the ground.

Chapter 37

Mike had no idea how they ended up on the ground or why his head was pounding. Someone rolled him onto his back and he looked up in that guy's face. He knew that face but couldn't remember why. And then he was punched again, this time left fist to right temple, with a more direct impact than the first strike.

Luke bent into the bleeding face stopping inches from Mike's nose and menacingly relayed, "And that's for Sarah, for putting your hands on her when you tried to force her into this very stadium that night, you little piece of shit."

Mike was offering no resistance, still not understanding that his plan was finished. He was bleeding and he never took pain very well. He was also shaking quite a bit. The adrenaline of his plans was wearing off and it had been almost 48 hours since he had a good drink, long drinks. He had the little flask, but that had been gone nearly in two swallows before he fell asleep in the storage unit. Oh, the storage unit. He wondered if that had exploded yet. But he wasn't going to offer anything up until he knew why they thought they were arresting him.

Luke looked over at Sarah, who was holstering her weapon and telling the house they got him - of course, their location was known and Rae had already selected four other cameras in the network that looked at the checkpoint once, so they saw the takedown from all angles, had even called Tam from the room across from them to watch it all. The two officers from the checkpoint arrived to cuff Mike in a nonchalant manner behind his back after they sat him upright, as all eight checkpoints' officers had been told what may happen. They four of them started to walk Mike toward city hall to take him up to the office and interrogate him there.

Mike lost his mind and started writhing in the officers' grip. Yelling things like, "Don't take me up there" and "It's still happening, we can't go up there," they stopped near the corner with the hot dog cart and decided to begin the interrogation there.

"What in the hell is wrong with you, Mike? And I mean that in more ways than one. Let's start with why can't we get out of the rain to ask you some questions and specifically why we can't go into city hall?" Luke was directly in front of him, as an officer would be in front of a low-level military fuck-up, screaming directives at him that, Luke hoped, would bring him back into line and rejuvenate the feeling of compulsory response when a commanding official was demanding answers.

"It's not done. It's not done. If we go in there, we'll get it, too. You were supposed to be in there and you're not. Who's in there? Why aren't you in there?"

Obviously getting nowhere, the officers agreed to essentially pick him up and drag him into the building as Sarah's unspoken request with her head nod towards the building. They wanted out of the rain as much as anyone else, and guarding the nut while he was being questioned by these people or others was a much more appealing option than standing in this weather. As they turned the corner and walked toward the front door of the building, they noticed the hot dog cart as any hungry officer on a long detail knows to be on the lookout for food. But they paused, as that wasn't on the plans for their checkpoint and the sign said it didn't have any more food.

Something wasn't right and they called Luke back from a few paces ahead. Indicating the cart and the strangeness, Luke and Sarah walked towards it while the officers stayed with Mike in a vice grip while on the sidewalk. At least the huge tree was providing them all with a little break from the downpour. It seemed like a good - and successful - position to hide something, so now the cart made them more uncomfortable than the rain.

As they approached, they noticed that the wind had caused the blue tarp to partially fall from where Mike had rigged it on the umbrella to cover the back wall. Definitely noticeable now that they were looking for anomalies, the tubing that ran up the side of the building from the cart was easily visible. It went into one of the windows in the ninth floor EOC. In fact, it went to the window where Sarah guessed it was the one where Marcus usually sat. Luke was already on the phone to Chad, and Sarah notified Tam back at the house. Something was being fed up into the building where Mike thought all of the leaders for the various first responders and homeland security personnel were located today.

Luke was hanging up the phone when he got back to Mike and the cops. Without warning, he nailed him with a right jab, causing his head to snap back and causing new swelling and a gash to his left chin. The officers had been ready for it, both in physical support of the suspect and that they had been briefed at roll call if they got into the situation that they were now in, they were under direct orders to <u>not</u> engage their body cameras. Surely the water of that day jammed them up or something - and the Feds backed them up on this one. Issue of national security, exemption to the freedom of information public records laws, so let it go.

Mike's head was spinning. He didn't ever really remember being punched before today. Never being in battle, and not having friends that would roughhouse when little, it was all very strange to him. He had ringing in his ears and knew his face was bleeding; he even thought maybe his nose was broken from the first punch, but he couldn't have access to his hands to feel anything beyond the throbbing and running of blood. Over the ringing in his ears, he thought Luke was asking him something.

He tried to focus, but really couldn't - he did, however, see Luke's lips moving and looked directly at them. Something about a tube. *Hot dogs. Binary munitions. Timer and compressor. Everyone supposed to be in EOC. Storage unit blows substation. I'll be here. Can save the day.* He thought he may be going in and out of consciousness, but then the loud sirens made his head straighten up and eyes bulge at how the sound worsened the ringing already in his head.

Chad was pulling up with the Hazmat team in three vehicles, coming against the normal flow of the one-way street that was part of the "no drive zone" for the event. Mike had actually been babbling aloud, so they pointed out the cart, tubing and discussed what may have happened. Chad's team rolled in their Class A's all ready to go except the head gear and oxygen activation (a very quick employ). Every first responder knew with the game, there wouldn't be time to waste if something went down. Entering the building, the two teams split into a search evacuation team and one to go to the ninth floor.

While they did that and Luke handled the city hall mess, Sarah took the lead in the supposed explosives in a storage unit near the substation. He didn't say where, but it seemed likely to be nearby. The police special operations division's captain sent the two bomb squad units to the two substations with storage units nearby and began sweeping them as well as evacuating the surrounding area near both power stations.

It didn't take long for the Hazmat team members to exit the building and return to their trucks. Chad got briefed and came back to the five of them standing under the tree. "Looks like whatever he intended didn't work. Building is clear - of people and VOCs or other weapon components. Team is switching some equipment and you can see they're coming for the cart."

It turned out to be another failure for Mike. The binary compounds never were opened to mix and be delivered by that compressor - which had stopped working - to the ninth floor. It was too close to kickoff and the mayor wanted to see it in person - so had paraded the media with him across the street to the stadium at fifteen minutes to kickoff, after making some statements about safety and world-class facility, blah blah blah. The timer did indeed count down to five, but the detonator didn't work and the canisters were still sealed. They'd handle the disposal of those units and everything would be gone by the end of the first quarter.

Sarah also got news back that while the second bomb team found the facility in question and detected explosives, when they cut the lock on the door and sent in the little robot, indeed there were boxes of things that could be explosive along the wall closest to the sub station. If they had blown, it would have been a mess. But the detonator wasn't attached and the materials were so old, from resold expired military ordinance, that they aren't certain if it would have blown anyway. Unstable, yes. Reliable for what he intended, absolutely not. Both squads would work together to clear that area of his mess, too, and let residents back in their homes before halftime. So close to one of the port access road entrances, they'd go out that way instead of down the busy street - and were hoping to catch the second half of the game.

Sarah, Luke, the two officers and Mike went into city hall and sat in the atrium of the council chambers. It was the one area they knew was not recorded by sound or video, where council members sometimes stepped out of meetings to get messages, take phone calls or to discuss things that could impact their decisions. Mike had essentially stopped bleeding and was somewhat awake enough to answer questions. Once they had him sitting in a chair, the officers took two chairs outside of hearing distance, so they could honestly answer "I don't know" if ever questioned in conjunction with what was about to go down.

Sarah and Luke remained quiet, considering how to proceed. She realized they hadn't told Jason yet, who would be with the mayor, so sent a brief text, "We got him. Still a screw-up. Enjoy the game."

A swift written reply, "Not on your life - get me out of here. Where are you?" Sarah chuckled as she showed her screen to Luke. They decided to let Mike wait in silence for the Colonel to arrive and handle this pathetic marine. Neither felt any pity for this man, and were actually looking forward to hearing what Jason could get him to say.

Seven minutes later, they heard him walking briskly down the entrance hall and then heard his voice before he turned the corner. "I told the mayor we may have caught a terrorist, but it could be one of his former employees so I had to leave. He was so stunned that I got out of the suite before he could say anything or come with me." Arriving to them both, who were standing behind Mike's chair that was facing across the room to the two officers, he cracked his knuckles and took a deep breath. He was trying to repress the Marine in himself and was failing. He figured he'd just go with it.

Marching over to Mike, he began dressing him down as only a Marine Colonel could to a lower-level Marine performing far under expectation.

When he had used what Sarah thought was only a hint at his colorful military vocabulary and Jason settled down a bit, he began more even-tempered phrases, but still was notably angry. "I can't even call you son as I would a real Marine. You aren't a real soldier. Real soldiers know what Mad Dog Mattis said was true - Be polite, be professional, but have a plan to kill everybody you meet. But hell, that was the General talking about war. We aren't in war. Who do you think you are, trying to start a war? Did you forget the code of conduct? Did you ever respect it, especially the part about Death before Dishonor? What the hell do you think this stunt was if not the ultimate display of dishonor? Damn oxygen thief. You qualify for extinction. "

And then the language deteriorated again into Mike being called upon to at least stand when a commanding officer was in a room and to look at Jason directly and do not speak until he was told to speak and more of the like. Sarah and Luke had never seen him like this, but Luke had seen the sort from other Marine commanders. They didn't use that approach exactly in his unit, but the themes were common across the board for addressing someone who nearly got you killed.

Jason left Mike standing (albeit swaying unsteadily) and walked over to them to ask if he gave a real confession or rationale yet. They explained that while he did give some testimony, if it could be called that, it was after a good blow to the head, so perhaps it should be reviewed again. Returning to Mike, he began with, "Hey, I'm talking to you. Look at me!" After some more screaming, he directed Mike to tell him what the hell he thought he was doing. He actually had to specifically prompt him to start speaking.

Mike still couldn't focus and he was feeling quite nauseated. He could only imagine how irate Jason would be if he were to vomit on him while he was dressed so pretty for the game.

He began getting worked up, defensive at the thought of having to be courteous to Jason, envisioning him getting sick all over him and using that as a way to escape. He actually felt he needed to tell him exactly how it should have been and why he was trying to get everyone out of the way, especially that bitch.

"Excuse me? Did you say something?" Jason was neither amused that Mike seemed to be mumbling to himself but was absolutely livid that he had turned toward Sarah and began venting expletives in her direction. You just did not do that as a Marine to a lady. Jason took one large step forward and yelled, "Now."

Mike's attention was returned to the man before him and he began seething in disgust. He had a speech prepared for a dying man's face, but this would do. He would be heard. They would have to see his logic was right.

"You are all a bunch of pigs," began Mike, which drew raised brows from Sarah and Luke widening his stance and tucking his fists into his crossed arms. They were slightly behind Mike. In fact, Mike showed some signs of dilution so he may not understand what was happening at all. Continuing, "I did everything around here. I made the plans, I found interns, I coordinated with the other areas. You never recognized me. You never acknowledged my good work. You didn't show me any loyalty that I deserve as a leader."

Jason did not move but smirked a little. He decided to allow the diatribe to continue a little while longer, and Mike certainly wasn't holding back now. "I knew how things should work. My whole career was about moving up and leading teams, helping out other guys, but you told me to leave. Then you wouldn't hire me and I had my own company to help you out. You spread bad things about me and ruined me. I had to make people understand that I was the magic behind the curtain of your office."

Taking a breath, he began talking so quickly he was spitting. "I know where your weaknesses are and what you should be doing. I planned the binary munitions release to get rid of you and your hoards of staffers and hell, if I was lucky it would take out the mayor, too. That device should have worked. Someone deactivated it before the cops took me around the corner. My plan worked. Someone interfered again and tried to make me look like a fool."

Jason uttered one word, "Why?"

"The world was watching. I would save the day. I could replace your whole office myself. I would have people reporting to me again. You'd just all be gone and I could get on with my life. But none of you were there. Someone told you about my plan. You guys happened to be in the right place at the right time to see me. You had someone deactivate my cart. I don't know what happened to the explosives uptown, but apparently you had someone stumble upon that so you could make yourselves look good again." He lowered his head and wove a bit on his feet.

"Mike, do you think that we could have just done our jobs and you made too many mistakes, couldn't perform as well as the others? How likely is it that someone else is responsible for all of your mistakes? Do you really think this is about a woman that got in your way and ruined your life?" Jason wanted to touch back to his comments about Sarah, to see if he had any other surprises that were directly mainly at her wellbeing.

"Women always get in the way. My sister was always in the way. She left nothing for me. Better grades, better in sports. My dad didn't pay attention to me. You didn't pay attention to me. She arrived and then you all paid attention to her. I just wanted to be a leader again. I didn't even think she'd still be around. Can I have a drink to settle my nerves?" He looked up at Jason again, totally deflated as it started to sink into his bloodied swollen head that he may be in serious trouble.

Sarah walked around to the front of Mike, and Jason stepped off to the side. All she said was, "I'm still standing," and as she took a little step toward him, he collapsed backwards with fear and loss in his eyes, falling into the seat.

He put his head down and started to cry.

Chapter 38

Sarah walked toward Luke and they headed toward the front doors. Jason asked them to wait up as he made a quick phone call. After he hung up the phone, he told the officers that the FBI was coming to read to Mike the list of charges and that would take a long time. They may or may not need to make statements, but were to stay with Mike and get him booked into the jail when the FBI said it was time, making sure he was placed on suicide watch since the man was still weeping and was apt to do something even more stupid than today's stunt. The Hazmat team and bomb squad would likely swing by, too, to give their statements and initial report to the FBI. He also said he'd send some food and hot coffee over for them as this would likely be a while, but at least they'd be dry. They thanked him and smiled. He returned their smiles and nodded, saying thanks and heading to the two at the end of the hallway, not even giving a second glance at the broken man in the chair.

"So, want to go to the game?" Jason asked them both. Sarah looked at Luke. Luke looked at Jason.

Sarah turned back to Jason, too, and said, "Do we have to sit with the mayor?"

Knowing they didn't have to was a great relief, and Jason was appreciative of them getting him away from the mayor, too. Putting the rain gear back on, the three walked back through the same checkpoint that snagged Mike and across to the gate where

Alex was standing. The four of them walked into the stadium, and Sarah let the house team know to stand down, go have a drink and get some sleep. The team would meet tomorrow back at the house for a debriefing, maybe around two or so.

Surprisingly, they were able to see most of the second quarter. Of course, they did make sure to get something to eat and Jason passed a flask to them each to take a celebratory swig, but they did all have souvenir cups of non-alcoholic beverages. They were also able to watch all of the halftime show, and they cut back outside at the middle of the fourth quarter. The game was a blowout and most people were leaving anyway (well, fans of the losing team). The fact that the departures were staggered was actually good for crowd management - between half the fans leaving already, the rest of the spectators and then staff, players and media exits would be much simpler. They already knew the waves would involve some of the food court staff leaving, then the rest of the fans, then the two teams and finally getting the media back outside.

As they were all heading down the ramp together, Sarah turned to Jason to quietly share with him that she was probably going to get pulled back by her real boss, would have to leave the region soon for an extended time on another job. She was surprised she had been allowed to stay this long, but figured things were so messed up that the "powers that be" decided her boots on the ground were better there. Jason nodded and said to let him know when she needed to pull out, and while they couldn't make a fuss, they would try to do something together before she left.

She began to give him a quick rundown of what needed to happen with the SNS storage location, and Jason cut her off with a laugh.

"Oh I forgot to tell you… Wayne was arrested."

Sarah stopped walking, so Jason stopped walking thus causing the other two in front of them to stop and look back. They didn't know what he said. But they heard the rest of the story.

"Yeah, so the mayor blurted it out bragging how he and his brother and his daddy worked out the other afternoon with Wayne to some group on Saturday. He was using it to make a point about his family connections to this group of whomever. Anyway, he also said how they got him to admit to some things and the U. S. Marshal came in and took him away. Was a beautiful setup, it seems. Makes you wonder if anyone that gets something on the mayor will stay out of jail long enough to use it."

"Well, that may make one part of your job easier," Sarah replied as they all continued out of the stadium again. At the bottom of the ramp, Jason went to the right back toward city hall as his car and driver were waiting across the street at that same now-infamous checkpoint. Luke needed to take Sarah back to her car, and Alex was parked around that way, too. They were all lost a bit in their thoughts as the two said good night to Alex, told him they were going to meet around two or so at the house tomorrow, and the two cars drove away in opposite directions.

On the way back to the team house where her car was located, Luke chuckled and said they forgot to have their safety meeting.

"What? Crap. What meeting?"

"No, don't worry. Remember during the last event when we evacuated everyone and some of us wanted to go have a drink but didn't want Mike to know, we said we had a safety meeting? We didn't want him to come drink with us and it sounded official to the other staff members since we went off to command meetings and section chief meetings all of the time. We forgot tonight to have a safety meeting. It would have been so appropriate to cap off the night that way, and I would be smiling from ear to ear."

"The last time, as I recall, we all had some sleep and we did that when the ten of us had those hotel rooms given to us - so we showered and then had the meeting. And didn't we lose two that literally ran off down the street since there was no one around? I remember looking for those two for about five minutes and deciding a feather bed was more interesting than whatever dark hole they found. We never did hear what happened to them after they ran off after the meeting, quote unquote. I think I actually slept four or five hours that night. It was lovely."

"I don't know if I slept that much but it was more than I had been getting. And the hot shower with decent water pressure was nice, too. Better than the tenth floor shower room - but that was better than the event prior to that one where you prayed for rain to cleanse you. Manna from heaven. And today, we couldn't get the rain to stop. It finally did as we left the arena tonight. But having the option to pick a shower back then or the dilution potential in this event, I'd take that rain today over then any time."

"It's funny how people come here and expect one thing and get something else. I wonder what those people at the checkpoint thought earlier when I pulled my gun on him. I just couldn't shoot him. I wanted to, even before he said he wanted to kill Jason and then all that anger he had toward me for some unknown reason. I just couldn't do it. But you tackled him. What did you growl at him after that second punch? I couldn't hear since I was on comms back to the house?"

Luke just smiled and blew it off with an, "Oh, nothing." He was about to go back to the safety meeting concept and suggest they go have a mini-meeting when her phone rang. She took her phone out of her pocket and said it was Marcus.

"So, how was your day, dear?" Sarah started and was immediately cut off by Marcus.

"Did you get the bastard?"

"Yes, we did. And he cried." As she was rehashing the events, she realized it took the entire time to reach the house and her car. She told Marcus to hold on a second and unfastened her seatbelt. Leaning over to Luke and giving him a hug, she thanked him for punching Mike. She didn't let him know that she heard what he had said, she just wanted to see if he would repeat it. Exiting the car, she said she'd see him tomorrow and shut the door, climbing right into her own and putting the phone back to her ear.

Luke felt like he missed his chance. He didn't blame Marcus at all, and it was fun listening to her relay the story of how it went down. He was glad Marcus was safe and was sure he'd hear at the debrief tomorrow right back here how his night went. For now, it was passing midnight and he decided to get a drink for the road and head back to his house after sending the kids at the 'avatar ranch' a thank you note from the parking lot, telling them they did a fantastic job and there would be a bonus coming, he was certain.

Sarah drove off while Luke was sending that message to the kids, and tried to get Marcus to start talking about the bust. He interrupted her though.

"Hey, are you hungry? I never eat before I go on a raid or serve a warrant. Never know if you have to run or if something happens, how long it's going to be before you can take care of things. Where are you? Can we get something to eat? I'm exhausted and hungry and really don't want to see any damn tourists or football players or certainly want to stay the hell away from public officials."

Sarah was actually between the place where she picked up her Lebanese food the other day and the team house. Restaurants here always were open late. Not as late as bars, but even they had some pretty decent food for the crowd that worked odd shifts in what they called SIN - service industry. Not the strippers or the hookers - that was a sin in lower case letters. She wanted to talk to him more, so suggested she pick something up as she was just leaving the house. They would arrive at her cottage about the same time and he could tell her about his night.

He had to pick Lebanese like she had the other day, Chinese (both of these were the best in town and neither was a bad choice), Thai (it was the second best in this category practically next to the Lebanese spot), pizza from the inn down the street or a po-boy… He stopped her.

"Too many choices. Chinese. Whatever. Do you have anything to drink or should I get something?"

Assuring him she had plenty on hand, she gave him her address and warned him to wait until she got there before exiting the car. "Don't park right in front of the house - the wife works nights and parks there; she should be home soon. And if I'm not there and the husband is reading on the porch as he enjoys doing on cooler evenings, he was former FBI and there will be a lot of stories if you are still kitted up. He also sits there while armed, just sayin."

Laughing, he agreed to wait and as it turned out, she arrived first, bags in hand waiting as he parked. The wife was already home, the dogs were in the house - husband, too. She really liked the couple and felt safe with them. No worries, no loud parties, and they kept an eye out for her. They invited her to join them for dinner sometimes and the food - usually prepared by the husband - was always very good, and always paired with superb wine. A very comfortable home, and her very charming cottage should be clean enough as she motioned for him to follow her back through the large plants with no lights along the path. She didn't anticipate having to ask him to wait a minute, making him wait while she cleaned up anything inside. Her grandmother told her to keep a neat house because you never knew when you might have company. Wasn't that the truth?

Walking through the little back gate, around the pool and onto the decking, they entered together, her just noticing that he had his duffle bag with him. Likely full of weapons that he didn't want to leave in the car, when he noticed her looking at it, he also shared that it had a change of clothes. He was still in his vest and full BDUs. She spun around, saying this was the first floor and walking over to the bathroom, completed with stone shower and very hot water, she pulled out towels and offered him to take a shower if he wanted. She would plate the food and open some wine.

Marcus was so relieved she offered a shower. He gladly and quietly accepted. It was wonderful to put on khakis and an oxford after almost eight hours in his gear. He remembered to not have the pale blue shirt when he threw extra clothes in the car that morning since she saw it at the wine bar. As he combed his hair, he knew whatever she would be pouring would be wonderful - and much better than a beer at his house. He buttoned the cuffs on his shirt that was amazingly not very wrinkled as he tucked it into his pants, his belt already fastened. Boots in the compartment made for that, rest of the uniform in over some other equipment and he emerged a bit refreshed, though still tiring quickly.

She had the food out on the coffee table in front of the couch. He knew if he sat there he would fall asleep and start snoring. He placed his duffle on the floor by the french doors through which they had entered, but behind the whatever the marble topped drawer thingy fancy furniture was. He was too tired to try to remember. The smell of the Chinese food took him to where she was standing. He accepted the glass of wine, and toasted to two great evenings.

He sat in the cream wingback while she sat at the edge of the cream fluffy looking couch. He took a deep breath and she told him to start eating, he must be famished. Not rushing but not being shy, he picked up his plate, sat back and started to tell the story of how this crazy drug bust came at the same time as Mike's stupid adventure.

Chapter 39

The DEA had done quite a bit of research based on a neighbor who was sick and tired of the increased activity - both generally in the way of foot and vehicle traffic, but also the violent crime that was increasing. Before the storm, there hadn't been any violent crime in that area for as long as some of the residents could remember. It had been a solid middle-class to upper-middle class area, where everyone worked or the parents lived after retiring. Afterwards, however, with only three out of every ten homes on a block still standing using a generous estimate, things took a turn. The person found a contact that vouched for him and he handed over a small notepad of all sorts of times, license plates, direction of people flow, descriptions of the people that went in the house - even an on-duty policeman's unit number as he would stop by every now and then, but nothing was changing. In fact, it was getting worse.

So once that introduction was made, direct texts of information were sent to the DEA. They began working their own investigation, and discovered with the help of this "assistant" - they didn't want to say informant because he wasn't inside the business - that this home and seven others around the city were purchased by a family that suddenly bought a million dollar home along the lake. The houses purchased by this couple in the various neighborhoods within the past two years all started seeing an uptick in murders. There were more carjackings. A pattern was beginning to be established, and it was obviously a big deal - it was just big enough that they couldn't get their arms around it quickly.

Meanwhile, Marcus' investigation had been looking at the areas where the deals were being made, not the flow of the drugs themselves. He was checking the crimes that happened near those same seven houses and a few other areas and speculated there was a connection. Not able to put any descriptions of shooters in multiple locations, he wasn't sure where to turn next. Once he got to know the kid from the grocery and got that text a few days ago, he and the DEA put it together that the kid was the oldest son of the matriarch of the whole damn cocaine funnel for the southeastern U.S. and even some big runs up to New York, that was the break both sides needed to cut the organization off at the knees, stemming the flow of nectar to the addicts for now.

Sarah took another sip of wine and tucked her feet underneath her on the couch. Marcus rolled up his sleeves and ate some more of the Chinese food she had picked up for him (obviously the cracked pepper beef was a smart decision), and she finished off her last spring roll before changing the music streaming softly from her phone. Just a bit of relaxing background sound - between that and the ceiling fan's rhythm, she was likely going to be asleep soon. He continued to tell her more about the boy and how they met down the street from where this all ended up taking place, backing up a little in time as he was collecting the thoughts most important to him rather than only the facts for the story he'd include for the police report.

He was glad the kid was at work that night. Marcus had told him to throw the cell phone away after he called him that everything was over. Since his college was almost finished, he asked the guy for whom he interned if he could move to another office out of state under the pretense of he wanted to see another new city in the United States. Marcus had put in a word for him, too, and the guy was more than happy to help out. The kid would finish his last class online, and was due to leave in the morning for his new hometown, away from all of this. He got what he wanted - a fresh start and an office job, practically all in one day. The funding for the move was arranged by the whistleblower law that gives a part of the tax evasion to the informants confidentially. Marcus had arranged a little upfront money for the kid and the Feds would follow up after they counted all they hauled in tonight… well, it was now early hours of the morning so actually last night.

Sarah chuckled as Marcus' mind was going in a million directions. She wanted to hear more about the actual house and what they found, but was too tired to ask. In addition, she knew when you were coming off an adrenaline high (just as she had earlier when they went to watch the game for a little bit), you just needed to ramble and let stuff out. He'd get to the interesting part of the story soon enough.

As though reading her mind, Marcus apologized for focusing on the kid. He told her he was just really glad the life of one kid was able to be saved from this city, which just sucked the soul from some people. It drew people from all over the world, like this kid from Guatemala, under the pretense of offering a relaxing fabulous life, with hardly a care. He was strong enough as things beat down on him to find a way to adapt and then overcome. Parties around town all the time, festivals galore, it seemed too good to be true; so many moved here thinking they could live like that everyday. And the hard reality was when you arrived at this gleaming palace in the sky, the underbelly started to reveal itself, sinking its fangs into your tender skin and slowly drawing the energy, the drive, even seemingly the intelligence out of folks. It wasn't a place where people could really see the vision of an easy life and ever reach it.

Then he realized he may be preaching to the choir. "Sarah, I still don't know where you grew up, and those questions driving across the lake where we focused on your tango lessons never did get me a straight answer. You have lived what I've just described. You were kind of dropped into the belly of the beast, weren't you?"

"And those questions and that story will wait until another day. But yes, this magical kingdom has turned into quite the haunted house of sorts, where skeletons of people turn up around every corner. Keep going about how you could roll on this house when so many empty lots are still in that area of town. How in the hell was it not an O.K. Corral when the team got there?" It was that graceful and effortless redirection, just as in the meetings on the ninth floor or elsewhere, that the story turned back to the speaker and away from herself. It was easier this way. Reduced attachments. Suspecting she was going to be leaving soon, she wanted one normal night with a friend. Even if she wanted more, it couldn't happen, wasn't fair to either of them. She sipped from her wine glass and found her eyes blinking slowly as Marcus began speaking again.

Moving up to that afternoon, they had decided that the old school yard behind the house would be the main route of attack. It had enough cover with the school being rebuilt and the large oak trees still speckled the property. As it wasn't a flat area, they would use the slight rolls and branches for cover, and even come along the back fence that was overgrown with cat's claw weeds. They were worried about the house next door because that man seemed to be a lookout for them - but never out of the back. Always out the front door, on the porch, up and down the street.

To counter the watchman at the front wouldn't be tough as the big party would be happening and he likely would be having a swell time rather than looking for people coming as so many people would be showing up. The bouncy things in the front were the largest concern as he explained how the drug dealers planned to use children as cover. Feds decided to rent one of those stupid party busses to drive down the street like it was headed to the drug house, music blasting and everything else and it would blare the horn, swing along the front of the suspect house knocking out the little balcony poles if necessary and parking between the front doors and the area where the kids would play. It eliminated an escape route for anyone inside. The team members inside were going to run the kids down the block to the day care center, hiding them along the cinderblock wall away from any potential projectiles.

The blaring of the horn would be the time for the teams along the fence line of the school and those in a city public transit bus near the day care to sweep into the party, rushing front and back; thirty cops came from the back and about fifteen more had the front sectioned off. The dealers had been so certain that they were untouchable they never expected cops to come through the construction area. They had blocked themselves in with an above ground pool blocking their own exit along one side of the house and the tail of the party bus left that side not really usable, either.

Had they not made sure to get so many officers aligned for this event, it would have been a lot worse. As it was, one guy entered the breach too early when he heard the party bus gun the engine and he actually was shot. DOJ was not happy about that, especially since someone forgot to notify EMS to have two units on standby. Second guy in covered him with his own body and all the others jumped through the hole in the fence (that the dealers probably cut for their own escape if they were every approached from the front) and surrounded the group in the back yard so fast that they really did surprise them even if the good guys were outnumbered by the bad.

When the other fifteen in the joint task force arrived from the public transit bus down the block, half came around back and entered the house. There were two distinct sides of the residence and getting people out of the bottom - which was hollowed out like a party hall - was no issue. The other half of the team squeezed in between the party bus and upper unit door, which luckily was a "push in" not "pull out." Carefully going upstairs, there were only two guys up there. They also realized to stay alive they should not reach for a weapon; their hands were held high when the first team member came around the top of the stairwell. There was so much cocaine and crack arranged like a high-tech warehouse there was no way they could flush or rinse any. The precision scales, the sophisticated airtight wrapping device normally used for preserving things that go in a freezer - bricks upon bricks of cut and uncut drugs. All lined up on shelving that made it look like a library. Labelled for purity, stacked and inventoried like a home supply store, it was crazy.

After they got everyone booked and loaded in the that public bus that was moved to the front of the house to serve as a huge paddy wagon, every officer went upstairs to look at the operation. It was unlike anything any of them had ever seen - even the DOJ and DEA guys in from Miami and El Paso admitted this was the most sophisticated operation they had ever seen. It was also the first time they ever had seen an operation run by women - and in particular, one woman.

They had kept the matriarch and her two sisters separate and under guard, not loading them with everyone else. The kid was right, the woman stepped up right away and the two sisters tried to explain their way out of it. The sisters didn't know much but were ready to roll on the older sister. They started talking about this tall gringo with greasy hair, who would show up to Bible Study or dinners or soccer. They relayed how scared they were at the soccer game when his driver pulled up with his lights and sirens. How her own son was in the car with them when it pulled up, even how her sons were the runners of supplies to staging areas around the city. Marcus was out front with the bus, trying to find out how the officer from another area was doing at the hospital when the guys interrogating the sisters told him about the "gringo" connection to his informant. Marcus stepped away and called the kid, told him everything was done. But asked him about the white guy and the lights and sirens to the soccer game.

"Sarah, you'll never believe who it was."

"So tell me because I will never guess with this much wine in me."

"Sean. The guy from the meetings on the ninth floor."

She shot forward and nearly spilled the little bit of wine left in her glass. He told her how they sent two guys over to arrest him at his house and made sure the media was around for that. Of course, neither of them cared to watch the news tonight, but she started laughing, barely bringing herself to stop before tears rolled down her face.

"And you'll never guess who was arrested on Friday afternoon while exercising with the mayor?"

"Payback - don't make me guess."

"Wayne, same meeting in question. He apparently admitted everything about his skimming and essentially assured himself a RICO conviction by admitting his plans while the one brother, you know the Fed, while he was on the treadmill right next to him. Apparently he thought he walked on water and was part of their old boys club. Wrong!"

They laughed some more and she topped off their wine glasses, toasting to the fact that comeuppance really does occur, even to the people that think they have an in with karma.

Chapter 40

Hours later, and somehow sleeping through the four-dog morning alarm as the neighbors left for work and well into the heat of the first day of a new workweek for most people, she only woke when her phone rang for the third time in a row, as the phone on silent would vibrate instead of ringing unless someone called three times. It was about to make her to throw it into the pool. She lost more than one phone to that salt water pool.

When she accepted the call on this third attempt, she just kind of moaned into the cell. She merely listened and said, "Give me an hour or so. I'll meet you there." She clicked off the phone and looking around tried to wake up. She realized she was on the down couch on the first floor with music still softly playing on loop. The acoustic songs always relaxed her and put her to sleep. It never failed, even when she tried to listen to that whole soundtrack in particular, she would usually be asleep before the end of the second song.

She couldn't believe she was so tired she fell asleep on the couch, with the hand knit Irish cable throw over her legs. Gotta get up, as she focused her eyes around the little cottage. Small, it was more than enough for her. It was thoughtfully rebuilt on top of the two hundred year old stable once used in the keyhole lot, where horses had been kept on its first floor and sleeping quarters were maintained on the second for servants - or slaves depending on the family. In fact, when they had to rebuild from the storm and the tree that nestled onto the back corner of the old one-floor cottage, they found original bricks from the first structure on that site as they excavated. They now formed the elevated footer that kept the door close to two feet above the pink pool deck and around three feet above regular soil.

Standing, crossing the room, she turned off the music and leaned forward to blow out the candle, but two things crossed her mind. First, she needed to talk to Luke about the bricks - she kept two, one for keepsake and the other for diagnostics to see how it was actually made more than two centuries ago. The privacy of the secure yard, with the pool nearly surrounding a third of the accessible two sides of the cottage with the four-dog hound alarm (literally, four hounds) gave a level of safety for sleeping, if not for much serenity. A gunny friend agreed it was well-guarded and well-placed (for many reasons) and that had increased her comfort level with the location.

The second thing she noticed was a set of keys that weren't hers next to the candle. Glancing at her phone she had slapped on the table next to the candle after that call, it was around eleven in the morning. She hadn't recalled taking a friend's keyring when she was out earlier. She had one friend within walking distance of the cottage that had wrecked numerous cars from drinking and driving. They all used to take turns after football games taking her keys. They'd even been known to work with bartenders to weaken her drinks, too, until she switched to drinking wine. But she kept coming out of flipped cars alive - and out of the courthouse rather than into jail. No, she hadn't taken keys last night.

Oh, she did recall Marcus calling after his scene cleared, about an hour after she cleared when the game had ended and Luke had been driving her back to her car. He told her that he was hungry and tired. Knowing from an earlier conversation that he lived too far out from the city center to get safely home, she told him to come to her place. Two glasses on the table to the right, but no other indication he was still around. But, there was a black duffle by the linen press at the french doors.

The first floor was an open plan, except the bathroom at the end opposite of the room from the maple staircase by her sofa. To conserve space, the bath area had a lovely pocket door with etched glass for privacy and to allow light to filter through. She checked the bath, and it was empty. Turning around to the front of the cottage, pulling back the window's sheer curtain, it was obvious that he wasn't poolside or on the wooden deck, either. Hot tub was also clear. But he had to be somewhere and the place wasn't that big.

She needed a quick shower to jumpstart the day as her hour was vanishing. The on-demand water heater was downstairs, moved in the rebuild so it wouldn't wake guests upstairs if someone was showering downstairs; the hot water felt good. She loved the shower as she had tiled it with the stones herself. It reminded her literally of rebuilding and it seemed she was about to embark on that same kind of path again based on the brief telephone conversation. Ten years in one city was a long time. Granted, the circumstances here were unique. It was a place with its own rhythm and rhyme, soul and smell, parades and pastimes. She was glad to have returned to live here again, to come to life here again. But things here weren't always real and she was about to be given her next dose of real by her boss in an hour.

Wrapped in her gold silk robe that was more like a full-length toga and her hair in a towel, she quietly went upstairs with a noiseless yawn. She needed more sleep after the eventful two days. With her eyes trying to close, she was passing the couch, she stopped to text both Luke and Chad while she thought of it, though on separate messages. To Chad, she wrote *Raincheck; being deployed elsewhere today. Touch base later. Be safe.* To Luke, she chuckled as she typed *Our Safety Meeting has to be delayed, heading to next mission out of town. Talk to you soon.* Replacing the phone on the coffee table, she climbed the three steps up to the right, then two on the angle, and eight to continue to the open second floor along the back wall. The second level was designed more like a loft space than bedroom - it perfectly complemented the building-wide second story porch overlooking the pool.

Both the first and second floor had full-length windows poolside as well as french doors. As she walked through the cottage, she was noticing details as if saying goodbye to the little things that made her smile. The back wall along the steps only had small windows upstairs, three scenes depicted in stained glass at the very top edge of the wall, with the outer two depicting matching forest scenes and the center one flowers. She had faced her bed along the floor-to-ceiling windows over the pool so she could wake up to the stained glass scenes every morning. She read in the well-lit nook at the far end of the room, which was above the pool and had windows all around, including an easy glance at the forest scenes to spark her imagination if she wanted to daydream.

Approaching the top step and looking at the bed over the half-wall, she realized that's where Marcus had gone. Clothes piled somewhat haphazardly on the floor, on top of his shoes. Everything was apparently piled there, as she caught a slight refraction of light on his badge. Weapon in holster on top, cuffs, wallet, phone - all next to the bed between him and the french doors. With twelve foot ceilings and no pillars for the porch (thanks to newly engineered wood beams), it would be mighty hard for anyone - even the neighbor's feral cat - to appear on that porch. But good training and habit make things easy, especially when exhausted.

She snuck past the bed to grab a suit hung in the closet and then padded in her bare feet back around the bed to grab a top and things out of the bureau. But she wasn't as quiet as she thought. As she opened the drawer, he laid in the bed and watched her, issuing a gravelly good morning to get her attention and smiled when she glanced his way.

"Don't even think about it. Well, think about it, but don't act on that look, Marcus. My boss called - my real boss - and I have to go over to meet him. Something's brewing, even though the last thing feels like it only just ended... without enough time to relax and recover. But know that I would enjoy recovering with you more, right where you are."

Marcus grinned and just watched her return across the room, passing the end of bed on her way back to the closet where she switched the suit on the hanger in her hand to a different one. This was light cream, heels to match, and had a soft lilac blouse, which she hung on the half-wall for a moment. Back over to her dresser to brush and style her hair, and though her hair was still damp, she twirled it up into a twist of some sort - it fascinated him to watch her transform herself so effectively, so rapidly.

She came over to the side of the bed where he laid watching her. Still in her gold toga, sitting on the side of the bed near his waist, she reached over his head. There were a few scarves on the bedpost. She chose the lilac silk and can carefully removed it with her right hand, putting it into service as a scarf for the day. "I will think of you as I wear this into my next battle." She leaned over and gave him a delicate kiss, like she really meant it but didn't have the courage to say she regretted saying goodbye.

He reached up to cup her face, then grabbed her left wrist, placing a kiss on her palm. Standing, slowly pulling away, she pattered down the stairs to finish getting dressed in the lower bath, finishing this step in rapid momentum and exiting the French doors. He knew then that she had wanted to stay. Her purposeful strides were nowhere to be heard, and he smiled as he heard the french doors close, drifting back to sleep again.

Her weakness was occasional self-doubt, and though she was better at avoiding temptations that spurred the practice, she rapidly realized that she would have enjoyed every minute of any time with Marcus. Duty called, and the door was still open for a leisurely exchange someday. This duty that called was literally her real boss, who did not like to be kept waiting, so she surprised herself with that departure from Marcus. Only she knew that was the last time he would see her for a long time, and she wanted to remember him just that way before she scampered to work. It would soften the self-inflicted blows for taking those few moments for herself, with a scene only she would remember.

Since this was her real boss, not a politician, she knew they had to meet *not* in her assigned office. She liked to meet in the park at the coffee house there, where she could get a bit of weak tea and he could get a cup of stale coffee. It was a tourist location, yet the park was pretty. He knew that's where she would want to go, and suggested it, so she had little to say when he called other than she needed an hour.

Feeling this was the ending of the tour here, she also wanted to be able to walk around a little to say goodbye to the place. She hated goodbyes. Being tough on the outside all of the time made her attach to places, scenes, and nature rather than people. Plus, in general, she didn't like many people. It was tougher in many ways for her to depart a place than a person.

She got her tea and began walking behind the museum in the sculpture garden, knowing that on the far side of where she started, he would be waiting. No reason to delay, they would walk through the paths on the fields, wander around a small pond as the ducks looked for bread, and he would give her the next assignment.

*

Hours later, when she reentered the cottage, he was gone. She knew he would be but she almost wished he was still here waiting for her. Wine glasses from the previous night were washed and on the counter; her hair towel that she left on the floor upstairs earlier now folded on the heated towel rack again, and his beside hers. Pillows straightened on the couch, remnants of their dinner yesterday now gone, she considered it thoughtful, pushing away any consideration that perhaps it was an erasure of what almost happened, the way it had to be moving forward.

Heading upstairs to begin packing, Sarah texted Marcus. *I have to go on assignment for a while. I'll make sure to bring the lilac scarf back when I see you again.*

She finished putting her things into the suitcases, left her car key there for her real office to handle, and she looked at the porch gas lamp for the last time. Gently closing the french doors of the cottage to the whirring of the pool filter, she walked out through the soaring colocasia plants and rambling gigantic hope philodendron, with bits of the evening dew dropping on her sleeve. Drops of hope, not tears of departure.

She exited the old iron gate that still squealed when it was called into service, and went to the car that was waiting for her.

Acknowledgments

I would like to sincerely thank my editing team, without whom we'd all be scratching our heads wondering what I was really trying to say - Karen Clevely, Shanan Guinn, and David Coffman (who also kept me afloat with Nan Nan's coconut creme pie!) Other friends have also been so supportive in many ways, particularly when I send a text entirely out of the blue for them but critical for my process when I forget an old medical term used once upon a time (Lara Christy), new equipment I got to see because her husband is a self-proclaimed technology geek (Tracy Davita Dowdy Mahood), ones who would just see how the book was coming along when they were working late and I was likely doing the same (Andy Bowman), and friends who prayed with me (June Wilder). There are others that helped me in various stages along this journey, some of which cannot be named or it will blow their cover, but you know who you are. And most of all, I thank my "hubby," Carlos Streber - mi pareja para obras de teatro en el jardín, películas tontas y horas de la noche de locura. ¡Te amo!

www.ingramcontent.com/pod-product-compliance
Lightning Source LLC
Chambersburg PA
CBHW020259030826
48979CB00026B/1555/J

* 9 7 8 0 9 9 7 5 4 1 4 0 3 *